"*Pointe of Pride* combines witty banter with elegant prose, and the tension between the sparring leads kept me turning pages until all hours of the night. The romance at the story's core is honest, tender, and truly lovely. Like any good dancer, *Pointe of Pride* digs deep and then soars."

—ANDIE BURKE, author of *Fly with Me*

"Chloe Angyal knows how to develop characters that you want to root for and shake by the shoulders in equal measure. Someone said the new grumpy/sunshine is chaos/spreadsheet, and this book delivers incredible chaos/spreadsheet tension, along with a great cast of characters and, of course, excellent ballet."

—KD CASEY, author of the Unwritten Rules series

"The tenacity of the joy and subtlety of the vulnerability in Chloe Angyal's writing makes it impossible to stop reading. *Pointe of Pride* is funny, romantic, sexy, and above all, so richly human that you will see yourself falling in love while reading. Angyal captures the things we love most about romance, and you'll be unable to put it down."

—DENISE WILLIAMS, author of *Technically Yours*

Pointe of Pride

Chloe Angyal

AMBERJACK
PUBLISHING

CHICAGO

Copyright © 2024 by Chloe Angyal
All rights reserved
Published by Amberjack Publishing
An imprint of Chicago Review Press Incorporated
814 North Franklin Street
Chicago, Illinois 60610
ISBN 979-8-89068-012-9

Library of Congress Control Number: 2024933576

Cover design: Jonathan Hahn
Cover illustration and hand lettering: Sarah Gavagan
Typesetting: Jonathan Hahn
Author photo: Vivian Le

Printed in the United States of America

For Molly, Whitney, and Jordan. I'd be lost without you.

Author's Note

This book features on-page depictions of pelvic floor dysfunction and painful consensual sex. I've tried to treat these issues with the care that they, and you the reader, deserve.

Chapter 1

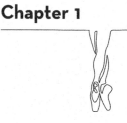

There was a special place in hell reserved for the people who designed the lighting in airplane bathrooms, Carly thought, glaring at her reflection in the tiny, grubby mirror. She'd already spotted three new gray hairs since she started brushing her teeth. After a full day in transit, she felt exhausted. And thanks to this mirror and the ghastly overhead lighting, she looked it. Her freckled cheeks were pale, her skin dry and pinched. Two purple-gray smudges under her eyes made them look swollen and sunken, and gave her whole face a vaguely undead vibe. Despite her lip balm's best efforts, it was no match for twenty-plus hours in a plane, and now her lips were chapped and flaking. And, *shit*, make that four new gray hairs.

Carly spat into the teeny sink and rinsed her mouth, scowling into the mirror while she swirled the water around her gums. *This is true friendship*, she thought, packing her toothbrush and toothpaste back into her travel toiletries case, *spending a whole day sitting upright in a series of tin cans full of recycled air so I can stand up with Heather at her wedding.* She was basically a lock for sainthood, she reasoned, as she opened the door carefully and slipped back out into the coach section, offering a quick, apologetic smile to the impatient-looking middle-aged man who had been seated across the aisle from her snoring loudly for the last twelve hours but was now waiting outside the door. He slipped past her, unsmiling, into the bathroom.

Of course, Carly conceded once she was settled back in her lumpy aisle seat, Heather would do the same for her—if Carly ever got married, which seemed unlikely. Heather had a habit of always showing up when Carly needed her, though. Like two years ago, when Heather's ex had gotten Carly fired and Heather had leapt into action to get Carly's job back. And it wasn't like Carly was sorry to be missing three weeks of a particularly slushy February in New York to drink champagne and go to the beach and hang out with her best friend. *So, maybe not sainthood*, she thought, swiping through the action movies on offer and wondering if she could squeeze in one more before the plane landed. *But maybe some kind of friendship medal. A plaque, at the very least.* Carly must have dozed off during the opening credits, because she jolted awake when the plane touched down. The hundred people around her seemed to heave a collective sigh of relief.

As soon as the plane came to a stop, the man across the aisle from her stood up and reached for the overhead bin. Carly rolled her eyes. Why did people do that? Did they not understand how lines worked? Did they think the first person to leap out of their seat back in row 56 would somehow be allowed to leave the plane before everyone else?

Trying to ignore the fact that his khaki-clad ass was now perilously close to her face, Carly pulled her phone from her backpack and turned it on. There were two texts waiting for her:

> *AusTel, 6:57 AM: Welcome to Sydney. You are roaming on Australia's largest network. Enjoy your Aussie adventure!*
> *Heather, 6:57 AM: WELCOME TO SYDNEY! Marcus and I will be waiting for you at arrivals and we'll have coffee. Can't wait to see you* ☕️ 🐨

Carly let out a little groan of longing. Coffee sounded so good right now. So did a shower, a nap, and any meal that hadn't been reheated into oblivion and served to her on a plastic tray. And a hug from her best friend.

She opened her emails, scrolling through twenty-two hours' worth of messages. There were a few ads about flash sales from her favorite brands—the Capezio leotard she loved was 25 percent off this week—and stopped suddenly when she saw one from Catherine Lancaster. Subject line: *Changes to New York Ballet promotion schedule.*

Carly's stomach lurched. Since Catherine had retired from her perch as a longtime principal dancer and taken the reins of the company from the recently dethroned Martin Koenig—that asshole—she'd changed very little at the company. Mr. K had retired abruptly after a long and authoritarian rule, and for the last year Catherine had been running things much as he had, albeit without Mr. K's cold disdain or hot temper. Carly had sometimes wondered if Catherine's recent experience as a dancer imbued her with a little more sympathy for the dozens of dancers now under her purview. Now, though, it seemed the Lancaster era was beginning in earnest. Carly's breath was a little short as she jabbed hastily on the message.

> *Dear company members,*
> *As you know, New York Ballet traditionally promotes dancers at the end of the spring season in June. However, in order to give promoted dancers more time to prepare for their new positions, this year promotions will be announced when we begin rehearsals for the spring season in March. My hope is that—*

Carly didn't read the rest of the email. She slumped back in her seat and let her phone fall into her lap, trying not to panic. Shit. Shit, shit, *shit.* She'd thought she had more time. Heather had scheduled her wedding so her maid of honor would be home in time to start rehearsals, and Carly had figured that when the trip was over, she'd be able to go home to New York and have a whole season to impress Catherine. But now she'd have . . . a week, if that? Her chances of proving to her new boss that she deserved to be promoted to soloist had just been slashed, and there was nothing she could do about it. She couldn't very well turn around and go back to New York. She wouldn't even consider missing Heather's big day, not after everything she and Heather had been through together. She screwed up her face and tried to take a deep, calming breath. It didn't work.

"Shit!" she hissed.

From the aisle, someone cleared their throat pointedly. Carly opened one eye and looked up to find the impatient man in khakis staring at her, looking affronted. Carly closed the other eye and went back to cursing internally.

She needed this promotion. She'd spent all thirteen of her years at NYB in the corps, and if being unceremoniously fired by Mr. K had taught her anything, it was that being one woman in a fifty-person corps made her disposable. She hated how that felt. As a soloist, she'd have a little more stability—to say nothing of the opportunities to teach, coach, or maybe even run a small company when her body gave out and she retired. But she was thirty-one, and there wasn't much time left.

She managed not to curse out loud again, and when it was finally time to deplane, she pulled her bag up off the floor and rose to her feet. Both her knees cracked loudly as she stood, and Impatient Khaki Pants glared at her, now truly appalled. She gave him a bright, plastic smile, and shrugged. *That's what twenty-five years of ballet sounds like, buddy,* she thought. *We might look like fluttering fairies on stage, but in real life our joints are wrecked, our muscles are spasming, and our toenails are peeling off. And we really like to curse. Oh, and our careers are fucking falling apart.*

Once she made it past the front of the immigration line—where the agent did a double take when he saw "ballerina" listed as her employment and looked her up and down with obvious curiosity—she found a loose luggage cart and pointed it toward the only moving carousel in the large, brightly lit arrivals hall. Hopefully, her bag would come out quickly and she could get out of here and go find Heather. And Marcus, and that promised coffee, but mostly Heather. It had been almost a year since she'd last seen her best friend, when the happy couple had come to New York for Heather's short guest run with her former company, but it felt like a decade to Carly. They'd gone from being roommates who took class together almost every day to living on opposite sides of the globe. While Carly was happy that Heather had found a company and a man that she loved down here, being apart all the time absolutely sucked. Which she planned to tell Heather as soon as she'd given her a hug that lasted between ten and fifteen minutes.

It was only after she'd thrown most of her body weight behind the stray luggage cart that she realized it was missing one wheel. It swerved wildly, jerking hard to the right, and then the plastic bar slipped out of her grasping fingers and the cart went reeling away from her, wobbling and rattling toward—

"Look out!" Carly shrieked. Khaki Pants whipped around and threw himself out of the way just in time, but it was too late for the person behind him. The cart careened into the back of their legs and sent them sprawling onto their stomach on the smooth, shining floor of the arrivals hall, bag and papers flying.

"*Shit!*" Carly breathed, shrugging her backpack off her shoulders and running toward the stirring body on the ground. The cart rolled away and into a pair of trash cans bearing a list of foods travelers were forbidden to bring into Australia.

"Oh God, I'm so sorry, are you all right?" she asked, on her hands and knees next to the body, praying she hadn't just caused an international incident. God, she'd been in this country less than half an hour and already screwed up in spectacular fashion. Classic Carly.

The body rolled over, and Carly registered for the first time that it belonged to a man. She looked into his face and felt her mouth go dry. Thick, wavy dark brown hair. Sharp, sculpted cheekbones above a long, straight nose. And deep blue eyes surrounded by the kind of full, dark eyelashes that would make Maybelline executives weep. He looked like he'd be a head taller than her when standing, and his merino wool hoodie clung to a pair of lean, muscled shoulders. Even in her state of distracted distress, she could see that he was extremely good looking.

He was also extremely angry looking. His cheeks were flushed pink with rage, and his mouth was twisted into a shocked grimace.

"*Putain de*— what the hell is wrong with you!" he snarled up at her. Carly flinched and straightened up to sit on her knees. "You nearly killed me!"

Carly looked him up and down, taking in the muscular thighs visible beneath his tapered black sweatpants. She couldn't see any blood. All of his joints seemed to be bending in the right directions. *Nearly killed* seemed like an overstatement. Still, he did look pretty shaken up.

"I'm sorry," she said again, "I lost control of the cart. Are you hurt?"

"No, but that's hardly the point," he snapped. "Be more careful next time, would you?" The pink blotches in his face were blooming red as he looked up at her disdainfully. Carly glanced around and saw that a handful of people were watching them from beside the carousel. Khaki Pants picked up his carry-on bag, which had toppled over in the chaos, and approached them. Before he could offer his help—or, more likely, his own reprimand—she waved him off.

"I said I'm sorry," Carly said to the man on the floor. "It was an accident. It could have happened to anyone." But of course, it had happened to her. Carly Montgomery, disaster on wheels. In this case, literally.

In response, he simply scoffed, and Carly's neck prickled with irritation. He sat up slowly, more slowly than he needed to, in her opinion, and rubbed his knees.

"I really am sorry," she tried again through gritted teeth. "Let me help you with your stuff." Her knees cracked again as she got to her feet, and she walked over to his satchel. When she turned around she saw he was getting up too, and she watched as he rose tentatively and brushed the front of his sweatpants. The fall had messed up his hair, but only a little. Dimly, Carly wondered how he managed to get off a plane as perfectly coiffed as he was. She was pretty sure she looked like she'd just crawled out of a dumpster. Still, he looked disoriented, as if he were unsure his joints would hold his weight as he walked. Guilt swirled in Carly's stomach as he took a few careful steps and crouched to collect his passport.

She made her way back to the man, who was tucking the passport safely into his pocket. When she reached him, she looked up into his face, met his eyes, and quickly averted her gaze again. God, it was like staring directly at the sun. If she was going to look at him again she'd need a paper plate with a hole in it.

"Here's your bag," she said to the zipper of his hoodie, and she held out the satchel. "Sorry, again. I hope you're not too bruised."

He reached out to take it, and her eyes followed his fingers again as they wrapped around the fabric strap, brushing briefly against her skin. She sucked in a quick, sharp breath at the contact, and at the rush of sudden heat that sparked where their hands met.

A second later, he yanked the bag out of her hand, and the strap caught a little on one of her fingers.

"Ow," she said, shaking her fingers out. She lifted her chin, and paper plate be damned, she met his eyes accusingly. Up this close, she could see that they weren't only blue but flecked with silver and ringed with dark, stormy gray. Thin lines had set in around them, and they only deepened as he glared down at her.

He slung the bag over his shoulder, moving with more confidence now, and Carly was relieved to see that she hadn't hurt him. But then he spoke again.

"Sorry, I hope you're not too bruised."

Carly felt her jaw drop, and for a moment she was speechless. It was a rare feeling for her, and not one she enjoyed. What was this guy's problem? At most, he'd have some bruises on the backs of his legs and where his knees hit the floor. And possibly one on his ego, which certainly seemed large enough to withstand the hit. She hadn't broken any of his bones or, she hoped, any of his possessions. But here he was acting like she'd run him down with an eighteen-wheeler. Deliberately.

"Oh, what, like you've never made a mistake in your life?" she said sarcastically. He glowered down at her imperiously, and she scowled back. "Tell me, you uptight asshole, is it hard being so perfect?"

"I'm not perfect," he growled. His voice was deep and a little hoarse, with an accent that sounded Australian but might have been British. "But my mistakes generally don't endanger other people's lives or limbs."

Carly rolled her eyes. Amazing how she could fly to the other side of the world and still find the most entitled asshole in a five-hundred-mile radius. She was like a bright, flashing beacon for shitty men. And she'd had enough. She'd tried to be nice to this man, tried to smooth things over. She was doing her best. And if he wasn't going to accept her apology, then he could, with all due respect, shove that apology up his very nice ass.

"You could just say, 'It was an accident,' you know! You could just say, 'Shit happens!' Because shit does, in fact, happen! Some of us are mere mortals who occasionally make mistakes!" She was aware that she was shouting, and that her voice was loud enough now to carry through the hall to the other passengers and the airport staff. But as usual, she couldn't seem to stop herself. He had to *know*. "I didn't realize the cart was busted, and I'm doing my best to apologize, so you don't have to be such a *dick* about it!"

His eyes widened, and for a moment she thought she saw regret flicker in his obscenely blue eyes, but Carly was past caring. She was exhausted, and she hadn't seen her best friend in almost a year, and she truly could not bear to spend another moment of this endless day in an airport. She seized her backpack, threw it over her shoulder, and stalked away. But after a few paces, she stopped. She turned around and went back to the man, who was watching her with his mouth slightly open.

"Oh, and I really am sorry," she hissed one last time. "Sorry I didn't hit you harder."

She gave him one last scowl for good measure, turned on her heel, and hurried toward the baggage carousel. Heart racing, she stood tapping her sneaker on the floor and casting around for her silver gray suitcase. Mercifully, she saw the conveyor belt spit it out after a moment, and ignoring the shocked stares of her fellow passengers, she pulled it off the belt and hauled it toward the exit in one smooth motion, feeling her curly ponytail bouncing aggressively behind her. A second later, she had walked under the large G'DAY MATE! sign that hung over the sliding exit door and out into the bright Sydney sunlight.

As soon as Carly walked into the arrivals hall, she spotted Heather amid a crowd of families holding flowers and balloons. She was hard to miss when she was holding a sign that read CARLY MONTGOMERY, WORLD'S BEST MAID OF HONOR. Even better than a plaque. Carly shrieked and launched herself into Heather's arms and hugged her as tight as she could.

"You're getting married!" Carly squealed. "And you brought coffee! I've never loved you more."

Heather laughed, handing over the to-go coffee cup, and Carly took a grateful swig before giving Marcus a quick hug. He took Carly's suitcase, and together the three of them walked out of the airport and into the damp heat of a summer morning in Sydney.

"Show me the rock again," Carly said, and Heather dutifully extended her left hand. Carly had seen the cluster of three enormous lab-made diamonds over FaceTime, but she needed to see it up close. She shook her head. "Phew. How do you even do port de bras with that thing on? It's huge."

Heather lifted her arms into high fifth as she walked. "I had to do some extra weights work with my left arm, but it was worth it," she smirked. " Obviously I'm not wearing it on stage."

"Because you'd blind the conductor," Carly teased. "Or take your partner's eye out."

"Obviously *you're* not wearing *those* on stage," Heather gestured at Carly's hands, and Carly lifted her fingers to her face and wiggled all ten neon-pink nails.

"I've been wearing the loudest, brightest color I could find since the day the *Nutcracker* run ended," she smiled. It was her ritual: the company didn't permit anything other than natural hair or nail colors on stage, so once the season ended, she'd paint her nails or dye her hair, something bright and forbidden that she'd have to undo before the next season began. A few years ago, she'd given herself green highlights, which had looked appalling with her red hair. These hot pink nails would have been visible even from the nosebleeds. They were perfect.

It was a forty-five minute drive in morning traffic from the airport to Freshwater, the beachside suburb where Marcus grew up, and where Heather and Marcus had been living in his childhood home for the last two years.

"You must have gotten up early," Carly said, through another yawn. Heather swiveled around from the front seat with a bright smile. "Worth it," she said firmly, her brown eyes sparkling under her high, messy bun. Her skin glowed like she'd been doing some serious pre-wedding skincare. Or, she was just really happy. "It's so good to have you here."

"I'm excited to be reunited with the infamous Carly," Marcus said, catching Carly's eye in the rearview mirror and grinning mischievously. In his accent, it sounded like *Cahhly*, like he was from Boston, or pre-gentrified Brooklyn. She met his green eyes and smiled back.

"Who says I'm infamous?"

"Are you not the woman who started a shouting match within

an hour of arriving in this country?" he asked, eyebrows raised in amusement. Carly had told them the whole story on the walk to the parking lot, down to the exact shade of pink of that handsome asshole's face as he'd dressed her down.

"I did *not* start that," she replied indignantly, or as indignantly as she could manage through a third huge yawn. That milky Australian flat white Heather had brought her had been fine, but what she really needed right now was a vat of industrial-strength bodega iced coffee injected into her veins.

Marcus chuckled, glancing over his shoulder before changing lanes. "Yeah, but I bet you finished it."

Carly could see why her best friend liked Marcus. He was funny, and kind, and he brought out the best in Heather. A tiny part of her would never forgive him for taking Heather so far away—literally the other side of the world—but she was happy for them. Even if she sometimes struggled to *feel* happy for them. Long-term relationships had never been Carly's strong suit, and lately it had become difficult to watch so many of her colleagues pair off and settle down, especially when the pickings on the New York dating scene seemed to get slimmer by the day.

Well, that wasn't her problem anymore, she thought, as she watched Marcus reach across the front seat to squeeze Heather's hand. She'd made herself a vow after Carter stopped texting back that she was done. No more fuckboys, and no more fuckups. That was her new mantra. No more men who didn't understand how her body worked. Which meant . . . no more men. And no more mistakes that endangered the career she'd worked so hard for. She would spend the next three weeks living up to the sign Heather had made—and figuring out how to get promoted, somehow. She'd figure something out. She'd managed to survive on a corps de ballet salary without taking a penny from her parents. She could figure this out on her own, too.

As the car rolled out of the gridlocked center of the city and out toward the suburbs, the streets became narrower and greener, and the traffic lightened up. The sky was pale blue and cloudless, the sun was already high, and the sidewalks were dotted with people out walking their dogs and jogging along the sidewalks. When they stopped at a traffic light, Carly watched a group of uniformed school kids traipse across the road, their giant backpacks sagging on their tiny shoulders.

"That's Marcus's old uniform," Heather said. "Freshwater Primary School. It's cute, isn't it? They make all the kids wear them here, even in public schools. The school's up that way." She pointed up the hill to their left. "Our place is just down there."

"Hope you like the flat we found you," Marcus said, turning the car down the hill. "It's small, but it's close to us, not too expensive, and near the beach, which Heather said were your three top priorities."

"Damn right," Carly replied. She was going to spend three weeks soaking up the Australian sun and traipsing all over the city doing whatever it was a maid of honor was meant to do. She'd never done this before, but she also had no doubt Heather had already made a detailed, color-coded list of tasks for them to complete between now and the wedding. She was a little surprised Heather hadn't already pulled it out.

A few minutes later, they arrived at a two-story brick building with a faded yellow front door. "This is it," Marcus declared. "You're in one of the top units." He popped the trunk, and Carly climbed out of the back seat into the salty morning air.

The sidewalk in front of the house was scattered with petals, and Carly looked up to see a large tree arching over the low brick wall of the front yard, its twisted brown trunk sprouting glossy green leaves and velvety white and yellow flowers. Frangipani, she thought, just like the ones in the garden at her parents' beach house on Maui. She took a deep inhale and smiled at Heather, who had taken her suitcase from Marcus and was watching her with evident satisfaction on her face.

"Not bad, huh?" She smiled. "Let's get you upstairs so you can shower and get a fresh change of clothes. And maybe a nap?"

"Yes, please," Carly groaned gratefully. She reached up and pulled a flower off the tree and tucked it behind her ear, the scent wrapping itself around her, filling her with contentment and excitement. Sure, her arrival had been a little bumpy, but she was here now, and the next three weeks were going to be perfect. She would make sure of it.

The rental apartment took up half the top floor, and by New York standards it was positively spacious. There was a kitchen with a breakfast bar and two stools, and the living room had a comfortable looking couch and an upholstered bay window that looked out onto the street. The bedroom was snug, but it had a huge window and a skylight. The owners had leaned hard into the beach house aesthetic, and Carly failed to find a single item of furniture that wasn't distressed and painted white, or a decorative item that didn't feature at least one seashell or starfish. But the bathroom looked like it had been recently renovated, and Carly almost whimpered with longing when she saw the rainwater shower head hanging over the tub. She had spent her entire career dancing through clouds of other people's perspiration and sweating through heavy stage makeup, but she couldn't remember ever wanting a shower more than she did right now.

Carly wheeled her suitcase into the bedroom and unzipped it, ready to grab her shampoo and bodywash. But when it fell open on the floor, she stopped cold. She stared at its contents, confused. The last thing she'd packed had been the teal halter bridesmaid's dress she and Heather had picked out together. After a few weeks of scouring the internet, she'd found it on super sale, and it had been the last thing she'd packed before closing her suitcase. But the dress wasn't here. In fact, none of her things were here. She grabbed the first item she could see, a black suit bag, and found several pairs of men's shoes tucked underneath it, along with what looked like a camera bag.

"*Fuuuuuck*," she breathed. "No, no, *no*." She slammed the suitcase shut and examined the outside of it. It was a dark silver gray, just like her suitcase, but it was, she could see now, definitely *not* her suitcase. And these were *not* her belongings. In her humiliated rush to get out of the airport, she must have taken the wrong bag. Heart racing, she seized the baggage tag on the handle and frantically flipped it over.

Nick Jacobs, it read.

"Argh," she groaned to the empty bedroom. "Who the *hell* is Nick Jacobs?"

"Nick," Nick said into the phone, as slowly and clearly and patiently as he could.

"And how do you spell that, sir?" asked the bored-sounding man on the other end of the customer service line.

"Euh," Nick paused as he pinched the bridge of his nose and fought down every smartass reply that came to mind. Instead, in his most polite voice, he managed to say, "The usual way? N-I-C-K?" He paced the narrow length of his hotel room, too irritated with himself to enjoy the view of the beach from the window. "His" suitcase lay open on the bed, brightly coloured women's clothes frothing out of it. Taunting him for his unusual carelessness.

"Please hold, sir."

Nick glared at the suitcase. How could he have forgotten to check the name tag on the bag before he grabbed it off the conveyor belt? So many bags looked alike, and he always made a point of checking. Always.

Except this time, because he'd been thrown to the ground by a runaway luggage trolley, and then upbraided by its tiny American driver. Unbidden, the memory of her flashing brown eyes, wide and angry in her freckled face, popped into his mind. She'd barely come up to his shoulder, and she'd looked as exhausted as he'd felt after his long flight from Paris. But he'd watched as she'd pulled herself ramrod straight and seemed to grow by half a metre. Then she'd opened her mouth and unloaded on him, radiating so much rage that her curly orange-red ponytail seemed to vibrate with it. Even though *she* had hit *him*.

And then she'd swept from the building, leaving him standing on bruised legs, almost speechless, like he'd been hit by a human hurricane. And he'd been so out of it he hadn't even noticed that he'd collected the wrong suitcase until he'd showered and changed, then gone to unpack it and found none of his belongings inside.

"Stupid, stupid," he muttered.

"Excuse me, sir?" The customer service guy was back, and Nick couldn't blame him for sounding salty.

"Not you, sorry," he clarified hastily. "I was talking to myself."

"Mmhmm," came the unconvinced reply. "Is there anything identifying or unique about the bag you took, sir?"

"Euh," Nick started, but he couldn't quite figure out how to answer the question. This bag was unique, all right. He'd found a greenish dress on top of a pile of clothes and strappy sandals, and beneath a pair of denim cutoffs, there, plain as day, was a Ziploc bag full of sex toys. Specifically, dildos. The real owner of this bag, whoever they were, had packed a *lot* of dildos. White plastic ones, half a dozen of them in varying sizes, along with a travel-size bottle of lube. He'd hastily replaced the shorts, feeling as if he had violated this mystery traveller's privacy, but the shiny plastic of the dildo bag was still visible, catching the sunlight and drawing his eye every time he glanced towards the suitcase. He cleared his throat.

"There's, euh, nothing identifying on the outside, and no name tag. But I think from what I saw when I opened it, it belongs to a woman." A woman who apparently planned to have a *very* good time on her travels.

"Well, at this time, our protocol says we have to treat your bag as lost, so all I can do is file a report in our system and wait. Hopefully it will show up some time in the next few days. We'll call you if anything changes." Nick had managed to hold his panic at bay until now, but these words set his pulse racing. His cameras were in that bag, along with his suit and everything else he needed for this trip. Everything else he owned, really. He rubbed a hand over his head and squeezed his eyes shut, trying to settle his breathing.

"Okay, but isn't there some way you can— " he stopped when the room phone rang on the bedside table.

For a moment, his heart gave a hopeful flutter. Delphine?

"Euh, thanks for your help," he said quickly, wishing he actually meant it, and then he picked up the landline. "Hello?"

"Mr. Jacobs, this is the front desk," said a man's clipped voice. "There's someone down here asking to see you. She says she has your suitcase."

Relief swooped in Nick's stomach. "Thank God, tell her to wait just a moment, I'll be right—"

"She's also asking me to inquire as to whether you have her suitcase," the man interrupted. In the background, Nick could hear the murmur of another voice that sounded as agitated as he'd felt before the phone rang. "Gray, hardside, with a teal dress on top? No tag."

No tag, but a bag full of dildos, Nick thought. Who flew without a luggage tag? He never got on a flight without one, and good thing, too—if he hadn't put his hotel on his tag, this mystery traveller never would have found him.

"I've got it," he confirmed. "Tell her I'll be right down."

He pushed the dress back into the suitcase and zipped it up, then hurried out of his room, already sweating. It had been so long since he'd been home during the summer that he'd forgotten how humid it could get, the way the hot, damp air clung to your skin from the moment you stepped outside. You could sweat through a T-shirt before 10 AM in February.

He dragged the suitcase over the dingy hallway carpet, feeling bruises starting to bloom where he'd hit the floor this morning. The Freshwater Hotel looked exactly as he remembered it looking when he'd left for Europe fifteen years ago. It was a fairly old place, and it was only a hotel in the loose, Australian sense of the word. It wasn't a particularly flashy place to stay; the bar and restaurant downstairs were the main attractions, and the guest rooms were more of an afterthought. But it had been the only accommodation he could find that was within walking distance of the beach and in his budget.

One of these days, some big hotel chain'll buy this place and upgrade the shit out of it, he thought, arriving in the dated lobby, with its dark wood trim and scuffed tile floor. They'd tear out the battered baseboards and replace the chintz furniture with sleek midcentury modern stuff or rattan Scandi boho decor, market the place as an exclusive beachside haven, and jack the prices up by 400 percent. Sydney real estate being what it was, it was only a matter of time.

Nick's stomach rumbled and he checked his watch, frowning in confusion until he realized he hadn't yet changed it from Paris time. He knew from experience that it was best not to think about what time it was in whatever city he'd just left and to focus instead on the timezone he was trying to adjust to. Which meant whatever meal his body was hungry for, it was going to get breakfast. Good thing, too, because the smell of grilling meat wafting into the lobby from the restaurant was agonizing. He'd get this bag swap done and then treat himself to a full cooked breakfast and a strong coffee. His stomach growled again in impatient approval.

Just then, he saw a petite woman sitting in a tired armchair across from the front desk. She was scrolling through her phone and tapping her sneaker impatiently against the tiles and *oh, thank God* there was his suitcase. He started towards her, but at that moment, as if she'd sensed him looking at her, she looked up and stared at him. Their eyes met, and all Nick could do was stare back.

Her hair was no longer in a ponytail but damp and darker and hanging down her back. And she no longer looked like she was about to ram someone with a trolley and then verbally disembowel them. But there was no mistaking: it was *her*.

Chapter 2

Every time they left on company tour, Heather told Carly to pack a change of clothes in her carry-on, but Carly almost never remembered. This trip had been no different. So she'd showered and climbed back into her grimy airplane leggings and hauled Nick Jacobs's suitcase down the street and into the hotel lobby, where a welcome wall of air-conditioned air met her at the entrance. For a few quiet moments, she sat on a sagging armchair, enjoying the chill and waiting for him to appear with her bag. But when she looked across the lobby and realized who was staring at her, her face went suddenly as hot as if she'd stepped back outside into the Sydney sun.

Of course, she thought, her pulse pounding in her cheeks. She stared back at him. *Of fucking course.* What else could an asshole magnet like her expect? The man whose suitcase she'd inadvertently stolen from the airport was the very same man she'd hit with her cart. *Unbelievable*, she thought. And yet so very her. Even halfway around the world, upside down and in an entirely new timezone, she'd managed to fuck up. Twice. In rapid succession.

At least she could stop thinking of him as Handsome Asshole Guy, because now, she knew his name. Nick Jacobs. Nick Jacobs, who wrote two different phone numbers, an email address, and a hotel name on his luggage tag. Nick Jacobs, who had a very nice collection of what looked like professional-grade cameras. Nick Jacobs, whose shirt neckline revealed a few dark curls of chest hair and whose stubble only accentuated his sharp cheekbones. Nick Jacobs, who probably looked irritatingly hot in that suit she'd found in his bag. Nick Fucking Jacobs, who was watching her from across the room with disdain on his face and her suitcase at his feet.

Best to get this over with.

Carly would just hand over his bag and grab her own, and then she could go back to the apartment, change into some clean clothes, and pretend this never happened. Her wedding beach vacation could start in earnest.

So she took a deep breath, squared her shoulders, and wheeled the suitcase across the lobby to where Nick Jacobs was still waiting for her, looking haughty and annoyed.

He eyed her closely as she approached.

"You must be Nick," she said briskly.

"Yep, Nick Jacobs." he nodded. "Which is what it says right on my luggage tag." His voice was less hoarse than it had been at the airport, but it still dripped with condescension.

Carly rolled her eyes. *This fucking guy.* Okay, so she'd accidentally absconded with his bag, but she'd made the effort to return it. And in the blazing Australian sun, no less. She gave him a sarcastic smile that felt more like baring her teeth.

"You could just say thank you," she said pointedly. Nick Jacobs gave a humorless laugh.

"What am I thanking you for, exactly? For mowing me down with a trolley? For screaming at me in an airport? Or for stealing my property?"

Carly willed herself to keep her cool. *Think of calm, good things, Carly. Raindrops on roses, whiskers on kittens. Magical pointe shoes that don't wreck your feet. A barren deserted island where we can send all the shitty men.* "I didn't steal it," she gritted out, "I took it by mistake." Because she'd been too enraged—by him, thank you very much—to think straight.

"Whatever," Nick Jacobs muttered, and she rolled her eyes again. She reached out to grab the handle of her bag, but at the very same moment, he reached over to grab his own. In an instant, the space between their bodies had all but closed and her face almost pressed against his shoulder. The air was suddenly full of his cologne, something citrusy and spicy that made her stomach flip over.

She looked up in surprise and saw him looking down at her. No, looking down *on* her, his stormy eyes narrowed with dislike and his forehead creased with a frown. She pursed her lips, and watched as his gaze flicked down to her mouth, then back up to her eyes. Hot irritation clawed at the back of her neck as she glared, unblinking, into his face, unwilling to signal weakness by stepping back first. His frown deepened, his face clouding with what looked like confusion as he kept his eyes locked on her. The heat of their bodies and the scent of his cologne formed a small angry bubble around them in the middle of the cool hotel lobby. He held her gaze, still. So he was stubborn. But she was stubborn-er. *Not a word, but I don't care*, she thought, lifting her chin and cocking one eyebrow.

His eyes widened, and he gave in, straightening up and stepping back. Carly allowed herself a triumphant smile as cool air rushed in and his scent was snatched away—but as she watched him pull the suitcase toward him and she caught a glimpse of his toned forearms, her stomach gave another irritating flip.

He would *look good in that suit*, she thought bitterly, as she pulled her own suitcase toward her, but he looked damn good in the plain white T-shirt and navy blue shorts, too. Clearly Nick Jacobs was the kind of person who always remembered to pack a change of clothes in his carry-on.

Not bothering to thank her or say goodbye, he took a step away from her, then stopped and looked down at his suitcase. "Is everything still in here?" he frowned.

Carly stared at him in disbelief. "You're asking if I actually stole from you? My God, what is your problem?" *Fuck this fucking guy!* "No, I didn't steal from you. I'm not a *thief.*"

He had the decency to look chastened, and she watched his cheeks turn pink again, this time from something other than anger at her. He ducked his head and placed a possessive hand on the side of the suitcase.

"I'm sorry," he muttered, "there's just some pretty expensive equipment in here and I was worried I wouldn't get it back."

Carly shook her head impatiently. He could keep his half-assed apology. "Are we done here? Or do you want to file a police report? Maybe call Interpol while you're at it? I heard MI6 has some time on its hands lately."

"We're done," he said shortly. And then, because apparently he couldn't resist condescending to her one more time, he added, "Next time you should put a tag on your suitcase. So this doesn't happen to anyone else."

"Next time you should put all your fancy little cameras in your carry-on," Carly retorted. "So you don't have to worry about thieves."

"Yeah, well, maybe next time I'll just fill my bag with dildos, how about that?"

Carly's jaw dropped, and her skin went cold. She stared at him open mouthed, rendered speechless for the second time today. He ran his hand over his head, seemingly uncomfortable under her furious gaze. *Good*, she thought. *You should be uncomfortable, you smug piece of—*

"You went through my bag?" It came out like a hiss, and he looked around them, presumably to make sure no one had overheard.

"Just enough to see that it wasn't mine," he said stiffly.

"And just enough to find my . . . very personal belongings? Are you kidding me right now?" Carly's heart was pounding and indignation pushed her voice an octave higher.

He ducked his head again, wincing slightly and shrugging his broad shoulders as she glared at him. Guilt nipped at her neck. Distantly, she told herself to calm down, that she was letting her temper get the better of her yet again, but she was too tired, too embarrassed, and too furious to heed any of it. She was meant to be relaxing, goddammit. She was meant to be on a beach with her best friend, or racking her brains trying to figure out how to escape the corps. And instead she was here with Nick Bag Tag Jacobs, who had managed to ruin 100 percent of her vacation so far. Who was standing here all hot and put together and mocking the most intimate contents of her luggage. Of her *life*.

She gripped the handle of her suitcase and glared at him. She knew she should stop and take a few deep breaths and count to ten, like her meditation app had told her to do. She should visualize a train slowing down instead of reeling out of control and off the tracks. But she couldn't make her brain do it. Her limbs were heavy with exhaustion, and her cheeks were burning with rage and humiliation, and right now Nick Jacobs's face looked like an amalgam of every hot, nice-smelling jerk who'd screwed her over in the last few years.

"I didn't go through it all," Nick Jacobs said, his voice low and urgent, as if it was important to him that she understood, "I just needed something to identify it for the airline, and since there was no tag—" he said, but she interrupted him. The train had come off the tracks and was plowing through buildings, causing millions in property damage—and she couldn't seem to stop it.

"Next time," she growled, "I hope someone does take your fancy little cameras, okay? You deserve it. And they're not dildos, you pompous perve, they're dilators." She grabbed her suitcase handle again, never once breaking eye contact. "Medical, therapeutic devices for people like me, with useless, broken vaginas. Hilarious joke, right? A real thigh-slapper. Have a nice life, asshole."

Humiliation burned her cheeks, and a new instinct took over. Carly turned and stalked across the lobby, yanked open the door without waiting for it to open automatically, and was gone.

* *

What. The hell. Just happened?

Nick stood planted to the lobby floor, shellshocked, for the second time that day, by the human hurricane that was . . . whoever that woman was. He didn't know her name, not that he'd ever need to. She'd stormed away from him after accusing him of rifling through her stuff and denouncing him as an asshole. Again.

The hand wrapped tightly around the handle of his suitcase was slippery with sweat, and his heart was racing. It had started thumping unusually hard when he watched her rise from her seat and had only sped up as he'd taken her in. Despite his bruised knees and dented pride—both her fault, by the way—he couldn't help but notice the length of her neck and her thick, expressive eyebrows. Watching her from across the room, he felt like he could read everything she was feeling on her striking face. Even when what she was feeling was exasperation, disgust, disbelief, and loathing. Towards him.

He'd known even as the words were coming out of his mouth that he shouldn't mention the sex toys. But her jab about his cameras had gotten him right in the gut. Those fancy little cameras had cost him so much. His whole government-supported retirement fund wiped out in just a few foolish, hopeful clicks of a mouse. And what good had it done? He wasn't a photographer, was he? He was just a retired dancer with a failed second career and no retirement savings. He'd been so panicked when he thought those cameras were lost, and now that he had them back, they only seemed to mock him. He didn't need a beautiful woman mocking him, too, especially not a beautiful woman who had already upended his morning so completely.

And it absolutely would have been an asshole move to go through her personal belongings, which was why he hadn't done it. He'd put the bag of—what had she called them, dilators?—back as soon as he'd realized he was looking at something very intimate. She was the one who'd rammed him with a trolley, taken his bag, and then rejected his very sensible suggestion of buying a fucking luggage tag. She was the one who'd shouted at him in public on two separate occasions this morning. So who was the asshole here, really?

He huffed out a sigh and loosened his grip slightly on the suitcase, his muscles and joints suddenly feeling every minute of the twenty-one-hour trip from Paris, and his trip onto the floor of the arrivals hall. His first thought as he'd gone sprawling onto his stomach had been *I can't break anything, I have to be able to dance.* A split second after he'd hit the floor, he'd realized that no, actually, he didn't have to be able to dance. It didn't matter if he shattered his kneecap or tore his Achilles or threw his hands out in front of him and broke both his wrists. He wasn't a dancer any more, and he no longer had any reason to be cautious with his body. No one would miss him if he wasn't in class or on stage; no one would reprimand him for being careless and missing a performance season. He would just be a regular man with a regular broken wrist.

He sighed again, more resigned this time, and pulled his suitcase across the lobby towards the hotel restaurant. It was hard to imagine a less auspicious arrival home than the one he'd had today. But he was home.

Well, kind of, he thought, settling himself at a small table and looking out the window at the road down to the beach. Sydney was where he'd spent his teen years, but it had been ages since he'd lived here. In fact, he'd been gone almost half his life; he'd left as soon as he'd graduated from the School of Australian Ballet at seventeen. Only a few boys in his class had been offered places at the Australian National Ballet, and the rest of them, Nick included, had to audition for jobs at other companies. Seeing as there weren't that many full-time ballet companies in Australia, that usually meant going to Europe—Eastern, Western, wherever they'd give you a job. His parents hadn't wanted him to go overseas, and he was daunted by the prospect, too. But what choice did he have? He had to go where the jobs were. They'd been furious when he told them he'd accepted a contract at the Munich State Ballet, and they'd been pushing him to move home ever since.

Those first few years away had been an exhausting blur of figuring out how to be an adult with a real job, on top of learning German and memorizing dozens of ballets' worth of choreography. But after a few years, he'd been promoted out of the corps de ballet, then made the jump to the Paris Opera Ballet, where he'd had the absurd luck to spend over a decade dancing as a premier danseur at one of the oldest and most prestigious ballet companies in the world. If Sydney was where he'd spent much of his childhood, Paris was where he had truly grown up. In Paris, he'd finally begun to feel like he knew how to be a working artist. Like he knew who he was.

He sighed and flagged down a harried-looking waitress, who tucked her hair behind her ear and dug her notepad out of her apron pocket as she approached.

"What can I get you?" she asked quickly, giving him a perfunctory closed-mouth smile before readying her pen.

"May I have the full brekkie, with brown toast and extra mushrooms? And a skim cappuccino with one sugar. Please." The waitress nodded, then hustled away to put his order in with the kitchen, and his stomach grumbled impatiently. Sure, he'd miss being able to get exquisite French pastry at a moment's notice, but as he'd told Delphine many times, Parisians, for all their fine cuisine, still hadn't mastered the art of the full hot breakfast.

Delphine. He drummed his fingers on the table and tried not to think about her. The woman who had loved him until he left the company and they stopped having work in common. Who had barely mustered interest in his new career, if he could call it that. Who had told him that no, she didn't want to go with him on this trip because actually, she didn't want to go anywhere with him, ever again.

And so he'd come home alone, and on a one-way ticket. What was left for him in Paris, anyway? Most of their friends were still dancing, so Delphine had kept them in the split. Simply buying a bunch of cameras and calling himself a photographer hadn't made it so, and no one in Paris had been interested in yet more pictures of dancers. His dreams of being a digital Degas hadn't panned out. And now here he was: thirty-two but retired, no longer a dancer but not a photographer, no longer totally Australian but definitely not French, no longer in love but not over Delphine. He wasn't anything. He was just . . . floundering.

The waitress returned with a large cup of coffee on a saucer, and Nick gave her a grateful smile. She did a quick double take, and then glanced down at the suitcase tucked behind his chair.

"Where are you visiting from?" she asked. A more complicated question than she realized.

"Euh, Paris, I guess," he said. Her eyes lit up.

"Oh gosh, I want to go there soooo badly. How long are you staying in Sydney?" Also a complicated question. The way she asked it, he could tell she hadn't pegged him for a local. Which, he supposed, he wasn't anymore. He picked up his spoon and poked it into the foam to buy some time while he considered his answer.

"I'm not sure, really. A few weeks, at least, and then . . ." he trailed off. And then what? For the first time in his life, he had no plan, no goal, no project. He'd spent his entire childhood trying to become a professional dancer, then his entire young adulthood trying to *be* a professional dancer. But since he'd retired, he had the distinct impression that he'd simply walked off a cliff and had spent the last eighteen months in an endless, scrambling freefall.

He said none of this to the waitress, who was watching him expectantly, waiting for him to finish his sentence. He forced what he hoped looked like a carefree smile.

"And then we'll see where the wind takes me," he said. She nodded, looking satisfied. *What utter shit*, he thought. He'd never once gone where the wind had taken him, and he had no idea how to do that. He'd always had a plan. Had always known who he was and what he wanted. And now he was just drifting, aimless and feeling empty.

"What are you going to do while you're here? See the sights? The Bridge, the Opera House?"

Nick chuckled and took a sip of his coffee. He'd seen the sights. He'd spent his teenage years in a dormitory not far from the Harbour Bridge, and done his graduation performance on the big stage at the Opera House. But there was no need to tell her that. He nodded, pretending to consider the idea.

"I might do. They're great to photograph." Then he straightened a little in his chair and met her gaze. "I'm a photographer," he said, feigning a certainty he didn't feel. What did a successful photographer sound like?

"Oh, very cool," she replied, tucking her hair behind her ear again and glancing over her shoulder.

"Don't let me keep you," he said quickly.

"Yeah, sorry," she replied, with an apologetic smile. "It's peak hour. But I'll be back soon with your breakfast, Mr. Photographer."

Mr. Photographer. Nick shook his head as she walked away. God, he was full of it.

Carly stalked along the baking sidewalk, tugging her suitcase over the uneven pavement. A familiar feeling of reproach crawled between her ribs and mingled with her hunger to make her stomach ache. Nick Jacobs's low, almost pleading voice echoed in her head, matching her pounding pulse. *I just needed something to identify it for the airline.* He'd looked sincere when he'd said it, but then, he'd also looked sincere when he'd dressed her down and snatched his bag from her hand. Still, if she had a nickel for every time she'd flown off the handle like that, only to spiral into guilt and self-reproach mere minutes later . . . Well, she'd have made ten cents today. And she'd never have to take another dime of her parents' money. She'd also spend way less of her life apologizing for her behavior.

She knew there was no excuse for it. She wasn't a child, and there hadn't really been an excuse for it even when she was. But it never made a difference to tell herself that in the moment, when her insides felt alight with anger and she knew the only thing that would put out the fire was to unload on the nearest available target. It was such a cliché, the hot-tempered redhead. And if there was one thing Carly hated it was—okay, there were lots of things Carly hated. But one of them was confirming anyone's stereotypes. She spent so much of her professional life quietly obeying instructions, and it felt good to open her mouth and talk back in her personal life. Or shout back. But once she'd done that, she'd be left smoldering and regretful. Even if, as in the case of Nick Smugface Jacobs, they totally deserved it.

She was smoldering now as she made her way from the hotel back to her apartment, sweating and squinting against the sun. As she darted across the street, she tried not to think about the insults she'd thrown at him or the mortifying things she'd revealed about herself. Even by her standards, that little rant was extreme. Carly Montgomery wasn't known for her subtlety or her self-control, but she'd never descended to yelling at a stranger about her pelvic floor before. She'd never even told Heather about her pelvic floor issues, and Heather had been her best friend for two decades.

But he'd found the dilators. The stupid, sterile, hideous dilators that she'd brought with her because her physical therapist said she had to work with them every day if she wanted to see results.

And she did. She wanted, more than almost anything, to fix her stupid, broken vagina.

For as long as Carly could remember, inserting anything into her vagina—tampons, specula, and definitely penises—had been agonizingly painful. Sometimes, it was simply impossible. It took nerves of steel to wear a pad under a white leotard and pink tights, but it was that or skip multiple ballet classes every month when she was a teenager, because no matter how many times she tried, no matter how many different sizes or applicators or angles or internet-recommended tricks she used, she simply could not get a tampon more than half an inch inside her. She'd spent hours locked in the bathroom of her childhood home, pressing the tip of the tampon against what felt like a brick wall of muscle. Her body just refused. It closed up, like there was no opening there at all.

And when insertion was possible, it was painful as fuck, even for someone with the kind of pain tolerance you needed to be a ballet dancer. The first time a boy had tried to put his fingers inside her, when she was fifteen, she'd wondered why his fingernails felt so sharp, and why they seemed to have battery acid all over them. When she'd winced and squirmed her pelvis away, he barely seemed to notice her discomfort; he'd just kept pumping his fingers into her as if touching her cervix would dispense a cash prize.

It had been the same story when she'd had sex for the first time, with a different boy. He'd slid his condom-clad penis into her, and she would have sworn the lube was made of fire. After a few minutes that felt like hours, he finally came, and her eyes burned with unshed tears. Her jaw hurt from clenching through the pain. Three weeks later, he'd broken up with her; they'd dated for almost a year before sleeping together, but sex with her hadn't been worth the wait, he said. *No shit*, she remembered thinking. *I'll gladly wait another sixteen years before I do that again.*

The first time she'd gone to the ob-gyn for an annual exam, at seventeen, she'd raised the problem with the doctor. He'd checked her age on the chart and told her, with a disapproving frown, that she was probably too young to be having sex anyway. When she'd raised it with a different doctor a few years later, she'd been told she wasn't relaxed enough and to drink an extra glass of wine before sex.

She remembered the frustration that had bubbled in her chest as she searched the doctor's face for more insights. She'd chosen a woman ob-gyn because she hoped that she'd be more sensitive and understanding than the last one.

"Is it really a good idea to impair my judgment and reflexes right before sex?" Carly had asked skeptically. Then the doctor had suggested that her tolerance for pain might just be a little low.

"I'm a ballet dancer. I basically break the bones in my feet for a living," Carly had told her, trying not to sound too annoyed. "What else've you got?" At that, the doctor had raised her eyebrows and told Carly that all her tests looked normal and she was probably just too tightly wound.

Another doctor had prescribed her a numbing cream to put on her vulva before sex. *I don't want to feel nothing*, Carly had thought in frustration, *I want to feel pleasure. Or at the very least, not pain.* Yet another doctor had told her that she probably wasn't aroused enough and should figure out what turned her on and incorporate that into her sex life.

"I know what turns me on," Carly had snapped across the small, brightly lit exam room, the least arousing place in the entire world. She'd never lacked for desire. She'd always wanted the sex she tried to have. Wanted it to feel good, wanted to give her partner what he needed, wanted it to please, please, *please*, this time, just *work*. It was maddening that even though her entire job, her entire life, really, revolved around controlling her body, around training it to do something so few people could do, she could not control this. She could make her body do things no human body was ever meant to, but she couldn't do this one thing. This extremely natural, normal thing that everyone else could do.

"It isn't that I don't want it," she'd told that doctor. "I just want it not to hurt like a motherfucker."

That ob-gyn had *tsk*ed and shaken her head, and then none-too-gently suggested that Carly see a therapist, because the pain was probably in her head. But Carly was already pulling her feet out of the stirrups and reaching for her bra. The doctor didn't believe her. That was the problem, she thought: the doctors never really believed her when she told them how bad the pain was, or how many supposed solutions she'd already tried.

And if her sexual partners ever noticed that she was gritting her teeth and faking it, they never mentioned it. Usually, she could switch off her brain and push the pain away, moaning and digging her nails into their backs in what they seemed to think was pleasure. Her mind would drift out of her body, and she'd sometimes feel like she was watching herself have sex, putting on a damn good show that none of her boyfriends seemed to realize was all artifice. When it was over, she'd struggle to come back to herself, her brain too slow and waterlogged to speak. One guy had joked, his tone barely concealing his unearned satisfaction, that he'd fucked the words right out of her.

After a while, she'd started to resent their credulousness, hating the fact that they could feel so much pleasure and not even notice that she was in pain. Or worse, that they could take their pleasure even when they suspected she might be in pain. It made her burn with fury that they could enjoy themselves and not notice or care that she sometimes sighed in relief and wiped away tears as soon as they came. Inevitably, after a few weeks—a few months, at most—she'd cut them loose.

It wasn't until a few months ago, when she'd read an article about pelvic floor physical therapy and made an appointment at a discreet, spa-like clinic in midtown, that she'd found a doctor who believed her. And more than that, a doctor who didn't find her complaints mystifying or her problem unsolvable. Angela saw clients like her all the time. Clients who had given birth or gone through menopause and now couldn't have sex without pain. Clients who, like her, had never experienced pain-free sex in their lives. Angela examined Carly gently with her well-lubed and rubber-gloved fingers, managing to slide a single finger two knuckles deep into her vagina before Carly winced and recoiled against the exam bed.

Angela explained to her that even though Carly's pain felt like it was on the surface, like her most delicate flesh was being ripped and torn, the problem was actually in her muscles. Her pelvic floor was too tight, Angela had said.

"But it's supposed to be tight. It's strong. My pelvic floor is working all day, every day," Carly had said, craning her neck up from the exam table to meet Angela's eyes. "You can't do anything in ballet without activating your core and your floor."

Angela had leaned back in her rolling chair and shook her head, her glossy brown waves flowing around her kind face.

"Your pelvic floor isn't meant to work all day every day. It needs rest. It's a muscle, and muscles get sore if you don't give them a chance to rest. If your pelvic floor is working all the time, it's never resting and relaxing. It's tight and spasming, which is probably why penetration is so painful."

Carly frowned. The explanation made a certain amount of sense. But resting wasn't really something dancers were encouraged to do, unless they were seriously injured. Once, when she was nine or ten, a teacher had told her that after a day without ballet class, the dancer would notice the difference. After two days, her teachers would notice it, and after three days, the audience would notice. The warning had stuck with Carly, and she'd never taken more than two consecutive days off if she could help it.

"So I need to learn how to rest my pelvic floor?" she'd asked Angela. How would one even do that?

"That's right. We can work on some exercises that will release the muscles, so they have time to switch off and become less stiff and sore."

Carly had nodded eagerly, wondering why it had never occurred to her to approach a physical therapist for this problem. PT was usually the very first port of call for any dancer in the company. There was a physical therapy room on site at the theater, and if not for PT, half the dancers at NYB wouldn't still be working—or walking. Plus, she trusted Angela. After years of blank faces and condescending suggestions from doctors, it was a profound relief to talk to someone who was so unfazed by her condition. But then, Angela said something that put a damper on her relief.

"And I would advise you to stop having penetrative sex for a while."

Carly felt her eyebrows rocket upward.

"Excuse me?"

"You can learn how to release the muscles, but you also need them to unlearn what you've taught them over the years. Your body is smart. Every time you force penetration even though it hurts, you're teaching the muscles that penetration is painful and they should try to protect you from it. They're seizing up because they want to protect you. It's a perfectly natural response."

Carly swallowed, her throat suddenly tight. *They want to protect you.* Her body had known, all this time, what she needed. Had sent her one screaming, burning message after another, all but begging her to stop forcing something that was hurting her. But she'd ignored it. On some deep cellular level, beneath her skin, she'd known better. She'd wanted better. She'd pushed through the pain anyway.

She swallowed again and sat up on the crinkling paper as Angela tossed her rubber gloves in the trash can and scribbled some notes on a clipboard.

"Isn't there some other way?" she objected weakly to Angela's back. "Could I just double up on the exercises? It's just that . . . I really want to have sex."

Was that true, though? If she was honest with herself, a tiny part of her was relieved that Angela had told her to stop. She'd known for years that something was wrong, but it had taken Angela's firm, compassionate order to feel like she had permission to do something about it. The kind of sex she was having now—the kind of sex she'd been having for years—wasn't what she really wanted.

What she really wanted was sex that felt good. Sex that didn't make her feel like her body was failing her, and like she was failing herself for continuing to have it. She wanted to want someone and have that want answered with pleasure and comfort, instead of with pain and disappointment. And if temporary abstinence could help her achieve that, then wasn't it worth a shot?

So Angela had sent her home with a pack of sleek plastic dilators, white cylinders with rounded tops, and instructions on how to practice releasing her muscles and then inserting the dilators slowly. The thinnest one was about the width of a pen, and the largest the width and length of an average-sized penis. Once she could consistently insert the smallest one without pain, she was allowed to move on to the next one. *Weirdest PT exercises ever*, Carly had thought. She remembered opening the package and seeing them all lined up, a parade of the most sexless sex aids she'd ever seen, and jokingly asking Angela if they had any purple sparkly ones in stock.

Angela had chuckled indulgently and sent her on her way after reminding her that her best chance at success was to be consistent with her exercises and not put anything except the dilators inside her for a while. Carly said she'd do just that, and left the clinic feeling optimistic and excited to make good on her promise.

And she had, so far. She'd been diligent about doing her exercises every day and had progressed to the second dilator, which was about the width of a thick finger. At the time, she'd just started dating Carter, a former college lacrosse player who now worked in private equity. Carter was perfectly coiffed, perfectly pedigreed, and could carry a perfectly good conversation about contemporary art or current events. Perfect, perfect. Her parents would have loved him. Carly had had sex with him a few times, but after her first appointment with Angela, she told him that she couldn't do that anymore and wouldn't be able to for a while. She'd taken a deep breath and explained that it was a medical issue and reassured him, with her best attempt at a sly and flirtatious grin, that there were still plenty of fun things they could do. He'd seemed fine with it. He'd certainly seemed fine when she'd pulled him into the all-gender restroom to show him what kind of fun things she meant. They'd had a perfectly nice meal after that, though they spent most of it pretending not to notice the knowing look on their server's face. And then he stopped texting her back.

After four days of unreturned calls and texts, Carly got the message. Men couldn't be trusted. Not to see her when she was in pain, and not to want her when she was trying to do something about that pain. Unless they could fuck her they way they wanted to, she was of no use to them. Unless she could give them penetrative sex—"real sex," Carter had called it—everything else she had to offer was worthless.

And that was when she'd made her vow. Screw Carter and all the men like him. No more fuckboys. No more men at all, if all they really wanted was something she couldn't—no, *wouldn't*—give them.

And then Nick Jacobs had come along, with his strong shoulders and his ludicrously long eyelashes. Pulling her suitcase up the front path toward the front door of her rental, Carly pictured him mocking her, that condescending smile twisting his mouth. Asshole. Somehow, being laughed at felt even worse than the ghosting or willful ignorance, she thought, as she shouldered her way into the apartment and rolled the suitcase into the bedroom. She opened it up and let out a sigh of relief at the sight of her teal dress.

Now, should she have called him an asshole to his face, even if he very clearly was one? No. Carly was willing to admit that.

Still, she thought, peeling off her leggings at last and stepping into a pair of denim cut-offs, most assholes didn't try to apologize right away. Didn't look mortified when they were accused of going through someone's private belongings. Either way, she was too old to have so little self-control.

She gave herself a little shake, trying to get the image of his face out of her head. She had things to do today, places to be and people to help. Besides, she reasoned as she buttoned up the shorts and looked at herself in the mirror, it could have been a lot worse. It wasn't like she'd ever see Nick Jacobs again.

Chapter 3

Carly had mostly calmed down by the time she and Heather walked into the ANB building a few hours later. It helped that it was a gorgeous summer day, the sky a saturated turquoise, clear and cloudless. A far cry from the damp gray skies and sleet she'd left behind in New York.

"You weren't kidding," Carly said, peering out the window of the empty rehearsal studio. "The water is *right there.*"

The Australian National Ballet performed at the iconic Opera House, but its studios and administrative buildings were a couple of miles away, Heather had explained, built on what used to be a working wharf. A few decades ago, the high-ceilinged warehouses that lined one long finger wharf had been converted into rehearsal studios and offices, while the wharves that flanked held condos and a hotel. A few feet away from where Carly stood, the harbor glittered in the sun, sloshing around the legs of the wharf. It was spectacular, and so strange. She'd mostly believed Heather when she'd described the studios, but seeing it with her own eyes—hearing it, she could *hear* the water lapping outside—was something else.

"There's something magical about dancing on water all day," Heather smiled. She sat in the center of the sunny studio, pulling a pair of legwarmers over her canvas ballet slippers. "You can see for yourself next week. Peter said you can join company class any time you want."

Carly turned away from the window and nodded in thanks. She had hoped to finally relax a little on this vacation, but Catherine's email had changed everything. She couldn't very well go back to New York out of shape and expect to be promoted. A tiny, treacherous part of her wondered if she should be here at all. Shouldn't she be back in New York, attending the optional classes the company put on during the break? Showing her face at every opportunity so she could impress Catherine with her commitment?

She banished the thought and looked over at Heather, who had started her usual pre-class warmup sequence of jumping jacks, crunches, and stretches. The same one she'd been doing since they'd joined the company together at eighteen. Carly had spent all of fourth grade begging her parents for a sibling, but once she'd met Heather, she'd stopped. It didn't matter they were about as different as possible on paper; from the day they'd met in a ballet class at eleven years old, it had felt like they fit together like two feet slotting into a perfect fifth position. Heather was the closest thing she'd ever have to a sister. Carly was right where she needed to be.

"Can I join you?" she asked, as Heather jumped up and down.

"If you want, but aren't you tired?" Heather lowered herself to the ground and began her crunches sequence.

Carly was tired, and she wasn't exactly dressed for dancing, but if she was going to stay in shape, she might as well start now. Besides, it had been ages since she'd been able to dance with Heather. Even if it was just jumping jacks and a short barre before the pianist and rehearsal director arrived to run through one of Heather's solos, Carly wouldn't pass up a chance for them to dance together.

By the time they'd worked through the sequence—crunches, stretches, and then a series of calf raises, a new addition that ANB apparently mandated to prevent ankle injuries—Carly's quads felt warm and liquid and her spine loose and long, as if the endless flight from New York had never happened.

"Ready to dance?" Heather asked, panting slightly from the rapid-fire bicycles that rounded out the crunches sequence.

"Ready," Carly grinned. "Music?"

"I have a playlist I usually use when I give myself barre."

"Let me guess, it's all *Giselle*," Carly said slyly.

Heather rolled her eyes. "I swear, if I never have to dance that ballet again, it'll be too soon. No, it's just standard music for class, piano covers of musicals, the usual."

"Not today," Carly shook her head, already pulling her phone out of her back pocket and pulling up the music app. "Today we're going to mix it up."

"Ha, of course we are."

"Today we're going to mix it up *and* throw it back," Carly said, typing and scrolling until she found what she wanted. She hit play, and a second later, Heather was laughing, the sound slightly drowned out by the tinny sound of Usher and Lil Jon coming out of Carly's phone.

"We cannot do pliés to a song about sweat dripping down someone's balls!" Heather objected, but she was grinning.

"Excuse me, that's a totally different song, and we can do pliés to whatever song we want. What's going to happen, the ghost of George Balanchine is going to haunt us? Swoop around scowling until we turn on Stravinsky?"

"You're ridiculous," Heather shook her head.

"You love it. And if you don't want this song, I've got the rest of the hits of the early 2000s all lined up and ready to go." It was the soundtrack of their years at the NYB school together. The songs they'd played over and over again in their dorm room. "You think Balanchine's ghost will like 'Hey Ya'? Or maybe he's more of a Ciara kind of guy?"

"Ridiculous!" Heather repeated with a laugh, but she peeled off her legwarmers and jogged to the back of the room. Carly followed her, and together they dragged a barre into the middle of the studio. Heather claimed stage right, as she always did, and Carly set herself up on the other side of the barre, turning away from the mirrors lining the front wall of the room. She glanced over her shoulder at Heather and smiled to herself. Right back where she belonged.

She put her hand on the barre, fanned her feet out into first position, and took a deep breath. They began.

As it turned out, they could do pliés to Usher. And "Goodies" turned out to be the perfect tempo for tendus. Alicia Keys was a good fit for ronds de jambe, and "Hey Ya" made for some very fast, very frantic frappés. By the time they got to grand battements—to "Freek-a-leek," by Petey Pablo, and Heather didn't even bother pretending to object—they were both sweaty and smiling, and completely unfazed by the prospect of being haunted forever by the ghost of the father of American ballet. Who, to be honest, had been a bit of a creep and probably would have enjoyed spending his afterlife haunting young women.

Glancing in the mirror, Carly saw that her hair had frizzed out from her nape, like it always did when she didn't wrestle it into a bun and subdue it with hairspray. She was flushed and her upper lip was beaded with sweat, and she hadn't enjoyed barre this much in ages.

They were just stretching in deep post-battement lunges, throwing in some ports de bras—with some help from Beyoncé—when a woman stuck her head in the door. Heather stood up hastily, her face sobering, and Carly took that as a cue to grab her phone and turn the music off. Judging by the sheet music tucked under her arm, this was the rehearsal pianist. Heather stood up straight and schooled her face into a serious professional expression as the accompanist walked into the room, eyeing them with bemusement.

"Everything all right in here?" she asked. "That's not music you hear every day at the ballet."

Right. Australian National Ballet's artistic director might be a reformer, but ballet still loved its traditions. And "Lean Back" was not exactly traditional barre music.

"Hi, Kimberly," Heather said. "We were just getting warmed up. Er, I was. I'm ready whenever Marie gets here." Kimberly nodded but didn't say anything. She looked over Heather's shoulder and ran her eyes questioningly over Carly. "And this is my best friend, Carly, visiting from New York."

"Hi," Carly waved at Kimberly, who didn't wave back. Time for Carly to make herself scarce. She pocketed her phone and went to retrieve her bag from the side of the room, while Heather sat down and busied herself with her pointe shoes and ouch pouches. "I'll go explore the neighborhood and come back in an hour, okay?"

"Sounds good," Heather said quietly. "Sorry we had to cut the party short."

"Don't be, you've got stuff to do. And that was hard work. I'm sweating. Like, it's dripping, all the way down my—"

"Oh my God, stop," Heather said, fighting a laugh.

Carly stuck her tongue out at her, then hoisted her bag over her shoulder. In the doorway, she stopped. "Hey, Kimberly, what are you rehearsing today?"

Kimberly looked up from her pile of sheet music and spoke over her shoulder. "*Firebird*," she said tersely.

Suppressing a grin, Carly met Heather's eyes. "Oh," she said, eyes wide and innocent, voice as even as she could keep it. "So, Stravinsky, then?"

The last thing she saw before she ducked out into the hallway was Heather snorting a laugh into her hand.

Nick rang Marcus's doorbell and smiled at the little golden plaque beside it. The sign was fashioned to look like the ones you saw on grand old-money Sydney houses, except he was fairly sure this one was a joke. The house was a one-storey brick place and one of the last unrenovated homes on the block, and it was called, the sign informed him, Sand Castle. All around it were hulking white concrete compounds and Hamptons-style beach houses in various stages of renovation and expansion, but this little brown house seemed to sit, calm and stoic, amid the madness.

He'd walked to his friend's place via the beach, kicking off his shoes to pad along the water's edge and feel the dense sand squish beneath his feet. Freshwater Beach was as beautiful as he'd remembered, the deep turquoise waves rolling in steadily, breaking on the jagged cliffs, and splashing water into the swimming pool cut into the rocks on the north side. He stood between the fluttering red and yellow flags and gazed out towards the Pacific Ocean, thinking about the famous ode to Australia's dramatic landscapes that he'd had to memorise in Year 4. Nick had loved it so much his mum had found a copy and hung it up in the house. *I love her far horizons, I love her jewel-sea / Her beauty and her terror—the wide brown land for me.* He'd thought about that poem a lot in his first few years away, and it always brought a fond, sad smile to his lips. It did again today as he stood on the sand, letting white foam fizz around his ankles. You couldn't do that on the banks of the Seine. Well, you could, but you'd probably contract some kind of infection.

Marcus's place was a few blocks from the beach, and Nick had been glad for the chance to stretch his legs a little after such a long flight. But now he was hot and thirsty and eager to get indoors. He was about to ring the bell again when the door swung open and Marcus appeared, a wide grin on his face.

"You made it!" Marcus said, opening his arms and pulling Nick into a hug.

"I made it," Nick confirmed, squeezing Marcus's shoulders tightly. He hadn't been able to come back for Marcus's dad's funeral a few years ago, and it had gutted him at the time. Richard had been about as good a ballet dad as a boy could ask for, and Nick had always liked coming to stay at Marcus's place when he wanted a break from school housing.

He'd dreaded picking up the phone and telling Marcus that he couldn't be there to support him, especially since Marcus had been badly injured around that time, and Nick knew that being left alone with his brother Davo wouldn't have made things any easier. But the company had been in the middle of its Paris season, and there was no way they'd let him fly to the other side of the world at such short notice.

Marcus gave him one last pat on the back and then released him. Nick looked him over. Marcus looked more tan than he remembered, and somehow just as lean as he'd been when he was dancing. If Nick had to guess, he'd say Marcus had taken up running or some other outdoor exercise. He didn't quite look like a dancer any more, but he looked fit as hell.

"You look great, mate. What have you been doing?"

"Surfing, every morning," Marcus smiled, gesturing Nick down the hallway to the back of the house. "It was the only thing I wanted to do once my Achilles was healed. And living down the road from the best beach in the city, it would be a waste not to."

Nick looked around the kitchen at the back of the house, which was familiar even under the fresh coat of mint green paint Marcus and Heather had given it. The old pine table still stood in the dining area, scratched and dented and bearing decades' worth of water marks. Nick had eaten many a meal at that table, when he came home with Marcus for holidays and weekends because it was too far for him to go home to the mountains. The table gleamed in the light that streamed in through the back windows, through which Nick could see the back verandah and the garden where he, Marcus, and Marcus's brother had fought pitched water gun battles in the summer and camped out under the stars in the winter.

Marcus went to the sink and filled a glass of water, handing it to Nick before throwing himself into one of the chairs. Nick sat down and took a grateful gulp.

"How was your flight?"

"Awful, thanks for asking. I swear, the older I get, the longer those flights are. And I have no idea what time it is in my body." He yawned.

"Best not to think about it," Marcus replied, catching the yawn from him. "Sorry, I was up late going over my notes from last semester. The new term kicks off next week. We tried to schedule the wedding around it, but between my classes, the ANB season, and the NYB season, it was all a bit of a nightmare." When he'd retired from dancing, Marcus had decided to become a physio and was now a few years into a five-year degree. "But we could have picked you up from the airport, you know. Carly's flight can't have gotten in much later than yours."

"That's the maid of honour?"

"Mmhmm. She got in this morning, then went to the studio to watch Heather rehearse *Firebird* for a bit. They've got Heather in rehearsal basically every day until the week before the wedding, so we need all the help we can get from you and Carly. They'll be back from the studios in a sec, and the four of us can talk about how to divide up the wedding tasks. Heather's got the master list around here somewhere, I'm sure."

"The master list?" Nick asked.

"I'd say planning a wedding is like planning a war," Marcus chuckled. "But slightly more complicated. After this, Heather will be ready to invade New Zealand."

"That bad?"

"The spreadsheets I've seen I can never unsee," Marcus deadpanned. "But I'm sure Heather's takeover of Wellington will be swift and bloodless. And the wedding's going to go off without a hitch. Especially with you and Carly here to help out. Although, Carly . . ." he trailed off.

Nick raised an eyebrow. "Not a fan of the best friend?"

"No, she's great, and she loves Heather to the hilt. So clearly she's got great taste. But she's just, sometimes she's a bit much, you know?"

"Ah," Nick nodded.

"She comes from some rich New York family, and she's pretty brash."

"Noted," Nick said. He'd dealt with brash rich kids before. Ballet was full of them.

"Heather calls her a force of nature. Don't get me wrong, she can be a lot of fun, too. She's just a bit of a live wire, you know? Like this morning when we picked her up, she comes storming out with her suitcase and gives Heather a huge hug, then tells us this story about how she accidentally ran some poor guy over with her luggage trolley and got into a screaming match with him."

Nick nearly spat out a mouthful of water. He swallowed it fast and wiped his mouth with the back of his hand, staring at Marcus, heart racing.

"What?" he said, suppressing a cough. No way. This could not be happening. He could not have burnt through a year's worth of unwelcome coincidences in one morning. Through his horror, he heard the sound of a key turning in the lock at the other end of the hallway.

"I know, way to make an entrance, right? Anyway, brace yourself." Marcus craned his neck to glance up the hallway, and Nick heard the front door open.

Muffled chatter filtered down the hallway, and Nick stared at Marcus in shock and disbelief. He kept staring as he heard two people making their way towards the back of the house, unwilling to turn around and confirm his suspicions.

" . . . come on, you can admit it, that woman had a stick the size of the Empire State Building up her butt," came a familiar voice. A *very* familiar voice. Deeper than you might expect from a woman her size, and a little scratchy, as though she'd spent the night before shouting to make herself heard in a crowded room. Or the morning shouting at complete strangers for no good reason. In any other woman that voice would be intriguing and a little sexy. In this woman it inspired nothing but dread. And, at this moment, it was right behind him.

Nick rose from the chair, more slowly than he'd ever stood in his life, and turned around.

Heather was laughing as she arrived in the kitchen. "We're here and we brought banh mi! Nick!" she exclaimed, a delighted grin on her pretty face. She stuck out her hand, and he shook it. "I'm so glad to meet you at last. I'm Heather."

Keeping his eyes on Heather to avoid looking at the woman next to her, who he could already sense was stone faced and furious, Nick managed a jerky nod and did something with his mouth that approximated a smile. Heather didn't need to introduce herself. The Heather Hays, ex-principal dancer at New York Ballet Theater, formerly one half of "America's ballet sweethearts," and the biggest hire Australian National Ballet had ever made? He still kind of couldn't believe that his best friend from ballet school, the gawky, daggy kid he'd once snuck off to a topless beach with, had managed to pull The Heather Hays. Or that she was even more beautiful in person than she was in publicity stills or on the cover of *Barre* magazine. *Well done, Marcus*, he thought, as she gave her fiancé a quick peck on the lips before setting a large brown paper bag on the kitchen table.

"Nick, this is Carly Montgomery, the maid of honour," Heather said, turning to face them again. She didn't seem to have noticed that Nick hadn't spoken since she'd walked in. He didn't know what would come out of his mouth if he tried. "Carly, meet Nick. Formerly a soloist at Paris Opera Ballet, now a very in-demand dance photographer."

He forced himself to look at Carly—he sure as hell knew her name now, and something told him he'd never forget it—and saw his own feelings reflected back on her face. Disbelief. Dread. Disdain. And a twinge of regret or shame or some other shadow he couldn't quite put words to. God, he should have known. With that posture, that carriage? He should have realized she was a dancer, too.

"Nick," she said stiffly. "Nick Jacobs." The way she said it, he was fairly sure she wanted to give him a profane middle name.

"Yeah," Heather said, looking at her friend in surprise. Nick saw Marcus's eyebrows rise. "Do you two know each other?"

Are you there Beyoncé? It's me, Carly. Why are you doing this to me? And can you just catapult me into the sun instead?

This was Marcus's best friend from ballet school? *This* was the best man she'd be spending the next few weeks with, and who'd be standing at the altar with her as Marcus and Heather said their vows? If she didn't love Heather as much as she did, she'd seriously consider changing her ticket and marching straight back to the airport this afternoon. Around the world in exactly one day.

She stared at Nick Jacobs—Nick! Fucking! Jacobs! The man she'd spent her entire morning fuming about!—and felt the seconds tick by as Heather's surprised question hung in the air.

All the elation she'd felt at dancing with Heather drained out of her as he stared back at her, his brow furrowed over those piercing deep sapphire eyes. Carly hoisted the sides of her mouth into a smile that felt distinctly like a grimace.

"No, we haven't met," she ground out. *At least I wish we hadn't.* She saw surprise and then understanding flicker across his face, and a second later he extended his hand.

"Nice to meet you," he said, sounding like the pleasantry was costing him as much as it had cost her. *Good.* He couldn't dress her down here, couldn't make her feel like a catastrophic failure for making a simple mistake. Couldn't reveal to Heather and Marcus how many times she'd screwed up in the barely six hours she'd been on this continent.

But she couldn't very well snub him here, either. If they'd never met, she didn't have any reason to be standing here stiffly, staring at him as he waited for her to accept his handshake. Grudgingly she took his hand and gave it one quick, uncommitted pump. His skin was soft and warm, because of course it was. She hated it.

"Nice to meet you, too," she said, in what she hoped was a convincing impression of politeness, then released his hand as quickly as she dared.

"Well, now that we're all here, we can get down to business," Heather said, eyeing Carly curiously. Carly swallowed and hitched her mouth up a little further, hoping Heather would chalk the strange tension in the room up to jetlag and fatigue.

"Let's get down," she agreed brightly. She was here for Heather. For Heather's big day. She didn't need to ruin this wedding with her new, burning dislike of Nick Fucking Jacobs. She would find a way to make nice with this man even if might pull her cheek muscles doing it. *World's Best Maid of Honor.*

"I'm going to go print off a few copies of the master spreadsheet, and then we can get started," Heather said. "Carly, help yourself to anything. I'll be back in a second."

"Okay," Carly smiled. Yeah, she was definitely going to pull a muscle.

"Just gonna run to the bathroom before we brief you on the invasion plans," Marcus said, giving Nick a knowing look. Nick replied with a nod and a close-mouthed smile, apparently as committed to this Nothing to See Here act as she was.

A second later, they'd both disappeared down the hall, leaving Carly and Nick alone in the kitchen. Carly glanced over her shoulder, waiting until she heard a door close, shortly followed by the whir of a printer starting up in the office she'd passed on her way in.

"I don't believe this," she hissed, just as Nick muttered to himself, "This is a nightmare."

Well, at least they agreed on one thing.

"I'd be happy to pinch you to make sure you're not dreaming," she shot back.

He glowered down at her. "A pinch would be minimal compared to the damage you already inflicted. Do your worst." He took a step toward her, squaring his shoulders, and once again she inhaled the scent of his cologne, something warm and spicy that on another man would have been tempting but on him was barely tolerable. Fine then, she'd hold her breath for three straight weeks.

God, three whole weeks with this man. Three weeks of pretending like she didn't want to roll her eyes every time he opened his mouth to talk. She would do it for Heather, because she'd do almost anything for Heather. But if this was going to work, he'd have to play nice, too.

"I swear to God, Nick Jacobs, if you ruin this for Heather, I will hunt you down and make your worst nightmare look like a dream come true," she growled.

"If *I* ruin it? *I'm* not the one you need to be worried about. Have I caused anyone grievous bodily harm today?"

"You seem to be walking and talking just fine," Carly retorted. "Unfortunately."

"You—"

"Listen to me," she said quickly, because Heather and Marcus would be back any second. "As far as they know, we have never met, which means we have no reason to absolutely loathe each other. And after this is over we never have to see each other again. But until that beautiful day, you and I are going to practice our fake smiles and get along when they're around, because I am making a huge professional sacrifice to be here and because this is meant to be the happiest day of Heather's life, and I will not let anything or anyone stand in the way of that. Do you understand me?"

He glared down at her, clearly weighing her words, and she willed herself to hold his gaze. If he wanted a staring contest he could have it, but he was going to lose. "You're right," he finally said, and it sounded like the words caused him physical pain. *Excellent.* "We've never met. But what a *pleasure* it is to make your acquaintance, Carly."

She opened her mouth to reply with any number of choice curse words, but at that moment, she heard footsteps and a toilet flush. Carly seized the back of one of the chairs and threw herself into it, and a second later, Nick seemed to uproot himself from the tiles. He sat down, and by the time Heather walked back into the kitchen, they were both seated, smiling amiably across the table while avoiding each other's eyes.

World's best maid of honor, Carly thought. Even if she pulled every muscle in her face.

"All right, I think that's the whole list," Heather sighed, leaning back from the table and passing the printed out spreadsheet to Marcus. "I know it's a lot to get done," Heather said, gesturing down at the paper in front of her, "but we're doing this whole thing on the cheap. Our vendors are all over the city, wherever the prices were best, so we'll have some running around to do. But between the four of us, we can do it. Divide and conquer."

Marcus studied the page for a few seconds. "Looks about right. Oh, you forgot to add the cocktail thing," he said to Heather.

"Right, of course. We wanted to have a signature cocktail, but neither of us really drinks cocktails, so we thought you might help us mix those up," Heather said, taking the spreadsheet back and adding yet another item to the already long list of wedding preparation tasks.

Nick nodded, looking down at the exhaustive spreadsheet Heather had handed him. Each wedding task was listed by chronological order and color-coded to mark who was responsible for it. His and Carly's initials were next to at least a dozen items. Nick now had full confidence that if Heather wanted to invade New Zealand, she could do it and make it look easy.

"This is Peak Heather," Carly teased, as she examined the battle plan, and Heather gave her a playful shove. "It's a compliment!" Carly replied.

This would be good for him, Nick reminded himself. He needed things to do, tasks to take his mind off the shapeless mess that was his life now. As long as he was focused on inventing cocktails and building playlists and picking up table numbers from the printer, he wouldn't have to think about his plans or lack thereof.

"As for getting around, we've got our car and we can borrow Alice's in a pinch, so we can split up and go wherever we need to," Marcus added. "Nick, can you still drive on the left?"

"Euhhh, probably," Nick hedged. Between the Paris Métro and his moped, he hadn't had much practice driving a car in the last few years, but hopefully the muscle memory would kick in once he sat on the right-hand side of a car.

"Okay, then you can borrow my mum's car," Marcus offered. "She's not using it much these days, and it mostly sits in her garage in Neutral Bay. Carly, I know you don't drive at all, so you can go with Nick."

"Sure," Carly said, throwing him a toothy smile that didn't reach her eyes. "That sounds like a great plan."

"Obviously I want you with me for my final dress fitting," Heather added. "But this way you two can get to know each other a bit."

"I look forward to that," Nick lied, returning Carly's wide smile and watching her nostrils flare in response. She'd said she wanted to play nice, so he'd play nice, but he had no interest in getting to know this woman better. They already knew each other just fine; being yelled at in public by someone, twice in one day, was a great way to get to know them. Especially when one of those yellings included information about their genitals. He felt his cheeks flush at that thought and hoped the other three didn't notice. He'd gotten to know Carly Montgomery well enough for a lifetime, thanks very much. Even if he didn't already know that she blew up basically any room she walked into, taking people and property with her, he knew her type. Rich, entitled, hotheaded. They didn't need to spend more time in each other's presence than was absolutely necessary.

"Oh, *me too*," Carly said. She was really laying it on thick now. If she wasn't careful, Marcus and Heather were going to start wondering if she was attracted to him. He nearly laughed out loud at the thought.

"Good," Heather smiled. "And while you're at it you can get to know the city a bit. Nick's a local; he can show you around. You don't mind, do you, Nick?"

Nick felt his fake smile falter. He wanted to correct her, but Carly's intense gaze and his stung pride stopped him. Heather was one hundred percent wrong, though. He did mind, actually. And he wasn't a local anymore, either.

Half the cafés and shops he remembered from when he last lived here, from his childhood, were probably gone now. Neighbourhoods had changed all over the city. Freshwater Beach used to feel low-key and hidden away, an overlooked and pleasantly rundown neighbour to the tourist-friendly Manly Beach, and now it felt kind of upscale and glam. The little hole-in-the-wall café inside the surf club, which used to only serve packaged ice creams in summer and hot chocolate from a machine in winter, was now advertising sourdough avocado toast with microgreens, and poached eggs with roasted heirloom tomatoes. He didn't really know this city at all anymore.

But he wasn't about to say any of this to Marcus and Heather, and he sure as hell wasn't going to reveal it to Carly.

"I don't mind at all," he lied. "Carly and I will make a great team." Heather gave him a grateful smile, and she and Marcus turned back to her list. Nick chanced a look at Carly, whose gaze had turned into a sharp glare. Her full lips were pursed, and her eyes slightly narrowed, as though she were wishing for the ability to shoot white-hot fire from her pupils. But he was just giving her what she'd asked for. He was playing nice. And if she could lay it on thick, so could he.

"I know Carly's decided she's going to be the greatest maid of honour the world has ever seen," he said through his wide smile, "and I'll do whatever I can to help."

The glare went from white-hot to blue fire at his words. She looked like she was mentally dismembering him.

That glare probably cowed other people, but Nick wasn't afraid of Carly Montgomery. She might be a spoiled, brash human hurricane, but for the next three weeks, she needed him. And it felt good to be needed for a change. Even if it was by someone who clearly despised him.

Chapter 4

When Carly woke the next morning, a pale yellow light was pressing itself against the shades of her bedroom window. It had been too hot the previous evening to sleep under anything more than a cotton sheet, but now the air in her bedroom had cooled, and she pulled the sheet up over her shoulders and her knees into her chest. She shut her eyes and listened hard to the sounds of Freshwater at dawn. A cyclist whizzing along the street. A garbage truck trundling down the block. Some kind of bird squawking in the frangipani tree in the front yard.

Under the sheet, she stretched her limbs out and groaned to herself. She was getting old. She woke up most mornings with her joints stiff and creaking now, even when she hadn't spent most of the previous day sitting in a coach plane seat.

You could have asked your parents to fund an upgrade, a voice in her head said. They'd have been only too happy, seeing how they had adored Heather since the first time she'd come to their home for a sleepover. Sometimes Carly wondered if her mother wished her own daughter could be more like Heather. So serious and focused, even at age eleven. Quiet. Carly wasn't quiet, had never known how to keep quiet. Heather had once said that when she was trying to be brave, she tried to be more like Carly. Well, when Carly was trying to be sensible for once, she tried to be more like Heather. And the sensible thing to do had been to pay her own way.

She'd saved up money for her ticket to Sydney, money she'd earned herself. Yes, she came from a wealthy family, even by New York standards. Edward Montgomery and Marlene Parker-Montgomery were both from old-money WASP families and had once taken Carly to the Metropolitan Museum of Art to show her all four of her grandparents' names engraved in stone on the list of the museum's major donors. And yes, her childhood had been one of privilege and ease.

But since she graduated from the NYB school and got her first paycheck from the company, she'd made a point of not asking her parents for financial help. When she and Heather had graduated from the company school and moved out of the dorms, they'd found a dingy little apartment near the Canal Street 1 stop and split the rent until Heather had moved uptown to live with her shithead ex-fiancé. Carly had stayed. She loved that apartment. She didn't love the lack of light in the bathroom, or the five flights of stairs up to her door. But she loved that it was her place. She paid the rent, made sure the landlord repaired the A/C unit when it broke down, and furnished the living room with secondhand furniture. Not vintage or antique furniture, of the kind her parents collected, but secondhand. She'd never deluded herself into believing that she'd made it all on her own—plenty of families couldn't afford the kind of ballet training she'd had as a kid, and without that training, she'd never have been able to join NYB. But now that she was an adult, she was determined to prove that she could fend for herself.

That said, there had been moments in the last decade when she'd been tempted to ask her parents for help. Just a little bit, to help smooth the way. Corps dancers were barely paid enough to get by in New York City. Two years ago, when Carly had been briefly unemployed, she'd been tempted to ask her parents for a loan, just enough to tide her over before she figured out what the hell she was going to do next. It would be so easy, she'd thought, and they'd be so happy to help. They'd never understood why she refused their money. "At least let us find you a place closer to the theater, honey," her dad had said, looking around in horror the first time he'd visited the apartment. She'd never been able to explain it in a way that made sense to them. And before she'd had the chance to give in to the temptation to go running to them, Heather had swooped in and saved her job.

Outside, the mystery bird squawked louder, and Carly opened her eyes. The clock on the bedside table (covered in seashells, of course) told her it was just past 5 AM. Heather had warned her that she probably wouldn't sleep through the night for a few days but that sunshine and time outside would help her body clock adjust. In other words, she should probably go to the beach. For medicinal reasons, of course.

Ten minutes later, she was padding down the sandy dune track to the beach. She'd pulled her hair into a low bun and slipped on yesterday's shorts and her favorite old NYB sweatshirt, which had a hole in the armpit but had been washed and tumble dried to soft, gray perfection over the years. The sand was loose and cool beneath her feet as she walked toward the water where, past the break, a handful of surfers were already out on their longboards.

She stopped halfway down the beach and sat down, breathing in deeply and feeling her body sink gently into the sand. Shit, it was beautiful here. None of the photos Heather had sent her had done this place justice. And how could they? A photo could capture the morning sky, all delicate mauves and watery blues, and it could show her the way the golden morning light made the water sparkle like a sumptuous costume under stage lights. But it couldn't capture the sounds of seagulls cawing overhead, or the fresh, salty scent of the water. Or the steady, comforting sound of the waves as they rolled endlessly in. Carly closed her eyes and listened to the water pound the sand, inhaling as it fizzed and receded, and exhaling with every crash. The soundtrack on her meditation app didn't do that sound justice, either. Love of her life aside, she thought, opening her eyes, it was no wonder Heather wanted to stay over here.

Out in the water, she watched two surfers preparing to catch a wave, looking over their shoulders as they paddled their hands over the sides of their boards. The wave took them, and one of them hoisted himself onto the board, angling his body along the wave and keeping his balance as the board twisted beneath him. The other surfer stayed on his stomach, and she watched his board come zooming into shore at an impressive clip, as the first surfer toppled off his board and landed with an unceremonious splash amid the breaking wave.

The second surfer climbed off his board and hoisted it under his arm, lifting his feet high to clear the shallow waves as he walked out of the water. Water streamed out of his hair and down onto his lean shoulders, drawing her eyes down to his broad and muscular chest, where more droplets caught in his chest hair and sparkled.

"Good morning," she muttered to herself, as he made his way out of the water, his clearly defined obliques shifting under his glistening skin with every step. A few moments ago, she'd been wondering what time the closest café opened, hoping she could get some caffeine into her system soon. Now, though, she was wide awake, and her mouth was watering slightly. She couldn't make out his face, but she ran her eyes down his body, shamelessly following the sharp V of his abs down until it disappeared into his small black bathing suit shorts. Wet and clinging as they were, they didn't leave much to the imagination, and she swallowed an appreciative groan as she let her eyes linger shamelessly on his crotch, then on his quads, which were flexing and releasing as he walked.

He stopped walking about fifteen feet away from her, and then, because apparently the Beach Gods had decided to smile on her this morning, he set his board down on the sand and turned around to watch the surfers who were still out in the water.

"Correction: best morning," she muttered, swallowing again as she traced the curves of his ass with her eyes and took in the deep vertical line of his spine, flanked by yet more lean muscle. He was cut like a dancer, but he looked like he was born and raised on the beach. She hoped he stayed there all morning watching the surfers so she could stay here all morning enjoying this view. Well, not all morning; in a few hours she'd have to go run wedding errands with Nick Asshat Jacobs. But she could endure his company as long as she had this breathtaking mental image to work with. She'd just pull this memory up every time Nick started talking, and it would be easy to smile vacantly into his stupid handsome face.

She was so busy committing every ridge of this hot stranger's muscled back and every inch of his wet, shining skin to memory that she didn't notice that he was turning away from the water. Before she could avert her eyes and pretend that she hadn't been gawking at him like the sex-starved weirdo that she was, he had turned around and looked at her. It was only then that she lifted her eyes above his shoulders and saw his face. His stupid, hand-some face.

In addition to everything else she was—loud, impulsive, chaotic, and a danger to everyone around her—Carly Montgomery was fucking *everywhere*. Inescapable. It was bad enough that he had to spend today with her, but Nick couldn't even go for a surf with Marcus without running into her. A force of nature, Marcus had said. More like Cyclone Carly.

He watched as she scrambled to her feet, spraying sand into the quiet morning air, still staring at him. Her eyes were wide and her mouth had fallen open into a large, mortified-looking O. After one more second of staring, she seemed to snap out of her frozen state, and she turned over her shoulder and hurried up the beach towards the dunes. She moved so quickly that she slipped a little on the loose sand, but she seemed determined to get as far away from him as she could, as fast as she possibly could. Except—

"You forgot your shoes," he called. She stopped dead, then whipped around to face him, her eyebrows scrunched into a frown. From this distance he couldn't be sure, but something told him she was clenching her jaw. She marched back down the beach towards the abandoned sandals, her bun bouncing at her neck, and yanked the shoes up off the sand. God, those fluoro pink nails were obnoxious.

"You could just say thank you," he said, just loud enough for her to hear over the waves, and she stood up and met his eyes, and even from here he could see the irritation and disgust etched all over her freckled face as he repeated her own words back to her.

He waited for her to snark back at him, but instead she simply turned and walked away again, her sandals swinging furiously from her hand. The prickled aliveness that had momentarily swirled in his chest faded as he watched her storm back up the beach and over the dunes. It snuffed out as she stalked out of sight.

"Was that Carly I just saw?"

Nick turned around to see Marcus walking out of the water with his board under his arm.

"Yeah, I guess so," Nick said quickly. He had the sudden feeling he'd been busted doing something he shouldn't have. He nodded out towards the waves, eager to change the subject. "Good swell this morning."

"No, yeah, it's been great the last few days. When it's like this I sometimes try to come back in the evening, too. My hair's never fully dry anymore." Marcus grinned contentedly and led Nick up the beach towards the surf club building, where two garage doors opened onto the sand and rows of empty storage racks stood ready to receive Nick's borrowed board.

As they rinsed and dried their boards, Marcus chatted amiably with a few other surfers he seemed to know quite well. They asked Nick where he was from, where he usually surfed, and it was such a relief to be able to speak to strangers here without worrying about his accent throwing them off or making him have to repeat himself. Nick's French wasn't bad for someone who'd only taken a year of company-sponsored formal classes, but his accent had caused frequent confusion among native speakers. He hadn't realized until this morning that he was usually bracing for confusion or repetition every time he opened his mouth to someone who didn't know him. That was what home was, wasn't it? A place you understood, and where you could be understood?

As Marcus waxed his board, he and another surfer began what sounded like an ongoing friendly debate about the merits of various wax brands, and Nick found his mind drifting. His friend had stopped dancing two years ago and had found himself an entirely new existence: Marcus had a new career path, a new hobby, new friends, and of course, he had Heather. Somehow, Nick had managed to fail completely at all of the above. Marcus seemed truly happy. He hadn't been dealt an easy hand in the last few years, between his dad's death and his injury and getting fired from ANB, but he'd come through it and built himself a full new life after ballet. Nick had done none of that.

"You need a coffee?" Marcus's question interrupted Nick's silent self-recriminations and brought him back to the cool, musty concrete room.

"Yeah, I need several," Nick agreed. He hadn't slept well the previous night. The noise from the bar downstairs filtered up through the floor.

A few minutes later, the barista at the surf club café slid their takeaway coffees over the counter—she'd started making Marcus's the moment she saw them coming—and they sat down on a bench overlooking the dunes.

"So what's on the docket for you today?" Nick asked. After lunch yesterday, Heather had divided up the tasks on her spreadsheet and given each of them a carefully ordered list of wedding tasks to attend to, complete with little checkboxes they could tick off when each job was done.

Marcus sipped his coffee and leaned forward on the bench, stretching his hamstrings with a quiet, satisfied groan. "I need to go to Randwick for my final tux fitting. But first we need to get you Mum's car. I can drive us both over there, then you can drive back on your own and collect Carly. Sound good?"

Not really, Nick thought. Not to him and not to Carly. Not if their brief and disastrous interaction this morning was anything to go by.

"You were right, she's kind of a lot," Nick muttered.

"Who, Carly? Yeah, I know."

"I mean, I've met some ballet brats, but she's on another level. Did you know she—"

He stopped. He didn't need to tell Marcus the whole story of yesterday's trolley-suitcase-dildo disaster. He took another sip of coffee and shook his head.

"I can see why you think that," Marcus allowed. "Like I said, she's a lot. But you should hear the way Heather talks about her. I reckon she'd trust Carly with her life. They're basically sisters. Did you know it was Carly who told Heather the truth about her ex?"

"About him cheating?"

"Yeah. She was the one who busted him with his girlfriend, and she came to Heather and told her about it, and then let Heather sleep on her couch for months after the break-up."

"Hmmm," Nick said, noncommittally, unwilling to admit to Marcus that he was impressed. Everyone said they'd tell someone if they knew they were being cheated on, but how many people chickened out when confronted with the choice to actually do it? He had the feeling Carly Montgomery never chickened out of anything. The idea annoyed him.

"Heather owes her a lot. So do I, come to think of it. If not for Carly, Heather would be married to that dickhead right now, instead of about to marry me. To Carly," Marcus said, raising his coffee cup and bumping it against Nick's.

"Maybe I'll put that in my best man speech," Nick laughed, and Marcus chuckled. "I've got a lot of embarrassing school stories to get through, though, so I might not be able to fit it in. Remember that time Justin dared you to do a whole class with your dance belt on backwards?"

"I do, and so do my balls," Marcus replied darkly. "But you wouldn't dare mention my balls at my wedding."

Nick swallowed a mouthful of coffee and gave Marcus an evil grin. "Wouldn't I?"

Marcus chuckled again and gave him a playful shove. "You go right ahead, then, but remember that I'll get you back with interest when your own turn comes. Speaking of which, how is the lovely Delphine? Are you going to put a ring on it any time soon?"

Nick felt his smile fade. He'd been hoping that Marcus would be so distracted by his own nuptials that he'd forget to ask about Delphine, but he should have known better. He cleared his throat.

"Euh, Delphine's kind of French about marriage," he dodged. "I don't think it's really for her. Sorry she couldn't make it, but rehearsals are just too intense right now."

He couldn't bring himself to tell Marcus the truth, not when his friend had his life so completely together. It was bad enough that he'd come back to Sydney with no job and his whole life in a suitcase. He couldn't bear to tell Marcus that once he'd stopped dancing, once they'd stopped working together every day, Delphine had decided they didn't have much in common. And that his post-retirement funk was getting *ennuyeux*. Boring. Better to play the French libertine card and let Marcus hear what he wanted.

Marcus nodded, apparently satisfied by his answer, and Nick took a relieved sip of his coffee. It had been a while since he and Marcus had really talked. But when they were kids, they spent almost every day together, and they'd known each other so well they barely needed more than grunts and body language to convey complicated ideas and feelings.

"You gonna see your parents while you're here?" Marcus asked.

"I haven't decided," Nick lied again. "Things ended so badly last time, and they were already pretty messy. They're just never going to forgive me for the way I left." His parents had never gotten over him going behind their backs to audition for Münchner Staatsballett. And after the fight they'd had when he'd last come home to visit—yet another row about him moving home—he didn't want to go out to Springwood to see them.

"What about Nina?"

Nick nodded. "Yeah, Neens and I are fine. Now that she's grown we've kind of got our own thing, separate from them." His sister had been so young when he'd left for Europe, and her parents had hidden a lot of their anger from her. But she was smart; she'd figured out that something wasn't right between them, and she'd spent years trying to bridge that gap, always reminding him whenever she called him that they *all* missed him, that he was welcome at home. But Nick didn't want to go home to Springwood, and he definitely didn't want to face his parents now.

He had been so cocky about his future back then, so sure he was going to go overseas and make a whole glamorous new life for himself, so sure that he was going to get away and stay away from Sydney, and even further away from his little hometown. He was so sure back then. So very, very sure.

He drained the last of his coffee and fiddled for a moment with the empty cup.

"Is, euh, is Carly bringing a plus-one?" he asked Marcus. He didn't know why he'd asked. He didn't care. It didn't matter.

"Nope, she's flying solo as well," Marcus said, and Nick ignored the prick of satisfaction that usually came from hearing the answer he'd been hoping for. "It's a good thing, actually, that you're both on your own. Makes the seating chart a little simpler."

"Do I want to know what that spreadsheet looks like?" Nick asked.

"No, but I see it in my dreams. And nightmares," Marcus chuckled. "I'm telling you, wedding planning is intense. I think Delphine might be on to something."

Nick forced himself to smile as he stood and tossed his coffee cup in the bin.

"Should we go get your mum's car?"

"Yeah," Marcus said, standing and yawning widely. "Let's get showered and then we'll go pick it up, okay?"

"Okay," Nick agreed. He didn't have to worry about Delphine today. He didn't have time to worry about her, actually. Today he had to remember how to drive on the left-hand side of the road. And he had to figure out how to spend the day with Carly Montgomery without one or both of them ending up dead.

Chapter 5

"We've circled this block three times already," Carly growled murderously, keeping her eyes straight ahead. "Do you even know where we're going?"

She gripped the seat and stared at the back of the car in front of them, determined not to let her gaze stray toward the driver's seat. It was bad enough that she was stuck spending her long-awaited vacation with Nick Jacobs, an insufferable snob who knew her biggest and most mortifying secrets. But this morning had made them enemies for life. First, she'd accidentally spent a good five minutes cataloging every mouthwatering detail of his mostly naked body, and *he'd caught her doing it.* And then, while she'd been waiting for the barista at the surf club café to make her coffee, she'd overheard him talking to Marcus.

I've met some ballet brats, but she's on another level.

Carly hated that *b*-word even more than she hated the other *b*-word. She'd spent the last decade of her life saving and budgeting and having the same argument with her parents every six months, all so she wouldn't be what Nick had called her. A ballet brat. An entitled princess who didn't live in the real world, who always relied on Edward and Marlene to buy her way into anything—or out of anything. Okay, so she sometimes lost her temper. But she was working on that, too. She was trying to be better. But of course Nick had seen none of that. All he'd seen was a *brat*.

"I know where we're going," Nick said through gritted teeth, accidentally turning on the windshield wipers instead of the blinker. He sighed with frustration. "We're going to the printer."

"I meant do you know where the printer *is*," Carly replied, although she already knew the answer.

"I know what you meant," he said, "and yes, I know where the printer is. It's on King Street, near the train station. That's what Marcus said."

"Do you want me to pull up a map? Google can solve this problem for us, you know."

"I don't need a map, I just need to find this place," he snapped, turning the windshield wipers on again.

Carly rolled her eyes. She'd always thought the whole men-don't-ask-for-directions thing was an old-fashioned cliche. Or was she simply a *brat* for not wanting to spend her day circling the same block?

"If only there were some kind of visual aid that could help you do that, perhaps guided by some kind of global positioning system?"

"*Putain de merde, je vais la tuer,*" he muttered.

"I wouldn't if I were you. I'm pretty sure Australia frowns on murder." There was a long silence as Nick stared out at the traffic, his jaw clenched. She watched him in satisfaction as realization dawned on him. "*Faut faire attention, Nick, on ne sait jamais qui parle français.*" There was another tense silence. Maybe she shouldn't have rubbed it in, but it was just so satisfying to watch the muscle in his jaw tick like that.

They inched forward through the traffic, through the same traffic lights she was quite sure they'd already waited at several times. "Since when do you speak French?" he finally gritted out.

"Since my least favorite nanny was Belgian. I learned it just to spite her. She used to mutter about killing me, too."

"Can't say I blame her," he shot back.

"Oh, you would have loved Nanny Sylvie," Carly said, as she scanned the storefronts on either side of the traffic-clogged road. "She was even more uptight than— Oh, there it is!" she exclaimed, pointing at a small sign in a second floor window that read UNIVERSITY PRINTERS.

Nick gasped and slammed on the breaks. Their bodies lurched forward, and her seatbelt caught her hard in the stomach.

"Shit, could you not scream in the car? You're going to cause an accident," he chastised her, once he'd straightened up. "*Another* accident."

Rubbing her stomach, she stared at him and wondered, for the hundredth time since she'd met him barely a day ago, what the fuck this man's problem was.

"I was just trying to help," she repeated, unable to keep some of her hurt out of her voice. And she had helped, by the way. She'd found the damn place, so now they could go pick up the menu cards and table numbers Heather and Marcus had ordered.

"Thanks for your *help*," he gritted out, turning on the blinker, on the first go this time, and turning down a side street in search of a parking spot.

She seethed in silence as he pulled into a spot and they climbed out of the car. Around the corner and back toward the storefront on bustling King Street, he walked a few paces in front of her, as if he were leading her to the place she had found. The street was lined with stores and cafés, and Carly spotted a cute-looking vintage shop next to a bubble tea place. If she hadn't been in the company of a prickly, judgmental ass, she would have asked if they could take a detour into both. Instead, she followed him up the stairs to the second floor of the building in the middle of the block and into the office of University Printers, taking care to keep her eyes on the stairs in front of her. She'd already been caught staring at Nick's ass once today, and she couldn't bear for it to happen again.

At the top of the stairs, they were met by an empty desk in a small, dimly lit reception area. The walls were hung with posters for performances by bands she didn't know at venues she'd never heard of, some of which looked like they were from the 1970s and 1980s. Carly could hear whirring activity in a nearby room, but this one was almost silent.

"Anyone here?" they called at the exact same time.

They looked at each other, and she felt her own face crumple in a scowl that mirrored his. There was no reply, so they stood there for a few seconds, staring each other down in rippling silence.

"Maybe everyone's left for the day, because it took us so long to get here," she said.

"Maybe they saw you coming and decided to save themselves," he shot back.

They glared at each other for a moment, and then she turned her back on him and examined a poster featuring a group of musicians with impressively big hair. She could almost feel his eyes boring disdainfully into the back of her head.

The whirring continued from the other room. Impatient, she looked over at the front desk and noticed a small bell next to a cup of pens. With a sigh, she strode across the room just as Nick started moving, but she reached the desk before he did, tapping the bell hastily before he could beat her to it. As a high-pitched ding reverberated around the room, his hand landed on top of hers, large and warm. Her stomach jolted, and a thousand hot, fizzling sparks radiated from where he touched her, up her arm and into her chest. She met his eyes, noticing that in the low light of this room they looked almost gray. For a moment, he looked down at her—no, she reminded herself, down *on* her, the ballet brat he'd been saddled with—and she watched a few tiny beads of sweat glittering over his top lip.

She snatched her hand away, knocking the bell off the desk as she did. She'd just stooped to pick it up when someone rushed into the room.

"So sorry to keep you waiting," the newcomer said, with one hand on her chest. She was tall and muscular and looked like she couldn't have been more than a few years out of high school. Her hair was cut in an enviable pixie, and her long blue dress revealed a tattoo sleeve on each pale arm. "I didn't hear you come in!"

"Sorry," Carly said, returning the bell to the desk. "We should have called out louder. We're here to pick up some wedding materials."

"Oh, sure," the woman said, turning to the computer in front of her and scrolling the mouse. "What's the name?"

"Heather Hays and Marcus Campbell."

The woman's face lit up. "Of course, the ballet dancers! I love the New York theme you went with, and it looks so good on paper, especially the table numbers." She looked over at Nick, beaming. "It's so nice to meet you both in person! You make a gorgeous couple. Only a few weeks to go now, are you so excited?"

"Oh, no," Nick started to say, "we're not—"

"We're not the bride and groom," Carly cut in. "We're just the wedding party, running some errands for them."

The woman's face fell. "Whoops! Sorry about that. It's just I love this stuff, and I thought, with the American accent . . ."

"It's fine," Carly shrugged. It was hardly an insult to be mistaken for Heather.

"You do make a gorgeous couple, though," the woman said, looking hopefully from Carly to Nick and back again.

"We're not a couple," Nick snapped from behind her. Carly turned around and gave him a deathly glare, then turned back to see that the poor woman looked very flustered.

"I'll just go get the order, it's in the back," she muttered, and she stood and hurried out of the room.

Carly whipped around as soon as she was gone.

"What the fuck is your problem?" she asked him, trying to keep her voice quiet and steady. "It's one thing to be an asshole to me, but you can't talk to other people like that."

He flushed and ducked his head.

"Sorry," he muttered. "I just didn't want her to think—"

"That you'd ever deign to date a *next level ballet brat* like me," Carly said. She saw his mouth drop open a little in what looked like shock and shame as she repeated his words back to him, but she was too annoyed to care. "That would be so embarrassing for you. You're lucky they've already printed all the stuff, or she'd probably put some obscene typo on it as revenge. 'Welcome to the wedding of Heather and Mucus,' or something. You'd better apologize to her when she gets back."

He nodded, avoiding her eyes. His cheeks were still pink. They stood in unfriendly silence for a few minutes, and then the woman returned from the back room holding a large box with HAYS + CAMPBELL scrawled on the side in black marker. She placed it on the desk.

"Here you go," she said quietly to Carly. "Do you want to take a look and make sure it's all correct and accounted for?"

"No, thanks, um, what's your name?" Carly asked.

"Geraldine," the woman said uneasily, keeping her eyes on Carly, as if she wasn't very eager for Nick to know her name. Carly couldn't blame her.

"I trust you, Geraldine. And I'm sure it all looks great. I helped Heather pick the New York theme, you know," she said proudly. "The street sign table names were my idea."

Instead of numbered tables, each table would be named for a different place in New York City, like Lincoln Center or Washington Square Park. It would be a little taste of Heather's home here in Sydney, surrounded mostly by Australian guests. Carly had joked that anyone Heather and Marcus didn't like could be assigned a seat at Port Authority Bus Terminal, or at A 4 Train Car Full of Drunk Yankees Fans. Heather had rejected the suggestion, saying that last one would be hard to fit on a mocked-up street sign. But now Carly wished there was a table called Fifth Avenue at Christmastime When You're Running Late for Something Important, so they could seat Nick there.

Geraldine pushed the box aside so she could check something on her computer. "It's already paid in full, so you're all set," she said.

"Thank you," Carly said, lifting the box and holding it against her hip. She waited for a moment, then cleared her throat and glanced over her shoulder, giving Nick a pointed look.

He ducked his head again, then took a few steps toward the desk until he was almost level with her.

"Euh, I'm very sorry," he said to Geraldine. "I was rude, and I'm sorry. It was an easy mistake to make."

She looked up and nodded at him warily. "No worries," she said quietly. Carly gave a small, satisfied nod—and then decided that actually, no, she wasn't satisfied.

"Nick actually doesn't date at all. He's never had a girlfriend," she stage-whispered to Geraldine, ignoring Nick's glower. "He's got a rare congenital condition. You see, he was tragically born without a personality, and it makes life very difficult for him. Doctors have tried everything, but it's incurable. There's a foundation named after him and everything."

Carly gave Geraldine a sly smile and arched one eyebrow, and Geraldine pressed her lips together, suppressing a smile. Carly could practically feel Nick's irritation raking down her back, but it was worth it. She hoisted the box against her hip and turned, feeling the heat of his gaze between her shoulders all the way down the stairs.

Chapter 6

The next morning, Nick met Marcus at the beach early again, but this time he had no intention of going in the water. As Marcus carried his board down the sand and paddled out into the waves, Nick opened his camera bag and pulled out his Canon 70D and a wide-angle lens. It had been the first camera he'd bought, before he'd officially retired but long after he knew the end of his dancing career was approaching. He'd started bringing it to the ballet studios every day, and whenever he had a free hour between classes and rehearsals, he'd stick his head into a rehearsal studio and ask whoever was dancing in there if they minded him taking a few photos. Before he knew it, he'd taken hundreds and hundreds of shots of his colleagues, capturing them in blurry mid-flight and laid out flat on the floor in exhaustion. Of those hundreds of shots, he'd actually managed to take a few he loved.

It had been months now since he'd taken a photo he loved. Or maybe it was that it was harder to love them when he knew almost no one else would. Still, yesterday, when he and Marcus had been out on the water, he'd been struck almost breathless by how beautiful this place was, and by how much he'd missed it without even realizing it. He raised the camera and took a few warm-up shots of the cliffs that hugged the south side of the beach, where an ever-growing number of luxury homes hung precariously over the water. Then he turned and faced straight out to the ocean, adjusting his focus to try to capture a single surfer with the vast Pacific stretching out behind her and the long horizon on either side of her board. He'd had plenty of practice photographing around the Seine, but a roiling surf beach was more challenging to capture than a river.

He kept an eye on Marcus's bright green board as he walked this way and that along the sand at the water's edge, trying to capture each surfer as they clambered onto their boards. They were strong and graceful, not unlike dancers, and it seemed to him that the only way they stayed upright on their boards was by attuning their bodies to the waves, the way a dancer in a pas de deux learned to read their partner's body. When they became unattuned, out of sync with the wave, they toppled off their boards and crashed into the surf. Unlike Marcus, he'd never learned to do more than bodysurf, but he made a mental note to ask his friend about his theory on the similarities between dancing and surfing.

After about fifteen minutes, he checked the screen and scrolled through the photos he'd taken so far, then sighed and turned the camera off. They were shit shots. Utter shit. For perhaps the hundredth time, he heard Delphine's exasperated sigh echo in his head. *Putain, Nick, on n'est pas photographe simplement parce qu'on achète un appareil photo et se declare photographe!*

He shook his head and put the camera back in its bag, and, slinging the case over his shoulder, strode back up the beach. His plan to spend the morning taking photos seemed stupid now.

He thought of the confidence he'd feigned for the hotel waitress the other day, how easy it had been to pretend that he was steady and successful and turning down jobs left and right. He could keep doing that. Fake it til you make it, right? As far as anyone here was concerned, as far as Marcus, Heather, and any random waitresses had to know, he was a professionally successful photographer. As far as Carly had to know, he was the Annie Liebovitz of dance photography.

Carly. She'd thoroughly shamed him at the printer's office yesterday. He'd seen her angry before—several times, in fact, and they'd barely known each other a few days. But it turned out that Carly angry on her own behalf was nothing compared to Carly angry on someone else's. The look on her face when she'd reprimanded him for being rude to the receptionist was something to behold. Before, when she'd been angry about something he'd said to her, she'd been indignant and loud and her anger had flared quick and hot, like a match catching and burning out a few seconds later.

But when she'd demanded an apology on the other woman's behalf, he was reminded of the blue flames at the very base of a fire, the hottest and longest-burning ones. Her voice had gone quiet and threatening, and her face had become eerily calm and still. As if she already knew that she was going to extract an apology from him and the only question was how well he was going to grovel. If she was a brat, he'd thought grudgingly at that moment, she'd also figured out how to use her brattiness for good. What would it be like, he'd wondered, to have someone that fierce willing to demand justice on your behalf? Not someone like Carly, obviously; she'd burn down an entire city block just to avenge him if another car cut him off in traffic. But, someone. And just as he had when they'd been staring each other down across the beach, he'd felt something long-dead stir to life in his chest. A flash of colour in the vast grey expanse that had been his life lately. So he'd apologised, and she'd seemed mollified—and then she'd turned around and embarrassed him in front of that woman, for no good reason. *Tragically born without a personality?* Better than way too much personality.

And he had to spend today with her, again. Their task today was to pick up the wedding bands from the jeweller, a job Carly didn't want to miss and that Nick didn't trust her to complete alone. So later that morning, he presented himself outside her apartment building, showered and shaved, fed and caffeinated, and ready to drive into the city. When he pulled up, he saw Carly sitting on the front steps of the building in a short, sleeveless khaki-green dress and sneakers. He honked the horn, and she glanced up and then made a show of reluctantly standing and walking to the car.

"Good morning to you, too," he said, after she had thrown herself into the seat, slammed the door, and crossed her arms tight across her chest. She said nothing.

"Can you buckle your seatbelt, please?"

"Just drive, okay? We've got errands to run." Her voice was scratchy and she sounded exhausted.

"I'm not going to drive until you buckle your seatbelt," he said. "Come on. Click clack, front and back."

She rolled her eyes and pulled the belt across her body, and he heard the sharp metallic snap over the sound of her sigh.

"Happy now? Drive." She leaned back in the seat and glowered out the window. He turned the radio back on and drove them towards the main drag and then towards the Spit Bridge.

"Ah, shit," he said under his breath, as they drove down the hill towards the bridge. Traffic was backed up on their side of the road, and the other side was empty. "It's about to open."

"What's about to open?" she asked, frowning. It was the first time she'd spoken in fifteen minutes.

"The bridge. It opens a few times a day to let boats through, and cars have to stop and wait. It only takes a few minutes, but we must have just caught it."

"So I get to spend extra time with you. Delightful."

Nick looked over at her as he stopped the car and turned off the engine. She looked paler than she had yesterday, and her eyes were puffy and pink lined.

"You look tired," he said.

"Gee, thanks," she replied sarcastically. "No need for euphemisms, Nick. You can just tell me I look like shit next time."

"You look like shit this time," he said, matter-of-factly. She scowled across the console, but she didn't fire back at him. She looked like she barely had the energy to play this game. "What, no snappy comeback? You're not going to make up a new medical condition for me?"

Carly said nothing. She turned and stared straight ahead at the unmoving cars, and he watched her profile for a long moment as she tucked her bottom lip under one of her teeth and worried it. He was about to resign himself to sitting here for another fifteen minutes in prickling silence when she spoke.

"What's retirement like?" She said it tentatively, quietly. Without snark or heat, like she was genuinely curious.

It's shit, Nick thought. *I don't know who I am anymore. Or where I belong. Or what's going to happen next.*

"It's fine," he said, doing his best to sound confident. "I was lucky that I got to choose to retire, rather than having it thrust on me by injury or something. And the French are generous about their pensions for dancers, which helped the transition." What hadn't helped was withdrawing that pension early and blowing through most of it, leaving him with a dwindling bank account and no idea where his next paycheck was coming from.

"Do you miss dancing?" Carly asked, still looking straight ahead. He turned in his seat and copied her.

"All the time," he said to the license plate of the car in front of him. "I miss the adrenaline rush of performing. And the feeling of working on something for hours in the studio and worrying right up until the moment you do it on stage that it's not gonna work, but then your body just does it, and it's perfect, and all the work was worth it."

Out of the corner of his eye, he saw her nodding.

"I love that feeling," she said quietly. "Like your body knew the whole time what it was doing, and you just had to let it."

Exactly, he thought. Like he could trust his own limbs, his own ligaments, to do what he needed them to do. He didn't trust his body now, didn't trust that he could take what he saw and translate it onto film. He used to be able to see a shape in his mind and make his body mimic it. Now, that connection felt broken.

"I miss the music, too. There aren't a lot of jobs where you can hear a world-class orchestra play five nights a week for free."

Carly scoffed. "Free, except for all the broken bones and messed up muscles, and the lack of a social life outside of work, and the hundred-dollar shoes."

"Okay, it's not totally free. But is there anything better than a full orchestra playing *Swan Lake* five metres away from you?"

"Ugh, I hate *Swan Lake*."

"What?"

"I hate," she repeated, enunciating every consonant, "*Swan Lake*."

"I heard you. Why?"

"Boy meets girl, boy promises to love girl forever, boy gets distracted by random enchanted hot chick and decides to marry her instead? And we're supposed to think this is some great love story? It's basically Hinge but with feathers."

Nick frowned. "Well, he does die at the end."

"They both die! And she dies first! You ever notice how all the women in ballet end up dead? Giselle, Juliet, Odette, La Sylphide, they all die at the end."

"Not true, Giselle dies at the end of act one."

Carly groaned and rolled her eyes dramatically. "God, you're a pedant. I knew you wouldn't get it."

"I get it. Ballet's not exactly a bastion of feminism. But you can't deny the *Swan Lake* score is spectacular."

"The violin solo is okay," Carly allowed quietly.

"What's that?" he said, putting his hand up to his ear. In front of them, the stopped cars had started to roll slowly down the hill. The bridge must be reopening.

"I said the violin solo is fine."

"It's better than fine, but we can agree to disagree." That was basically all they did. But at least this disagreement hadn't resulted in bodily harm or property theft.

"Do you think it gets better? The missing it?" She turned her head against the seat, and he turned, too. She looked him full in the face for the first time since she got in the car. Her face was pinched and pallid, but the sun found gold threads in her orange-red curls and turned her eyes a liquid, maple syrup brown.

Nick sighed. *Fuck if I know.* "I hope so. But, you know," he added quickly, feigning confidence again, "I landed on my feet. There's life after ballet, if you know where to look."

She rolled her eyes again, with more disdain than drama this time, and looked like she was about to retort when the car behind them honked. Nick and Carly both jumped and turned back to face the road, and Nick hurried to put the car in drive. Next to him, Carly slumped back into her seat as they rolled down towards the water. Whatever rejoinder she'd had ready for him never materialized.

Twenty silent minutes later, they pulled into an underground parking lot in Sydney's central business district, just over the other side of the Harbour Bridge. The Bridge, at least, looked exactly as it had when he had left Australia. Still a smooth slate-grey curve flanked by four stout sandstone pylons. Still a dizzying geometric kaleidoscope of shapes formed by the criss-crossing steel bars at the sides and over the top. The lanes were still narrow, designed as they were for cars from the 1930s, and over the left-hand side, the sleek white sails of Opera House still sliced into the sky, odd and elegant as ever.

When they came aboveground, they found the city buzzing with pedestrians in business and business casual clothing, hurrying from high rise office buildings to cafés and back again. He led Carly along the crowded footpaths, past clothing stores and upscale restaurants.

"Once again, we walk on the left here," he said, the second time her body listed away from his and towards the right-hand side of the footpath.

"I know, I know," she sighed, stepping quickly out of the way of a young man who was scurrying down the street balancing a tray of takeaway coffee in one hand and holding out his phone in the other.

"Oh, and I know where I'm going this time," he told her. He didn't add that he'd looked the shop up three times until he could visualize the map and could be assured he wouldn't get them lost again.

"What a nice change," she said, through a wide yawn.

He looked down the block to the corner where he knew they'd find the jeweller. "This shouldn't take long. Then you can go home and take a nap."

"I don't need a nap," she grumbled, sounding a lot like a tired child who needed a nap.

"Uh-huh," he said, injecting as much skepticism as he could into the two syllables.

"Fine, I need a nap, but I can't take one. It'll mess with my jetlag adjustment." She yawned again, bringing a hand to her mouth and squeezing her eyes shut. Was it possible for a yawn to be stubborn? Because if it was, Carly had just yawned stubbornly. With her whole body, too, her shoulders lifting and rolling and her ribcage expanding as she yawned dramatically into her hand. Carly Montgomery never did anything by half measures, he thought, even yawning.

The jeweller had the rings boxed up and ready to go and informed them that there was still plenty of time to have them resized if for some reason they didn't fit. To Nick's relief, no one mistook them for the happy couple this time, although that might have been because Carly made a point of introducing herself to the jeweller by name before asking for Marcus and Heather's rings.

"Are you in a rush to get back?" he asked her as they left the air-conditioned cool of the shop and reemerged onto the baking footpath. Something had just occurred to him. "There's a shop I want to visit. It won't take long, and then you can go home and not take a nap."

In response, she simply yawned and shrugged, which he took as a yes. He steered them down the street for a few blocks, reminding her periodically to keep to the left, until they came to a narrow laneway he remembered from all those years ago.

"Excuse me, but I generally avoid going into dark alleys with strange men," she said, after rounding the corner and peering past him down the lane.

"A good policy, but this alley isn't dark, and I'm not strange," he replied, and barreled on before she could come up with a snarky retort. "Stay here if you want, I won't be long."

She sighed but followed him down the laneway anyway, staying a few paces behind him as it twisted behind the hulking office building, just as he'd remembered it. Only, when he arrived at the little hole-in-the-wall shop front he'd remembered, it wasn't a camera shop anymore. It was a café.

"You wanted to visit the Piccolo café?" Carly asked, drawing even with him and frowning up at the white neon sign over the tiny door. "What's so special about this place?"

Nick watched as a woman in a white button down and a sleek office skirt hustled out of the shop, a takeaway coffee cup in each hand.

"Euh, no, it wasn't a café before," he muttered, running a distracted hand over his head.

He'd only visited it a few times, but the memory of the place was still crisp in his mind. A grey-haired Greek man had sat at the counter, and shelves of cameras and film and photography books had extended up to the ceiling and all the way to the back of the narrow store. The place was fluorescent lit and smelled a little musty, but the inventory and displays were spotless, not a speck of dust or grime in sight. The man, who he'd assumed was the proprietor, let him leaf carefully through the huge, heavy art photography books, after making him leave his drink at the cash register and checking that his fingers were clean. It was quiet in there, and to a teenage Nick, who was still getting accustomed to the bustle and speed of city life, it felt like a refuge. He'd been excited to return and talk about cameras with the man behind the counter, now that he was a man and a photographer himself.

And now it was just another café churning out flat whites and macchiatos for office workers. When had that happened? What had happened to the proprietor? Had he moved the shop elsewhere? Had he sold up? Died?

"What was it?" Carly asked.

Nick said nothing. He stared, a little disoriented, at the shop-front.

"Nick? Hello?"

"It was a camera shop," Nick said quietly. "I guess that was a long time ago."

"Did you want to buy a new camera?" Carly asked through another yawn. "There have to be other camera stores in Sydney, right?"

"No, it's not that," he muttered. "It's—Never mind. Not important." He'd missed so much in the fifteen years he'd been gone. This city's secret places had changed and vanished, and he hadn't even been here to notice it happening.

"Tell me," Carly said. She said it as though she was curious, and as though she resented that curiosity. She was looking up at him expectantly, the way she had when she'd been awaiting his apology at the printer's the other day. Like she was going to get this information out of him as a matter of principle.

"I came here a lot as a kid, is all. And when I was trying to figure out what to do after I stopped dancing, I kept having dreams about this place." Nick didn't believe in the universe sending him signs, but those dreams had felt like a compass pointing him in the right direction. Of course, it turned out to be a disastrous direction. Even if the old man had still been here, Nick probably would have been too ashamed to go inside and lie to him about his new career. His stomach twisted with the familiar anxiety that had haunted him for months now, coupled with a new guilt at lying to Marcus, to Heather, to everyone around him.

"I'm going to go in and get a coffee," Carly said suddenly. "You stay here." It was as though she had intuited that he didn't want to go inside and see the place gutted and renovated, unrecognizable to anyone who remembered what it had once been. The ride here had created some kind of fragile peace between them, he thought, which she confirmed when she stopped a few feet from the shop door and turned to him. "What do you want?"

After she'd gone inside, Nick leaned against the rough concrete wall of the office block, staring across the laneway at the storefront. Based on the steady trickle of customers in and out, the place seemed to be doing all right. He thought back to the quiet hours he'd spent in the photography shop, when he was often the only customer. Not even a customer, as he'd never had the money to purchase anything. But the proprietor had let him wander and browse as though he did, showing him lenses and film like he had money to burn. In truth, Nick realized now, the man was probably happy to have someone to talk to, a little company in his quiet, tucked away shop. And Nick had been happy to spend a few hours away from the ballet school and the dorms, relieved to think about something that wasn't ballet.

He glanced down the alley, thinking about all the times he'd snuck back here and felt like he'd unlocked one of the city's secrets. It felt so strange now, to be a tourist in the place that had been home. Eventually, he supposed, he would feel that way about Munich, and about Paris, too. He'd be a tourist everywhere and a local nowhere.

A few minutes later, Carly reappeared with a coffee in each hand. She handed him a hot cup with "SK C +1"—a skim cappuccino with one sugar—scrawled on the lid, and he thanked her, making a mental note that the next round of coffees would be on him. Carly held her own plastic cup up to show him, a victorious smile on her face. Like everything else about her, Carly's smile was a lot. She smiled with her entire face, and every crinkle and freckle lifted and lit up as she showed a dozen white teeth, gleaming to match her brown eyes. Like him, she'd spent her life performing in heavy stage makeup, probably false eyelashes and deep red lipstick. But he had a feeling her smile would reach the cheap seats without any help from L'Oréal.

"Finally, I found iced coffee in this town. I've been dying for a bodega iced coffee for days, but it's not on any menu here. These guys had it and I'm so excited."

He was about to warn her when she lifted the straw to her lips and took a sip. Her eyes widened in surprise and she swallowed quickly, then gave a spluttery cough.

"What the hell is in this thing?" she exclaimed, peeling the lid off the cup and peering in at its contents.

"Ah, Australian iced coffee is a bit of a different animal," he said, suppressing a smile. "It's more like a coffee-flavoured dessert. There's probably ice cream and chocolate syrup in there. Maybe whipped cream, too." He looked down into the sweating plastic cup and nodded. "Yep, whipped cream. I used to love a good iced coffee when I was little."

Carly raised her eyebrows at him. "So is there any actual coffee in here? Or is it just a milkshake pretending to be caffeine?"

"Probably the latter," he shrugged, and she groaned with her whole body, throwing her head back and letting the sound bounce off the walls of the laneway. It was petulant and ridiculous, and some people might have found it endearing.

"What does a girl have to do to get a plain, unadulterated, nuclear-strength iced coffee with half and half around here? I'm not drinking this. It might as well be a sundae."

"I'm sure we can find you one somewhere in Freshwater. In the meantime, drink your milkshake."

On the drive home, Carly sipped at her iced coffee until she was making quiet slurping sounds and moving the straw around to catch the final drops of it.

"I see you hated your milkshake," he said drily, as they sat in traffic on Military Road.

"Shut up," she grumbled, stashing the empty cup in the car door. She leaned back in her seat and sighed, and when he glanced over he saw that she was once again slumping dejectedly and worrying her bottom lip again, all traces of her sparkling megawatt smile gone.

"What's wrong?" Because something did look really wrong.

"Nothing," Carly said, too quickly. Nick didn't bother telling her he didn't believe her. Subtle she was not, and her body language was a dead giveaway. "Fine," she said mulishly after a long silence, and Nick suppressed a triumphant smile. She couldn't win every round.

"I need to get promoted this season."

"Okay," Nick said, not following.

She ran her hand through her hair and exhaled a sharp, exasperated-sounding sigh.

"Like, *before* the season starts, which is in a few weeks. But I'm here, and as long as I'm here, I can't make a good impression on the AD before she makes her decision."

"And you won't go back any earlier." It was a statement, not a question. He knew a few things about Carly Montgomery now, including a few rather intimate things he suspected she'd rather he didn't know. And he knew that she wouldn't even consider leaving Heather in the lurch on her wedding day.

"Of course not," she muttered, confirming his assumption.

"Why the sudden urgency?"

She groaned and beat the back of her head against the headrest a few times. "Okay, look, you know how this works. I'm thirty-one. I've been in the company since I was eighteen. I've done my time in the corps, and I'm one of the oldest girls there now. Women. I hate when they call us 'girls.' And I love dancing. I even loved it under Mr. K, and he ran the place like a dictator. But I'm tired. My body's a bowl of Rice Krispies."

"I don't follow."

"You know, snap, crackle, and pop? I'm getting old, and I'll have to retire soon. I've got maybe two, three years left in me, if I don't get injured. And I don't want to retire as a corps member. I want to get promoted and dance a few great roles before I'm too busted and broken to get out of bed in the morning. You know?"

Nick nodded. Yeah, he knew. He felt busted and broken, inside and out, and retirement had only made it worse.

"You know why I hate *Swan Lake* so much? It's not just because Odette dies at the end. It's because I've danced it basically every season for thirteen years and all I ever get to be is a random swan and a random villager. Do you know how tiring it is to stand there in a straight line and keep perfectly still for five minutes while Odette and Siegfried dance their pas de deux? Or to spend most of act one flitting around in the background holding a broom while everyone watches the principals they actually came to see? I could walk off the stage in the middle of the performance and no one would notice that one of the peasants was missing. I might as well be part of the set."

It had been years since Nick had danced in the corps, but he didn't remember it being that bad.

"So, that's what's wrong," she sighed, sounding defeated. "Either I get promoted soon, or I finish my career as Peasant Maiden #4 and no one even remembers I was there at all."

Nick shifted a little in his seat and kept his eyes on the road. So that's why she'd asked about retirement. He couldn't blame her for being afraid of it. He should have been more afraid than he was, but he'd been so cocky about photography, so sure that he could make the transition seamlessly. It turned out that even with his connections in the dance world, he didn't have the talent for that.

"Retirement's not that bad," he lied, his stomach twisting again.

"So you said."

"Really," he insisted. "And just because we never get to see Peasant Maiden #4 do much besides wave a garland back and forth doesn't mean she doesn't have a rich inner life. It just happens off stage. And at least she lives to the end."

Carly didn't dignify that with more than a scoff. Okay, so it wasn't his strongest argument.

"I know dancing in the corps can be repetitive and unrewarding at times, but the corps is really important," he tried again.

"Easy for a former soloist to say."

"But it's true. There's no ballet company without a corps. Imagine *La Bayadère* without all the Shades, or even something modern like *Rite of Spring* without a corps. You hate *Swan Lake*, but imagine how much worse it would be without the swans. It would just be . . . *Lake*." He glanced over at her, hoping she'd crack a smile, but she looked unmoved. "The corps is what makes those ballets as impressive as they are. Principals are great, but the corps is what really fills the stage."

"Oh, so we're filler?" she retorted hotly. "Like I said, I don't want to spend my entire career as a glorified set."

"That's not what I said," he said quickly. It wasn't what he'd meant, either. But he could feel the fragile truce that had developed between them starting to crack. He could sense another Carly Montgomery Shit Fit coming on.

"I just mean that the corps is essential. And it's where some dancers do their best work."

Carly turned to him, and even without looking at her, he could feel dislike rolling off her, filling the entire front seat. "Some of us are just destined to live on the bottom rung forever, while the special ones are destined for bigger things? Do you know what an asshole you sound like right now?"

"I—That's not what I'm saying!" God, she was impossible. "I'm just saying that lots of talented people spend their lives in the corps because the corps needs talented dancers."

"Oh, I get it," Carly said, suddenly baring her teeth in the wide, sickly fake smile she'd been using with him whenever Heather or Marcus was around. "I should be grateful? I've spent a decade as one of thirty-two interchangeable Shades, and never getting to dance Sugarplum, because I'm so talented and fortunate?"

"Yes! Getting to dance that long is a privilege! Just ask Marcus, or anyone else whose career ended early because of an injury. Or are you too much of a brat to see how lucky you are?"

Carly inhaled sharply. Nick kept his eyes on the road, ignoring the stab of guilt in his gut at the sound. They were over the Spit Bridge now and not far from Freshwater. She didn't say anything for a long moment, and the silence swirled around him, thick and uncomfortable. Nick heard her take three slow, deep breaths in and out.

When she finally spoke, her voice was quiet and lethal, that blue-hot rage again, and it shook slightly. "How convenient for you that you were one of the chosen ones, Nick. But being stuck in the corps means no one notices when you retire, and no one cares when you get fired on a whim, either. You are dispensable."

"I—"

"I don't want to talk about this anymore. Especially not with you."

Fine, he thought. *You win*. But a few minutes later, when he pulled the car up in front of her building and she shoved the door open and climbed out without so much as a see you later, nose pink and eyes watering, she didn't look like she was relishing the victory at all.

Chapter 7

"Here you go," Carly said, placing the jeweler's small glossy bag carefully on the kitchen table. "Two wedding rings, sized, polished, and ready for the big day. Marcus, the jeweler said you should double check that they sized yours right, because they can resize it pretty easily if you need. Heather, the jeweler said you should have included more diamonds."

Heather laughed and rolled her eyes. "He didn't say that."

"No, but it's true. That ring needs more sparkle."

Heather pulled the bag towards her and fished the two small boxes out. "It doesn't need more sparkle," she said, slipping the ring onto her left ring finger and admiring her hand. "It's simple and under-stated, and it matches Marcus's ring. I love it." She leaned over and gave Marcus a kiss on the cheek, then slid the second box toward him.

The two rings did make a perfect set, Carly thought as Marcus opened his box. Marcus had chosen to use his late father's wedding ring, a plain yellow gold band, as his own ring. Heather had chosen a two-tone braided band, which made it look as though Marcus's ring had been wound around a white gold one.

Marcus put his ring on and rotated it a few times. Then he cleared his throat. "Fits just fine," he said. "Thanks for picking them up, Carly. I know you probably didn't imagine spending your holiday running errands for us."

"Actually, that's exactly how I imagined it," she said brightly. "That's what a maid of honor is for, right?"

"Right," Heather agreed, "but you should take this afternoon off. Want to go to the beach?"

"Fuck yeah, girls' day at the beach!" Carly almost shouted, and both Heather and Marcus laughed.

Carly took a deep breath as she watched the water sparkle and lap at the white-yellow sand. Shelly Beach was a small, sheltered cove surrounded by dense green forest. Sydney's best kept secret, Heather had called it. It was a beautiful little haven on the very edge of the world. Looking out at the water, she'd never have guessed there was a city of four million people behind them.

"You're never coming back to New York, are you?" she said, letting the breath out on a sigh. She said it to the water, and she said it with a smile, but Heather wasn't fooled.

"I miss you, you know. A lot." Heather put her arm around Carly's shoulders, and even though it was too hot to be touching another person, Carly didn't move away.

"I know," she nodded. "I miss you, too. New York misses you. The company's not . . . It's just not the same without you." Heather gave her a wistful smile and squeezed her arm around the back of her neck. Her palm was sweaty against Carly's shoulder, and Carly didn't care.

"I don't miss the company. It never felt like home, even when it was my entire life. And I've got a new company now, and it feels like where I belong. But I'll never have a new Carly. There's only ever going to be one Carly."

Carly nodded tightly, surprised to find that her eyes were watering. She'd known all this was true, but she hadn't realized until she heard it out loud how badly she needed to hear her best friend say those words. Heather had her whole new life, with her fiancé and her secret beaches, and Carly's life had stayed exactly the same, except that now her best friend lived on the other side of the world.

"How's Melissa doing?" Heather asked, and Carly gave her a shaky smile. Now that Jack had left the company, never to be heard from again, his ex-girlfriend had really come into her own. She and Melissa weren't exactly friends, because you could never truly be friends with someone who had cheated with your best friend's fiancé. But they'd been cast in a few dances together this year, and Carly had come to enjoy Melissa's presence in the studio. Certainly, now that Jack was gone, Melissa seemed more sure of herself. She was a consistent dancer, she listened closely when other people were talking, and she wasn't afraid to tell a choreographer when a step wasn't working or when she and the other dancers needed more rehearsal time.

"She's doing okay, I think."

"Just okay?"

"Better than she was. I think she was in pretty bad shape after Jack left. He casts a pretty long shadow."

"Don't I know it," Heather replied with a humorless laugh.

"I think she might run for union rep, actually," Carly said. "She's organized, she's opinionated. I think she'd be a good advocate for the other dancers."

"I wonder who she learned that from," Heather said, her tone arch but admiring.

Carly twirled an imaginary mustache. "Someone has to take my place as resident troublemaker when my knees finally give out. Mwahahaha!"

Heather chuckled. "Come on, let's go cool off," she gestured toward the water. They walked down the warm sand and dropped their bags, then stripped off their clothes and jogged into the water. It was blessedly cool after their walk under the relentless sun. Up to her waist, with the water lapping gently at her ribcage, Carly turned to her friend. Might as well tell her.

"Catherine's changed the promotion schedule, and now she's announcing before the spring season."

Heather's eyes went wide. "Oh, wow, that's a big change."

"I know," Carly nodded, hitching her mouth up into a *no big deal* smile and trying to project the confidence of someone who had everything under control, even as a hot wave of panic rose in her gut. Time was running out before she walked away from ballet—or was pushed again. "But I'll figure something out." *Please, God, let me figure something out.*

Heather looked over at her, and even through the reflective sunglasses, Carly could tell Heather's eyes were narrowed in skepticism.

"What?" Carly said defensively. "It's fine."

This time Heather pulled her glasses down so Carly could see just how little she believed her.

"Honestly, it's—"

"It's not fine," Heather interrupted. "This messes up the whole timeline, and you're freaking out."

"No I'm not," Carly said, too hastily. Heather lowered her chin and gave Carly her patented Heather Hays *cut the crap* look. Carly let out a sound that was half groan and half sigh.

"Fine, I'm freaking out," she admitted. "But I'll figure something out. I will." Some time in the next two-and-three-quarter weeks, she would solve this problem, she told herself, trying to hold another small wave of panic at bay.

"I know you will," Heather said soothingly. It was her Big Sister voice, which meant a Big Sister offer of help was coming. "But if you don't, will you let me help? I could put in a good word with Catherine, at the very least. I have a pretty good relationship with her. She was very eager to mend fences as soon as she took over from Mr. K."

"No, you've already done so much," Carly argued. She didn't want her best friend to have to swoop in and save her again. It had been hard enough last time to ask Heather to put her own career on the line to save Carly's job.

"I'm just saying that I would if you wanted me to. But I hear you." Heather frowned pensively, then pulled out her hair tie and ducked down until the water came up to her chin. Carly did the same, lying back in the cool water and letting it flood her scalp as her hair floated around her shoulders.

"Obviously, asking your parents is out of the question," Heather said after they'd floated in silence for a few minutes.

"Obviously," Carly agreed. She knew damn well that a sizeable donation from Edward and Marlene, perhaps enough to bankroll a new three-act ballet or update an entire warehouse worth of costumes, would make the board lean on Catherine to promote her. It would only take one phone call to them, and they'd be so happy to do it. She'd call them, and they'd write a check big enough to have every square foot of carpet in the theater replaced, or something, and just like that she'd be a soloist. And she'd never forgive herself. "It wouldn't be real. It would be like I bought my place— No, like they bought it for me. I've made it this far without asking them for help, and I'm not going to cave now."

"Mmm," was all Heather said. She'd heard Carly give some version of this speech many times.

They floated for a few more minutes, and Carly let the sound of the water and the seagulls and the distant buzz of a boat motor wash over her. "You know what you need?" Heather said.

"A beach this clean in Manhattan?"

"You need something to boost your profile. Catherine already knows how you dance. She's been watching you in class and on stage for years. But you need to show that you're a box office draw, too. That way, promoting you is good business for them."

"How would I do that?" Carly frowned up at the cloudless blue sky.

"I don't know, get famous? Book an endorsement deal with a dancewear company? Rack up a million Instagram followers?"

Carly sighed. It was true that dancers' Instagram accounts had basically become part of their resumes now. It had been a long time since she'd auditioned for a dance company, but she knew that these days, when you showed up to an audition, companies didn't just want to see how good your extensions were or how many pirouettes you could do. They also wanted to know what kind of an online following you had. And Carly had basically no following. She only used Instagram to keep up with her friends' lives and to follow funny ballet meme accounts.

"So, what, I magically amass 999,900 followers in the next three weeks, and Catherine will have no choice but to promote me because some of those hundreds of thousands of internet strangers will buy tickets at Lincoln Center?" Carly asked.

"I think that's the theory," Heather agreed.

Carly exhaled an impatient breath. It took years to develop a following of that size, and it wasn't like she would have any rehearsal or performance footage to post in the next three weeks.

"Okay, but how do I do that?"

"You mean outside of full-frontal nudity?"

"Ha," Carly said humorlessly. "I'm not doing that."

"Well, there goes my first and only idea," Heather shrugged.

Carly stood up and slapped her hand along the water, spraying Heather in the face.

"Hey! Not cool!" Heather cried, but she sent a splash right back.

Carly giggled and dodged the spray, then dived sideways, closing her eyes and letting the cool water envelope her face at last. It felt glorious after the beating sun, and for a moment she let the water hold her, enjoying the feeling of weightlessness and silence. It was clear enough that when she opened her eyes, she could see the rippled sand below, and she spotted a few silvery fish darting away from her.

When she broke the surface and wiped the salty water away from her eyes, she found Heather standing right where she'd left her, with a triumphant grin on her face.

"I've got it," Heather said. "I've got an idea."

"Oay," Carly said warily, hoping Heather wasn't going to suggest calling Catherine on her behalf again.

"You need new followers, which means you need new photos. Really good photos, right? And we know someone in Sydney who takes really good photos."

"We do?" Carly asked.

"We do. We know Nick."

Carly stared at her. "Nick . . . Jacobs?" she managed, her heart thudding.

"Yeah, Nick Jacobs! He's a big deal photographer now, right? Marcus says he's killing it."

Carly gave a mirthless laugh. "Absolutely not."

"Why not?"

"Because he's so—" *Pretentious. Uptight. Smug. Judgemental.* Carly swallowed all those adjectives and searched her brain for something neutral. "Busy. He's busy doing wedding stuff." *And making me miserable.* She schooled her face into the easiest and breeziest it had ever been, hoping it was enough to fool Heather. "I told you, I'll figure it out on my own. You don't need to worry about this. You don't need to worry about anything, you're the bride!"

Heather gave her another skeptical look, confirming Carly's suspicion that she might have slipped from easy and breezy into maniacal and crazed. She tried to pull it back a little.

"Nick is great," she lied, "but I don't think he'll want to help me."

She could just imagine how he'd respond if she asked. *Euhhh, no.* She blinked hard so she wouldn't roll her eyes at the memory of his verbal tic, which he threw around like he was desperate for everyone to know he'd danced at POB. *We get it Nick, you're a smoking hot success with an Australian accent who also speaks fluent French.*

"You could at least ask."

I could also dance the entire second act of Swan Lake *wearing nothing but dead pointe shoes.*

"I don't think so," Carly said, and she turned to face the beach and started to wade back toward the sand.

"Why not?" Heather said, following her. "Do you not like him or something?"

Oh God. That wasn't good. Carly didn't need Heather worrying about her career prospects *or* about her desire to feed the best man to a hungry shark. She needed Heather happy, carefree, glowing. After everything Heather had been through, that's what she deserved.

"I like him just fine," Carly lied again, exiting the water and heading for their bags and towels. She picked up her towel and prepared for the acting performance of a lifetime. "I see why Marcus likes him so much." A lie. "And he's been a great guide to Sydney." Also a lie, the man was allergic to maps. "And he's not bad to look at." Not strictly a lie, but irrelevant.

Heather nodded as she dried herself off. "Right? I'm engaged and everything, but my eyes work. And uh, yum."

Sure, if you like your men haughty and superior. "Mmhmmm," Carly said, hoping Heather took the sound as agreement and not as an unwillingness to open her mouth in case she blew her cover. As far as Heather needed to know, she and Nick were getting on famously.

"Marcus is so glad to have him back. He's been gone forever, and they were really close when they were younger. Marcus considered asking Alice to be his best man, but she called dibs on officiating about five seconds after we told her we were engaged, so Nick was the obvious choice."

Carly smiled, hoping she looked charmed and touched. If only Alice had demanded to be best man. "Well, Nick and I are going to make sure this wedding is everything you've dreamed of. Which won't leave any time for photography."

"If it's going to get you promoted, you should at least give it a try. What's the worst that could happen?"

One of us could end up mysteriously devoured by a crocodile?

"I don't . . ." she started, but she had no idea how to finish the sentence. No idea how to tell her friend that the last person she wanted help from was Marcus's condescending, big deal best man. Instead, she threw Heather what she hoped looked like a confident smile, as though that thought didn't make her queasy. "I promise that if I can't think of a solution myself, I'll ask him."

Which meant she would absolutely, positively, have to think of a solution herself. Something that didn't require help from her best friend or her parents, she thought, as she dried herself off, a little more vigorously than was strictly necessary. Or from a man who'd made his disdain for her very clear.

Except that, by the time she got into bed that night, she hadn't figured something else out. She sat on the bed in her apartment, staring at Catherine's email. Then she pulled up her calendar app and swiped, yet again, through the weeks until she arrived at the start of rehearsals for the spring season. Not even a month. She went back to the email, even though she had it memorized by now. Asking Heather to put in a good word for her was out of the question. So was letting her parents "help her out a little," which was how they would describe donating several new Steinways for NYB's accompanists.

She sighed and opened Instagram. One hundred and three followers, and most of them were company members or cousins. She tossed the phone down onto the covers and groaned petulantly at the ceiling and accepted the awful reality. Heather was so sensible, so wise, so right all the time, goddammit. But did she have to be right this time, too?

Chapter 8

Nick's stomach grumbled as he pulled his T-shirt over his head. He'd woken up well before his alarm and laid in bed, unable to go back to sleep. And now he was suddenly ravenous. He'd decided to give up on sleep and head downstairs for breakfast and was just reaching into a drawer for a pair of shorts when there was a slow, quiet knock on his door.

"One sec," he called. He pulled his shorts on hastily, noticing as he did that the bruises on his knees and at the backs of his legs had turned an unpleasant vomit-green colour, and zipped up his fly as he walked to the door.

He pulled the door open, one hand still on the button of his fly, and felt his head jerk back in surprise.

It was Carly, a takeaway coffee cup in each hand, and a brown paper bag hanging from her wrist. She was wearing denim shorts and a loose pale blue linen blouse, under which he could just see the thin black straps of a bra. Her hair was pulled up in a high bun this morning, but a few curly red strands had already fallen out and were stuck to the sides of her long neck. It made her look frazzled, an impression reinforced by the serious little frown on her face.

"Hi," she said quietly. "I brought you breakfast. Well, breakfasts, plural, because I wasn't sure what you'd want. But I figured Australian cafés have taken over New York for a reason, and it's because any Australian breakfast is a good breakfast. So I figured that since I'm jetlagged you're probably also jetlagged so you may be down for a bit of breakfast right now since some places aren't even serving breakfast so we could have, like, breakfast together because why not. And I've just said the word *breakfast* so much that it no longer has any meaning."

Nick stared at her and said nothing, first because surprise stole his words, then because her rapid-fire blathering was irritating, and then ultimately because he didn't particularly have anything to say to her. From the moment he touched down in Sydney, Carly Montgomery seemed to have made it her personal mission to make his life a living hell. Why would a surprise breakfast together at 6 AM be any different?

"I don't want breakfast," he said gruffly and watched as her face fell. But then his stomach grumbled loudly, and the ghost of an evil smile curved her mouth. She schooled it quickly and returned to her serious, determined expression.

"Just in case you do want it in the near future, then, can I interest you in some avocado toast? Or a bacon and egg sandwich on a brioche bun?" Carly lifted her arm gently, so that the paper bag swung and the smell of cooked bacon wafted towards him.

Nick's treacherous stomach gurgled again, and she grinned. Damn it.

"I'll take the sandwich.," he said. His mouth was already watering.

"You got it. And the coffee? Skim cappuccino with one sugar, right?"

"Yeah," he said slowly as she nodded and handed him the right cup. She remembered his coffee order? "Thanks."

Then an awkward silence stretched between them.

And stretched.

And stretched . . .

"Can I . . . come in? Just for a few minutes?"

"Why?"

"Please?"

"*Why?*"

"*Please?*"

Carly's voice had ticked up several octaves, and Nick arched an eyebrow, calmly taking a sip of coffee. He was starting to enjoy this. "No, tell me why first."

With a huff and a roll of her eyes, Carly blurted, "Because I have something to ask you, and I'd feel really stupid laying it all out and asking it here, in the hallway, outside your door when I'm trying my hardest to be nice!"

Nick hesitated for a moment, tempted to take the bag with both breakfasts and slam the door in her face. It was basically what she'd do to him if he were to ask her for any kind of help. But the serious look on her freckled face and the fact that she'd shown up unannounced with a peace offering at the crack of dawn were enough to tip him into the realm of mild curiosity. Nick stepped aside and tried not to notice the smoky floral scent that trailed behind her as she entered his room. Once inside, Carly set the bag down on the desk and fished out a lumpy package wrapped in aluminium foil.

"Bacon sandwich," she said. He nodded his thanks, then sat down on the bed and unwrapped the package on his lap. When he looked up, it was to see her perched on the desk, watching him.

"I wanted to say that I'm sorry about yesterday," she said. This time her voice was firm and steady, nothing like the rapid and breathless spilling out of words she'd arrived with.

"Which part?" he said, unable to resist the retort. He bit off a mouthful of the sandwich. Shit, it was good. Another thing the French didn't do all that well. Sure, they invented brioche, and they knew how to make a croque monsieur, but a bacon and egg sandwich with barbeque sauce just tasted like Australia. Like home.

"All of it. It was nice of you to listen to me vent, and I should have heard you out. I know you were just trying to . . . help." She rolled her shoulders back as she said the last word, as though she was trying to wriggle away from it. "I have, uh, a bit of a temper, as you've probably noticed. I'm working on it."

He swallowed his mouthful of brioche fast, because part of him wanted to reply, *Work harder.* But another part of him realized that this apology, right now, was part of that work. She was trying.

"Apology accepted," he nodded. He took another bite of his sandwich and washed it down with a swig of coffee. "But you really do have an Anne of Green Gables–level problem."

Her eyebrows shot up in question.

"You know, Anne of Green Gables? Red hair? Major temper? Smashes slates on boys' heads?"

"I know who Anne of Green Gables is," she said. "I just didn't think you would."

"Please. I have a sister who was a big time horse girl. I know who Anne Shirley is."

"Um, right," Carly said, with a little shake of her head. She took a sip of her coffee. "I've been thinking about the promotions calendar problem. And I think I've come up with a solution. Well, Heather came up with a solution."

He raised his eyebrows in question, and she took another gulp of her coffee, then swallowed hard.

"I need to boost my profile. Show NYB that I've got lots of people who are interested in me and will want to come see me dance bigger roles. And I was thinking that social media would be one way to do that."

He nodded and tossed the final chunk of the sandwich into his mouth. Social media was like a second, part-time job for some dancers these days, especially Instagram, because it was so visual. He'd mostly stayed away from it as a dancer, but once he'd started his photography business, he hadn't really had a choice. He also hadn't had much success convincing people to follow his account, and he doubted his posts there had translated into any business for him.

"So as it turns out, I need your help," Carly went on. She sighed the words out, as though it caused her deep spiritual pain to say them. "You're a photographer. And I need photos. I know we've got wedding stuff to do, but I thought that in between, we could do some shoots around Sydney. It could be good for both of us."

Not likely, Nick thought. They couldn't get through a single wedding errand without an explosion of some kind. And now she wanted to *work* together? He crumpled up the sandwich wrapper and tossed it into the bin next to the desk, but it bounced off the rim and hit her sandal.

She bent at the hips the way dancers did—the way normal people, with normal hamstrings, found totally bizarre—and deposited it in the bin. As she bent, her blouse lifted at her waist, revealing a small expanse of smooth skin stretched over rigid lines of muscle. For a split second, he wondered what it would be like to have those muscles in the grid of his camera, how her small but steel-strong body would look balanced in an attitude—or even more dramatically, a penché—her hair unbound and flowing like living fire with the ocean waves crashing behind her. *Golden hour would look great with her complexion. Wide aperture setting, f/2 probably, to not wash her out. Rim lighting, if we can time it right. Maybe a few long exposure shots, capture her movement. Some close-ups. I think I have the right bounce cards and color gel to really showcase the gold in her eyes . . .* Suddenly Nick found his heart racing, and he quickly pushed the thought away, averting his eyes so that when she straightened up, his gaze was on the floor.

"So, what do you think?" she said hopefully. He looked at her frankly.

"I think it sounds like you're asking me for help, but you haven't actually asked me anything yet." Her eyes widened, as though she'd been on the verge of rolling them and barely managed to stop herself.

She took what looked like a deep, calming breath. "Nick Jacobs, will you please help me with this, by doing something that will also be quite beneficial to you?"

"That's more like it," he said with an approving nod. "And no."

Her face fell and she let out an exasperated kind of growl.

"Why not?"

He shrugged. "How many reasons do you need? I don't want to. I don't think we'd work well together, seeing as every time we cross paths it's a total disaster. I've got best man stuff to do. I don't think your plan will work anyway. And lastly, unlike you, I don't need to boost my career." He'd told that final lie a little too forcefully, a little too unkindly, and he instantly regretted it. He could reject her request without being a dick about it.

Carly seemed to agree, because her cheeks flushed, and then she closed her eyes and nodded almost imperceptibly, as though she was counting silently in her head. When she opened them again, he was surprised to see a look of desperation in them, and a sheen of tears that made the golden brown shimmer more brightly than usual. Regret twisted in his gut again, and he shifted uneasily on the bed. She might be a human hurricane, but Carly Montgomery was still a human, and he'd clearly hurt her feelings.

"Please. I wouldn't ask if I didn't really need your help," she said quietly. "I don't have any other ideas. And I know you don't need this, but I do."

Telling him that he was her last resort hardly helped her case, he thought.

"I don't think so." He said it firmly, hoping he didn't sound cold or unkind.

"Well, I do think so," she insisted. Her voice was a little louder now, and just as firm as his, and he was starting to realize that she wasn't going to be put off by his insults or by his attempts to let her down gently. He remembered the way she'd yawned the other day—stubbornly and with her whole body. "Don't you want to boost your profile, too? You barely have an Instagram presence. I checked."

"I . . . I don't need one. I'm in demand enough without one."
What utter shit. As if it was a secret sign of success to be almost
unfindable online. It wasn't. His tiny follower count wasn't some
power move, it was a sign of how miserably he'd failed so far. But...
If he did this for Carly, he'd be able to add a whole new series of
photos of a dancer from one of the world's best companies, taken
on the other side of the world. The few jobs he'd managed to book
had all been in Paris. It would make him look like an international
photographer. No, it would actually *make* him an international
photographer.

He bit his lip. Sensing he was wavering, Carly pressed on.

"I was thinking you could take some photos on some beaches,
maybe out in the bush Heather is always telling me about. I don't
know, on the Harbor Bridge or something?"

He rubbed one hand over his head, thinking of all the picturesque
places in this city where he could photograph her. Even though
she'd probably find a way to get them both drowned, or to accidentally push him off North Head. He shuddered.

"If you want to boost your followers that much, I don't think
dance photography in nature is what you need. What you need is—"

"Save it," she said. "Heather's already made the nudity joke, and
it's not that funny. Please, Nick. I'm desperate, and I wouldn't ask
if I didn't think there was something in it for you. If nothing else,
you could write your ticket off as a work expense."

Well, she had him there. Even one-way tickets to Australia were
steep, and now that he had no reliable source of income, he needed
every write-off he could get. And it could be an interesting addition
to his portfolio, a location rarely seen. And if he could compose
the shots just right . . .

He shook his head and sighed, knowing he would regret what
he was about to say, and probably very soon. But he also had the
distinct impression that if he didn't say it now, she'd keep arguing
with him until he finally caved. Better to save them both the time
and the headache and just get it over with.

"Fine. I'll do it," he said, and she gasped.

"Really?" she asked, eyeing him closely, as though she half expected him to wait a beat and then say "just joking."

"Really. As long as it doesn't interfere with wedding stuff. I really don't want to let Marcus and Heather down." Though it occurred to him, as he said it, that there was some appeal to having another task in front of him, another project he could work on and hopefully succeed at. Even if he also had to work on this one with Carly.

"It won't get in the way, I promise," she grinned, and Nick imagined that same joyous smile captured by his lens, her freckled face turned towards the sunrise as she casually tied her pointe shoes on the steps of the Opera House. He studied her for a long second, took in the way her eyes sparkled with excitement, relief radiating from her face. It made his heart race again, and it set off a strange throb in his chest.

"We're going to make you an even bigger photography star, and we're going to get me promoted. When can we start?" It had been a while since he'd made that expression appear on a woman's face.

"Um, we can probably start tomorrow," he ventured. "Tomorrow afternoon." Maybe by then she would have figured out some other plan and convinced some other sucker to go along with it.

She raised her eyebrows at him, looked out the window. "It's not even 7 AM. Why waste two whole days?"

For God's sake, this woman was relentless. "Because I might have things to do?" he said, rising from the bed and throwing his empty cup into the bin. "I might already have plans for how I'm going to spend this whole day."

She frowned at him, skeptical. "And do you?"

He paused. "No," he admitted under his breath.

She grinned again, triumphant, and there was that throb in his chest again.

"Then we start today. Let's shake on it." She thrust her hand out, and he took it without thinking, wrapping his fingers around her palm and feeling it clammy with sweat.

She gave his hand one enthusiastic downward tug. He returned it, a little more gently, and she gave a strange, relieved little giggle. He looked down into her delighted face and couldn't keep himself from smiling. Maybe this wouldn't be a total disaster.

Chapter 9

"Well, this is a total disaster," Carly muttered, brushing her hair away from her mouth, only to have it blown right back into her face for the hundredth time. A few strands stuck stubbornly to her lip gloss as the wind whipped around her.

Their first attempt at a photo shoot wasn't going well at all. The location Nick had chosen was a rocky cliffside in a national park near Manly, with sweeping views of the harbor hundreds of feet below. It was beautiful and forbidding, with clumps of gray-green scrub that looked like the only plant life that could survive up here. It was also extremely windy. Why had Nick decided that it was a good idea to hike to the edge of a cliff on a windy day and ask her to do an arabesque on a craggy rock? Carly had no idea.

"Make it an attitude. And can you cheat it a bit to the left?" he called from ten feet away. Carly obliged, bending her free leg and pulling her hip back so that her foot rose a little higher into the air and less of her torso was facing the camera.

"*My* left," he called, sounding annoyed. She rolled her eyes as she made the adjustment. "It's a pretty good lens, so I saw that."

She rolled her eyes even bigger this time, to make sure he really got the shot. He pulled the camera down, then squinted at the screen. "Nice, really nice," he yelled sarcastically. "You look like you're about to faint."

Or get thrown into the ocean by the next strong gust. *Maybe*, Carly thought, *that was his plan.* It would look like an accident if she toppled into Sydney Harbor in the middle of an arabesque. She brought her foot down and crossed her arms over her chest.

"What step is that?" Nick called.

"Pas de douche," Carly muttered as the wind plastered several of her curls to her cheek again. She pulled them out of her face and glared over at him.

"Can you give me a Giselle penché? The big one, from the second act?"

He must be out of his mind. If she stood out here on one leg, with her free foot pointing at the sky and her body lowered almost to the ground, she was going to be swept off the side of the cliff for sure.

"I've never danced Giselle," she yelled back. One of twenty-four identical wilis? She'd danced that role plenty of times, standing stock-still in a line along the side of the stage while Heather or one of the other principals danced in the middle of it.

It was Nick's turn to roll his eyes. "You still know how to do a penché, though. Or is it just not very good?"

Carly scowled. Nick didn't know what he was talking about. She had an excellent penché, thank you very much. She took a step forward, making sure there weren't any loose rocks under her supporting foot before lifting her other foot behind her, raising it as high as she could before she needed to lower her body to accommodate the movement. When her leg wouldn't go any further, she stopped, and for good measure she clasped her hands in front of her chest, just as she'd seen Heather and all the other Giselles do in the second act pas de deux.

"See, was that so hard? You've got a very nice penché," Nick called, sounding smug.

I know I do, she wanted to yell at him, but she'd lose her balance if she turned her head. The sneaky bastard had goaded her into doing exactly what he wanted, and he knew it.

After a moment, her lower back began to ache with the effort of holding the position, and she brought her leg down slowly.

"Okay, try the Odette thing, with the wings," he called, putting one foot behind him and raising one hand to the sky, resting his head against his bicep.

"Also never danced Odette." A nameless swan? Many times. But before he could goad her into doing it, she did her best impression of the famous swan pose, with her front leg in a deep bend and her other leg extended long behind her. She raised one arm like Nick had, placing the other hand in front of her body, hovering over the place where a white tutu skirt would have been had she been in costume. "How's that?" she asked, as though Nick's opinion mattered. There was a long silence as he scrutinized her.

"Tilt your chin up," he called eventually, and she ignored the absence of praise and lifted her head slightly.

"Up and to the right," he corrected, and she tried. "No," he called, and Carly closed her eyes to keep from rolling them. Presumably, being a stickler for detail was an asset in a photographer, but surely it wouldn't be good for him if his model got blown off a cliff while he fussed about the precise angle of her chin.

She was about to say all this when she caught a waft of spice and citrus, and when she opened her eyes, Nick was a foot away from her, his stupidly handsome face creased in a frown.

"Like this," he said, tilting his own chin up and to the side. Carly held her breath and did her best to imitate him, then raised one eyebrow impatiently. He merely frowned down at her, as if nothing about her pleased him. Well, the feeling was mutual. And she was losing patience.

"Just show me, then," she snapped, gesturing to one of his hands.

"Fine," he replied shortly, and before she could think better of her suggestion, his hands were on her jaw, guiding her into place. His fingertips were cool and his touch light, but Carly's skin was suddenly burning in every place he touched her. Out of irritation, she thought. Because he was pedantic and fussy and refused to be satisfied. She swiveled her eyes up to his face, careful not to move her head at all, and saw him looking at her with intense focus, a shallow frown between his eyebrows. Up this close, she could practically count each of his unfairly long eyelashes.

"Am I perfect yet?" she asked sarcastically.

Nick's fingers froze on her face, and he pulled them away. It didn't stop her skin from buzzing. "That'll do," he replied tersely, taking a step away from her, and she gritted her teeth.

"Get the shot, then."

"One second, I just want—" Just then, a huge gust of wind swept over the cliff and slammed into Carly's back. She let out a little shriek as she toppled over, grabbing Nick by the shoulders and sending him stumbling backward. For a moment she thought they were both going to tumble onto the hard, rocky ground, but Nick regained his footing and righted himself, and she was able to stop herself from falling.

"You're a menace," he muttered

"That wasn't me, that was the wind," she objected. "And I'm not the one who wanted to take photos in the eye of a hurricane."

"The eye is the calm part. It's the rest of the hurricane that's dangerous," he shot back, and as she let out a frustrated growl, he turned away and she heard him mutter something that sounded a lot like *human hurricane.*

"Can we please go somewhere less windy? I don't want to die today." *But I might commit murder.*

"Sure," he said shortly, sounding defeated, and then he was stalking away from her back toward the car.

"God, that was a nightmare. Why did you want to trek all the way out there?" she asked, joining him in the front seat a few minutes later.

He stopped and looked over at her, his eyes a dark inky blue now that they were out of the sun.

"I thought the shots would look good," he said simply, putting the keys in the ignition. As if the discomfort and danger were irrelevant as long as the photos came out well.

"That's the most ballet dancer thing I've ever heard," Carly said. "Who cares what it feels like, as long as it looks good?"

He gave a grim laugh, and Carly idly wondered if he ever laughed for real. Like a good, from-your-gut, throw-your-head-back-and-cackle kind of laugh. Or was it all sharp, humorless laughs like that one?

"Anyway, do they?" she asked.

"Do they what?" he said, as they rolled down the hill and back, she assumed, toward Freshwater.

"Look good? The photos?"

"God, you're not impatient at all, are you?" he shook his head. "You can't wait until we get back?"

"Only if you drive faster," she said. In response, he pumped the brakes, and they both lurched forward in their seats. He winced, and she had a feeling the sudden stop had pressed on his bruises.

"Serves you right," she said tartly, and his silence suggested he agreed with her. "Can I please just see what you got?"

"Fine," he sighed, and he pulled the car to the side of the road and threw it into park. He reached behind him and pulled his camera case off the back seat, and she reached for it.

"Absolutely not," he said sternly. "I'm not letting you hold it."

"Why, you think I'm going to try to *steal* it?" she shot back sarcastically, her eyebrows raised and her eyes wide. "I already tried that, remember, and you caught me, Interpol."

"No, but I'm sure you'll find some other way to wreak havoc," he replied, "and I can't have that. None of this works if my camera doesn't work. So just let me hold it, okay?"

Carly looked at him, torn between irritation and impatience. This close to him, she could see a few fine creases around his eyes and smell the spicy cologne she was coming to associate with him. And with this very particular blend of frustration. He was watching her, waiting to see if she was going to accept his terms.

She gave a small eye roll of assent, and he gave a reluctant little nod, then opened the bag and switched the camera on.

Nick busied himself with the camera, taking his time putting the bag back on the back seat and pulling up the photos he'd taken of Carly on the North Head cliffs. He'd been planning to drive home as slowly as possible, to put off the moment when he'd have to show her the photos. But he should have known that her fierce impatience would wreck that plan. So he'd insisted on holding the camera and counted on her being insulted. With any luck, she'd get into a signature Carly huff and decide that she didn't want to see the shots after all, if he wasn't going to trust her with his Nikon. But she'd surprised him—well, her annoyed little eye roll hadn't surprised him one bit, but the rest of it had. She'd stared him down, her mouth set in a firm, stubborn line and her eyes locked on his, and then given in.

His thumb shook slightly as he scrolled through the images now, and he hoped she wouldn't notice. He wished he'd come up with another excuse, and another one after that, but he'd been caught off guard. Everything about Carly seemed to catch him off guard, and now here they were, each with one elbow on the armrest, craning their heads over the camera so she could look at his photos right in front of him.

His pulse sped up as she scrolled through the first few shots, some warm-ups he'd taken of her before she'd started posing. It had been an unpleasant walk up to the edge of the headland, and it had been windy as hell up there, but the view from the edge of cliffs was as striking as he'd remembered. The Sydney skyline in one direction, and the vast expanse of the Pacific Ocean in the other. As dramatic and iconic views went, he'd thought it was a good place to start.

But now, this entire exercise seemed like a colossal mistake, and his heart was hammering in protest. It had been months since he'd let anyone see his photos, and it was hard not to think about the last time he'd tried. He'd shown Delphine a shot he'd taken during a dress rehearsal at the Opera Garnier, one of the best he'd taken since he'd gotten serious about photography, or so he'd thought. She'd frowned down at it for a good thirty seconds and finally managed a "beuhhhh," the French verbal equivalent of a shrug. After that, he'd stopped asking her if she wanted to see what he was working on, and so she never saw another of his photos. It wasn't like she'd made a practice of asking to look at them.

He swallowed hard, and reminded himself that it didn't matter if Carly hated the photos. He didn't need her good opinion, and if they were truly terrible, they could go to some other location and try again. She needed this as much as he did, and as she'd told him this morning, he was her last resort. So she wasn't in a position to criticise or get picky. Still. He swallowed again.

After a few tense seconds of scrolling, she stopped and leaned closer to the camera, squinting slightly. She was close enough that one of her errant curls bobbed close to his face when she cocked her head, threatening to tickle the tip of his nose.

"Hmmm," she mused. He couldn't tell what the sound meant, and he was too anxious to ask. She saved him the trouble. "I really like this one," she said, and as relief bloomed in Nick's chest, she pulled back so that he could see the screen.

He'd caught her at the height of her attitude, balanced on one leg with the other one raised and wrapped behind her body, her hair blown back off her face and away from her long neck. He'd been right to get her to cheat to the left; it made her look like she was a second from tipping over and toppling off the rock. But the look she was giving the camera made it clear that she wasn't coming down until she decided to. Despite his anxiety, he'd gotten at least one good shot out of this day.

She leaned forward to look at the camera again, and this time her hair did catch him on the nose. It smelled like the bouquets of roses the stage managers kept stashed backstage to give to principal dancers on opening night, but smokier somehow, and less delicate. He became aware that the sun was beating down on the little car, making the air feel stuffy and the backs of his knees itch with sweat.

"I look really good here," she said, leaning back and gesturing at the camera. "I mean, you made me look really good. And the view from the cliff looks incredible behind me, and even the wind really works. It's so dramatic."

"Euh, thanks?" he half asked, the stream of compliments making his cheeks flush and something uncomfortably pleasant crawl in his chest.

He looked at her, waiting for the other sarcastic shoe to drop. Surely she was going to find something to criticise or complain about, some way to blow up this otherwise perfectly nice interaction. All available evidence would suggest that was what was about to happen. But instead, she just said, "Let's post it."

"Oh, I should edit them first," he objected. It was one thing for her to see them, but he needed to make sure they were perfect before anyone else did.

"We don't have time for that," she said, shaking her head dismissively. "And who cares if it's not perfect? Let the people see my grubby sneakers and stretch marks on my inner thighs Authenticity is what clicks anyway, right?"

"Euh," he started, but he had no idea what to say to that. He hadn't noticed any stretch marks on her inner thighs, but suddenly they were all he could think about. Maybe he should start the car and put the air con back on.

"Come on, we don't have time to tinker and retouch. If this plan is going to work, we have to start posting these photos ASAP," she said. "Besides, this is really good; it doesn't need editing. I promise you. Can I see the rest?"

He knew she was only praising him because she was in a hurry, and she wasn't really praising him at all, just this one photo. Still. He picked up the camera and held it out to her.

"You're sure?" she asked, eyeing him skeptically.

"Sure," he said. "How much damage can you possibly do?"

"You'd be surprised," she muttered, taking the camera.

"No. I wouldn't," he said archly, and she chuckled, but turned her attention to the camera.

He watched as she scrolled through the images for a few minutes, watching her forehead crease and her lips purse as she assessed the other photos he'd taken. He'd just realized he was staring when she burst out laughing, tossing her head back as the loud, joyful sound filled the car.

"What's so funny?" he said, craning his neck to see which photo had incited that response. She giggled, the high-pitch sound so different from her deep, almost scratchy voice, and held it up for him to see.

She'd stopped on a frame he'd taken just as a gust of wind had thrown her hair right across her face, so her entire head looked like a red curly blur. But beneath the fuzzy red ball that was her head, her body was all sharp, long lines. Her arms were thrown out at a low angle at her sides, energy radiating from her shoulders all the way down through her fingertips, just the way dance teachers always demanded. One of her legs was extended behind her, her foot pointed in her sneaker, and a slight bend in her front leg was making the muscles in her thigh bulge beneath the hem of her shorts. She was a picture of utter chaos and absolute control.

"Not the best shot in the set," he said. "Maybe we shouldn't post that one."

"I think it's hilarious," she replied, grinning back at him, her lips glistening and her eyes alight with amusement. "Is that really what I look like?"

Yes, he thought, as he turned away from her and turned the key in the ignition. *That is exactly what you look like.*

Chapter 10

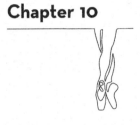

That evening found Carly pacing the length of the bedroom, swiping back and forth between the photos Nick had agreed to let her post. She'd hoped the windy morning would result in more than just three usable shots, but he'd been so precious about making sure she only posted photos that he'd decided were perfect. Amazing that even three of them had lived up to his impossible standards. Clearly the man never did anything or bothered with anyone who wasn't perfect, which raised the question of why he'd agreed to spend any time with her.

She squinted down at the middle photo and noticed again how precisely he'd manage to position her between the distant spiky skyline and the yawning bright blue sky over the ocean. She was in the center of the frame, arching into an attitude and fixing the camera with a determined kind of look, but she appeared to be dancing on the edge of the world. She'd meant what she'd said in the car, however grudgingly she'd admitted it, and however surprised he'd seemed to hear it. He was good at this.

Her thumb hovered over the phone screen. *Just pick one*, she thought. *Pick one, hashtag it, and post it. What's the worst that could happen?*

"Ha," she said to the empty room. *This plan could fail, and I'll have begged Nick Jacobs for help for nothing, and I'll retire in obscurity at thirty-two with no marketable skills. And I'll have no choice but to take money from my parents.*

Anxiety prickled at the back of her neck, and she took a deep breath through her nose, trying to keep it from spreading through her whole body the way she knew it could. Exhaling slowly, she walked over to the little window and peered out at the ocean. She could do this. And if she couldn't, she would figure something else out. She was good at figuring things out. She'd figured out how to support herself without her parents' help, and how to get Heather out of the country after her asshole ex-fiancé, Jack, had destroyed her best friend's sense of self, *and* how to get her job back when Jack had gotten her fired. She could do this. She took one more deep breath, then tapped on the middle photo and pulled up Instagram.

> *@carlymontgomery: Soaking up the Sydney sunshine at North Head National Park! Photo by the talented and in-demand @NickJClicks #ballerinasinthewild #sydneytourism #attitude*

She scanned the caption for typos—God forbid she posted Nick Jacobs's photo above a misspelled word—and was about to hit POST when her phone buzzed and a text popped up. It was from the number she'd saved under the name "Nickhead."

> *Nickhead: Sunrise is at 6:30 tomorrow. Do you want to get some early shots on the beach?*

She stared at the message. Was he insane? She was on vacation, and supposedly so was he. Who got up at 6:30 AM on vacation, and who looked good enough to be photographed if they did? She was about to tap back a snarky message to that effect when she paused. She was still jetlagged, so a 6:30 AM call time wouldn't be so hard. Nick Jacobs was offering to help her—volunteering, even, after she'd had to wheedle help out of him this morning. And she wasn't in a position to turn him down.

She glanced over her shoulder out the window. The beach would look spectacular in the golden hour right after the sun came up. She sighed.

Carly: Sure. I'll meet you in the lobby. Coffee's on me.

The first round, at least, she thought, turning back to the photo. She took one last look at it, exhaled a shaky breath, and then hit Post.

Carly: I just put the first photo up. Please share it with your tens of followers.
Nickhead: Dozens. I have *dozens* of followers.
Carly: Pedant.
Nickhead: I wouldn't say I'm pedantic, per se, I'm just precise.

"Oh my *God*," Carly muttered, wondering if she was going to pull a muscle from rolling her eyes at this man.

Nichead: OK, that was pedantic.

Carly laughed and restrained herself from texting back in amused agreement, but only just. She changed into her pj's and brushed her teeth. Then she slipped one of her dilators and a little bottle of lube out of their clear plastic bag and got comfortable under the covers.

Angela had told her to start with some breathing exercises, a few deep inhales and slow releases to get her muscles to relax—the exact opposite of the kind of short, shallow breathing she'd expect to be doing right before trying to have sex. Once that was done, she lubed up the sterile white dilator and slipped it under the blanket. Shifting against the pillows so she could reach, she slipped the dilator slowly and steadily inside her, reminding herself to breathe deeply as she did. *Picture a flower opening*, Angela had told her. *Imagine your muscles letting go instead of clamping down.*

Once the dilator was all the way in, she released her head back onto the pillow and took a few more deep breaths. It didn't hurt tonight, but she could feel a tight, stretching sensation as she laid there and let her muscles adjust to it. Still, this counted as a Good Vagina Day. She was having more and more of those lately, sometimes two or three of them in a row, but she'd learned not to get her hopes up that she was magically cured now. Sometimes Bad Vagina Days just came out of nowhere. So did Very Bad Vagina Days and Fucking Awful Vagina Days. That was the most infuriating, exhausting thing about chronic pain: there was no consistency, no control, no way to know when a string of good days would end or a string of bad days would start.

But today was a Good Vagina Day, she thought, letting her eyes drift closed. A good day all around, even if she'd spent it with Nick Jacobs instead of with Heather. He'd agreed to help her, and they'd gotten at least three usable photos out of the morning, and there would be more tomorrow. A good day.

Unbidden, the image of Nick's long, agile fingers swam to the top of her mind, the way they'd fiddled with the camera before he'd reluctantly handed it over in the car this morning. And his intense blue gaze, fixed on her as she posed on the cliffside, his eyes watching her closely but seeing everything else, too. And the deep, muscular channel that ran down his back to his round, unforgivably muscular ass. Her muscles gave a needy throb around the dilator, and her eyes popped open.

She froze on her back, staring up at the ceiling in horror. She'd never once had a sexy thought while doing her dilator exercises, because the whole thing was so profoundly unsexy. Sure, the end goal of all this was pain-free sex, but the exercises themselves were about as sexless as the planks she did to warm up her core before morning class. She reached down to pull the dilator out as quickly as she dared, and her muscles throbbed again.

She propped herself up on one elbow and threw the blanket off her body. "Absolutely not," she declared, glaring down her body at her vulva. "Not a chance in hell. Don't even think about it."

Carly slept fitfully, and far too soon, her phone was vibrating rudely against the nightstand, blaring "God Is a Woman" at top volume. She groped across the bed to silence it, growling in exhausted irritation. "Sorry, Ariana," she muttered and laid back down, wondering how long she could snooze the alarm without making herself late. God forbid she keep Nick Jacobs waiting. But before she could reset the alarm, something on the screen caught her eye. A notification from Instagram.

"Shit," she breathed, staring even though the bright screen made her want to squint. "God *is* a woman, and she works *fast*."

Ten minutes later, she'd pulled on her faded old NYB sweatshirt and a pair of bike shorts, rubbed some brightening moisturizer on her face, swiped on two coats of mascara, and twisted her hair up into a rushed bun that she hoped looked messy-chic and not just messy. She dropped her phone and wallet into her shoulder bag and hurried out the front door in the direction of the Freshwater Hotel.

She found Nick waiting in the lobby, his camera bag slung over his shoulder. He was wearing jeans and a slate gray polo shirt, and he looked both sleepy and impatient. His eyes were a little puffy, but his posture was impeccable as always.

"Did you see?" she said, without preamble.

"Good morning to you, too, Carly," he said, and she ignored him, pulling her phone out of her bag.

"It is a good morning!"

"Speak for yourself," he grumbled.

"I always do. Nick, it's working," she said. She pulled up her Instagram account and held her phone up for him to see. "About two hundred new followers since I went to sleep. Which wasn't that long ago, seeing as *someone* wanted to get up at the ass crack of dawn to take more photos."

"Weird way to say thank you, but okay," he interjected, and she stuck her tongue out at him. He stared at her mouth for a split second, as though a grown woman sticking her tongue out at him was an affront to his most delicate sensibilities, then rubbed a hand over his hair and redirected his gaze to the lobby door. "Let's get started."

Nick walked down the dunes in groggy silence, and he let her get a few paces in front of him so he could get a few shots of her walking down the slope, the back of her long, freckled neck exposed by her high bun. A few wisps of curly red hair had already escaped it and were floating behind her on the morning breeze. He had a sudden urge to reach out and brush them away. Tuck them back into the bun. Let his fingertips slide over the smooth, downy skin and tangle in the rebellious orange-red chaos that was her hair.

That's insane, he told himself. *You're only thinking that because you've seen her tongue this morning. And not in a sexy way, in a juvenile go-to-hell kind of way.*

He cleared his throat, and she turned to look at him, eyebrows raised.

"Is something wrong already? Is this perfect morning not perfect enough for you?" She swept one arm out to gesture over the almost deserted beach. The sky above the horizon was a promising golden pink, and there were already a dozen surfers out on their boards.

"No, it's great," he said tersely. "Why don't you go stand between the flags, and I'll stay up here?"

He'd get close-ups later. Right now, he needed to put some physical distance between them, and wide shots seemed like an obvious way to do it.

He cleared his throat again as she dropped her tote bag and shoes on the sand next to him and walked away, casting him a curious look as she went. He fiddled with his camera, keeping his eyes averted so that he wouldn't have to watch her calf muscles flex under her skin as she walked down the beach. After spending an hour poring over the photos he'd taken yesterday—an hour was all she'd give him for editing, queen of patience that she was—he felt like he had her legs memorized. Which meant he knew that, yes, she had stretch marks on the insides of her thighs. And a constellation of freckles on her right shin that formed a small isosceles triangle. And he had noticed all these things not because he wanted to see them or know them but because he was a photographer, and because he'd promised to try to help her. To help both of them, really. He hadn't woken up to as many new followers as she had this morning, but he'd picked up a few dozen. This professional marriage of convenience might actually pay off.

"What are you waiting for?" her impatient voice drifted up the beach, and he started.

"Sorry, your highness," he called back, and he sensed rather than saw her epic eye roll.

He raised the camera and found her, positioned precisely between the red and yellow surf lifesavers' flags, which were rippling gently in the placid morning breeze.

As he watched, she knelt in the sand and extended one long leg behind her body, arching her spine back until she was looking straight up at the sky.

"Nice," he murmured to himself, snapping half a dozen shots of her there. "Do that again, but slower," he called down, and when she righted herself and then leaned back again, he caught the whole, languorous movement frame by frame. The motion had lifted her sweatshirt at the front, and he could see a wide strip of exposed skin above the waistband of her shorts.

"That'll do," he called, and as she straightened again, the skin disappeared. Scooping up her things, he headed down the beach to join her. Above the churning waves, the sky was brightening to a rich, glowing peach, fading into a cool inky blue. They probably had a few more minutes until the sun came up and the light changed all over again. Perhaps they should try a few shots over by the ocean pool before then.

"Heather said there's a pool down there," Carly said, squinting towards the north end of the beach. "Could be an interesting backdrop."

He nodded, resisting the urge to tell her it had been his idea first. They made their way to the end of the beach and towards the little concrete track that led around to the pool. Lots of Sydney beaches had lap pools built into the cliffs like this so you could swim laps in calm saltwater that was continually refreshed by the waves. It had been years since he'd been in one, but he still remembered the eerie feeling of being so close to the roiling crashing waves and spraying foam but being entirely safe and protected in the water.

Again he let her walk in front of him, and again he couldn't keep his eyes from the stray strands of hair that danced around her neck as she moved. He clenched his jaw, pressed his fingers against the hard plastic of the camera, and dragged his eyes away to look out over the water.

When they arrived at the pool, they found it empty except for a lone swimmer, a woman in a one-piece swimming costume swimming slow, lazy laps of backstroke. Carly watched her for a few seconds, then took in the entire view: the pool built into the cliff-side, the waves moving steadily towards the beach, the blue sky shot through with wide streaks of pearly pink and glowing orange.

"Hell of a way to work out," she said, shaking her head in awe. "No wonder Heather fell in love with it, all of it."

"Mmm," he said noncommittally.

She turned over her shoulder and looked at him appraisingly, her cheeks and forehead bathed in the warm morning light. "Why did you ever leave again?"

"Not a lot of dance jobs going in Australia," he said grimly. He'd had no choice but to leave—first his hometown and then the whole country. He'd been thrilled to do it, too, eager to go off in search of the kinds of adventure he was sure he could never have if he stayed home. But now he was back, and not the same person he was when he went away. And this place wasn't the same place he had left, either.

"Interesting," she said skeptically. "I just assumed they kicked you out."

"We aren't all lucky enough to have multiple world-class ballet companies in our hometowns," he said. "Australia's small, and sports obsessed. Lots of artists leave and never come back. Marcus is a rare exception."

She opened her mouth to reply, no doubt with some kind of quip, but he cut her off.

"We'll lose this light soon. Let's get back to work." She straightened up and gave him a mock salute, then dropped her bag at his feet and walked around to the other side of the pool. Honestly, the cheek on this woman, who just yesterday had begged him for his help. Wasn't he the one who'd volunteered to wake up at some ungodly hour to do this for her? He switched the camera back on and followed her around the pool, stopping about five feet away from where she stood with one hand on the railing that separated the even concrete pool deck and the jagged rock formations.

"Nice place to do barre," she said, arranging her feet in a tight fifth position and lifting her chin. In her bike shorts and faded old NYB jumper, she did look ready to start a morning ballet class, and when he lifted the camera up to his face, she pulled her shoulders down and looked into the lens with such intensity that he wouldn't have been surprised if she'd made piano music materialize on the beach out of sheer will.

"Go on, then," he said from behind the camera, unable to stop his mouth from curving into a smile. She grinned, flashing straight white teeth, then lowered herself into a demi-plié, letting her free arm drift languidly out beside her. It was the simplest movement, something the both of them had done every day since they were children, but there it was again: the same energy he'd seen in the photos he'd taken yesterday. She had probably done thousands, maybe tens of thousands, of pliés in her life, but she looked delighted to be doing this one. Whatever else Carly Montgomery loved or hated in this world, one thing was clear from watching her complete a single demi-plié: the woman loved to dance.

She carried on with a modified barre, brushing her bare feet gently over the concrete in tendus as he snapped away. Behind her, the sky was shifting into a steady cornflower blue, promising another bright and punishingly hot day.

After a few more minutes, she stopped moving and shook her legs out. "This is where there'd be grand battements, but I'm not warm enough for that," she said, and he nodded.

"Lean your back against the railing for me?" he said, and she obliged, crossing her feet at the ankles and resting her elbows on it and the railing. He eyed the lens as he came closer to her, picking his way around the edge of the pool. He zoomed in and saw that her cheeks were slightly flushed, either from the wind or the exertion, and the freckles across her nose seemed more pronounced today than they were even yesterday.

He was so focused on her face that he barely felt the ground disappear from under one of his feet, but he saw through the lens as her eyes widened in alarm, and what came next happened so fast that he had no chance of preventing it: he wobbled perilously on the foot that was still on the concrete, she lunged for him with grasping, open hands, he tumbled backwards and felt the strap yank sharply at his neck, and then his back hit the water with a huge, ungainly splash.

A second later, he scrambled to his feet and his head broke the surface. His nose was full of saltwater and his back stung, but he ignored all of that and spun around, looking desperately for his camera. He grabbed a deep gulp of air as he searched for a telltale blob of black, perhaps floating next to him or already sunk to the bottom of the pool. In the back of his mind, he knew it was hopeless, knew that being submerged in seawater would have ruined it beyond repair—*fuck*, how could he have been so careless, *again?*—but he cast around for it anyway. Maybe he could salvage the SD card, he thought desperately, his clothes swirling and dragging around him. Or maybe he was just a giant failure who had walked away from the only career he'd ever known and was floundering in his new one as spectacularly as he was floundering in this pool.

"Where is it?" he growled, exasperated. Furious at himself and at this entire miserable situation. "Where did it—"

"I've got it."

Nick froze and looked up. Carly was standing a foot from the edge, clutching his camera to her chest like a child with a stuffed animal.

He sloshed to the side of the pool, hauled himself out of water, and stumbled towards her, reaching for the camera, desperate to check that it hadn't been damaged. Carly took a step back and turned her body away, shielding the camera from him.

"Let me see it!" he said breathlessly.

"No, you're all wet!" she objected.

"Carly, I swear to God—"

"I just rescued this damn thing from going down like the *Titanic*; I am not going to let you get water all over it!" she said, outraged.

Nick stopped and took a deep breath. He breathed out, feeling saltwater rattle unpleasantly in his nose.

"Please, just hold it up so I can look at it."

Carly eyed him warily, then turned her body back towards him. He examined it from a foot away, careful not to drip on it. It looked fine. He couldn't see so much as a drop of water on the lens or anywhere else. But if he could just dry off and get his hands on it to check, he could—

"It's fine, Nick. I wasn't going to let anything happen to it." She sounded annoyed.

"Sorry, I just—"

"I know, you care about your cameras more than life itself. Why do you think I saved the camera and let you fall into the pool? You weren't very graceful, by the way."

Nick narrowed his eyes. "I wasn't trying to be graceful."

"Clearly."

"I just want to dry off and check that it still—

Click. Carly lifted the camera to her face and snapped a photo of him. "Say cheese." She didn't wait for him to smile, which was a good thing, because she'd be waiting a while.

"Can you please stop taking photos of this?"

"In a second." *Click, click, click.* Carly snapped away, no doubt delighted to capture this mortifying moment. Nick looked down at himself, at his grey T-shirt plastered against his chest and his shorts clinging to his thighs. He lifted one foot and felt his sneaker squelch against concrete. He must have looked like an absolute disaster. But the camera was apparently working just fine. Now that the adrenaline of the last few minutes was wearing off, he could think back and replay the seconds right before the fall. He'd watched Carly's face transform into a mask of horror as she realized what was happening, and then, right at the last second, she'd lunged for him. No, not for him. For his camera.

"Carly, stop."

"No, I'm making art here. Soggy, drowned-rat art."

"Carly!"

"What?" she finally pulled the camera away from her face. She cocked her head and raised an eyebrow, the posture Nick was coming to think of as trademark Carly, all challenge and sarcasm, and a thin layer of humour draped over spikes of anger. She had a few droplets of water on her jumper and on her face, and they sparkled in the rising sun, decorating her flushed, freckled cheeks. In the warm golden light, her eyes were a deep, luxurious brown, and even though they were currently regarding him with skepticism and impatience, Nick couldn't unsee the alarm he'd seen there as he'd teetered on the edge of the pool and she'd reached frantically for his Nikon. Saved it for him.

"Thank you."

"It's nothing," she shrugged, raising the camera again, but he stepped towards her, unwilling to touch the camera but trying to get her to stop so he could do this properly.

"It's not nothing. It'd be ruined if you hadn't done that," he gestured down at the camera, which she was still clutching tightly, her fingertips white around it, "and I'd be in big trouble."

Carly swallowed hard, then looked him up and down. "I don't know, you look like you're in pretty big trouble now."

He looked down at himself again, then held his hands up in surrender. He really did look like a drowned rat. "Fine. Don't let me stop you from capturing this glorious moment."

She flashed him a quick grin as she raised the camera, and his stomach gave a strange jolt. Leftover adrenaline from the near-miss, he told himself, as she started snapping again.

Chapter 11

By the time Carly presented herself at Heather's place that evening, she had posted two more of Nick's photos and added almost a thousand new followers. It wasn't a lot compared to some dancers she knew—there was one principal in her company with 250,000 followers—but it was a damn good start.

She checked her account one last time before she rang the doorbell, because she needed to know the current number. She wasn't stalling. She certainly wasn't dragging out the minutes until she had to be in Nick's company again, just like she definitely hadn't spent the day dragging her mind away from the memory of the way Nick had looked as he'd clambered out of the pool this morning. She'd spent the entire day regretting her decision to save the camera. She should have kept Nick on dry land and let his Nikon fly into the pool. Sure, it would have destroyed an expensive piece of equipment and broken Nick's heart, and sure, it would have set their little project back. That would have been regrettable, obviously. But at least she wouldn't be walking around Sydney with the mental image of a sopping wet Nick, his shirt clinging to his broad muscular chest, looking down at her like she'd saved his life rather than his camera. Looking at her as though, for the first time since they'd met, he actually wanted to look at her.

She was distracted by the memory of it all day. She barely managed to hold up her end of the conversation as Heather drove them to ANB ballet studios, and she screwed up the frappé combination on both legs because she hadn't paid attention when the ballet mistress was setting the exercise. As she and Heather walked the aisles of the supermarket, collecting ingredients for a family dinner, she couldn't stop seeing it: Nick, sunlit and soaked, gazing at her with unmasked gratitude.

She hoped some of those photos had turned out well, because otherwise all she'd have to show for this morning was a very unwelcome memory of Nick with his shirt plastered to his shoulders and droplets sparkling on his eyelashes. *Yum*, Heather had said the other day, but that didn't even begin to describe the roaring hunger Carly felt when that image popped into her mind for the four hundredth time that day. Or the unsettling stab of concern she'd felt when she'd seen him about to topple into the water and had to decide, in a fraction of a second, what to do. It had been an easy decision.

He'd been so panicked as he'd scrambled around the pool searching for the camera, and in that moment she'd had a sudden and unwelcome flash of realization, which was that for all his pedantry and pretention, Nick Jacobs wasn't a monster. He'd looked like a kid in that moment. A scared kid terrified that he'd messed everything up, and Carly had felt a strange, aching sense of recognition as she'd watched him splash and struggle. She knew that feeling, the way dread and self-recrimination slammed you in the chest when you discovered you'd screwed up yet again.

It would be easier if he were a monster, a fuckboy. Monsters and fuckboys she could handle. If he were a fuckboy, she would have let his camera sink to the bottom of the pool without a second thought. But he wasn't. He was just a person—a person who was helping her, even though he could barely stand her. A person who had thanked her earnestly and hadn't noticed that she'd played his thanks off with a laugh, then brought the camera up to her face so he wouldn't see how her cheeks were burning at the unbearable combination of a soaking wet man and a sincere apology.

She pressed the doorbell and the door opened almost immediately to reveal a curvy white woman with tight brown curls and flawless makeup above her flowing hot pink caftan.

"Hiya!" she chirped. "You must be Carly. I'm Izzy. Come on in!"

Carly returned her smile and stepped over the threshold to follow her down the hallway into the little kitchen, which was crowded with people. To her relief, none of them was Nick.

"It's Carly!" Izzy called into the room, spreading her arms wide and bellowing the words like Oprah announcing her next guest.

"Oh my God, finally," someone said, and Carly wondered for a moment if she'd arrived late. But then the speaker, a petite Asian woman, definitely a dancer, stepped away from the kitchen counter and smiled at her.

"I'm Alice," she said, grinning as she wiped her hands on her shorts. "So excited to meet the famous Carly. Heather was actually counting the days until you got here." She held out her hand and Carly shook it, returning Alice's smile. Alice had been Marcus's best friend in the company, and Carly knew she and Heather had become good friends since Heather had joined ANB.

"I'm excited to meet the famous Alice," Carly said. "Aren't you the one who told Heather to get her ass back to Sydney to make things right with Marcus?"

"The very same," Alice said proudly. "And I was right, wasn't I? God, I love being right. I was just about to pour Iz a drink. Do you want a drink? You look like you could use a drink."

"Once again, you are right," Carly smiled, and Alice let out an honest-to-God cackle. Carly liked her already. "Heather said you're injured. What happened?"

"Standard dancer's fracture," Alice shrugged, lifting her right foot a few inches off the floor. "I've been putting in my hours in physio, but I'm going to miss the season. So I could use a drink, too."

While Alice was pulling wine out of the fridge, Carly placed her bag on the couch, then returned to the kitchen, where Heather was standing at the counter next to a woman Carly suspected was Marcus's mother.

"Anything I can help with?" Carly asked.

"No thanks, dear, we've got it under control," the older woman said, and she turned around to face Carly.

"This is Marcus's mom, Leanne," Heather said over her shoulder as she chopped up a cucumber and tossed the pieces into a large bowl where they joined the greens they'd bought earlier.

"The maid of honor!" Leanne smiled, the tanned skin around her green eyes wrinkling deeply as she smiled warmly at Carly. Marcus had the same eyes, and the beginnings of the same wrinkles. Leanne wiped her hands on her apron and extended a hand, which Carly shook carefully; she knew that Leanne had moved out of this house when her worsening osteoarthritis made the stairs too much of a challenge.

"Nice to meet you, Mrs. Campbell," Carly said politely, accepting a tumbler of white wine from Alice. As she turned to thank Alice, she let her eyes dart around the kitchen and living room. No sign of Nick. Where the hell was he? Maybe she'd get lucky and he wouldn't show up at all.

"Oh, please," Leanne chuckled, waving a dismissive hand. "Mrs. Campbell is my dad. Call me Leanne."

"Okay, Leanne," Carly laughed. When she joked, Leanne's eyes took on the same wry twinkle that Marcus's did. A kind and funny husband, a house on the beach, a principal dancer job, *and* a cool mother-in-law? Heather really had won the lottery.

Heather dropped the last of the cucumber into the bowl, then turned around and looked out the kitchen window. "The guys are outside arguing over the barbecue," she said, and then all four of the women around Carly said, in unison, "Again."

Carly looked around at them, eyebrows raised questioningly.

"This happens every time," Izzy explained, pulling out a seat from the dining table and flopping down into it. "Marcus and Davo go twelve rounds over the right way to arrange the coals and the best way to arrange the meat and whatever else there is to argue about. The food tastes the same whichever way they do it, so I'm not sure what the point of the argument is," she shrugged.

Carly met Heather's eyes, and Heather gave her head a tiny shake. *It's fine.* Carly knew that Marcus and his older brother had had some serious shit between them in the past, and based on what Heather had told her, it had only gotten worse after their dad had died. But a long-running dispute over the best way to light a grill seemed harmless enough. Some brotherly bickering over the barbecue was apparently just a Campbell family tradition.

"The food would get done quicker if Marcus and David didn't do a song and dance about it every time," Leanne said, reaching for her own glass of wine and taking a sip. "But since we've added Nicholas to the equation, we might get to eat before midnight."

Carly swallowed a mouthful of wine too fast and tried not to cough. Throat burning, she gave Leanne a polite, interested nod, then turned slowly around and looked out the window. On the back deck, crowded around a smoking old-fashioned barbecue, were Marcus and a pale, freckled man who must be Davo. And between them, gesturing calmly with a pair of tongs, was Nick. She watched him for a second as he waved the tongs gracefully in the air, his shoulder muscles shifting visibly under his T-shirt.

"We've known Nicholas since all three of them were shorter than me," Leanne said. "He's always been the peacemaker between my two. He's so levelheaded and sensible, nothing seems to get to him." *Nothing except me, apparently,* Carly thought. She seemed to have a unique ability to piss him off, to get under his sensible, levelheaded skin.

"So, Carly, how are you enjoying Sydney so far? And how many checklists has Heather given you to work through?" Alice asked, her hand on Izzy's shoulder.

"Um, I really like it here. And just one checklist . . . so far," Carly said ominously, and Izzy and Alice laughed.

"Excuse me for being organized," Heather said. "You'll all be thanking me at the open bar. Marcus's plan was to have everyone BYOB. To a wedding."

"Hey, you said you wanted it to be low-key," Marcus said. He'd opened the sliding door just in time to hear Heather's comment. "What could be more low-key than everyone bringing a six-pack?"

Carly laughed. When Heather and Jack had been engaged, they'd talked about getting married at his parents' house in the Hamptons, surrounded by the biggest names in New York arts and philanthropy, with a champagne fountain and a performance by the first chair violinist of the New York Philharmonic. Carly had once caught her lovingly scrolling her mouse over a pair of white Chanel pumps that cost as much as a month's rent. Now she was planning to marry Marcus barefoot on the beach and have the reception right here in their backyard. Apparently she'd drawn the line at BYOB, but still, it was hard to imagine two wedding plans more different than the two Heather had made. Then again, it was hard to imagine two men more different than Jack and Marcus. Thank God.

"Is the meat nearly ready?" Leanne asked.

"Another five minutes or so," Marcus said, slipping inside and closing the door behind him, but not before Carly caught a whiff of barbeque smoke and frangipani. Marcus took three cans of beer from the fridge and kissed Heather on the cheek on his way back to the door. Carly watched as Heather grinned, then tried to school her smile, then gave up and grinned even wider.

"Oh, get a room," Alice groaned dramatically as Marcus pulled the back door open and stepped onto the deck, but then she stooped down and kissed Izzy's cheek, to Izzy's obvious delight.

"Speaking of checklists," Heather said, when she'd stopped blushing, "we need to nail down our cocktail recipes so we can put in an order at the bulk liquor store. Carly, do you and Nick have any ideas?"

Carly took another sip of her wine and swallowed it slowly, buying time to pull her mind away from the vaguely jealous thoughts that had occurred to her.

"We can schedule a time to test out some options," she said. "I'll talk to him tonight."

Heather nodded, and Carly could almost see her rearranging a color-coded spreadsheet in her head.

"Will has the cake design all set," Alice told Heather. "My brother," she said to Carly. "He opened a bakery last year. His *Bake Off* obsession escalated until he was taking days off work to bake, so he quit his IT job and went all in. Now all he wants is to be the Australian Paul Hollywood, but Chinese."

"And less of a prick," Izzy chimed in.

"Right," Alice agreed.

"And Alice has been writing her remarks for the ceremony since the day after you got engaged," Izzy said, smiling up at her girlfriend. "She's going to do a brilliant job."

"I'd expect nothing less," Leanne said.

"What's your role in all this?" Carly asked Izzy. It seemed like everyone at the table had one, along with a string of in-jokes built up over weekly Sunday dinners.

"Oh, I'm basically a professional wedding guest at this point," Izzy said with a proud smile. "So many of my friends have gotten married in the last few years that I've got wedding guesting down to a science."

Carly looked over at Heather. "I think you're the only bride in the world who'd be reassured by that approach."

"That's correct," Heather said cheerfully, and all five of them laughed. "But she's also doing my hair and makeup on the day. Yours, too, if you want a little something extra."

Carly was about to reply when the back door slid open and Davo stepped into the room. He was taller than Marcus and had a broad, muscular frame, and with his pale face, dark brown hair, and watery blue eyes, he looked nothing like his brother and mother.

"Meat's done," he said, stepping aside to reveal Marcus holding a plate of cooked steaks and sausages in each hand.

"Thanks very much, boys," Leanne said as Marcus set the plates on the set table. Behind him, Nick walked in carrying two more plates of roast vegetables and what looked like plant-based meat. Carly's eyes were drawn to his forearms, which were straining under the weight. "And thank you, Nicholas, for keeping the peace out there."

"No problem, Leanne," he smiled, putting the plates on the crowded table. "I'm glad I could negotiate in a situation with such . . . high stakes."

His smile widened as six groans erupted in unison at his pun, and Carly chuckled despite herself. He looked over at her before she could wipe the smile off her face, and their eyes met amid the cacophony of *terribles* and *ought to be ashameds*. Carly felt suddenly shy as they looked at each other, and it occurred to her that if they had met each other like this, instead of in a series of billowing dumpster fires, they might have actually liked each other. If she'd met this version of Nick—surrounded by people he knew and liked, loose and a little goofy—maybe she wouldn't have immediately decided he was an asshole. Maybe he wouldn't have decided she was an insufferable ballet brat. They could have become friends during this trip, instead of unwilling errand buddies who tolerated each other long enough to take photos. Yet again, the memory of his face this morning, awash with gratitude and relief, swam unbidden into her mind. He'd been drenched in sunlight and water, and he'd stared at her like he could actually see her. Like he actually liked what he saw. Carly looked down at her drink and caught her breath, but when she glanced up again, he was still looking.

Chapter 12

A lot had changed since he'd left Sydney, but at least this one thing was the same: Marcus's place felt as comfortable and welcoming as it had when he was fifteen years old and here for a sleepover. Even though Marcus and Heather had given the place a fresh coat of paint, it was just as warm and homey in here as he remembered. Leanne was still kind and no-nonsense, and they still had the old barbeque Marcus's dad, Richard, had fired up seemingly every time Nick had come over. He had always felt like he could uncoil a little here. Breathe a little deeper. Relax more than he could in the dorms.

Another thing that hadn't changed in his absence: Davo Campbell was still kind of a tosser. Davo had always had a knack for making his younger brother feel like the least important person in the room, and the last fifteen years clearly hadn't broken him of his need to find little ways to dig at Marcus and try to get under his skin. The first time Nick had witnessed it, he'd wondered why all Davo's seemingly friendly comments seemed to have an edge to them, a mean bite to the laughter. Now he understood that this was what passed for bonding for a lot of Australian men—taking the piss out of each other and saying "I'm just joking" if anyone called foul—but Nick had never had much patience for it. His tolerance was even lower after the years away. Leanne had called him the peacekeeper, but mostly he was there so that Davo could pull that shit on someone else, and give Marcus a break for a change.

No wonder Marcus hadn't wanted Davo as his best man, Nick thought, as they all crowded around the table, drinks in hand. His toast would have been a nightmare.

"Leanne, Davo, why don't you take your usual spots," Heather called over the chatter, and Nick watched as Leanne took a seat at the head of the table and Davo took the chair opposite her, at what he remembered as Richard's old place.

"I'm next to Izzy," Alice said, pulling out the chair next to her girlfriend's and placing her drink down.

"Oh, *get a room*," Marcus said, and all the women laughed, including Carly. She was clutching her wine glass tightly, eyes wide, as though she was a little overwhelmed by the whole scene, and it took him a moment to realize that the only person she really knew here was Heather. Well, he supposed that if bickering constantly with someone and letting them take photos of you was a way to know them, then she knew him a bit, too.

He'd spent most of the day hunched over his computer editing photos of her. He'd had plenty to work with, because this morning's photos had turned out really well. Not the ones Carly had taken, where he looked damp and bedraggled, his expression a strange mix of exhausted and exhilarated. But the ones he'd taken of her were the best work he'd done in months, in his opinion. Perhaps he should have been photographing dancers outside all this time. He'd done so many sessions in the studio, trying to capture intimate moments in rehearsal and class, but even the Paris Opera Ballet, which rehearsed in a studio with a soaring domed ceiling on the top floor of the famed Opera Garnier, didn't have light like this.

Heather had mentioned something about how the light was different in Sydney than in any other place she'd been—sharper, brighter, more saturated—and looking at the shots he'd taken at the pool and on the beach, Nick had to agree.

The shot of Carly in that deep kneeling backbend looked good in colour—the red and yellow flags, the pink horizon, and Carly's red bun all made for a sense of warmth against the huge expanses of blue sky and water. But it looked striking in black and white, he thought; removing the colours made Carly look like a pale bird on the beach, a creature he'd just happened to capture as she stretched on the sand.

The ones he'd taken by the pool, though, were even better. He'd stared for a full minute at the best of the bunch, a shot of Carly with one foot extended in a tendu and her supporting leg slightly bent. Her free arm was extended at forty-five degrees, and she was looking up at her hand as she prepared to sweep the arm, and then her whole body, down over her stretched leg. Her lips were slightly parted, and he could almost feel the breath she was taking and would sigh out as she folded over. The warm morning light caught all the oranges and golds in her curls and made her brown eyes glow as she watched her own fingers, her face lit with anticipation and pleasure. Once again, he was struck by how happy she looked when was dancing, even if it was just a simple barre exercise by the beach. She looked content and in control. She might be pure chaos the rest of the time, but something happened to her face when she danced. No wonder she didn't know what she was going to do once she retired: *this* was the thing that brought her joy so deep it all but screamed off the screen. Even her ridiculous hot pink nails looked right in this light.

Tonight, her curls looked damp from the shower, and she was wearing a sage green linen shirt-dress that stopped just above her knees. Against the green fabric, the orange-red of her roiling curls looked brighter and more saturated than usual. The dress was loose and somewhat shapeless, but low-cut enough to reveal her sternum, which he knew from staring at photos of her was paler than her arms and legs, with freckles scattered across it. He tightened his jaw and told himself that he probably shouldn't be thinking about the freckles on her sternum.

She met his eyes over the table as the laughter petered out, and he swore he saw her grip on her glass get even tighter.

"Uh, I'll sit next to Heather, if that's okay?" she asked the room, and Leanne nodded her approval. Carly pulled out her chair and took a big swig of her wine.

"And I'd like to sit next to my future wife," Marcus grinned, dropping a kiss on Heather's temple and shooting a challenging, amused look across the table at Alice. That left Marcus to take Heather's other side and Nick to squeeze in alongside Izzy. Directly opposite Carly. She smiled a little as she sat down, and it wasn't the too-wide, just-for-show smile she'd thrown his way every other time they'd been around Heather and Marcus. It was quiet, just a flash of white teeth visible above her full bottom lip, and before he could think better of it, he felt himself return it.

With some difficulty, he pulled his chair out and folded himself into it, and Izzy leaned into Alice to make space for him. Still, it was a tight squeeze; this table was probably fine for a six person Sunday dinner, but eight was pushing it.

"All right everyone, no need to stand on ceremony. Just dig in," Leanne said, and then the table was a mess of arms and hands and tongs as all eight of them passed platters around and loaded up their plates. He watched as Izzy heaped salad onto Alice's plate and Marcus took a few seconds to select the best-looking piece of grilled eggplant for Heather. Meanwhile, Heather served Leanne a bit of everything, saving the older woman from having to deal with the tongs or the salad servers. Davo had already started cutting into his steak.

"So, Nicholas," Leanne started, once much of the food had been transferred from serving dishes to plates, and Nick sat up a little straighter at her tone.

"Am I also about to get grilled?" he joked, and Leanne chuckled. Alice and Izzy groaned in unison, and Carly gave her head a tiny shake as she cut up a piece of meat.

Leanne gave him a warm smile. "It's not a grilling, I just want to know how life has been since I last saw you, what was it, a decade ago?"

"Something like that. Right before I moved to Paris, I think."

Leanne's face took on a dreamy, faraway look. "Paris," she sighed. "I've always wanted to go. Tell me everything. Do you have a collection of striped shirts and a bike with a bread basket on the back?"

Nick tilted his head skeptically. It was like the reverse of what French people sometimes asked him when he revealed he'd grown up in Australia—*Est-ce que vous aviez un kangourou en lieu d'un chien?*—and about as far removed from reality.

"I think I only have one striped shirt, and I had a moped for a while, but it's mostly the Métro for me."

Leanne sighed again. "Even public transit sounds more romantic in French."

"I don't know, taking a bus over the Harbour Bridge every day is pretty romantic," Heather piped up. "Oh, that reminds me, Carly, we should take a ferry into the city this week. Best commute in the world. No offense to the Métro, Nick," she added.

"None taken," he said quickly, as Carly nodded at Heather. He shoved some grilled zucchini in his mouth, hoping Heather would keep talking so that Leanne couldn't ask any more questions about his life in Paris. His *former* life in Paris. His former commute to his former job from his former apartment with his former girlfriend.

But instead Heather kept eating, and Leanne did have more questions.

"And what have you been doing since you got to Sydney?" she asked, peering at him curiously over her wine glass. "Marcus mentioned you've become a photographer since you retired from dancing."

Nick lifted his mouth into an imitation of her smile. It felt like work. He pulled his shoulders back and did his best impression of a confident, well-established photographer.

"That's right. It's been a fun challenge." That was only half a lie. There was nothing fun about going from knowing exactly what he was doing, and knowing he was good at it, to feeling like a lost, floundering failure.

"I imagine it's a difficult field to break into." He nodded in confirmation, hoping the heat creeping up his neck wouldn't reach his cheeks. It felt crappy to lie to Leanne, crappy and dangerous. The woman hadn't spent decades as a nurse and raised two sons without developing an extremely sensitive bullshit detector.

"Well, goodness knows you've got some experience with that," Leanne said.

"That's true, and at least this time around I don't have to wear tights to work."

"You could if you wanted to," Marcus said, his mouth half-full of steak. "Might be a nice trademark."

"You've been helping Carly out with her promotion project, in between wedding errands, right?" Heather spoke up. "How's it going?" Carly looked up from her plate and smiled at him—that small, real smile again, and she cocked her head ever so slightly to the side, awaiting his answer.

"Euh, it's going swimmingly," he said, and Carly's eyes sparkled with amusement. Okay, so she was probably remembering how ridiculous he looked climbing out of the pool soaked to his skin, but he didn't mind. She'd saved his camera, they'd gotten good shots, and so far, their plan was working.

"That's good of you," Leanne said. "And when the wedding's over, you'll head back to Paris?"

Nick turned to Leanne, away from the glittering warmth of Carly's mischievous gaze. He couldn't quite bring himself to meet Leanne's eyes.

"I'm still figuring out my options," he said. He swivelled his body towards the other end of the table, desperate to engineer a subject change. "So, uh, Davo, how's the contracting business these days?"

Davo took his time chewing and swallowing. Finally, he spoke. "Yeah, good," he said, before taking another sip of his beer. Then, nothing. Why had Nick counted on the most taciturn person at the table to help him divert the conversation?

"Effusive as ever, Davo," Alice said drily. "I think what Davo means to say is, 'The contracting business is going gangbusters because the homeowners of Sydney love nothing more than knocking down their expensive houses and turning them into even more expensive houses in a never ending real estate arms race that keeps everyone but rich people with rich parents from ever owning property.'"

God bless Alice Ho. She'd been a few years behind them at the ANB school, and Nick remembered her as quiet and serious, but she'd clearly grown out of that.

"Right, and meanwhile, the rental market is also absolutely bananas, so we're totally trapped," Izzy added. "When Alice and I moved in together I thought it would mean a bit of a break on rent, but the way rents are rising, it's hardly anything."

"There are other advantages," Alice objected, holding up her fingers and counting off. "Love, companionship, a hook-up to Will's endless baked goods."

"I'm mostly in it for the baked goods," Izzy grinned, and Alice gave a faux-wounded gasp.

Nick laughed, and soon everyone at the table, well, everyone except Davo, was engaged in a lively conversation about which newly renovated house in the surrounding neighbourhood was the most hideous. Once the conversation got going, Carly met his eyes across the table.

Swimmingly? she mouthed, punctuating the silent word with a tiny shake of her head. He replied with an equally tiny shrug, and she flicked her eyes upward in an abbreviated roll. He huffed a quiet laugh, and for a moment it felt like they were friends. Or at least, they were not two wildly mismatched people who could barely tolerate being in each other's presence.

Soon the platters were being passed for seconds and Alice was warning people to save room for dessert because her brother had sent along a spectacular pavlova, and Nick was full of good food and relaxed for the first time in what felt like months. The rest of Sydney had changed, but this small pocket of the city seemed to have been waiting for him, warm and recognizable, since the day he left. Across the table, Carly and Heather were laughing about something, and Nick watched as Carly threw her head back, the pale column of her neck arching gracefully toward the ceiling, drawing Nick's attention to the deep V at the front of her dress. Once again, he had to remind himself not to think about the spray of freckles across her sternum.

When their plates were empty, Heather stood and began to clear the table.

"Sit," Marcus instructed her quickly. "We'll do this."

Heather opened her mouth to object, but Carly pushed her chair back and grabbed the plates from her hands. "Don't argue," she said firmly. Carly cast a look over her shoulder, summoning Nick to his feet with a lift of her chin. Not daring to disobey her, he grabbed the nearest empty plate and took it into the kitchen.

He, Marcus, and Carly ferried the empty platters and used cutlery off to the kitchen, and Alice went to the fridge and pulled out an enormous pavlova. Nick started rinsing plates, and after a moment, Carly arrived at his side.

"You rinse, I'll load," she said, holding out her hands. For a moment they worked in silence, the comfortable, happy noise of the conversation at the table washing over them.

"'Swimmingly' wasn't any worse than 'Heather and Mucus,'" he said quietly, and she laughed. It was a lovely sound, all surprise and genuine amusement. She bent to put the plates in the dishwasher, and this time he wasn't successful at keeping his eyes from her skin where her dress gaped slightly at the neckline.

"How did the photos come out?"

"The ones you took of me? They're prime blackmail material. I look ridiculous."

"I know, I was there," she chuckled. "I meant the ones of me."

"They're good," he said quietly. An understatement. *They're the best work I've done in months. I managed to capture the way you soak up and reflect all that light, and for a moment today it felt like I'd finally captured reality.* He didn't say any of that. "They're very good. You're, euh, easy to photograph."

Carly looked up at him, her hands full of knives, which a few days ago would have made him extremely nervous. She usually looked at him like she wished she had a knife or two handy. But now she was giving him that same shy smile, like she was testing the shape with her mouth.

"I think that's the first nice thing you've said to me, asshole."

"Probably the last, brat," he volleyed back, but he was smiling, too.

An hour later the pavlova—just as spectacular as Alice had promised—had been demolished. Izzy had threatened to lick the crumbs of meringue and remaining blobs of cream off her plate, and then made good on the threat. After the chorus of *eww*s and *come on*s had subsided, and Izzy had smacked her lips in defiant satisfaction, a warm, sated silence fell over the table.

"That was one of Will's best, I reckon," Marcus told Alice. "If the wedding cake's anything like that, we're going to eat the whole thing ourselves."

"Oh, are we making this wedding BYOC, now?" Heather asked, amused.

"It's not the worst idea in the world," Marcus shrugged.

"No, it is," Alice deadpanned, and everyone laughed. "You have to serve them cake. It's basically the law."

"All right, we'll let them have a little," Marcus conceded. "I hope Delphine knows what she's missing by staying behind in Paris. The French are good at patisserie, but I bet they haven't mastered the perfect pav. Nick's girlfriend couldn't make the trip," he added for the benefit of Leanne and Davo.

Across the table, Carly's head snapped towards him and Nick froze with the remnants of a laugh still curving his mouth, the mention of Delphine making his stomach lurch. He managed a non-committal nod in Marcus's direction, and the conversation moved on. He could feel Carly's eyes on him, sharp and focused as Izzy regaled the table with how she'd been the first to know Marcus and Heather were sneaking around, because they'd made out in the fitting room in her shop.

He looked across the table at Carly. She was smiling, but it wasn't that shy, genuine, teasing smile. It was the making-nice smile, wide and toothy and completely for show. Foreboding crept across the back of Nick's neck as he met her eyes, which had gone cold and dead. She looked away, fixing her gaze on Izzy, who was dramatically demonstrating the way Marcus had snuck out of the fitting room, apparently totally unaware that Izzy was watching him and had definitely clocked his messed up hair and rumpled shirt. Heather had her face in her hands and was groaning in embarrassed amusement. Nick watched as Carly kept her eyes stubbornly on Izzy, even though he was sure she could feel him watching her. Her cheeks were slightly flushed, her posture rigid.

As the laughter died down and Izzy finished her perform-ance—"All's well that ends well, but you guys are the reason I hung PLEASE DON'T MAKE OUT IN HERE signs in all my fitting rooms"—Carly yawned widely.

"I'm beat. Do you mind if I call it a night?" she asked Heather, still studiously avoiding looking his way. He watched her, trying to catch her eye, but it was pointless. She didn't look at him as she stood and said her goodbyes to Leane and hugged Alice and Izzy, and she didn't glance his way as Heather stood and walked her to the front door.

What had just happened?

"Euh, back in a sec," he muttered to the table, standing quickly. "I need to ask Carly something about tomorrow's shoot."

Carly leaned against the warm bricks of the front of the house, taking deep, calming breaths. In for five, out for five. In for five, out for—nope, not working. She was still fucking furious.

She didn't even know why. All she knew was that Marcus had mentioned Nick's girlfriend—because Nick had a girlfriend, apparently—and her stomach had dropped to her knees, and a series of unwelcome emotions had swept through her. Embarrassment, because she should have known. He was a hot, successful photographer who was occasionally funny and borderline bearable. Of course he had a girlfriend. Humiliation, because a small, stupid part of her had been starting to enjoy his company and had thought he was enjoying hers. Fear that he'd known that was what she was thinking—or worse, think she was attracted to him—and would look down on her even more now. And then, the fury.

This was what she got for letting herself forget, even for a second, that despite being enjoyable company when he was loose and goofy, Nick Jacobs was an asshole. She took one more pointless deep breath. She'd take a long, angry walk on the beach and try to clear her head. She was about to push herself off the wall when the front door opened, and she turned and found herself face-to-face with the loose, goofy, asshole himself.

"I was just going," she said.

"Wait a sec. Can we talk?"

"I don't want to talk to you right now. Ideally ever. But at least not until tomorrow." They still had work to do, God help her. She still needed him. The thought only made her more furious, and she moved to leave.

"You're upset," he said. He said it like it was a matter of fact, like he was so sure, and she hated his certainty and hated that he was right.

"Yeah, that happens a lot around you," she snapped.

"I've noticed," he said slowly, observing her closely. Giving her his damn photographer look, like he was piecing together a whole picture together around her.

"I'm starting to think it's not a coincidence," she shot back.

He took a step toward her, and she wanted to step back, keep the space between them constant. Or better, put an entire beach between her and Nick Jacobs. An entire continent.

"Probably not. But you were fine back there, and then you weren't. What's wrong?"

"Just the usual, proximity to you."

"Carly." Again, it wasn't a question. He took another step toward her, and she pressed her back against the hard, warm bricks. She wanted to run; she wanted to melt into the wall. She wanted him to stop looking at her like that.

"Nick," she hissed back.

"What's wrong?" he repeated.

"Why do you even care? I'm a big-time ballet brat, remember?"

"And I'm an uptight asshole. But we're stuck with each other." He was stuck with her, he meant. He had taken pity on her. "And if we're going to keep working with each other, you either need to get it together or tell me the truth."

She stared at him furiously for a few seconds, then forced the words out. "You could have told me you had a girlfriend." She hated how plaintive and pathetic she sounded.

There was a long silence, and her words hung in the air. Nick was giving her that look again, and she watched as realization dawned on his stupid, handsome face. She wanted to screw her own face up and squeeze her eyes shut so she didn't have to watch a knowing smile creep over his mouth, but she willed herself to stare him down, desperate to hold on to some scraps of dignity. It was physical attraction, what she felt. That was all. He was objectively good looking. She could think that without *liking* him. The world was full of objectively good-looking men, literally millions of them, and plenty of them were unlikeable assholes and—oh God, he would hold this over her forever, she thought as she watched him.

But the smile she was expecting never materialized. Instead, he rubbed a hand over his head and sighed.

"I don't have a girlfriend," he said quietly.

"Oh, bullshit," she retorted.

"I *don't*," he said, more firmly this time. "We broke up a few months ago."

"Marcus doesn't seem to think so."

"Yeah, well I lied to Marcus," he shot back hotly.

Carly frowned. "Why?"

"I— It doesn't matter. It's complicated."

"Uh-uh, no way," Carly crossed her arms. "If we're going to keep working together, you either need to get it together or tell me the truth."

Nick narrowed his eyes at her, but after a moment, he spoke. "She broke up with me. We were together a long time. I was hurt, and I wanted to lick my wounds on my own. And, I didn't want to make my break-up Marcus's problem when he had a wedding to plan. Okay?"

Carly shrugged, as if this information was neither here nor there to her, as if she wasn't alight with curiosity. How long was a long time? Had they talked about marriage? What was she like? What was Nick like when he was in love? *It doesn't matter. He doesn't like you, and you don't want to like him.*

"Okay," she said, pushing off the wall at last. "Are we done here?"

"Maybe," Nick said. "If you can tell me why you'd be so upset if I had a girlfriend."

"I wouldn't be," she gritted out. Her pulse was suddenly fluttering in her ribcage again.

"But you were. We established that already."

God, he was infuriating. "Fuck off, Nick."

"I'll fuck off if you tell me why you were were so bothered by the idea of me having a girlfriend."

"Fine," she snapped. "I'm angry because for one very brief, very idiotic second, I thought you weren't a complete asshole, and of course I was wrong, and I hate being wrong."

"Interesting," he said, taking another step toward her. There was barely a foot between them now, and if he came any closer, she wouldn't be able to avoid smelling his cologne. "Because for one very brief, very idiotic second, I thought you weren't a complete brat. And I don't think I was wrong."

Carly stared at him. He watched her, studying her face while she scrambled for words. He was so close. She pressed her lips together and watched his eyes flick to her mouth and stay there. "But if you really think I'm an asshole, then you wouldn't care about that. Right?"

"Right," she said faintly, determined not to look away from him even though he was so close and so beautiful it almost hurt to meet his eyes. God, those eyes. In the dusk light the blue was almost gray, the lashes casting shadows on his cheeks. Those eyes could see things in her face she didn't want him to see. Things she didn't want to be true. But they were. The knowledge that Nick wasn't single had made her furious for reasons she hadn't wanted to think about. But he'd known. He'd looked at her and he'd known. "Right, I don't care about that," she murmured, with a swallow.

"And you definitely wouldn't care if I had a girlfriend. Isn't that right, Carly?"

"Oh, shut *up*," she sighed, and then she grabbed a fistful of his shirt and pulled his mouth down to hers.

At first it was more collision than kiss. He stumbled forward in surprise, his nose squishing hers slightly, and his teeth glanced against her bottom lip gracelessly. But then he braced himself against the wall, a hand on either side of her body, and righted himself. Suddenly there was almost no air between their bodies at all. She was so aware of the smell of him, all spice and citrus, his mouth pavlova-sweet and reassuringly firm against hers. She felt his tongue slip past her lips, and as it met her own, a small sound, somewhere between a sigh and a groan, escaped from her throat.

The sound seemed to spur Nick on, because a second later, his large hand found the side of her neck and he pressed his hips against hers until Carly was deliciously trapped between the hard bricks and the solid wall of his chest. She had started this, but Nick was in charge now, holding her and kissing her insistently, like he wanted to prove a point. She answered by tilting her head and dipping her tongue deeper into his mouth, where it clashed with his as she arched her body against his chest. She felt him shudder as her breasts pressed against him, and looped her arms around his shoulders, desperate for more of his body against hers, more of his mouth, more of his scent.

Nick's fingers slid up her neck and into her hair, while his other hand was splayed against her hip, keeping her body flush against his as she kissed him deeply, fiercely, unthinkingly. He pulled gently at her hair, and her body answered with a hot, needy pulse between her legs. He must have heard her whimper, because he did it again, and for a moment she wanted to scream because *how dare he* be so good at this? She vented her frustration by nipping at his lower lip and felt his fingers tighten around her hip. So she did it again, because *she was damn good at this, too, thank you very much.*

Someone laughed loudly inside, and Nick broke the kiss, chest heaving. Carly was panting. She looked up into his face and saw that his lips were swollen, and when she brought her fingertips to her own lips, they felt tender and a little puffy, too. It had been a long time since she'd been kissed like that. Had she ever been kissed like that? With so much need, but so much care? His eyes were trained on her fingers, and when she looked closer, she saw they were a little glassy, like he was dazed or drunk. *Drunk on her.* The sight of it made her feel a kind of whole-body hunger—and a ripple of self-satisfaction. She had done that. She had gotten this uptight, annoyed man drunk off her mouth. Broken vagina or not, she had done that.

Suddenly, her fingertips felt cold against her lips. She swallowed, trying to push away the truth that had just floated into her head, sweeping away the lust and the reckless need. Her broken vagina. It started like this every time: they wanted her, and she wanted them, and she wanted so badly to give them what they wanted. And she never could. And it hurt like a motherfucker. And it ended like that, every time. This time would be no different. The only thing that would change would be that she would end it before it could truly begin.

She dropped her hand and leaned back against the wall, putting half a foot of space between them. Nick carefully extracted his hand from her hair, and she missed it the moment it was gone. His other hand was still on her hip, radiating heat through the fabric of her dress. Just a few inches lower and he'd have his hand on her thigh, she realized, and the thought of his palms on her bare skin made her want to scream in frustration again. *Shut it down, now.*

"Let's not make that mistake again," she said, in as businesslike a tone as she could muster. It sounded unconvincing, but she meant it.

He frowned down at her for a moment, studying her face. He looked more alert now, and confused. "You kissed me," he said slowly. He peeled his fingers off her hip even more slowly, and took a step backward.

"I did," she nodded, hating the clipped sound of her own voice. "But I don't want to do it again." A lie. Her heart was still racing, and she could still taste sugar and strawberries.

She saw something shift in his gaze, a curtain falling.

"Okay, well, thanks for letting me know," he said, matching her tone. "I should go back inside. I'll send you the photos from this morning's session so you can post them tonight." His eyes were sharp again, and before she could say anything else, he was turning away from her and toward the front door. She watched him open it, wishing she could explain. But what would she even say? *I'm broken? I can't give you what you want, and you don't want to give me what I need? It's only a matter of time before we disappoint each other?*

"Nick, wait," she said, grabbing the door before it could swing shut behind him. He was already halfway down the hall.

"Goodnight, Carly," he called over his shoulder. His voice was aggressively friendly, like he knew the others might hear him from the kitchen.

It was better this way, she told herself. This way, he'd remember that he actually hated her, and they'd go back to a prickly, barely functional partnership.

"Okay, see you tomorrow," she called back, just as cheerfully, just as fake.

Because they still had to work together. She'd made a promise to Heather, and she would not break it. And she would not let one kiss stop her from doing what she needed to do to get promoted. One idiotic, ill-advised, knee-melting, *never-to-be-repeated* kiss.

"*Fuck*," she sighed, closing the door and turning to slump against it. After a long moment, she walked down the front steps. This was a mess. She was a mess.

But at least this mess had a few hundred more followers than she'd had yesterday.

Chapter 13

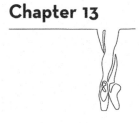

Carly couldn't sleep. She didn't know if she'd ever be able to sleep again. How could she, when every time she closed her eyes she was back on Heather's front porch, pressed against the wall with Nick Jacobs's hand in her hair? His hand gripping her hip, need pulsing in his fingertips. She rolled over onto her back and stared at the ceiling, her body buzzing even though she knew she was tired.

There was no refuge here, either. Even with her eyes open, she could still smell him on her skin, could still hear the way he'd hissed with desire when she'd bitten his bottom lip. She arched her back under the sheet, remembering how badly she'd wanted to press her entire being against his tall, lean body.

But she knew where that led. It led to more kissing, and then to the kind of sex he'd want and she couldn't give him. She gripped the sheet hard in one hand, feeling almost as frustrated now as she had in the moment. He'd want to put his fingers inside her, and his cock, and she would be left with two choices: stop him just like she had last night or pretend that she wasn't in pain. A few months ago, she would have chosen the second option. She would have kept kissing him—because *God*, that kiss—and she would have gritted her teeth through whatever came next. But she knew better now. Which was why a kiss like that could not happen again. Why she'd pushed him away and watched him walk back down the hallway, pretending nothing remarkable had happened.

Here in the dawn light, though, alone with the ache between her legs, she couldn't pretend. She wanted Nick Jacobs, and he wanted her. She didn't understand it, but she couldn't deny it, either. But what would be the point of giving in to it? She had a broken vagina, and they had work to do. The wedding was two weeks away, and then she'd go back to New York and he'd go back to Paris. *Get it together, Montgomery. You came here for Heather.* To spend time with her best friend and help her pull off the perfect wedding she deserved. Not to fuck around with the best man, and certainly not to screw up her best chance of getting promoted.

She groaned at the ceiling and rolled toward the bedside table, reaching for her phone. Desperate for a distraction.

When she'd come home from Heather's last night, she'd had just over a thousand followers. She pulled up her account and saw that now, she was closing in on three thousand. Still a far cry from viral fame and guaranteed promotion, but clearly she and Nick were doing something right.

She scrolled through the comments on the latest photo she'd posted, another one from yesterday's session at the pool. She'd turned toward the railing and closed her eyes to let the morning sun warm her cheeks and her eyelids, then come up onto relevé and lifted one leg into a high arabesque, leaning her torso ever-so-slightly forward to get her working leg as high as she could. It had come out beautifully; Nick had captured the movement of the water below her and the breeze that had caught a few strands of her hair as she held the position perfectly still. The jagged, surf-swept rocks were a perfect contrast to the smooth, geometric lines of her legs. Her skin looked like it was glowing, and her body looked strong and in control. It might have been the best photo yet, and she'd posted it without hesitation this time, complimenting Nick's talent and making a point of tagging the official accounts of the tourism boards for Sydney, New South Wales, and Australia. And clearly, she wasn't the only one who'd appreciated it.

> @PlieForPasta: Wow, i'd literally kill for extension like this
> @shaydoesballet: feeeeeeeet!
> @VisitSydney: Looking good @CarlyMontgomery, and Freshwater Beach looks pretty nice too!

She clicked on the profile picture for Sydney Tourism, and her heart leapt: the account had reposted the photo, and it had thousands of likes on it. That explained the sudden increase in followers. It also explained the tone of some of the comments on her own post.

> @jjmiller965: Sydney's always been on my bucket list, and now I think this chick has to go on my fuck-it list lol
> @GainsInMaine: I wanna found out just how flexible this bitch is

Carly made a face and deleted the comments as quickly as she could. Ugh, men were garbage. And men on the internet were garbage monsters. The internet was where the fuckboys of the world really let their fuck flags fly and said things to and about women they'd never dare to say in real life. Even though the internet was actually real life, and it wouldn't take a forensic genius to track these guys down. She deleted a few other gross comments and then pulled up some of the other photos Nick had sent over.

She swiped through them, then stopped on one of the black-and-white shots he'd taken yesterday morning, when he'd told her to go down to the water without him. She'd dug one knee into the sand and extended the other leg behind her, then arched backward until her chest was parallel with the sand. She could still feel that pose in her lower back, but it had been worth it; this shot was art. She smiled down at the screen, zooming in and noticing how Nick had captured the moment the wind had grabbed her hair and made it stream behind her just like the lifesavers' flags above her. He really was good at this.

And really good at kissing. Like, annoyingly, unfairly good. Confident and commanding, like he knew exactly what his body was capable of. She wondered if he danced like that, when he was still performing. He'd been attentive and careful, too, like he was studiously collecting information about her body. Listening to it. She wondered if he'd partnered like that.

She had to stop thinking about kissing Nick Jacobs. Needed to stop *wondering* about him.

Maybe she could get out of seeing him today. Maybe she could conjure up some excuse, some wedding errand that only she could do, and then she wouldn't have to spend all day with him.

As if in answer to her prayers, a clap of thunder sounded overhead, followed by the ticking of rain against her window. She rolled over and looked out; the early morning sky was a swirl of full gray clouds, and the rain was falling steadily. Halle-freakin-lujah. No chance of photography today. She smiled grimly to herself, then hastily tapped out a caption and posted the photo. There. That was done. She'd have a whole day to herself, and by the time she saw Nick again tomorrow, she'd have stopped thinking about kissing him.

Nick spent the night refusing to think about Carly. Refusing to think about the idiotic decision he'd made to kiss her. Refusing to think about the inexplicable disappointment he'd felt swell in his gut when she'd pulled away from him and declared that kiss a mistake. Kisses, plural, really. Lots of them. Lots of hot, needy kisses that made absolutely no sense to him. They'd been glued to each other like horny teenagers, and if he hadn't been on the front veranda of his best friend's childhood home, he knew he would have been grinding his hard-on against her, desperate as he was to feel as much of her body against his as was humanly possible. He hadn't kissed anyone that way in years, perhaps since he'd actually been a teenager. Maybe not ever. He hadn't ever felt desire like that, desire that blacked out all the sensible parts of his brain, the parts that knew that Carly Montgomery was a walking hand grenade.

And then, of course, the grenade had gone off. She'd pushed him away and told him that the entire thing had been a bad idea, and even though he agreed, because again, *hand grenade*, he'd been confused and disappointed when she'd said it. And he didn't want to think about why.

It was for the best, he told himself, as he stared at the ceiling. Yes, that kiss had crackled with heat and desire, promising that anything more would be truly explosive. But that was the problem, wasn't it? Carly was explosive. Predictably unpredictable. He needed to stay far enough away from her that he didn't get grazed by any more shrapnel.

But they had work to do. Kissing or no kissing—and she'd made it clear, there would be no more kissing—he still needed photos for his portfolio, and he wouldn't mind a little viral popularity, either. And there were still plenty of items left on Heather's spreadsheet.

Which was why, after a night of restless sleep, Nick climbed out of bed, got dressed, and made a stop at the hotel café before heading out into the splattering rain. He had just raised his hand to knock on Carly's when it was flung open, and there stood Carly in jean shorts and a tank top, looking slightly disheveled from sleep and very surprised to see him.

"It's raining," she blurted, by way of greeting. "I figured we couldn't shoot in the rain." She met his eyes, and he thought he saw a flicker of panic before her gaze darted away and landed on the takeaway coffee cup in his hand.

"It's supposed to ease up in a few hours. I thought we could cross a wedding task off our list then head out once the rain stops."

"Oh. Okay." She sounded almost disappointed, as though she'd been counting on a day without him. Which shouldn't bruise his pride, obviously. It didn't. What had happened on the front porch at Marcus and Heather's last night . . . it was irrelevant. He certainly hadn't tossed and turned all night thinking about what could have happened if they hadn't been interrupted.

"Come in, then," Carly conceded, yawning and not meeting his eyes. "I'll be back in a minute. I was just about to run downstairs and get myself a coffee."

"This, euh, this is for you," he held out the cup. "I already had one."

She glanced up at him in surprise, her brown eyes wide and still puffy from sleep. "Thanks?" she said, like she wasn't sure if she could trust him. "Is that another milkshake?"

"No, it's a simple iced coffee. Just coffee with ice. I asked for nuclear-strength, and the barista had a tattoo on his forearm that said DEATH BEFORE DECAF, so I suspect he delivered."

She laughed softly, and the sound shouldn't have been sexy. "Thanks," she repeated, and this time he heard the full stop at the end of it. It was grudging, but it was there. She took the coffee from him and turned back into the apartment, waving him inside.

He followed and was met by an explosion of beach decor that made his eyes water. "Really laying it on thick, aren't they?"

"It's growing on me," Carly said, flopping onto the couch. She closed her eyes and took a long sip of the coffee. He tried not to look at her lips pursed around the straw, and failed. "Oh, God, caffeine," she groaned, and again, it shouldn't have been sexy.

Casting around for a distraction, Nick sat at the small round dining table and pulled out his phone, which had the list he'd assembled. Googling "best wedding dance floor songs" had helped him settle down last night when all he could think about was the moment Carly had grasped his shirt and closed that last, desperate inch of space between his mouth and hers. About the rough, hungry moans that had drifted out of her when he touched her and—no, not thinking about that right now, he reminded himself. Or, ideally, ever.

He cleared his throat. "I thought we could take care of the playlist this morning. I already started building it, but I thought you might have some opinions to share."

Carly opened her eyes and threw him a skeptical look. "You *thought* I *might* have some opinions?"

"Yeah, I had an inkling," he said, allowing himself a smile.

"Hmmph." Carly took another long pull of coffee, then pushed herself off the couch and crossed the room, holding out her hand. "Show me what you've got so far."

For a moment, he considered refusing, but he knew her well enough by now to know that she'd get her way eventually, so he handed the phone over. He watched as she scrolled through the list, her forehead wrinkling deeper with each swipe of her thumb.

"No, no, no. Absolutely not. We are not putting "Uptown Funk" on this playlist. If people want to dance to that song they can go to every other wedding on the planet. And have you actually listened to the lyrics of "Hey Ya"? That is not a happy song. And while we're at it, you can take "Happy" off here. What is this, 2014?"

Yeah, he had an inkling she might have some opinions. "What do you suggest, then?"

"We need some classics on here, stuff the older guests will recognize. Earth, Wind & Fire, Lionel Richie, Wham!"

"Wham."

"Wham!" She said it with so much enthusiasm he could hear the exclamation mark at the end of it.

"I don't like Wham."

"Everybody likes Wham!, Nick," she rolled her eyes.

"Not everybody." This was fine. This was good. They were back to bickering, and no one was thinking about kissing anyone.

"Everybody with an ounce of good taste, then." Her thumbs flew across the screen, and a second later "Wake Me Up Before You Go-Go" was blaring out of his phone.

Nick gave her his coldest, stoniest stare, and she grinned back, putting one foot in a bevel and bouncing her hip, phone in one hand

and coffee in the other. When he didn't respond, she got her shoulders involved, shimmying until her ponytail shook. Nick watched her, realizing with horrified interest that if she was wearing a bra under that shirt, it wasn't a terribly supportive one. He shifted uncomfortably in his seat, and when she didn't stop dancing, he reached out and snatched the phone back, fumbling slightly as he hit pause.

"Fine, you win, you win. I'll put this on the list." Carly gave him a smug smile, and he looked back down at his phone. Looked anywhere but at her. "What else do we need, then?

Carly pulled out the other chair and sat down across from him. "Some newer stuff for the young people. Beyoncé, Lizzo, Taylor Swift. Obviously some songs about dancing. ABBA, Whitney Houston, Robyn, the Bee Gees. Half the guests are ballet people, which means they're going to want music from the dance movies they love, which means that Jamiroquai song from *Center Stage* and 'I've Had the Time of My Life.' Oh, and 'Yeah!' by Usher."

"What dance movie's that one from?"

"It's not from a movie, it's just Heather's favourite song."

He looked up at her, eyebrows raised in skepticism. For a second, Carly's smile looked vaguely evil, but then she widened her eyes innocently and took another sip of her coffee. This felt like a trap.

"Heather's favourite song includes the lyrics 'bend over to the front and touch your toes?'"

"Hamstring flexibility is very important, Nicholas," she said, her innocent act so unconvincing that he couldn't suppress a laugh. "Just trust me, she'll love it. What about Marcus? What songs will he want to dance to?"

"Euh, it's been a while, let me think." When they'd been teenagers, Marcus had been into Australian rock. Powderfinger, Cold Chisel, INXS. He didn't think those were particularly good to dance to, but— "Oh, Kylie Minogue. 'Spinning Around.'"

Now it was Carly's turn to look skeptical. "Really?"

"Pirouette technique is very important, Carly," he said, imitating her wide eyes.

Impossibly, her brows rose even higher.

"Fine, maybe not the song, but definitely those gold hot pants. He had a poster of her in them stuck up in his locker at the ANB school for years." Marcus hadn't been the only one. Those hot pants had had the entire country in a collective wet dream for most of the year 2000. "If you want Usher on this playlist, then I get to put Kylie on it."

"All right, fine," Carly said. "What else?"

Nick thought about the weddings he'd attended in the last few years, a few of them in Germany but most in France. Delphine's friends from high school or from the Paris Opera Ballet school. A few of their colleagues from POB, almost all of whom had grown up in France, since the company rarely hired people who hadn't come up through its school.

"'Les Sunlights des tropiques,'" he said. It played at basically every French wedding, and it always got people on the dance floor.

"Never heard of it."

"Trust me, if you like Wham, you'll like this song."

"Once again, everyone likes Wham!"

Nick didn't bother with a comeback, he just pulled up the song and hit play. It had a rapid, tropical beat and lyrics about feeling the sun on your skin on a beach at the edge of the ocean. He watched as Carly listened, lips pursed again, like she was reserving judgment.

"I don't like it."

Not reserving judgment for long.

"Give it a chance; listen to it for more than ten seconds."

"I am listening! He just said he has a bongo in his heart and a bird in his head!"

"'Don't leave me hanging on like a yo-yo' isn't exactly poetry." He stood and struck the same pose she had, with one foot propped onto demi pointe and his knee crossed coquettishly over his standing leg, and popped his hip to the beat. "Viens danser," he sang along.

"Non," she replied, staring up at him like he'd lost his mind.

"Viens danserrrrr," he sang louder, and maybe he had lost his mind a little. He was being ridiculous, he knew, but maybe the only way to best Carly Montgomery was to beat her at her own game. He grabbed her hand and tugged it, and she stood reluctantly, letting him hold on to her fingers and swing her arm back and forth to the beat. She rolled her eyes, but a few seconds later, her feet started moving, and she was stepping side to side as Gilbert Montagné sang about the magic of the Pacific Ocean, the waves and the sky. Then her hips and shoulders joined in, and Nick dropped his showgirl posture and started moving like Carly was, like they were on a dance floor with a foot or so between them, enjoying the silly '80s beat of this silly '80s song the French loved so much. *Y a rien à faire qu'à rêver. Prends-moi la main viens danser*, Montagné crooned. *There's nothing to do but dream. Take my hand and come dance.*

The last time he'd danced to this song, he'd pulled Delphine into his arms, him in a sharp linen suit and her in a chic backless dress. They'd swayed under the night sky at a vineyard in Provence. About as far from Freshwater Beach as you could get, he thought, as he and Carly bopped together, her in her cut-offs and him in a pair of board shorts he'd never have worn in Paris.

"All right, fine!" Carly sighed loudly after a moment. "It's a good song."

Nick chuckled and kept dancing. "So I was right?"

Carly rolled her eyes, somehow managing to roll them in time with the beat. Well, New York Ballet School was known for prioritizing musicality.

"Sorry, Carly, didn't quite hear that," he teased.

"You were right," she grumbled, though there was no real resentment in it.

"A little louder, please? So I can hear you over the good song?"

She shot him a lethal look, but he just laughed and held out his hand, only half expecting her to take it. But she did, and in his surprise, he spun her around a little harder than he'd meant to. She gasped and toppled a little, falling towards him, but he put his other hand on her waist and steadied her. Once she'd regained her footing, they kept dancing, a few inches closer than they had been, and he could feel the muscles in her waist shifting under his hand as she swayed. Smell her shampoo clinging to the curls that had slid out of her ponytail as she danced. He swallowed, thinking that he should step back and restore the space between them. He should.

He was about to do it—really, he was—when the song ended and the next one began, a slower beat. *On va s'aimer*, Montagné sang. *We're going to love each other.*

He knew better than to pull Carly even closer, but that was what you did when a slow song came on, wasn't it? You pulled your partner closer, so that her hips touched yours, and you could run your hand from her waist to the small of her back. You watched her press her lips together, probably unconsciously, as the movements became less like dancing and more like breathing together. You let her slip her hand out of yours so she could twine her arms around your neck and bring your faces even closer together, until your pulse was pounding hard enough for her to feel it through your ribcage.

Human hand grenade, he thought. *Back away slowly. No sudden movements.*

She was so near now, just like she'd been last night. And just like it had last night, his body screamed for him to close the gap. Cover her mouth with his and taste her. She'd taste like the coffee he'd brought her, he thought, and suddenly he'd never craved coffee more than he did at this moment.

Let's not make that mistake again, she'd said. But the way she was looking up at him through her lashes now, shy and nervous, made him hope she hadn't meant it. Or that she'd meant it and was having trouble sticking to it. He sure as hell was.

"Carly?" he asked quietly, as their swaying slowed to almost nothing.

"What?"

"Last night . . ."

She swallowed, and he watched her throat work, watched the muscles shift under the smooth skin. His mouth watered.

". . . was a mistake," she finished his sentence. She lifted her chin and met his eyes, her face a picture of determination. But she didn't remove her arms from around his neck, and he didn't miss the way her gaze slid over his mouth on the way up.

"That's right. Shouldn't happen again."

"Right," she said, so quietly he almost didn't hear her.

"Right," he echoed, but she didn't move away.

"Because you're an asshole," she breathed, and it almost sounded like she was saying it to herself. Reminding herself.

"And you're a big-time ballet brat," he said, just as quietly, letting the words flutter over the top of her ear. She shivered and bit her lip, and that was when he knew he wasn't alone in this insanity.

"Swear to God, if you call me that one more time, I'm going to—"

"What? What are you going to do, kiss me again?"

For a moment Carly said nothing. She looked up at him, eyes glittering with defiance and unmasked desire. When she finally spoke, her words sent a thrill of triumph and anticipation racing up Nick's spine.

"Try me."

Nick looked down into her face, at her full lips and flushed, freckled cheeks, and those wide golden-brown eyes. Carly Montgomery had no poker face whatsoever. And she wanted him to call that bluff. He lowered his head until his mouth was barely an inch from hers, hovering there and testing his own resolve. For a moment neither of them moved. Neither of them breathed. And then he spoke, just like they'd both known he would.

"Brat."

This time, when she kissed him, he thought he was ready for it. But no one could ever be ready for the human hurricane that was Carly Montgomery. She claimed his mouth, her tongue darting in with swift determination, and heat swept through him, desire making his skin pulse and buzz with every stroke of her tongue.

He couldn't keep himself from groaning as her fingers tightened in his hair and she pulled him harder against her body, kissing him furiously. She tasted like coffee and sugar, and he lapped at her mouth like it was the first shot of caffeine he'd had in weeks.

Desperate for more, he grabbed her waist and spun her, walking her backward until her legs hit the back of the sofa, swallowing her gasp as he pressed himself against her and she tightened her grip on his hair. It stung deliciously at the roots, and he pinned her to the sofa with his hips, reveling in the breathy mewling sound she made when she felt his hardness through her shorts. It took all his self control not to sweep his other hand up her leg and run his fingertips over the smooth, hidden skin of her inner thigh, over those silvery pink stripes he'd seen during those hours of torturous editing. Instead, he gripped her waist, feeling her muscles shift beneath the fabric as she arched into him, tilting her head to gain better access to his mouth.

Nick completely lost track of time. He forgot about the spreadsheet and the playlist, and about all the very good reasons this was a bad idea. He didn't hear the rain hitting the windows or the cawing of birds outside. He heard nothing but Carly—Carly's sighs, Carly's gasps, Carly's whimper as his lips left hers and traveled down her neck to her sharp collarbone. In this ridiculous seashell-orgy of an apartment, they were their own tiny world, pressed against the couch and each other for what could have been hours or mere minutes. Her smooth, freckled skin tasted faintly of sunscreen and rose petals, and he wanted nothing more than to peel those denim shorts down her spectacular legs and find out what the rest of her tasted like. His cock was painfully hard, pressing against his shorts and demanding release, desperate for more of her.

He ran his hands down the sides of her body, tracing the curves of her small breasts before skimming his fingers over the taut skin between the bottom of her shirt and the top of her jeans. She gasped and broke the kiss.

"I can't have sex with you," she blurted.

Nick froze and pulled his hands from her hips, taking a step back for good measure.

"I'm sorry," she said, her face screwed up. "We have to stop. And we can't do this again. I can't have sex with you."

Nick took another step back, and Carly's stomach dropped. He was already walking away from her.

Good. Fine. She'd known he would. God, men were so fucking predictable it was almost funny.

"No one said anything about sex," Nick said, sounding a little out of breath.

Carly crossed her arms, then looked him up and down pointedly, raising her eyebrows at the very obvious bulge at the front of his shorts.

"Fine, I was thinking about it," he conceded. "But can you blame me? That was . . ."

Incendiary. Atomic. And obviously leading to sex. "I know. But I can't. I mean, I promised I wouldn't."

"Promised who?" he said, cocking his head. "Shit, are you . . . do *you* have a—"

"No, I'm single," she said hastily. "Very single. Extremely single."

"Okay, so, who did you promise?"

"Me. I promised me."

He nodded slowly, as though he understood. But then he spoke. "So are you, uh, waiting for marriage?"

Carly snorted. "Absolutely not. That ship sailed a *long* time ago. And it sailed many times. A whole fleet. An armada, even."

Nick frowned, either at the image or out of incomprehension, she couldn't tell. "I'm not following. What promise are you talking about?"

Jesus, he was really going to make her say it, wasn't he? It was bad enough that she'd lost her cool and blurted it out at him, but now she had to explain it to him? Here, in this increasingly small living room?

"I have a health condition that makes sex impossible."

Nick nodded in comprehension. "The broken vagina."

Carly felt her cheeks heat. It was one thing to throw around those words jokingly, like a kind of armor over her hurt, but it was another to hear Nick say them. He sounded so serious, as if they were talking about a natural disaster or the national debt.

"That's not the technical term for it, but yes," she said, shifting against the couch. "And it doesn't really make sex impossible, it just makes it . . . unbearable." Even though she'd borne it. Made herself do it even when it hurt. Consented to the pain.

"Is it vulvodynia? Vaginismus? Dyspar— I don't know how to pronounce that one, but I've read about it."

"Dyspareunia," she whispered, staring at him. Her heart was suddenly racing. "How do you know about that?"

He leaned against the edge of the table and gave a tiny, elegant shrug. "Google exists. I Googled it."

She raised her eyebrows. "You . . . Googled it?"

"I searched for 'broken vagina' and 'dilator,' and a bunch of stuff came up, and I read it."

Carly burst out laughing. She couldn't control it. It was half amusement, half discomfort. He Googled it. It was the kind of thing Heather would do, she thought, and then she pictured it, and only laughed harder. The idea of Nick Jacobs sitting down at his computer and typing in the words she'd yelled at him, tapping in "broken vagina" and letting Google take him down the pelvic floor rabbit hole—it was too much for her at this hour. But then she thought about the last time she'd had this conversation with a man, and what a disappointment that had turned out to be, and a laugh died in her mouth.

"Well, I'm glad you finally learned that Google is your friend," she said, once she'd collected herself. When she'd first tried to find information about painful sex online, when she was still a teenager desperate for answers, there'd been almost nothing out there. What a difference a decade made.

"I learned a lot, though I think my algorithm is a bit messed up now," he said, smiling. His biceps flexed and relaxed as he crossed his arms over his chest, and she had to will herself to look somewhere else.

"And now you know why this can't happen again. I can't have sex with you." *Even though I really, really want to.*

He didn't say anything in response. He just watched her, and she kept talking to fill the silence. Just to put off the moment when he'd do what she needed him to do, which was to concede that she was right. That there was nothing here and couldn't ever be.

"I made myself a promise that I wouldn't have sex with anyone until I'm better, and there's so much other stuff I need to focus on right now, with the wedding and the promotions schedule, and I don't break my promises," she went on, reciting the words she'd repeated to herself all night. Hearing the words come out of her mouth without really feeling them on her tongue. "So, yeah. That's why it can't happen again."

He leaned back and nodded slowly, like he understood. His eyes looked a little puffy, she noticed, and she could have sworn he was still wearing the same shirt he'd worn last night. She had a feeling she wasn't the only one who'd slept poorly.

"Can I ask you a question? You don't have to answer if you don't want to."

"Okay," she said warily.

"According to Google, there are different kinds of, uh, broken vaginas," he said, and she couldn't help but smile faintly at the words. "Some people can't handle being touched at all, some can't even wear tight clothes. Some can do those things but can't handle penetration." He paused and swallowed, and she watched him gather the courage to ask. "Which are you?"

"The third one," she said. "I wear tight clothes for a living, with no problem, thank God. I can be touched. And it's not like I can't handle penetration," she said.

"The armada."

"Right," she said, with a grim smile. "I can handle it. It just hurts like hell when I do it. But I can do it."

"Spoken like a true dancer."

She nodded. Angela had said something similar during their first appointment. In a gentle voice, a voice that seemed calculated to probe but not to blame, she'd asked why Carly hadn't stopped sooner. Hadn't listened to her pain sooner. Angela knew the answer, of course, but she'd wanted Carly to know it, too: she'd spent her whole life pushing through pain, ignoring discomfort, dancing even when her body begged for rest. Ballet had taught her to keep going even when she knew something wasn't right.

"And I don't want to hurt like hell anymore. Every time I do it, it only makes things worse, and I'm working really hard to make things better." No one could ever accuse her of not trying. She might be a mess and a menace and occasionally a brat, but no one could say Carly Montgomery didn't try. Just like no one could say she didn't keep her promises.

"That's why you have the dilators," he said. It wasn't a question.

"Yes," she sighed, looking over her shoulder at the door to the bedroom, where the white plastic columns were stashed in their ziploc bag in her nightstand. "I guess you read about that, too."

He made a noise of assent. "How's it going?"

She looked back at him sharply, remembering the pointed questions that had lain just under Carter's words when he'd asked something similar. *How long are you going to make me wait? How long am I going to have to settle? How long will I have to put up with this?* Her answer then hadn't satisfied Carter, but it was the only answer she had to give Nick now, so she gave it.

"Slowly. I think it'll be a while before I can have sex again, if . . . if it ever happens." It struck her as extremely strange that she was having this conversation with Nick Jacobs, someone she'd known for less than a week, and liked for even less than that.

He was watching her again, his face impassive. Except for his eyes, which were the color of the waves at dawn, and were fixed intensely on her face. She wanted to look away, wanted the conversation to be over, but she made herself hold his gaze.

"So, anyway, that's that. We have more important things to do, and there's only two weeks until the wedding, and I have a broken vagina. Plus, I'm a menace and *tu veux me tuer*." She said all of this as briskly as she could, squeezing the back of the couch and feeling the stuffing contract beneath her fingers.

"That's not true," he said quietly.

"Yes, it is," she replied firmly, almost relieved that they were back to bickering. "We absolutely have more important things to do, and the wed—"

"The last part's not true," he interrupted.

She felt her eyebrows jerk up, and for a moment she couldn't think of what to say.

"Nick," she started, but he interrupted her.

"Don't get me wrong," he went on, leaning cockily back against the table and lifting one side of his mouth ruefully, "I absolutely think you're a menace, and I fear for my safety every time you walk in the room. But it's not true that I can't stand you. Actually, I can't stop thinking about you."

"About how much you want to throttle me? Or push me off the Spit Bridge?" she tried to joke.

He raised his head and met her eyes with a hot, hungry look. He swept his gaze down her body so slowly and so deliberately that she almost felt it like a physical touch. Her mouth went dry as his eyes returned to her face.

"No," he said firmly, his meaning unmistakeable, and the word reverberated in her bones.

She scoffed. "That's not liking me. That's wanting to fuck me. And as I've already told you, I can't do that. I can't give you what you want." *Please don't ask me to.* Why was he making this so difficult?

Carly stood up from the back of the couch and walked out of the living room and into the kitchen, sucking down gulps of her ice coffee, then tossed the empty cup in the trash. She leaned against the cool granite counter and took a few breaths, knowing that she'd have to go back into the living room and face Nick again.

But before she could turn around, he came into the kitchen and approached her cautiously, like he thought she might bolt if he moved too quickly. He stepped toward her until the tips of his shoes met the front of her flip flops, and looked down into her face.

"I know we've both acted badly, what with the trolley ramming and the public dressing downs," he said, and she stared down at their shoes as he spoke. "I'm sorry for my part in it. But I can't stop thinking about you."

Carly swallowed hard and looked up at him, feeling heat radiating from his chest. She wanted more than anything to pull him against her, bring that heat closer and let it mingle with her own, but she willed herself to stand straight. Still, she couldn't stop the truth from tumbling out of her mouth.

"I can't stop thinking about you, either. It's very irritating, isn't it?"

He chuckled, and she felt the low rumble in her toes and in every nerve ending.

"I wouldn't say irritating, per se, but it's very distracting."

"Nick Jacobs, you're a pedant," she said with a smile.

"I'm not a pedant," he said, not taking his eyes from her mouth. "I am precise."

She rolled her eyes, and he responded by leaning forward slowly, so slowly, and putting one of his hands on the counter next to hers. A tiny movement, but one that took all the remaining air from her already breathless lungs. She turned away, giving him her back and regretting the decision immediately. There was no escape here, either. His body bracketed hers, and even though only their hands and feet were touching, she swore she could feel his pulse hammering along her spine. His long, graceful fingers were loose on hers, but she could feel the tension that pulsed in his arms and imagined it wrapping around her shoulders.

"Nick," she said as firmly as she could manage, clinging desperately to the purpose of this conversation. "I can't give you what you want."

"I want whatever you have. Whatever you can give me," he said, barely louder than a whisper. His breath flickered against her ear as he spoke. "Whatever we can do together. I want that. I want *all* of that."

He lifted a hand and swept his fingertips across the nape of her neck, pulling her hair away and exposing the skin to the cool morning air. Then he repeated the motion with his lips, sending hot sparks racing under her skin. She shuddered and arched her back, not wanting him to break contact, and he didn't. He took a step closer and kept his mouth on her neck, hot and ravenous and raising goosebumps with every sweep of his tongue, and trailed his fingers lightly up her body from her hip to her waist and up the side of her breast. Desire gathered between her thighs, and she arched her back again, wanting as much of him pressed against her as possible. He obliged, and she felt the hard length of him against the base of her spine.

"*Fuck*," she breathed, and she felt him smile against her skin.

"We don't have to. I don't want to if you don't want to. So the question is, what do you want?"

She didn't know how to answer, so she tipped her head back and tried to kiss him, but he stopped her. He put his hands on her waist and gently turned her around. Now the counter was the only thing hard against her back, but she looked into his appallingly handsome face and saw him gazing down at her with dilated eyes. She was breathing rapidly, but he seemed to be holding his breath.

"What do you want?"

She nodded, then grabbed a handful of his shirt and tried to pull him toward her, but he resisted, standing firm and letting her tug fruitlessly on the fabric.

"You're going to have to say it," he said, looking into her face and raising his eyebrows, challenging her. "With words."

She glared up at him and pulled his shirt again. "Nick," she pleaded, and she was annoyed, but not surprised, to hear the whining note in her own voice. Her heart was hammering against her ribs, and the want between her thighs had become an insistent, throbbing demand.

"I said words, plural. That was one word."

"Pedant," she growled, and he chuckled, low and throaty. A real laugh, not something sharp and grim, but loose and warm and just for her. The sound made her breath catch in her chest, and when he lowered his head and ran his hand up the side of her body again, she had to remind herself to exhale, then inhale.

"I'm not a pedant, I'm precise," he said, his mouth half an inch from her ear. "And I want you to tell me precisely what you want from me."

"No," she said stubbornly, releasing his shirt. For a moment he froze, taken aback, but then she grinned wickedly up at him and stepped sideways and away from the counter. He wanted her to be in charge here? *Fine then, I'll be in charge*, she thought, and she sauntered as casually as she could out of the living room and into the bedroom. *You think I'm a brat? Fine then, I'll be a brat.*

She heard his footsteps follow her, and then stop. When she reached her bed, the sheets pushed down and the throw blanket tossed in a heap at the foot, she turned around to see him standing in the doorway, his hands pressed flat against the door frame. He seemed to be holding himself there, unwilling to enter the room. *Fine*, she thought again, meeting his gaze and refusing to break it. *We'll see how long that lasts.*

She sat down and settled herself back on the pillows. He didn't speak, and didn't move, so she slipped her thumbs under the waistband of her shorts and slid them slowly off her hips. When she lifted herself off the bed slightly to get them over her ass, she saw his sharp intake of breath and felt triumph flicker beneath her sternum.

"Carly . . ." he started, but she shook her head.

"I don't want to tell you," she said, sliding the shorts down her thighs, then over her calves, and kicking them off. "I want to show you."

Chapter 14

Nick had only ever passed out once in his life, when he was eighteen years old and had shown up to a dress rehearsal with a raging flu. It had been his first year in the company, and he'd been too scared to call out sick. He'd danced the first run through of Balanchine's "Rubies" without incident, but as the orchestra began to play at the top of the second run-through, his vision had swayed and all the blood seemed to drain out of his body. His legs swam and he stumbled, and a second later he was falling, and remembered nothing more until he woke up in the theater's tiny medical room with an icepack on his forehead.

He wondered if he was about to pass out again now, as he stared at Carly's discarded shorts on the floor. She hadn't spoken loudly, but he heard her words echo around the bedroom as if she'd screamed them into a megaphone.

I want to show you.

He pressed his hands a little harder against the doorjamb to ensure that if his legs did give out, if all the blood did in fact drain out of him, he wouldn't collapse again. On the bed, Carly was playing with the strap of her tank top, rubbing it between her fingers and sliding it over her collarbone. Holding his gaze, she grasped the bottom of it and, arching her back, peeled it off and over her head. He didn't see where it landed after she dropped it off the bed, and he'd never cared about anything less. She lay back on the pillows in a pair of black boyshort panties and a flimsy-looking pale blue lace bra, and all he could think in that moment was how furious he would be if he did, in fact, pass out. If he missed this, or whatever happened next.

What happened next was that she ran her hands up her thighs, her fingers tracing up her body and snagging gently on the legs of her panties before continuing over her muscled stomach. She broke their shared gaze and closed her eyes, and for a moment he regretted it, until he saw the way she flinched and arched into her own touch as her fingers fluttered over her bare ribcage. She gasped and let out a tiny sigh, and the sound made every cell in his body flare with heat and scream for him to get closer to her. As close as it was possible to be.

He stepped into the room, and by the time he was standing at the end of the bed, Carly's hands had reached her bra and she was gently squeezing her small breasts, sighing louder now and pressing her head back into the pillow. He stared, trying to take in every mouth-watering detail of this picture, trying to catalogue every shift and pull of her stomach muscles under her pale, freckled skin. But when the fingers of one hand slipped under the lace and he saw the fingers of the other hand pinch at her small, hard nipple through the thin fabric, he knew it was pointless to try to remember. He'd never be able to forget. He would go to his grave with the sound of Carly's breathy moans, and the stretch of her skin over her ribs as she writhed, etched into his memory.

His erection was pressing against the fly of his shorts, hot and heavy and impossible to ignore. It took all his self-control not to pull down the zipper and touch himself, but he had asked for this. He had asked her to tell him what she wanted, what her body could take, and even though she'd agreed, she had done what she always did: unleashed utter chaos. He heard the sound of his own rapid breath mixing with Carly's moans, heard the jaw-clenched, strangled sound that escaped him as she extricated her fingers from her bra and slid her thumbs under the waistband of her panties. Carly Montgomery was going to kill him, and he was going to enjoy every second of it.

In a matter of seconds, she'd shed her panties, and he watched, almost shaking with need, as she returned one hand to her breast and ran the middle finger of the other up the inside of her thigh and between her wet, glistening folds. Her groan of relief nearly undid him, and all he wanted was to wrap his hand around his cock, or better yet, wrap her hand around it, but he would not interrupt her. He willed himself to watch, to memorize the way her fingertip circled and dipped in wide sweeps and then in tight, rapid rings. He wanted to learn every step in this dance the first time. And if he couldn't learn it all by watching, he fully intended to learn the rest by doing.

Her breaths were coming in jagged gasps now, her heels making deep, round imprints in the mattress as she rolled her hips against her hand. His pulse was booming in his ears as he watched her, every inch of his skin hot and tight and desperate to be touched.

"Oh God," she gasped to the ceiling, and oh *God*, he didn't have enough eyes to watch all of her at once. Her hand flickering over the lace, teasing her nipple with the pad of her thumb. Her torso arching, her thighs tensing. Her middle finger rubbing and receding, dancing on her clit. Her beautiful face, twisted and perfect and surrounded by her riot of red curls.

"Fuck, Carly," he moaned, aching for her release and his own. "I want to see you come."

She opened her eyes and pulled her head up off the pillow, meeting his eyes with a look of sheer desire. Next time, he decided, through the hot, dense fog of want, he would be the one to put that look on her face.

"Oh God," she gasped again, and then her mouth opened in a moan of ecstasy, and she shuddered and bucked, writhing and rolling against her hand until the moan became a whimper, and then a sigh.

A ringing silence filled the room, broken only by Carly's panting and the thunderous sound of Nick's pulse, which he wouldn't be surprised if she could hear. He was so hard it hurt, but he didn't take his eyes off Carly's. She gave him a sly, flushed smile and removed her hand from between her legs.

"Does that answer your question?" She sat up and pressed her back against the pillows.

All Nick could do was nod. She'd won this round, and he'd never been so happy to lose.

Nick's nod was restrained and dignified. Well, as dignified as a man could be with his shorts tented by what appeared to be a massive hard-on. Carly gave him another sly smile and raised her eyebrows in invitation.

She'd never touched herself in front of a man before. She wasn't shy—and if anyone knew that by now, it was the man standing, looking slightly dazed, at the end of her bed—but she'd never imagined doing what she'd just done. Then again, no man had ever asked her how she liked to be touched before touching her. No man had ever understood the truth about her body.

But Nick knew. Nick had Googled it, for Chrissake. And then when Google hadn't given him all the answers he needed, he'd asked her. And she'd been willing to provide them. For a moment, as she'd been peeling off her shorts and preparing to call his bluff, it had occurred to her that with another man she might have been embarrassed. But Nick Jacobs had already seen the worst of her, so what was there to be embarrassed about?

"Nick? Did that answer your question?"

He nodded vaguely again, and she grinned. "You're going to have to say it, Nick. With words."

"You're impossible," he breathed, and she let out an evil giggle. Then she scooted to the end of the bed and rose to her knees in front of him.

He pulled her into his arms in an instant, placing one large hand at the back of her neck and the other on her ass, pulling her body against his. She became aware of how almost naked she was, as the fabric of his shorts slid against the damp skin of her bare thighs, and she decided to even things out a little. She seized the bottom of his shirt and tugged it upward, and he leaned back to pull it over his head with one hand, keeping the other hand on her ass and their hips pinned deliciously together.

One he'd tossed the shirt on the floor, he returned his hand to her neck, pulling gently at the roots of her hair. Her clit throbbed in response, but before she could even moan her encouragement, his mouth took hers. His tongue was hot and decisive as it swept between her lips, and it tangled with hers in an urgent dance that only intensified when she ran one hand over his chest and let the other trail up his thigh and over the hot, hard bulge in his shorts.

His body was just as she remembered it from that first day at the beach, all shadows and lines where the muscle shifted under his smooth skin. She let her fingers linger over his stomach, and the lean bunches of muscles over his ribs, and the firm, neatly cut lines of his pecs. All the places ballet had molded and made him, pleasantly softened by retirement. He groaned into her mouth when she ran her fingertips across the deep, muscular channels that disappeared into his shorts, a whisper-light touch that made him grind against her other hand. Taking the crystal-clear hint, she nipped at his lower lip and then set to work undoing his shorts, but a second later, his hand covered hers, stopping her.

"Don't you want . . . ?" she asked, punctuating the question with a squeeze of his cock and a quick series of kisses to the place where his neck met his jaw.

"I do," he groaned, tipping his head back to grant her more access to the tender skin there. "But not yet."

He moved his hands to her hips and pushed her gently, and she let herself fall backward. In a second, he was on the bed with her, above her, his body bracketing her with heat and muscle as his mouth found hers again. She took the opportunity to run her hands over his back, feeling the sinew shift gloriously under her fingers as he kissed her mouth, her neck, the hollow of her collarbone. She arched under him, hoping and praying his lips would keep moving lower, and he did not disappoint her.

He shifted his body to lie beside her and pulled the lace of her bra aside, and the sound that escaped her when he flicked his tongue over her nipple was one of sheer rapture and relief. He teased the tight, tender skin with his lips and tongue, sending bright, hot sparks of pleasure rocketing through her body and straight to her clit. She gasped for air, eager for more, and once again, he obliged. His other hand ghosted over her rib cage, just as hers had done a few minutes earlier, and then his fingers were on her other breast, the pad of his thumb caressing her nipple through the flimsy fabric. She whimpered and swore in response. Carly had never been the kind of dancer who could pick up choreography simply by watching it. Nick clearly was.

"Don't stop," she gasped, and just to make sure he'd understood her, she grasped his wrist and dragged his hand down her stomach. But instead of following her between her legs, his hand stalled at her hip and held tight to the place where her skin stretched over the bone there. He lifted his mouth from her breast, and her eyes flew to his. Before she could ask what was wrong, he spoke.

"I want to stop if it hurts," he murmured, and her heart flipped over her chest. "I don't want to hurt you, Carly. If it's hurting, I want to stop, okay? You have to tell me right away."

She nodded, struck by the intensity in his gaze. His eyes were dilated and his lips swollen from kissing her, but his mouth was set in a determined line.

"Promise," he whispered firmly.

"I promise," she nodded. "Right away."

He gave her a half smile, and her heart flipped again as he returned his mouth to her nipple. She sighed in relief and took his hand again, guiding it down her body and between her thighs. The sound he made when he touched her for the first time was like nothing she'd ever heard.

"Shit, you're so wet," he groaned against her skin, running his middle finger between her folds just the way she'd shown him. The movement sent an electric thrill through her, quickly followed by a hot throb of pleasure as his finger arrived at her clit and began to circle it in an uncanny imitation of what she'd shown him. Pedant, precise, whatever he was, this was perfect. She sighed and arched into his touch, grinding against his hand and chasing the climax that had begun to build the moment he'd started teasing her nipples. His finger sped and slowed, its circles widening and narrowing, and she heard her own breath become ragged and needy.

"Don't stop," she moaned again, and this time, he didn't.

"I won't stop until you come," he said, his voice low and husky with need. She could feel his erection pressing against her hip, hard and ready, and her mouth watered at the thought of what she could do to it as soon as she came.

"Fuck, I'm so close," she gasped, and she snaked her hand in between their bodies to wrap her hand around his cock. The sound of his groan, hot and desperate around her nipple, pushed her over the edge. She bucked frantically against his hand, wishing the glorious, heedless free fall could last forever. But soon it was over, and Nick's fingers stilled against her, her breath became steady, and normal sensation returned to her limp, exhausted limbs.

She opened her eyes and saw a shaft of golden morning light splayed across the ceiling. Perfect photography light, she thought, but what photograph could ever capture this moment? She gave Nick's cock another squeeze and was rewarded with that same delicious sound. Grinning, she reached down and took his hand, then gave his shoulder a gentle push. He rolled onto his back and she followed him, straddling him easily and going straight for his fly. He'd waited long enough for this, and so had she.

Carly had laid on her back panting for all of three seconds—just long enough for him to wonder how she'd react if he slipped his slick finger into his mouth to taste her—before she sat up and pushed his shoulder until he was the one on his back. She straddled him and pulled off his already-unbuttoned shorts, pulling them down his legs hastily and laughing when he pointed his toes so she could get them over his feet.

"Thanks, ballet," she muttered as she tossed his pants onto the floor, and then she turned back and looked down at him, stretched out on the bed in nothing but his underwear. "No, really, *thanks, ballet*," she said. She bit her lower lip and squeezed one of his quads appreciatively, and the sight of her hand on his thigh, so close to his hard, aching cock, was torment. As if she'd heard his thought, she slid her fingers up his leg, the movement slow but the pressure firm.

The first time she stroked his cock through the fabric, he let out a sound somewhere between a groan and a hiss, and she looked down at him with an evil smile. She repeated the movement, and this time he couldn't stop himself from thrusting against her hand. The smile widened into a grin, and for a moment he thought she would stay there, straddling him with her bra askew and her pussy bare and wet, until he couldn't take it any longer. But to his bottomless relief, she reached forward, extricated his cock, and wrapped her hand around the base of him. He growled and pressed his head into the pillow, more desperate to come than he could remember being in his life. Her grip was firm, but her hand was still. After a second, he looked up at her and saw that her eyes were wide and her mouth slightly open in what looked like surprise.

"Are you okay? Do you want to stop?"

"No, no," she said quickly. "I just . . . um . . . I'm really glad I don't have to try to fit that inside me," she explained, and he laughed to the ceiling. She squeezed his cock, and pleasure streaked up his spine. "That is some Big Nick Energy."

He laughed again, but the sound was strangled when she started stroking him in earnest. He wanted to close his eyes and let the sensation drag him under, but just as he was about to, she took her hand off him and put it between her own legs. A second later, her fingers returned, wet and slippery with her arousal, and all he could do was stare as she stroked him, her tempo increasing as his breath quickened.

"Shit, Carly," he groaned as she ran the pad of her thumb around the head of his cock, smearing a drop of pre-come over the swollen, unbearably tender skin. She kept stroking him, and now he matched her rhythm with his hips, thrusting up into her slick hand and chasing the orgasm that was gathering at the base of his spine. She worked him faster, her eyes fixed on his face and her other hand braced against his flexing thighs as he groaned and gasped beneath her. Then she moved that hand between his legs and gently squeezed his heavy, clenching balls, and he was dragged under.

The release was so intense that he slammed his eyes shut and momentarily saw white. He was drowning in pleasure, hot and fierce, and Carly kept pumping her hand over his cock, wringing every last moment of his orgasm out of his body. When he opened his eyes, every inch of his skin buzzing and burning, he saw her sitting over him, her hand still wrapped around him and a wicked smile on her face. Carly Montgomery was a menace, but she was a menace who'd just handed him the most breathtaking orgasm of his life. He couldn't remember ever coming so hard, and certainly not from a hand job.

She moved to climb off him, but he shook his head.

"You're not going anywhere," he said, surprised he was able to get the words out.

"I was going to get you a tissue," she objected. She glanced down at the thick spray of come on his lower abdomen.

He shook his head, then reached for her wrist and pulled her hand toward him.

"What are you—" She stopped talking and gasped when he ran his tongue lightly over her palm. He swirled it around her middle finger and then his own. He could taste her on his hands, and on her own, and it was intoxicating enough to make his dick twitch against his stomach.

"Big Nick Energy," she said with a weak laugh, pulling her hand away from his mouth and putting it back on his cock.

It rained all day, and Nick didn't even mind that it meant missing an afternoon of shooting. They found plenty of ways to pass the time. When they finally stumbled out of Carly's bedroom shortly before noon, Carly grabbed her wallet and dashed downstairs in search of lunch. After she closed the door loudly behind her—as he'd learned in the last few hours, Carly did just about *everything* loudly—Nick flopped onto the couch, head slightly foggy.

A holiday fling was, if he was honest with himself, not his best idea. He'd known that as he was buying her an American-style iced coffee, as he was climbing the stairs to her apartment, as he arrived at her door. It seemed like the kind of idea that would only create more mess and more hurt. A few weeks of messing around, and then the wedding, and then what? They'd go their separate ways, he supposed. Her back to New York, and he back to . . . well, he still didn't know. Would he stay here? Go back to Paris? Try to make a home and a career somewhere else entirely? He had no idea, and he should have been using this time to figure it out. And yet, he couldn't stop himself from walking to that café, handing over his card, and rushing up the steps. And then she'd opened the door looking sleepy and rumpled and charmingly annoyed at him, and he wished he'd come over sooner. He couldn't remember ever feeling so bewitched by a woman, not even Delphine.

With a jolt of surprise, he realised that until Marcus had mentioned her last night, he hadn't thought about Delphine in days. When he woke up in the morning, the first thing he checked on his phone was Carly's follower count and then his own. He didn't hope for missed calls or new texts from Delphine Delacroix, and when he pulled out his phone to check Instagram now, he didn't find any. What he did find was that Carly's latest photo, the black-and-white one of her on the sand between the flags, had racked up thousands of likes. Over on his own page, the same image had been liked a few hundred times, and the comments below it were effusive.

> @BonAperture: Amazing shot, @NickJClicks! This light is to die for.
> @dancersinthewild: Hard to take a bad photo when you've got this kind of backdrop . . . and this gorgeous dancer!
> @DSLDiva: Damn, Sydney looks stunning, I gotta get down there

He closed the app and smiled sleepily to himself. The plan was *working*.

Every objection Carly raised this morning had been correct. They had work to do, and not a lot of time to do it. Well, almost every objection. She had seemed determined, hopeful almost, that he would lose interest as soon as she told him about her condition. But he'd known about it for days, had pieced together the words that she'd shouted at him that first morning in the hotel lobby and had let the internet help him figure out the rest. It hadn't stopped him from kissing her last night. It hadn't stopped him from lying awake last night wondering what she sounded like when she came. What she looked like when she stopped moving and talking and fighting him, and just slept. What it would be like to fight alongside her, rather than against her.

He lay back on the couch and closed his eyes against the bright late morning light, letting his head sink into one of the many beach-themed throw pillows. Between the lack of sleep last night and their exertions this morning, he was in need of a nap or an espresso or both. He must have dozed off, because next thing he knew, Carly was prodding his shoulder impatiently and saying his name.

"Nick. *Nick.* Come on. There's lunch, and we need to finish the playlist."

"Tired," he mumbled. He opened his eyes to see her crouching next to him in a pair of shorts and a striped T-shirt, looking down into his face. He was reminded of the very first time he'd seen her, when their bodies had been arranged in a similar position, except that time he'd been on the floor, and she'd had a look of sheer horror on her face. He liked this better.

"Come on," she said again. "If we can't take photos, we need to get wedding stuff done." She seized one of his limp hands and gave it a fruitless tug. She sighed and went to drop his hand, but he held tight to her fingers and gave a tug of his own. She gasped and lost her balance, and he caught her hips as she fell towards the couch, guiding her down slowly until she was on top of him.

"This is the opposite of what I asked for," she said, but again, he could see a smile curving the edges of her mouth. He ran a hand up the side of her body, the back of his knuckles brushing over her ribs, and she closed her eyes with a sigh. He repeated the movement, and she squirmed against him.

"You're right," he murmured, his lips so close to hers he could feel each little puff of peppermint breath that passed between her soft pink lips. "We should stop right now. We definitely shouldn't stay on this couch all day."

"Definitely not," she agreed, but as she spoke she opened her legs a little wider so that her knees dug into the couch on either side of his body. She had him.

"So let's go," he whispered, not meaning a word of it, and then she kissed him. Not hard and fierce this time, but slowly, almost cautiously. As though she was testing a theory, gathering data.

Her tongue slipped between his lips as the scent of her wrapped itself around him, and he knew he'd never smell roses or taste peppermint without thinking of her. His tongue answered hers just as delicately, letting her set the pace, letting her explore his mouth and move her body against his. But within moments, the kiss turned hot and urgent, and her hands were everywhere—on his chest, in his hair, gripping the arm of the couch—and she twisted and ground her hips against his inevitable erection. He groaned against her mouth as she moved up and down his hard length, and he lifted his hands to her breasts, eager to put this morning's learning to good use again.

She broke the kiss and looked down into his face, and the sight of her kiss-swollen lips and her flushed cheeks under her freckles made him want to stay on this couch with her on top of him all morning, all day, all week.

"I can't come again," she smiled ruefully.

"Wanna bet?" he asked, and she laughed.

"You like a challenge, don't you, Nick Jacobs?"

"Why else would I be spending time with you, Carly Montgomery?"

She opened her mouth to retort, then closed it again, as if conceding the point. Then she nipped at his lower lip the way he loved, and placed a hand on each of his shoulders.

"In that case," she said, as she ground against him, sending pleasure and need spiralling through him, "I'll take that bet."

Chapter 15

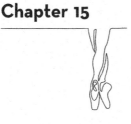

By the next morning the rain had cleared, and when Carly met Nick in the lobby of his hotel, the sky was a bright, blazing blue, promising a cloudless, pitilessly hot Sydney day. It would be cooler up in the mountains, he promised, but right now it was midmorning and there was a lot of traffic on the roads. Today, though, Carly found that she didn't mind being stuck in Leanne's hot little Honda Accord with Nick, especially now that she didn't have to keep her eyes off his fingers as they fiddled and danced on the steering wheel at a long red light.

His words from yesterday morning echoed in her head as the car inched along a busy street, just as they had as she'd been falling asleep last night.

I want whatever you have. Whatever you can give me.

She'd dated plenty of men in the last decade. While Heather had been settling down with her ex Jack, Carly had been on the dating apps, swiping and hoping and always ending up disappointed by the men she met there. Always watching them be disappointed by her. For them, it wasn't enough that she was smart and funny and had managed to get and hold onto a spot in one of the best ballet companies in the world. She couldn't give them everything they wanted from her—for some men, the *only* thing they really wanted from her. And they sure as hell couldn't give her what she needed. It had taken a long time to realize that she deserved more, and muscle memory was powerful. She couldn't shake off a decade of feeling like an unfuckable disappointment overnight.

When she'd heard Nick all but beg for whatever she was willing to give him, when he made it sound like a precious gift and not like a runner-up prize, she'd realized that she'd been waiting years to hear it. Without ever knowing that it was what she needed. Without ever understanding how healing it would be—or how hot.

"How was the lamington?" Nick asked, interrupting her thoughts.

"Sublime," she smiled. They'd grabbed coffees and baked goods to go, and Nick had urged her to try another Australian delicacy, a cube of sponge cake covered in chocolate and flaky coconut, with a layer of berry jam in the middle. Carly had demolished it a few minutes after they'd gotten into the car, and she had half wanted to ask him to turn around so she could buy another one.

"Good," he said, tapping on the steering wheel as the cars crawled. "If we ever make it up to the mountains, we can get lunch up there. And tomorrow we should hit one of the beaches on the other side of the Bridge."

"Yes, I need to see as many of Sydney's four hundred perfect beaches as possible."

"It's only 398," he said, and she rolled her eyes. Pedant. "I think we should go to Bronte. It's an underrated gem. Everyone knows Bondi and Coogee, but Bronte's between them, and it's got an even better pool than Freshwater. In my humble opinion."

She snorted. "When has your opinion ever been humble?"

"Fine. It's not humble, it's just right. Bronte was one of my favorites as a kid. It's a straight shot on the bus from the ANB dorms, and it was a nice way to escape the craziness of a hundred teenage ballet students all living on top of each other."

"Sounds like the NYB school. One huge dorm full of hormones, hairspray, and the most competitive and tightly wound humans you'll ever meet. Who are all exhausted and sore and starving half the time."

"Exactly. So I'd go there and just be by myself. Or Marcus and I would go across the bridge to Balmoral Beach, which was a favorite for another reason." He smiled to himself.

"What was the reason?" Carly asked, suspiciously.

"Ah, well, two reasons, really," he allowed. "It's a topless beach. At fifteen, we thought we'd struck gold."

"You little pervs!"

"Yeah, that's basically what Leanne said when she found out. We only went a few times before she busted us. Mostly when I wanted to get away from the dorms for a bit, I'd go to Marcus's place."

"Not home? Where is home?" She watched him as he flicked the blinker and joined a long line to get onto a highway.

"What do you mean?"

"What do you mean, what do I mean?" Carly thought it was a pretty simple question.

He didn't answer. The lights changed and he just made it through and merged onto the highway. Carly eyed him closely. He still looked a little underslept, but even when he was tired he was annoyingly handsome, his deep blue eyes bright and shimmering in the hot sunlight and his long lashes casting tiny shadows on his cheeks.

"Hello?" she asked.

"Hang on a second, I'm concentrating. It's been a while since I drove on a highway on the left-hand side."

Carly narrowed her eyes and watched his face, but he kept his eyes on the road. If she didn't know better, she would say he was stalling.

"You haven't answered my question," she reminded him a few minutes later. Traffic had eased up and the car was speeding along the highway, which was flanked by clusters of eucalyptus trees and big-box stores.

"What question?" he asked, checking his mirrors. She gave him a skeptical look. He was definitely stalling. And he should definitely know by now that she wouldn't be put off that easily.

"Where's home?"

He sighed and looked over at her, his face a picture of amused disbelief. "You're relentless, you know that?"

"I do," she grinned. "And you're bad at dodging questions, you know that?"

He sighed again. She was starting to like the sound, even if it was the sound of exasperation.

"I'm not dodging the question, it's just not a very interesting answer. I grew up in a little town west of here, Springwood. It's about half way up the mountains. We'll drive through it today."

"Springwood," she repeated, rolling the name over her tongue. "Sounds pretty."

"It is. Quiet, and surrounded by bushland."

"How old were you when you left?"

"Fourteen. My ballet teacher, Miss Rosemary, had an old colleague who ran a summer intensive just for boys here in Sydney. She submitted an application for me without telling me or my parents, and I got in. Which isn't as impressive as it sounds—they took just about anyone who applied, and there weren't that many boys doing serious ballet back then. I think it's changed now."

"Right, now ballet is *overrun* with boys," Carly replied sarcastically.

"That first year I think there were only twenty of us," he went on, ignoring her retort. "From all over New South Wales, including a few other boys from the country. Talk about a building full of hormones. We were all gangly and pimply and we all had huge chips on our shoulders, especially the country boys, because we put up with so much shit at school for dancing. Everyone assumed we were gay, and they didn't take kindly to gay kids in those days. I think that program was a real eye-opener for a lot of us. Made us feel a bit less freakish. I'd never met another boy who did ballet until that summer. By the second day, I knew I wanted to go back every year, just to get away and to feel like I was normal for a few weeks."

"Did you? Go back?"

"I didn't have to. At the end of the summer they brought in some people from the ANB school, and they handed out a few full-time scholarships. I got one. So I went home to Springwood, packed up my things, came back to Sydney, and stayed all year. Only went home for Christmas and Easter breaks after that."

"Did your parents mind letting you go?"

He leaned back in his seat and glanced over at her, as though he was deciding how much more to tell her. Frankly, she was surprised she'd gotten this much out of him, relentless or not. After yesterday, though, a wall seemed to have come down.

"It's complicated," he said after a moment, and she made a buzzer sound.

"Errrhhhh, try again."

He gave her a rueful smile, as if she'd responded just as he'd expected. But when he spoke, there was no levity in his voice. "Honestly, I think they were relieved. I'd been pretty miserable at school, and I think Miss Rosemary explained to them that there was only so far I could go at a little local dance studio. And I was so eager to go, I didn't give much thought to what it would mean in the long term."

"What do you mean?"

"What do you mean, what do I mean?" Stalling again. She stared back at him, waiting, with a stony expression that she hoped said *nice try, but do better.*

"I mean I haven't lived with my parents since I was a kid. I barely went home, and they had my little sister to look after, so they didn't visit very often."

"Ah, so you're a big brother," Carly couldn't help but smile. Imperious, always right, exasperated, protective even when he was exasperated. Of course he was a big brother.

"Yeah. Nina. She's four years younger than me, so I haven't lived with her since she was ten. After school, I went straight to Europe, and I've been there ever since. They're still in Springwood, in the same house. I come home when I can, but there's so much of my life they weren't there for and that they don't understand. And that makes things . . . complicated."

"When are you seeing them?"

Nick paused. "I'm not sure. I might—" he checked his mirrors again and changed lanes, preparing to exit the highway.

"You might what?" she asked.

"I might not see them. I haven't told them I'm home."

"Yet," she said.

"What?"

"You haven't told them you're home yet. You're going to tell them, right? You came all this way."

"I came all this way for Marcus," he said stiffly, and she widened her eyes.

"You're not going to go home and see them?"

There was another pause. "It's—"

"Complicated, right," Carly finished. "So you've said."

He cut her a sharp look across the car as he took the exit, pulling them onto a two-lane road, but he didn't contradict her. There was something he wasn't telling her—yet—that much was obvious. Still, she decided not to press any further and busied herself with looking out window at the new landscape. The road crossed over a narrow winding river that was dotted with speedboats and even a few crew teams, and then it began to climb.

"What about you? Where's home for you?" Nick asked a few minutes later. Carly's ears had just popped.

"Depends on who you ask," she replied, leaning forward to fiddle with the air-conditioning.

"I'm asking you." She stuck her tongue out at him, and in response he gave her a remarkably accurate impression of her *nice try* face.

"New York City is home. Born and raised, and I'll probably die there, too. I live downtown, in Chinatown, in a crappy little apartment that I love and that my parents hate."

He raised his eyebrows curiously. "And where do your parents think you should live?"

"Uptown with them. Broadway at Seventy-Eighth Street." In the six-bedroom apartment where she'd grown up, knowing but not understanding just how abnormal their lives were. It wasn't until she got to the NYB school and became friends with Heather that she realized most eleven-year-olds in New York City didn't have a credit card to take cabs wherever they went or a housekeeper who kept their kitchen pantries stocked with gourmet snacks and bottled water from the Swiss Alps. Or that most families didn't have a house on Nantucket and a ski-in chalet in Vail. Or that most parents couldn't offer their grown children an apartment within an apartment, a little home inside their home with her own kitchen, bathroom, and private entrance.

Nick was looking at her appraisingly, probably trying to follow her train of thought. She didn't know how well he knew New York City, or whether "the Apthorp" would mean anything to him.

"Your parents are . . . comfortable?" he asked.

Carly snorted. "No, they're rich. The whole family is, including me, I guess. And comfortable. Actually, they've never been uncomfortable in their lives. Well, until I came along. I make them pretty damn uncomfortable."

"Why?"

"Too loud, too stubborn. They put me in ballet hoping it would make me quieter and more ladylike."

"And it worked like a charm," Nick chuckled.

"I am ladylike as fuck, thank you very much."

"That's definitely the first word that comes to mind when I think about you," he agreed sarcastically.

"I'm ladylike enough on stage, okay? Offstage, I like to do things my way. And they don't appreciate that."

"What does your way look like?"

She shrugged. "I like to fend for myself. It's not that I'm ungrateful. It's more that I know how lucky I am, and I think we only get so much luck in this life. I was born into mine, and now I want to do what I can with it. But I want to do it for myself, and I want to do it my way." She lifted her chin stubbornly, daring him to argue with her, but he didn't. Which was a good thing, because she'd had some version of this argument with her parents enough times to know how to win. Or at least wear someone down.

"Sounds reasonable enough to me. I'm guessing your parents don't feel the same way."

"They don't. If you ask them, they'll say that yes, they were born into money, but they've worked hard. They don't understand that their work has carried them further than everyone else's because of where they started. They don't seem to understand that hard work alone can't get a person to where they are. Or that even if they *didn't* work hard, they'd still be fine. Better than fine, because they'd still be wealthy. They don't get that. And they don't get me at all. So we have that in common, I guess," she added, with a half smile.

He was looking at her with the same kind of intensity she'd seen the first day he was photographing her, as though he was seeing her but also seeing past her. Trying to compose the picture around her. He turned back to the road but was silent for so long that she started to wonder if she'd said something to offend him. It certainly wouldn't be the first time.

"Does the company know about your parents?" he asked finally. Like he had put the picture together perfectly. Of course he had.

"It does. They used to give generously to the school and the capital fund and all the other worthy causes when I was still a student. After I graduated I asked them to redirect their giving to some other cause. It took some convincing, and I'm sure the company's development team wasn't happy about it, but NYB has plenty of rich donors, and I really wanted to—"

"Fend for yourself," he finished.

"Right," she said. "Isn't that what you've been doing all this time? Isn't that what everyone else does? It's what Heather's done most of her life. I want to be like everyone else."

He chuckled and shook his head, and she widened her eyes. "What? You think I'm naive? A poor little rich girl?"

"No, no," he replied. "Well, a little bit, but no. It's just, please don't take this the wrong way, but you're nothing like everyone else. I don't think you could be like everyone else if you tried."

She leaned over and put her elbow on the center console, closing the distance between them until she could see his pulse fluttering in his throat. He inhaled deeply, then looked down at her briefly, a smile in his blue-gray eyes.

"You know what Heather once said to me?" she said in a quiet, serious tone. "That the easiest way to get me to do something was to tell me that someone, somewhere, had decided that I couldn't."

"That sounds about right," he grinned.

"So tell me again that I can't."

There was a brief pause, and for a moment Carly worried that he wouldn't play along with her flirtatious bit.

"And watch you be like everyone else just to prove me wrong?" he eventually asked, his voice deeper and more serious than she'd anticipated. "Never."

Chapter 16

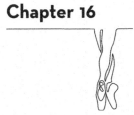

The road twisted and climbed, taking them through towns with names like Lapstone and Warimoo, and the charmingly named Knapsack Reserve. Carly wanted to pull over and investigate that one, but Nick insisted they keep moving. In each village, they drove through a small strip of stores—a café, a newsagent, a supermarket, a bottle shop, which she had learned was what Australians called a liquor store—before passing clusters of old houses and the occasional public school. Signs in each town informed her she was on Darug and Gandangara land, and as they kept climbing and one town gave way to the next, the forest that encroached on the scattered buildings became thicker and thicker.

After almost an hour of winding roads, Nick pulled off the highway, and a sign announced their arrival in Leura, the "Jewel in the Mountains' Crown," and Carly breathed a sigh of relief. Her knees were tight and achy, and she needed to pee.

"I loved this town as a kid," Nick said after they'd parked and found their way to the pretty little main street, a slope crowded with cafés and antique stores. "It looks exactly the same as I remember it, down to the quilt shop and the lolly shop. And the view of the valley." He gestured toward the bottom of the street where the bush took over again, and Carly could see down into a vast gully full of dense trees and dotted with orange terra-cotta roofs.

When Carly returned from the public restrooms, it was to find Nick with a coffee in each hand and his camera around his neck. Without the ocean breeze, it was even hotter up here than it was in Sydney, and she hadn't realized until she saw the sweating iced coffee that she was parched.

"Ready to work?" he asked, holding out the cup to her.

She took the coffee in one hand and gave him a mock salute with the other, and he led her down the street toward the bush.

"Remember my policy about going into dark alleyways with strange men?" she asked as the shops and pedestrians dropped away.

"I do," he said.

"I have the same policy about going into deserted forests with strange men," she said.

"Well, this isn't deserted, it's a very well-known track to a very well-known lookout," he replied, gesturing toward a sign that read Bridal Veil Lookout. There was a group of outdoorsy-looking people walking their way, having apparently just come from said lookout. Which sounded very pretty, and very on theme.

"You're still a strange man," she said as they turned down the path, and she was rewarded by the sight of Nick Jacobs *sticking his tongue out* at her. Like he'd been bodysnatched or something. Or like he was just in a rare good mood.

I want whatever you have. Whatever you can give me.

The track snaked down through the ever-thickening forest, the many gum trees that hung over them still and silent in the unmoving air. In addition to their own footsteps, she could hear the high pitched trill of some unseen bird, and the throaty, reproachful cawing of another bird that almost sounded like it was arguing with the first. As they walked, the grasses and ferns along the path occasionally rustled with sudden movement.

"Just small marsupials," Nick said when she started and stepped into the middle of the path. "Or lizards."

"Or deadly snakes," she added, picturing a snake taking a bite out of her ankle and wishing she'd worn something other than shorts.

"Nah, if it was a deadly snake, you'd be dead by now," he said, as if that was supposed to be reassuring.

After about ten minutes of steady decline, they came to a set of uneven stone steps with a handrail that had been drilled into the rock. Nick climbed down first, then turned at the bottom of the steps and waited as she stepped down carefully. As she reached the last few steps, he held out his hand, and she took it, letting him guide her down onto a steel viewing platform that hung improbably off the face of the mountain.

He gestured to her right, and, following his gaze, she gasped.

About a hundred feet away, a waterfall was tumbling and spraying over the rocks and into the valley below. The water was narrow and dense at the top, but it widened as it fell, stretching thin and diaphanous over the rocks, looking just like delicate, shimmering lace. Bridal Veil Falls. The mountain was too high to see where the water landed, but Carly knew that somewhere in the dense green eucalyptus forest below them, there must have been a creek or a river flowing through the enormous valley that was laid out in front of them, interrupted by rolling tree-covered hills and dotted with jagged rock formations. Above it, an ultramarine sky stretched forever, cloudless and triumphant.

"Damn," Carly whispered. "Beats the Lincoln Center fountain."

"Say cheese," Nick said beside her, and she turned her head, grinning. He was waiting with his camera up, and she heard it click rapidly.

She turned back to the waterfall and watched it for a few minutes, taking in the sound of tumbling water and bird calls, and the smell of earth and eucalyptus. And then the sight of Nick. Face half-obscured by his camera, his forehead visible but damp with sweat, his hands wrapped around the device like it was a part of him. A natural extension of his muscular forearms and long, agile fingers. Beneath it, she could see half of his smile, just his full bottom lip. She wanted to bite it.

But instead, she slipped off her sneakers and yanked off her sweaty socks, and walked to the very end of the viewing platform. Just like at the Freshwater pool, there was a railing here. She fanned her feet out into first position and slowly lifted one foot into passé, then extended it until it landed on the railing. She heard the camera click again, and heard Nick padding behind her to find the best angle, and after a while she rotated her hips and pivoted on one foot until she was facing the spectacular waterfall and the barre was holding her foot up in an arabesque. Then she lifted her arms into a high fifth position and pressed the ball of her other foot down until she was on relevé.

"That's perfect," Nick said from behind her. "Can you lift it off the railing?"

She was going to retort that if she somehow fell off this little lookout and down the side of a mountain, she'd haunt him forever, but instead she pulled up through her obliques and lifted her foot until it hovered a few inches above the warm metal. Peering down into the valley, with just the ball of her foot tethering her to the earth, she felt like she was almost floating.

Nick walked around her, clicking away and murmuring encouragement, and she let the sound wash over her, along with the birds and the water and occasional rustle of a feeble breeze in the leaves.

Forty minutes later, though, her face was beaded with sweat and no longer fit to be photographed. Nick had shot her from every conceivable angle, in a range of positions, though he'd refused to let her do any jumps, muttering something about the platform giving out and her haunting him forever.

"No more," she groaned, dragging herself up off the ground and brushing dirt and pieces of leaves off her knees. Hunched over and sweaty, she paused when she heard the camera click and looked up at him.

"Don't get this," she frowned up at him.

"But you look so graceful and elegant," he chuckled, but he put the camera down.

"Can we please find some shade, and some water? Maybe a nice cold beer?"

"In a second," he said.

"We've taken every photo it's possible to take, Nick. What more could you want?" she whined as he lifted his camera up over his head and set it down carefully on the steps.

He turned around and walked across the platform in a few short, determined strides and didn't stop until they were face to face and the railing was prodding lightly at her back.

"Oh, I see," she said, with a knowing smile. All thoughts of shade and icy beer vanished as his hands found her hips and pulled them toward his. His gaze was as hot and intense as the sun on her shoulders, and as much as she wanted to hold it, to stare back until he broke first, she wanted his mouth on hers more.

When she got it, when her tongue slipped between his sweat-salty lips and claimed his mouth and he pulled her even closer, until their damp bodies were flush against each other, she had a fleeting, absurd thought. *I could get used to this*. Which was ridiculous, she knew. Whatever Nick said, whatever he thought he wanted from her, this arrangement of theirs had an expiration date. In two weeks the wedding would be over, and she'd go back to New York, back to real life, just in time for Nick to realize that he wanted more from her than she could ever give him. Before she had to watch him be disappointed, before he could go back on his word that he'd take anything she had and didn't need more, she'd be gone. It was a perfect arrangement, really. Heavy on making out in beautiful public places, light on any Carly-esque failures. And if her climbing follower count was anything to go by, it would be a professionally fruitful arrangement, too.

After a few minutes, he pulled away, panting and hard, and

swallowed with what looked like a lot of effort. She watched his Adam's apple bob and resisted the urge to lick the stubbled, salty skin there.

"We should go," he murmured, undercutting his point somewhat by putting a hand in her hair and tugging lightly until her head tipped back and he could kiss her where her neck met her jaw.

"You first," she groaned, squinting against the sun. "Don't we have cocktail testing to do?"

His only reply was a growl against her skin.

"A compelling counterargument," she replied, putting a hand on each of his shoulders and pushing him away. "Come on, Heather and Mucus are counting on us."

With a reluctant chuckle, he took a few steps back, then retrieved his camera from the steps, and they returned the way they came. But not before she'd taken one last look at the falls and the valley, wondering if she'd ever smell eucalyptus again without thinking of Nick's lips on her skin.

They climbed back up the hill to Leura's main drag, and Nick scrolled through his photos as they walked. He'd gotten some great shots, and some that could be improved with editing. Certainly a few that were worthy of his portfolio. Behind him, Carly was checking this morning's Instagram posts and reading him some of the more effusive comments. Her follower count was steadily rising, and they hadn't had a squabble in almost twenty-four hours. It was hard to bicker with their tongues in each other's mouths.

"Listen to this one: 'This photo belongs on a billboard or an ad for Australia.' Pretty cool, right?"

Nick nodded, still scrolling back to the beginning of the after-noon's work. "Very cool, and let's hope that Tourism Australia agrees with—"

"Nick?"

He raised his head at the new voice, and his fingers slipped around the camera. Nina. What the hell was Nina doing here?

"Uh, hi," he said awkwardly. His sister stared back at him, mouth half open, eyebrows scrunched together in confusion.

"Uh, hi, yourself. Aren't you meant to be in Paris right now?"

"I . . . Marcus is getting married," he said, running a hand over his hair.

"I heard. I just figured you weren't gonna come home for it. After last time—"

"Well, I did," Nick said, a little too abruptly, and he felt, rather than saw, Carly's frown and the sharp sideways look she threw at him.

He forced himself to meet Nina's eyes, which were the same colour and shape as his own. She'd cut her hair to her shoulders since he'd seen her last, and it was darker, too. She was looking up at him, an expression of mingled confusion, expectation, and disappointment on her face. Nick felt sweat gathering at the base of his spine, his T-shirt clinging to his skin there, and knew it wasn't all from the summer heat. Nina's eyes darted from him to Carly, then back again.

"This is Carly Montgomery. She's the maid of honour, from New York City. We're, euh, running some wedding errands and working on a project. Carly, this is Nina. My sister."

He watched as Carly gave a little nod of confirmation, as if she'd suspected just by looking at Nina they were family. "The horse girl," Carly smiled, extending her hand. Nina looked confused for a moment, then shifted her shopping bags to shake it.

Nick watched uncomfortably as his sister performed the polite, perfunctory pleasantries with Carly, asking her how she was enjoying Sydney, where she was staying, what sights she'd seen so far. All the while, he could feel her watching him in her peripheral vision. Nina lived a few towns down the mountain, in Blaxland, and worked as a nurse at a dental practice in the city, and he hadn't expected to run into her here in Leura. Then again, he realized, shame creeping up his spine, regret squeezing his chest, he had no idea how his younger sister spent her weekends. For all he knew, she went shopping up here every week.

"What, euh, what are you doing up here?" he asked, once Carly had finished telling Nina that she'd eat a lamington for every meal if she could.

Nina raised an eyebrow and levelled a cool look at him. She looked annoyed, and hurt. "I live here, Nick. What are *you* doing up here?"

"I told you, we're running errands and taking some photos," he said. He'd wanted to take Carly to one of his favourite mountain towns, the most picturesque place he could think of, but he realized now it had been a huge mistake, a stupid risk.

"That's not what I . . . *argh*," Nina replied, cutting herself off in frustration. "Carly, would you please give us a minute?" she asked, without taking her eyes off Nick. Nick felt Carly's questioning glance and answered it with a stiff nod.

"I'll go get some coffees. Nina, do you want one?" When his sister shook her head, Carly hoisted her bag up over her shoulder, walked quickly to the nearest café, and disappeared inside. Nick watched her go, but his attention snapped back to Nina as she spoke.

"Were you seriously going to come home, after all this time, and not tell any of us you were back?" she asked, shifting her bags again so she could put her hands on her hips.

"Neens," he started, but the nickname only made her glower more fiercely.

"Don't 'Neens' me, Nicholas. Answer the question."

"I was going to text you; I just wanted to get through the wedding first. I'm staying down near Marcus's mum's place, and I've been busy with—"

"Yes, errands and projects, I heard you." Errands, projects, and the human hurricane who had been distracting him from both, and from how hard and complicated it felt to be home after so many years. Distracting him enough that he would take her to this place where they risked running into all the things he'd been hiding from.

"I was going to text you when it was over, when I had a little more time." She didn't look like she believed him, but it was the truth. He'd thought about it as they'd driven up to Leura, Carly's "yet" fresh in his mind.

"Uh-huh," Nina said, the sound dripping in skepticism. He glanced over her shoulder at the coffee shop, hoping Carly would emerge soon. She might be a hand grenade, but for once she wasn't the angriest woman in his vicinity, and he wanted her back beside him.

"I was planning to text you, I promise, but like you said, last time . . ."

"Last time was between you and Dad and Mum, not me. I wasn't even there. Don't cut me out just because things are hard between you three. You and me, we're a whole separate thing. Or I thought we were."

Nick ran his hand over his hair again and sighed. She was right. As stilted and infrequent as his contact had been with his parents since his last trip, things had been okay with Nina. They texted; they did occasional video chats. He sent her birthday cards, mailing them a month in advance to make sure they got to her on time. When she called him, she provided vague updates about his parents' lives—Dad had retired and joined the local men's shed, Mum's ladies' bushwalking group was planning a big trip to Victoria—but mostly they talked about safe topics. Work, travel, TV, podcasts.

"I'm sorry. I should have told you I was coming."

She shrugged, the paper bags at her side crackling with the movement. "How would you like it if I came to Paris and didn't tell you I was there?"

He tipped his head to the side, a smile sneaking into his voice. "Who would you stay with? Who would you force to go to a rave with you even though they had company class in the morning and needed more than an hour and a half of sleep?"

Her face cracked into a sly grin, possibly against her will. The whole family had come to visit him in Munich for his mum's fiftieth, and Nina, newly eighteen and celebrating the end of high school, had stayed an extra week, dragging him out on the town every night. The morning after that rave, no amount of spotting could have kept him from feeling dizzy and nauseated during pirouettes. He'd never let her hear the end of it.

"Fair point. But I don't do raves anymore. I'm a tired old lady."

Nick rolled his eyes. "You're not even thirty."

"How long are you staying?"

"Up here? We're not. We were about to drive back down to Sydney."

Nina gave him a look that said she knew he'd understood her question, even if he'd chosen to answer a different one.

"I don't really know yet. Work is—"

"Skim cappuccino for you, and an American iced coffee for me," Carly called from a few metres up the hill, and a second later she appeared at his side.

"Thanks," he said automatically, giving her a grateful smile. She'd saved him from having to invent some lie to tell Nina about his work. Or worse, from telling her the truth. And as far as he knew, her career was on track, steady and reliable. Unlike his. Their fingers brushed as Carly handed over the warm cup, and Nick watched as Nina's eyes flicked from their hands to his face, then to Carly's.

"How's Delphine going?" she asked pointedly. Shit. Yet another thing he'd hidden from her. Nick swallowed, then glanced sideways at Carly. What choice did he have? He couldn't stand here and lie about still being with Delphine right in front of the woman he'd kissed barely half an hour ago. He looked down at his sister and told her the truth.

"I don't know. We broke up a few months ago," he said, keeping his voice level and matter of fact. Which it was. It was a matter of fact that he and Delphine Delacroix were no longer together. That she no longer loved him. And that since he'd met Carly, since Carly had half killed him with her luggage trolley, he'd barely thought about his ex-girlfriend.

"Crap, I'm sorry, I didn't know," Nina said, and he nodded. She didn't know because he hadn't told her.

"It's okay. I'm okay." She raised an eyebrow and looked like she was about to ask about him and Carly, but he was too quick for her. "We should get going; we've got another wedding errand to take care of tonight. But I'll call you after the wedding and we'll hang out, okay?"

"Wait, you should stay for dinner. I'm going to Mum and Dad's. I know it's short notice, but they can make enough for two more."

Nick's stomach somersaulted and he felt his pulse speed. "Neens, I can't. Not today."

"Come on, please? I'll be there. And I know they'll be happy to see you, even if . . . even if things are off."

"I—"

"You came all this way and didn't tell us. Now you're not even going to come home for dinner?"

Fucking hell, Nina Elizabeth Jacobs was good. Were all younger siblings like this? Did they all come out of the womb with guilt-tripping, will-bending genes that didn't stop working even if you lived on the other side of the world? Nick looked over at Carly, who was watching him expectantly, the late afternoon sun washing her face in warm, low light and turning loose strands of her hair into fiery gold.

"Fine, fine. I guess cocktail testing can wait." Even though he'd love to be a little bit buzzed for what was about to happen.

"Great!" Nina chirped, not even bothering to conceal her self-satisfied smile. "I'll text them now and pick up an extra bottle of wine on the way there, just in case. I'll see you soon. You still remember how to get home, right?"

"Yes," he said irritably. Though perhaps he'd conveniently forget and just keep driving down the mountain.

"Well, call me if you forget. Again." Nina fished around in her purse and pulled out her car keys. "Carly, any dietary restrictions?"

"No, I eat anything," Carly said distractedly, looking curiously between them. Nick groaned inwardly as he thought about how much he'd have to explain to her and how unpleasant dinner was going to be.

"Great!" Nina said again, and Nick wanted to scream at how happy she looked at the idea of the whole family being together again, when the same thought made his stomach clench and anxiety grip at his throat.

"See you soon," he said weakly as she turned and walked up the hill towards her car.

She waved over her shoulder, keys jingling in her hand. "See you at home."

Chapter 17

Carly waited to speak until they were both buckled into the baking-hot car, but her patience didn't extend much further than that.

"Do you want to tell me what that was about?"

"No." Nick turned the ignition with more force than was necessary and turned the AC up so that the vents blasted warm air into their faces. Carly lowered her window, keeping her eyes on him. His cheeks were flushed, and she was willing to bet it was more than just the heat of the stuffy car.

"Yeah, I wasn't really asking. What's going on? And if you tell me one more time that it's 'complicated,' I swear to God."

He leaned back in the driver's seat, eyes closed and jaw clenched. He looked so tense, and so miserable, and she had an urge to reach over and stroke the stubbled skin along his jawline until it released. Kiss his pinked cheeks until their normal color returned.

She reached over and turned the fans down so he couldn't pretend not to hear her. "You can tell me. Think of all the things you know about me. It can't possibly be worse than that." She let out a quiet chuckle, thinking of all the things he knew about her now, and could have sworn she saw the side of his mouth twitch.

"Let's try this," she started again. "How long's the drive to your parents' place?"

"About twenty minutes," he said, almost under his breath.

"Okay, so talk until we get there, and then I won't ask any more questions. Come on, you have to tell me what I'm walking into."

He turned his head, looking across the front seat at her. "Do we have to go? Can't you suddenly get sick or something? Or realize you forgot something really important in Sydney?"

She shook her head. "And piss Nina off, again? No, thank you."

At the mention of his sister, he pressed the back of his head into the headrest and sighed at the ceiling. "For Nina."

"For Nina," Carly agreed. She'd watched as a series of emotions had washed over the other woman's face, so like Nick's in its shape and coloring. Surprise, then disappointment, frustration, hurt, and anger, all expressions she recognized after a week in Nick's company. Except usually *she* was the one causing them. And she'd watched as Nick told Nina the truth about Delphine, taking a breath to steel himself first, but then delivering the information without any fuss. He might still be hiding the truth from his best friend, but at least he'd told his sister.

Nick lifted his head and turned on his blinker, then pulled out of their parking spot. He was silent for a few minutes, and she thought he might simply ignore their agreement, but then he turned the car onto the highway and sighed.

"You asked me earlier if my parents were happy to let me go away for school," he started, and she swiveled in her seat so she could look at him as he spoke. "They didn't mind that part, but when it was time to graduate and audition for jobs overseas, they balked. They were willing to let me go as far as Sydney, but Europe or the States was too much for them. I tried to make them understand that it was the only way to find a full-time gig, but they wouldn't listen. They wanted me to stay here and try to find dance work closer to home."

"But you ended up in Europe."

Nick's hands clenched around the steering wheel. "I auditioned behind their backs. Lied to the school, told them my parents were fine with me auditioning. And when I got the offer from Munich, I accepted it without telling Mum and Dad. When I told them I'd signed the contract and the company had already sent me a plane ticket, they were furious. My dad was a primary school principal, and so it takes a lot for him to lose his temper, but when he does . . . it can be downright scary." Carly watched him talk, surprised with every emerging detail that the uptight, rule-abiding Nick she knew had ever done something so rebellious.

"But there wasn't much they could do," he went on, sounding grim but a little proud. "I was eighteen; they couldn't stop me from going. So, I left. Mum bought me a calling card and we talked on the phone every weekend, even though I barely got more than a few words a week out of Dad that first year. And I always told them I was fine. I had to be fine, even when . . . even when I wasn't fine. Because I'd been so insistent about leaving."

Because he'd broken their hearts when he left, Carly thought. She thought about how proud Nick was, how stubborn. She understood a little, now, why he was like this. Why he didn't want his best friend to know his girlfriend had dumped him. And why he didn't want to call his parents and tell them he was home. She had a sudden urge to fake sick so he could keep driving, take them all the way back to Sydney where he wouldn't have to look all this ugly history in the face. But then she remembered the delight on Nina's face when he agreed to dinner. Nina seemed just as stubborn as he was, but at least they were on speaking terms. If Nina was there, and she was there, together they could get Nick through one meal.

"So, that was it? You haven't talked since?"

Nick glanced at her, the warm evening light throwing shadows across his face, making his cheekbones appear even sharper than usual.

"No, things got a little better. They came to Munich after I'd been there for a few years, and I've come home once or twice. I was here when Nina graduated from uni. It wasn't as bad as it was when I left, but it was . . . tense."

Carly stole a look at the clock on the dashboard. She didn't know how long they'd been driving, but she suspected they didn't have much farther to go. A moment later, Nick confirmed her suspicions, turning off the highway and driving slowly along a tree-lined street that took them down the ridge.

"But then . . . Nina mentioned last time?"

Nick heaved a deep sigh and didn't say anything for a long moment. "It was five or six years ago. It was really cold for September that year, and I had to borrow a beanie from Dad. The night before I left, I went to give it back to him, and he said, no, no, hang on to it for next time. They always talk about when I come back, when I come back. Like they're just waiting for me to come home with my tail between my legs. Admit that I was wrong when I was eighteen and ambitious and scared shitless but willing to give it a go, you know? It was like that the whole trip, even at Nina's graduation ceremony. Mum said something about how when I come back I could go to uni here and get a degree, too." He flicked the turn signal hard and they continued down the hill, past small brick houses with terra-cotta roofs, early evening sunlight glinting off their front windows.

"So Dad said, keep the beanie for when you come back, and I just lost it. I told him that I didn't know when I'd be back again, and maybe I wouldn't ever come back."

Carly exhaled loudly.

"Yeah. I meant that I didn't know if I'd ever move back for good, not that I'd never come see them again. And I expected him to lose his temper like he did when I was a kid, but instead he just looked . . . so hurt. Like I'd said the worst thing he could think of, but he thought about it all the time. I felt shitty, but I was so mad. It always feels like they're just waiting for me to fail."

Carly stared. She knew that feeling. And she liked to think she'd pissed her parents off more than a few times, but Nick had her beat here. "You were right, that is complicated."

"Yeah, it is. So, that's what you're walking into. Because my darling sister, who stayed here and only ever moved two towns down the mountain, and went out and got a job they actually understand, insisted that we come to dinner. And because I love her, and because she's a world champion guilt-tripper, here we are."

He pulled the car over and threw it into park. They'd stopped in front of a squat brick house, painted pale green with a terra-cotta roof and a white front door. The front garden was neat and ordered, and the hedges separating the property from the street looked freshly trimmed.

"This is home?"

"This is where my parents live."

"Okay, this is where your parents live. And they are?"

"Rod and Narelle. He was a principal, she still works part-time as a bookkeeper for local businesses."

Carly nodded, tucking the names away. There was a pause, and she watched as Nick stared at the house. "And we are?"

Nick looked at her, his face a mixture of gratitude and dread, and she couldn't help but reach across the front seat and give his hand a brief, encouraging squeeze. "We're best man and maid of honor. Business partners. Friends. Maybe lie if they ask how we met."

Carly pulled her hand away. She shouldn't feel let down by his answer. That was what they were, after all. Best man and maid of honor. Uptight asshole and ballet brat. Who had made each other come repeatedly this morning, who had kissed at a beautiful lookout barely an hour ago. But he was right. They were business partners who were helping each other out. Tonight, helping him out meant sitting next to him while he faced his parents and maybe lying about how they met. She could do that.

"Understood. Let's go," she said, undoing her seatbelt and turning to open the door. "Oh, but Nick?" she turned back and gave him a sly grin. "If you need me to run anyone over with a luggage cart, you just say the word."

In the five years since his last visit, the outside of the house had barely changed. The garden was still neat as a pin, the brass knocker on the front door still gleamed in the fading sunlight. And standing on the welcome mat still made his heart race. He'd been grateful to see Nina's car already parked outside; at least he wouldn't have to face his parents alone.

Beside him, Carly reached forward and lifted the knocker.

"It'll be okay. And if it's not, I *can* fake sick," she said over her shoulder. She put a hand over her stomach and faked a convincing gag, and he felt the tightness in his chest ease slightly. Not alone, even if Nina wasn't there.

Carly tapped the door three times, and it opened almost immediately. There stood his mother, an apron tied around her waist, her grey-streaked hair clipped up in a familiar twist. Her face was more lined in person than it looked on their rare FaceTime calls, especially when she smiled, which she did as she took the two of them in. A strained smile, but a smile nonetheless. Nick's throat was dry and tight, and he attempted to clear it before he spoke.

"Hi, Mum."

"You're a sight for sore eyes," she said, stepping forward and hugging him snugly around his waist. A little taken aback, he stood frozen in her arms, then wrapped his own arms around her shoulders and squeezed gently. She sniffed quietly, stepped back and hastily wiped her eyes with the backs of her hands, and ushered them inside.

"Welcome home," she said, sounding pleased. "And you must be Carly."

"Hi, Mrs. Jacobs, nice to meet you. And thanks for having me," Carly said, flashing a wide and toothy smile as she followed Nick into the front hallway. They'd replaced the carpeting since he was here last; it had been beige for as long as he could remember, and now it was a pleasant powder blue.

"How did you know her name?" Nick asked, glancing up from the carpet to take in the familiar art on the walls: a photo of his parents on their wedding day, a photo of him and Nina after an end-of-year ballet concert, and that long printed poem he'd liked so much as a kid. His chest constricted at the sight, at once alien and achingly familiar.

"Nina," his mum shrugged. Of course. Nina kept him updated on their lives, and she served as a go-between in the other direction, too. For the first time, it occurred to him that shuttling bare-bones information between people who barely spoke must have been a strain on his sister. If it weren't for her, he'd know almost nothing about his parents' lives, and they'd know very little about his.

His mum put her hands in the pocket of her apron and looked him up and down.

"You've filled out a bit," she said, sounding pleased. "Retirement suits you."

Nick felt irritation prick at his gut. Of course she thought that. They'd been waiting for him to retire ever since his career began. And she had no idea how little retirement suited him, how he'd been floundering ever since he stopped dancing. He pushed the bitter thoughts aside and tried to smile back.

"It's a new challenge," he said noncommittally. "What's for dinner?"

"Roast chook, lots of veggies. The usual."

Nick smiled despite himself as he and Carly followed her down the hall. No one roasted a chicken like his mother. For years in Paris he'd tried and failed to replicate it. He'd brined, he'd spatchcocked, he'd bought freshly harvested rosemary from the shamelessly flirtatious old woman who ran the herb stall at his local street market, but he'd never been able to get it right. He breathed deeply and let the scent of the bird in the oven fill his chest as they arrived in the kitchen.

They found his father reading the newspaper as Nina set the table around him. Nick felt his smile drop as Rod glanced up from the paper and looked him up and down.

"Nicholas. I thought you were never coming back." Nick heard Nina's disappointed sigh, and just managed not to let out one of his own. Why had he let her guilt him into this? Why hadn't he insisted on getting in the car and driving back to Sydney, back to safety?

"Hi, Dad," he managed. There was no point in returning fire so early. He'd get through the evening by making pleasant conversation with his mother, and then he and Carly would get the hell out of here. When he didn't say anything more, his father simply looked at him across the table. Nick looked back, noting the toll the last few years had taken on Rod's solid, square face. His beard was more salt than pepper now, and his neat dark brown hair had thinned noticeably. But even though he was retired, he still looked every bit the school principal, leveling a cool and assessing gaze at Nick as though he was wondering how many lunchtime detentions to give him. After a silent moment, Rod lowered his eyes back to his paper and turned the page. Well, Nick hadn't expected a warm reception for himself, so he had no business feeling disappointed. But his dad could at least acknowledge Carly.

He was about to introduce her himself when she spoke, her grin back in place, and her voice sweeter than he'd ever heard it.

"Hello, Mr. Jacobs, I'm Carly Montgomery. It's so nice to meet you. Thank you for welcoming me into your home." She stepped forwards and thrust her hand into his father's peripheral vision.

Rod looked up at her in surprise, unable to ignore her hand when it was right in front of his face. He shook it briefly, apparently too taken aback to do otherwise.

"Hello, Ms. Mont— Er" he started.

"Montgomery," she supplied, her voice syrupy sharp. "I'm Heather and Marcus's maid of honour and Nick's business partner." Rod frowned up at her, then glanced over at Nick, who was suppressing a grateful smile. Then he dropped her hand and went back to what looked like the real estate section.

Across the table, Nina had paused in the middle of setting out cutlery to watch the interaction, and she looked up at Nick with a smirk. Her eyes widened as if to say, *She's a live one*, and he tipped his head ever so slightly to the side in reply. *Oh, you have no idea.*

Carly watched as his father turned the page again, her smile stretching so wide it looked like it hurt, and a thrill of mingled delight and dread shot through Nick. This could go very wrong, very easily. He of all people knew how quickly Carly Montgomery could explode when someone disrespected her. But when she turned to face Nick, her smile shrank to something genuine and reassuring. She handed him her bag and joined his mum in the kitchen.

"Can I help with anything, Mrs. Jacobs? I'm not much of a cook, but I can chop with the best of them."

A few moments later, his mum had handed her a knife and a salad bowl and set her to work chopping vegetables. Nina went back to setting the table, watching Rod pointedly as she worked. When he didn't look up from his paper, she rolled her eyes and picked up the bottle of wine in the centre of the table.

"Wine?" she asked Nick.

"Please," he muttered, reaching over and taking the bottle from her. "But what are you going to drink?"

She giggled, and his heart lifted at the sound. In the kitchen, Carly glanced over her shoulder and caught his eye. She held his gaze and flicked her eyebrows up, checking on him, and he raised the bottle of wine in her direction. In response, she lifted the knife, looking beautiful and threatening and like a woman who would cheerfully slide a blade between someone's ribs, smiling the whole time. He'd seen Carly detonate before, but tonight he had a feeling he'd get to watch her kill with kindness.

For the next ten minutes, he and Nina sat on the couch, drinking their wine and chatting about her life. Her work, her friends, the true crime podcast she'd been listening to on her commute into the city. His dad sat at the table and ignored them, and barely looked up when Carly deposited the salad bowl on the table in front of him with that same rictus grin on her face.

"Thank you," he murmured, so quietly that Nick barely heard him.

"Oh, you're so very welcome, Mr. Jacobs," she said, in a sticky-sweet voice that said *I definitely didn't poison this salad.* As she straightened up, she caught Nick's eye and winked, and he squashed another grateful smile. Carly Montgomery was A Lot, but tonight, it was just the right amount. He looked back at Nina, who had been in the middle of telling him about how the serial killer in the podcast was eventually caught, and found her watching him curiously.

"Is there something you want to tell me?" she asked, almost under her breath, but a second later the over timer dinged and his mum pulled the chicken out of the oven. *Saved by the chook*, Nick thought as she heaved it onto a plate and carried it to the table. Nick stood, but not before Nina rolled her eyes again in a knowing way that told him he wasn't off the hook at all. Carly trailed behind his mum, carrying the carving fork and another large knife, and they all took their seats as his mum began to carve the bird and his father folded up the newspaper and tossed it into the basket next to the sideboard.

"That smells amazing, Mum," Nick said, inhaling deeply again. And it really did. The spices and the crisp, browned skin, it smelled perfect. It smelled like—fuck, his chest was tight—it smelled like home. He swallowed hard and busied himself serving Carly.

"It really does smell amazing, Mrs. Jacobs," Carly agreed, as a drumstick landed on her plate. "I haven't had a homemade roast chicken in years."

"You're too kind," his mum said, waving the compliment away as she served herself salad. "And these vegetables are very well chopped."

"Well, I'm glad I didn't screw up the one thing I know how to do in the kitchen. Though there was a fifty-fifty chance I was going to lose a finger and bleed all over the counter."

Nina laughed, and Nick felt his shoulders relax a little even as his father silently served himself and began eating.

"Fortunately, I know first aid," Nina said. "And better a finger than a toe when you're a dancer. You are a dancer, I assume?"

"Sure am. So I need all ten toes for now. But once I retire I can take up knife juggling, just like I've always wanted."

Nina and Narelle both chuckled. Nothing from his father, as Nick had expected.

"Where in America do you dance, Carly?" his mum asked, after a quick, tense glance at Rod. At least she was trying.

"New York Ballet. I've been there my whole career, so, thirteen years now. And I was at the school before that."

"Wow, that's a top-notch company, isn't it? Very impressive," his mum nodded. "And do you like living in New York?"

"I've never lived anywhere else," Carly shrugged. "I don't think I ever want to."

"So you grew up in New York," his father said suddenly. It was a statement, not a question. All four other sets of eyes at the table swung towards him as he set his cutlery down and looked Carly full in the face for the first time. Nick's shoulders tightened again at the tone of his father's voice, firm and ready for a fight.

"Yes, born and raised," Carly said, her pride audible even through the tight smile she was reserving just for him.

"And your parents, they still live there? Nearby?"

"*Rod*," his mother hissed out of the corner of her mouth, but he ignored her.

"They do. On the same subway line, in fact."

"And how do you think they would feel if you packed up one day and moved to the other side of the world without telling them?"

"Dad, come on," Nina said. When he didn't respond, keeping his eyes fixed on Carly, Nina shook her head and took a large swig of wine.

Carly glanced at Nick, who had already opened his mouth to tell her she didn't have to answer the question. But she placed her hand on his, just like she'd done in the car earlier.

"My parents want me to be happy and successful, Mr. Jacobs." Nick was impressed by how level her voice was, even though she must be furious by now. "They're not interested in holding me back. And if I had to go to the other side of the world to have the career I wanted to have, they'd want to support me."

Financially, at least. Nick knew full well that her parents barely understood her decision to move to the other end of Manhattan, but he appreciated her willingness to stray from the absolute truth for him.

His father looked unmoved, but he didn't reply immediately, and Nina jumped into the silence.

"Nick, why don't you tell us about—"

"And how do you think they would feel if you stayed away for years, Ms. Montgomery," his dad interrupted, in full principal mode now, "and threatened to never come home again?"

"Rod, that's enough," his mum said, louder this time. She shot a look of mingled apology and exasperation at Nick. "You know that's not what Nicholas meant. You were both angry, like you are now, and you said things you shouldn't have said." Nick wanted to agree with her, though part of him never wanted to come home again if this was what it was going to be like. But he said nothing, and she kept talking.

"But for heaven's sake, it was years ago, and Nicholas has come home, and now that he's retired, maybe he'll stay a while. Or forever," she added hopefully. "You can be a photographer anywhere, after all."

Nick's mind went numb with rage, and for a moment all he could do was stare at his mother. He blinked, trying to muster up a response, but Carly had found one first. When she spoke, her voice hot and furious, every ounce of sugar and syrup evaporated.

"Your son went out into the world when he was basically still a child and managed to find a job in one of the best companies in one of the most competitive industries in the world. He held on to that job and was so good at it that he was promoted within just a few years, then got *another* job at the oldest and most respected ballet company on the whole planet. And then he retired and carved out an entirely new career in *another* extremely competitive industry, where he's absolutely killing it, and—"

"Carly, it's okay, just—" Nick started, his cheeks warm from a miserable cocktail of gratitude and shame. He appreciated that she was defending him, but the thought of her defending a lie—a lie he'd let her believe—made his skin crawl. He shook his head, trying to get her to stop, but he should have known that once she started, there was no stopping her. She pushed her chair back and stood, back rigid and knees locked.

"No, it's not okay. It's not okay at all! They should be proud of you! You worked so hard for this, you sacrificed so much, and maybe you've done things differently from how they wanted you to do it, but you're fucking *doing it*, Nick, and you're good at it. And they should respect that!" She glared at his father, who was staring up at her with his fork suspended a few centimetres above his plate. Nick glanced at his mother, whose eyes were glassy. Next to her, Nina was clutching her wine glass and watching Carly with a mix of alarm and awe.

Carly turned to his Dad, face alight with righteous fury. "Your son is talented. Really, really talented. I mean, do you know how good you have to be to be a *ballet photographer* in *France*? The country that invented ballet *and* photography? Most parents would kill for a kid like this, someone who's serious and smart and successful at whatever they decide to do—"

"Carly, let it go," Nick said, louder this time. "You don't have to— Let's just go." He got to his feet, heart racing with adrenaline but his limbs heavy.

"Yeah, let's go," Carly agreed, looking down at him, eyes blazing. Her cheeks were pink under her freckles, and her chest rose and fell with her rapid breaths. She grabbed her bag from the back of her chair and tossed it over her shoulder, then threw one last, disgusted look at his father. "I feel sick."

She turned on her heel and marched out of the kitchen, and Nick followed, a little dazed, as she stalked down the hall to the front door. He'd never been one for storming out, but maybe Carly was onto something. This felt damn good. She wrenched open the front door, and he was about to follow her through it when Nina came dashing down the hallway calling his name.

"Go, I'll meet you in the car," he told Carly. She looked for a moment like she was going to ignore him, but then she turned and marched down the front steps and threw herself into the front seat.

"I'm sorry about them," Nina said quietly, once Carly was out of earshot. She looked almost as miserable as he felt. "And about him, especially. I don't know what his problem is. I've tried to talk to him about it. I warned him before you came, but you know how stubborn he is."

"It's okay, Neens. You can't fix this. I love that you tried, but it's not your job, okay?"

She nodded, her eyes watering. "We really miss you. I really miss you."

Nick swallowed. "I miss you, too. Come here."

He pulled her into a tight hug and kissed the top of her head. When she pulled away, he saw tear tracks streaking down her cheeks.

"Come back soon?"

Nick opened his mouth to answer but couldn't find any words. How could he promise that? When he didn't know where his life was going, and when this was what coming home felt like?

"I—I'll try." Even as he said it, the promise felt like a lie, but she looked reassured by it, and her hopeful little nod made his heart splinter. He gave her another quick hug, inhaled the scent of chicken one last time, and left the house.

He found Carly in the front seat, still radiating anger.

"Let's go back to Sydney," she said, once he was buckled in.

"I've got a better idea." He didn't want to be driving right now. "Let's go find a hotel and get very, very drunk."

Chapter 18

Thirty minutes later, they found themselves at the front door of a tiny sandstone cottage surrounded by a rambling garden full of wattle bushes and stone statues of horses. Leura House was a charming-looking B&B, and even if it hadn't been, it was the only place on the mountain that had a room available at short notice. The affable middle-aged man who checked them in was all too happy to provide them with toothbrushes and a few other essential toiletries and only looked slightly curious when Nick hauled three plastic bags full of clinking liquor bottles into the lobby.

The horse theme continued as they walked up a creaky stairway. On the wallpaper, stallions raced, and a series of watercolor ponies kept them company as they climbed. Once they turned the key and let themselves into the last bedroom in town, Carly was entirely unsurprised to find several horse figurines over the fireplace.

"The Australian tourism industry sure loves a theme," she muttered, taking in the small rearing horses on either end of the mantle piece.

"I think they're trying to encourage horsing around," Nick dead-panned, and behind his back, Carly rolled her eyes. They'd both calmed down a little on the drive back up to Leura, though she could feel the aftermath of the adrenaline that had shot through her body as they'd left his parents' house, like a lingering exhaustion in her muscles.

"Whereas my place in Freshwater doesn't care what you do, as long as you shell out some money?" she replied, sitting down on the bed with a grateful sigh. She kicked off her shoes with a groan.

Nick snorted as he joined her on the bed, and she laid back until her head landed on a lumpy throw pillow. She reached behind him and pulled it out to find it was shaped like a horse's head.

"This is disturbing. Haven't these people ever seen *The Godfather*?" She frowned at the pillow and tossed it on the floor, then laid back on the firm mattress. Next to her, Nick had lain down and closed his eyes with a deep, heavy sigh. She looked over at him, tracing the sharp lines of his face and studying the dark creep of his five o'clock shadow. She kept waiting for the usual self-recriminations that followed an outburst like the one she'd just had, but they hadn't arrived. Nick's parents, and especially his dad, had had it coming, the way they'd talked about Nick. That pointed question his dad had asked about her parents had rankled her, but she knew it wasn't really about her—it was about his son, and the irritating but unavoidable truth, which was that Nick Jacobs was remarkable.

"I'm sorry I lost it back there," she said quietly, even though she wasn't, really.

Nick opened his eyes and looked at her for a long moment, his face unreadable. "It's okay," he said finally, even though it didn't sound like it was, really.

"Wanna get drunk?"

"I really, really do. Let's get drunk in the name of science and wedding planning." He climbed off the bed, reached for the bags of liquor, and began lining the bottles up on the antique wooden desk by the window.

"But we don't have our spreadsheet!"

"We'll make do. We can take notes on quantities and stuff, and Heather can enter all the data into her system when we get back."

"Sounds very scientific," Carly nodded, getting off the bed to join him. Together, they surveyed the bottles. Nick had gone a little nuts in the liquor store, and they had an entire bar cart to work with. Gin, vodka, tequila, and bourbon. Tonic water, a half bottle of prosecco, bitters, and small bottles of sweet and dry vermouth. Carly had had fun in the flavored liqueur section and had cajoled Nick into buying a few little fruity flavors in brightly colored bottles.

Nick stepped into the bathroom and returned with two glass tumblers. "What's your poison?"

"I like whiskey," Carly offered. "It's what I drink after a really bad day. And champagne after a really good one."

"Well, today was a really bad day," Nick said, reaching for the bourbon.

Carly watched as he unscrewed the cap and deposited a heavy pour in each glass. "I don't agree with that. It was a really bad night. But before that, it was a really good day."

Nick paused, then picked up the tumblers and handed her one. He looked exhausted, but he managed a small smile. "That was pedantic."

"Says the pedant. And besides, I'm right. We had a good day, right? We got some great shots; we both picked up a bunch of new followers."

Nick's smile widened, and Carly was relieved—and, okay, a little aroused—to see a mischievous spark in his eyes. "We did have a good day."

She took a sip of bourbon and stepped closer to him, near enough to brush a light kiss along the side of his neck. He groaned quietly and tipped his head, giving her more of the stubbly skin and the taut muscle beneath it. She kissed it again, her mouth open this time, and the sweat-salt taste of him mingled deliciously with the sweet bourbon.

"And the night's not over, Nick," she murmured against his skin. "We can turn it around."

In response, he wrapped one arm around her waist and pulled her tight against him, making her breath catch in her throat. She nipped at the place she'd been kissing, and he groaned again, louder and darker, and the sound made her nipples tighten and ache.

"We've got work to do," he said with a sigh.

"We can work later." Carly ran her free hand up the back of his neck and slid her fingers into his hair, pulling his face down to hers.

"And piss Heather off? No, thank you," he retorted, and she whimpered in frustration. She pulled away from him and looked at the bottles on the desk.

"For Heather," she said, echoing his concession from earlier in the evening.

"For Heather. Let's get to work."

"Fine, fine." Carly stepped backward, putting a few feet between them, and picked up a pen and notepad from the desk. The B&B's stationery had a chubby little pony on it, naturally. "The wedding theme is kind of a mash-up of New York City and the beach. You saw the table signs. So, it's kind of a cliché, but a Manhattan?"

"Two parts rye, one part vermouth, dash of bitters," Nick nodded.

"How did you know that?" Carly liked a good cocktail every now and then, but she didn't have their ingredients memorized.

"I know things," Nick said after a pause. "But we don't have rye."

"I think if you'd bought one more kind of grain alcohol the guy behind the counter would have called for a welfare check."

"Please, this is Australia. He would have reminded me to grab some rum."

Carly laughed and took another step backward. They had work to do. The faster they got it done, the faster she could get back to exploring Nick's neck with her mouth.

"Can we make a Manhattan with bourbon?"

"I don't see why not. It would be sweeter, but maybe if we go easy on the vermouth?"

"Let's try it. Bourbon is kind of southern, and Australia is the south. The deep, deep south. Like, get to Louisiana and keep going."

Nick looked skeptical at her reasoning, but he reached for the vermouth and the bitters and eyeballed the measurements. She watched him carefully, taking in the movements of his fingers, the flexing muscles of his forearms and wrists. For scientific reasons, obviously. So they could recreate the recipe later.

"We're supposed to add a cherry, so imagine there's a cherry in here," he said a moment later, handing her the tumbler full of rich red-brown liquid. "And it should be cold."

"Got it," Carly said, jotting down notes on the pad. *2 Bourbon, 3/4 vermouth, dash bitters, cherry, cold.* She took a sip and widened her eyes. "Holy crap, that's good."

As she watched, Nick took a slow sip of his creation, nodding thoughtfully as he savored the taste. She watched his mouth, biting her lip as he ran his tongue over his bottom lip. He watched her watching him, then repeated the movement with his tongue, and there went her nipples again. God, this man was a tease. How had she ever thought him uptight? He was playing with her. And he was *winning*.

"How does it taste?" she asked, her voice huskier than she intended.

"Perfect," he replied, downing the rest of the drink in two quick swallows. "You want more?"

Fuck yes, she did.

Nearly an hour later, they'd perfected the Deep South Manhattan—less vermouth and more bitters, to counteract the bourbon—and Carly's handwriting had deteriorated significantly. She hoped she'd be able to read it in the morning.

"'Kay, 'kay, we got it, on to the next one," she giggled. They were out of vermouth, anyway.

Nick was sprawled in the desk chair, swinging it back and forth gently. He wasn't quite as tipsy as she was, but he looked relaxed for the first time since they'd run into Nina that afternoon. He surveyed the remaining alcohol.

"What's Heather's favorite drink?"

Carly thought for a moment. "White wine. And light beer. She's not a cocktail person, and we're not serving white wine spritzers. I'd lose my maid of honor card for that."

Nick chuckled, then picked up the prosecco, which was sitting in a puddle of condensation. "We could do a twist on a French 75. That's sparkling, gin, lemon juice."

"A Freshwater 75," Carly said triumphantly.

"Yeah, I like that," Nick grinned up at her, and her pulse picked up at the sight. They needed to get this second drink done before she'd drunk too much to do all the things she wanted to do to him tonight. She turned her attention to the little bottles of liqueur. There was nothing lemon flavored, but she had bought some strawberry liqueur, which seemed promising.

Nick rinsed his tumbler in the bathroom sink, then opened the gin and popped the bottle of prosecco.

"Three parts sparkling, one part gin," he said under his breath, and once again she was impressed, if a little perplexed, by his knowledge of cocktails. She was about to ask about it when he handed her the bottle of strawberry liqueur. "Why don't you pour until the color looks right?"

She poured until the drink was a dark pink, and then they repeated the experiment in her glass, but with less liqueur.

"To a good day," she offered, holding one glass up in a toast. He looked at her for a long moment, his eyes a deep, unreadable blue.

"To a good day, and a bad night that got better. Thanks to you," he said, clinking their glasses gently, and desire tugged in her chest.

They sampled the paler drink, then the darker one.

"Oof, too much," Nick said, screwing his face up and setting the drink down.

If I had a nickel, Carly thought tipsily, scribbling the proportions of the paler version on her notepad.

"I think we're done here. I'll text Heather so she can cross this task off her master list." Nick nodded, looking satisfied, and started packing away the undrunk liquor. Carly padded toward the bed, drink in hand, hoping she looked sexy but feeling more sleepy than seductive. The hours in the sun had taken it out of her.

She settled herself against the pillows and sipped at the cocktail, watching him tidy up, then drained her drink.

"Nick. Let's have a really good night."

He looked up from the desk and let his eyes rake slowly down her body, lingering on her thighs and hips. Then he looked down at his own body and ran a hand through his hair.

"Stay right there. I'm going to take a shower, and then we'll have a really good night."

She pouted, and then remembered everything they'd done today. They both probably needed a shower.

"Fine, fine," she conceded.

"Unless you want to join me in the shower?" he raised one eyebrow, and the effect was unforgivably sexy.

Carly yawned widely despite herself. "Get the water warm, I'll join you in a second."

She adjusted a pillow beneath her and slipped her socks off, letting her tired feet sink into the perfectly firm mattress. Just a few minutes, and then she'd go into the bathroom and help Nick get clean, so they could both get very, very dirty. She was going, in just a second. Just . . . one more second . . .

Carly never joined Nick in the shower. He waited, letting the warm water beat some softness into his tense shoulders, enjoying the thick and luxurious lather of the B&B's shampoo, and gently palming his cock, hungrily anticipating Carly's hands and fingers and mouth taking over. But she never arrived. After a few more minutes of waiting, Nick realized he was wasting water and got out of the shower with a twinge of disappointment in his gut.

"Changed your mi—" he started to ask, stepping out into the bedroom wrapped in a fluffy white robe. The question died in his mouth as he took in Carly, who was curled up on one side of the bed fast asleep. She was barefoot, and as he moved closer he saw that the top button of her shorts was undone. But she was out.

As quietly as he could, he switched on the bedside lamp on the empty side of the bed, then crept across the room to turn off the overhead light. The moon and the streetlights now shone through the lace curtain, which was fluttering slightly at the open window.

Nick tiptoed to the window and carefully pulled the lace aside. The air outside was cool at last, and the lightest of breezes made the leaves in the gum trees rustle and sway on the other side of the street. The night up here belonged to the bush, to the croaking of frogs and the eerie, mournful cries of curlews. To the high-pitched chatter of ringtail possums and, somewhere not too far away, a barking that could have been a dog or an owl.

He stood there and inhaled deep breaths of eucalyptus and blooming night jasmine. It smelled like his youth, like life before his life really began.

Carly didn't stir as he lowered himself gently onto the bed, and for a moment he watched her, her chest rising and falling steadily, like calm water after a storm. The stillness after the hurricane. He slipped under the covers, still watching her. Her full lips were pursed and pouty against the pillow as though she was arguing with someone in her dreams. Which, he reminded himself, was definitely something she would do.

What a beautiful, infuriating, surprising woman. Not a brat but a force, an uncompromising warrior for the people who earned her trust. He thought about the way she'd defended him in front of his parents tonight. It had felt just as he'd imagined it would: like standing inside a hot, high ring of fire that burned between you and all the things that frightened you. His stomach clenched with guilt at the realization that he'd somehow fallen into the circle of people she trusted, despite having no business being there. She still didn't know the truth about his photography career; none of them did. And none of them would be as furious as she would be when she found out.

Nick sighed heavily, and she stirred, pulling herself into a tighter ball. "Mmphmmmph," she muttered into the pillow, and he smiled in the semidarkness. It sounded like she was winning this round.

He pushed the guilt away. He would tell her. He would. Just not tonight. Tonight they'd sleep in this strange bed in a horse-themed B&B in his favourite mountain town, in this country that was and wasn't his home. And tomorrow he'd wake up and make a plan to tell her the truth without losing her trust.

"You should get under the covers," he whispered.

"Mmmphmmph."

"I know, I know," he agreed. "But the nights get chilly up here, even in summer." He pulled the comforter out from under her limp body as gently as he could, but she simply cinched herself into a tighter ball. He kept tugging, determined to get her under the covers. With one last firm pull, he managed to get them out from under her, and he pulled them over her body.

"Niiiiick," she whined, in a tone some people might have called bratty, "'m tryna sleep."

"I know, *ma puce.*" He froze at the sound of the endearment, which had fallen out of his mouth before he could stop it. For a second he watched her closely, waiting to see if she'd registered what he'd said, but she was too wrapped in sleep to do anything but nuzzle the pillow and pull the covers up around her shoulder.

Force of habit, he told himself, as he settled onto his back and stared up at the ceiling. But then, he'd never called Delphine that, had he?

"Nick?" Carly said, her voice muffled by the pillow.

"Yeah?"

"You should tell him the truth."

Nick's eyes widened in the dark, and he looked over at her. Her eyes were barely open, and her hair was a rumpled mess around her face.

"Tell who what?" he asked, tentatively.

"Marcus. Tell him about your ex. He's not going to judge you."

Nick let out a quiet sigh of relief. "Maybe not."

"He's your best friend. Just wants to be there for you, like you are for her," Carly said.

"Him," Nick corrected.

"Mmhmm, that's what I said. And you have a whole new life, too," she went on. The note of grudging admiration in her sleepy voice made something sharp and wonderful twist in his chest. "You're a big shot pain in the ass photographer now."

He chuckled, then swallowed hard when he realized what she'd said. He thought about how enraged she'd been when she found out about Delphine, the look of disgust on her beautiful face. Disgust at him, but at herself, too. What would she say if she found out that he really had lied to her? That he wasn't a big shot at all?

Determined not to think about that any more tonight, he reached out to pull her body closer to his. She grumbled quietly, but as soon as her head was on his chest, she nuzzled into it like she'd done to the pillow.

"Heather's your best friend. Isn't there anything you don't tell her?"

Carly was silent for a moment, and her eyes drifted closed. For a long moment, he heard nothing but deep breaths and birdsong.

"Yeah, there are things I don't tell her," she said, so quietly that she could have been talking to herself. "But I told you."

He put a hand into her hair and held her until her breathing evened out, her inhales cool on his skin and her exhales warm and damp, soothing the aches he'd grown accustomed to living with. Tired as he was, essential as he knew sleep to be, he tried to stay awake to feel her breath on him.

* *

Carly woke to the sound of twittering, cooing birds outside the window. For a moment, she lay still and listened, trying to pick out the differences between mountain birdsong and beach birdsong. Then she stretched under the covers, feeling all of the previous day in her muscles. The drive, the photo shoot, the sun. The cocktails. She had a vague memory of intending to have sex last night, but then . . . nothing. In the middle of the night, she'd woken for a few minutes and found herself curled into a snug ball with Nick's large, solid body wrapped around her, his arm slung over her shoulder. It had felt alien and intimate, and she'd shifted slightly, putting a few inches of warm air between them. But a moment later, his arm had tightened, and he'd pulled her toward him, closing the distance and pressing his chest against her back. Deep in the haze of half-sleep, she'd been too tired to pretend she didn't like it.

She smiled to herself and turned to see if Nick was awake yet. But his side of the bed was empty.

Carly frowned, remembering the time she'd dated a guy for three months, only to wake up in his bed one morning and find him gone. When she'd wandered out of his bedroom, she'd found his roommate, perched on the kitchen counter in his boxers, eating mac and cheese out of a crusty-looking pot. When she'd inquired about the man she'd been seeing, the roommate said he'd left town on a two-week business trip that he'd never once mentioned to Carly. It wasn't her worst experience of the New York dating scene, but it was up there. Still, she was fairly certain Nick hadn't simply abandoned her in this B&B that not even the most dedicated horse girl could have dreamed up.

And to her relief, she was right. On his pillow was a note written on hotel notepaper. *Gone for coffee, back ASAP*, he'd written. His handwriting was neat and upright, just like him.

She stretched again and thought about the next two weeks. They needed to take more photos and keep up the momentum on their joint project. She'd need to go to company class every day. They had more wedding prep on their respective lists. And in their spare time, they could do . . . whatever it was they were doing. Whatever it was Nick had done the other day to make her quads and adductors ache so pleasantly this morning. Her muscles warmed and pulsed at the thought.

She heard footsteps outside the door, and a second later the door swung open and Nick backed into the room with a coffee cup in each hand and a piece of pale blue fabric slung over his shoulder.

"Good morning," she yawned as he handed her the larger of the two cups. Iced coffee with plenty of milk. He smiled at her, looking surprisingly well rested for someone who'd conducted an extensive semiscientific cocktail study the previous night.

"Good morning. The car's gassed up. The coffee is strong. And," he pulled the piece of fabric off his shoulder, "I even found you a spare shirt, in case you really want a change of clothes."

She smiled back, then took a grateful sip of the coffee. So he hadn't vanished on a surprise business trip. Quite the opposite, in fact.

"Thank you," she said, reaching up and pulling the shirt off his shoulder. She unfolded it, then guffawed. Leura House, Est. 1907, it said, in flowing teal screen-printed letters, which were surrounded by photographs of half a dozen rearing and racing horses. It was the most impressively ugly thing she'd ever seen.

"Wow." She couldn't think of anything else to say.

"Like I said, it's in case you *really* want a change of clothes." He grinned. "The front desk guy sent it up for free, because he noticed we came in without any luggage."

Carly stared at the shirt. "You sure it's not because he ordered five hundred of these things, and still has four hundred and ninety-nine left?"

"I am not," Nick replied, and she shook her head, then looked up at him, unable to keep a grin off her face.

"I love it," she declared. "I'm going to wear it to the wedding. I'm going to wear it on stage. I'm going to wear it in my new head shots when Catherine promotes me."

"As long as you don't wear it in any of *my* photos, that's fine," he chuckled, as she threw off the cover and pulled the shirt over her head. "By the way, lots of new followers this morning. And we haven't even posted yesterday's shots yet."

"Nice!" Her phone had died overnight, and suddenly she was in a hurry to get back to Freshwater so she could charge it and see how much progress they'd made. She climbed out of bed and struck a pose in her underwear and T-shirt. "What do you think?"

Nick let his eyes trail over her bare legs and her jutted hip, and then her T-shirt-covered shoulders. He took a slow, thoughtful sip of coffee, a small frown creasing his forehead.

"Well, as Miss Rosemary used to say about some of our costumes, you are a beautiful girl with a beautiful body. And that shirt is doing everything in its power to make it appear otherwise."

"Rude!" she gasped in mock outrage, flicking the horse head throw pillow at him.

"True!" he gasped back, catching it and pulling hard, reeling her toward him. And then she was pressed against him, up on her tiptoes, hip to hip and nose to nose. She kissed him, tasting coffee and milk, and his tongue met hers gently, carefully, as though they'd woken up and found each other in the sleepy dark. She moaned quietly and tightened her grip on her coffee, but before she could deepen the kiss, he pulled away.

"This place has a pretty early checkout time," he said, pressing a kiss against her hairline. "And we need to get back."

"Fine," she sighed. "But I'm not taking this shirt off."

Downstairs, the man at the front desk took one look at Carly and his round face split with a wide, delighted grin.

"I told you she'd love it," he said to Nick, approvingly. Nick smiled back and nodded, seemingly unable to come up with a polite response.

"I do love it," Carly enthused. "Thank you for sending it up. I can't wait to wear it in New York City."

He looked even more pleased at that. "The room is $282 for the night, and that includes taxes," he said, and Carly swallowed. That hadn't been in her budget.

"Exchange rate," Nick murmured from just behind her. "It's not as bad as it sounds. And we're splitting it. Fend for ourselves, right?" He pulled his wallet out of his pocket and put his card down on the glossy wooden desk.

"Right," she squared her shoulders and reached into her bag to get her own wallet. "Fend for ourselves."

Chapter 19

A week later, Carly's wedding prep list was down to almost nothing. After their unexpected overnight stay in the mountains, she and Nick had helped Marcus place the bulk liquor order, and over the next few days, they'd picked up tablecloths and napkins, driven to an event-rental warehouse to pick out folding chairs for the ceremony, and gone to a massive hardware store called Bunnings to buy several hundred feet of twinkling lights that the guys had strung all over Heather and Marcus's backyard.

Last night, they'd recreated the Deep South Manhattan and the Freshwater 75 for Heather and Marcus's final approval, and today Nick and Marcus were going to the discount liquor store to pick up all the supplies they'd need on the day.

"It's basically a French 75," Carly admitted to Heather as they drove over the Harbour Bridge, "but a little pink, like ballet. Trust me, people will love it." She yawned widely. She'd enjoyed a few too many Freshwater 75s last night and was regretting it this morning. It was Company Day at ANB, meaning that morning class would be taught by a member of the company instead of by a ballet mistress or the artistic director. It was Alice's turn to teach, and from what Heather had told her, Alice's classes were no joke. Assuming she was still alive at the end of it, she and Heather had the best wedding errand of all still to run: Heather's final dress fitting.

Carly had never been the kind of kid who dreamed about their wedding day. She'd never pictured herself in a big white gown or imagined a faceless but presumably handsome man lifting her veil to reveal her shining face. Even now, as her friends coupled up and married off, she didn't exactly want that for herself. Heather, though, was different. Practical and even keeled as she was, Heather wanted to be married, and she wanted a wedding—one of the reasons, Carly thought, that she'd stayed with Jack for so long. And if Heather wanted a long white gown and a veil and something borrowed and something blue, well, Carly wanted her to have it.

But first, she wanted to survive this ballet class.

For the last week, ANB had agreed to let her join company class every day, so every morning she'd woken up early, sometimes leaving Nick in bed asleep and sometimes finding that he'd already left to go surfing with Marcus. The classes Carly had taken with ANB's ballet masters and mistresses had been staid and predictable, in a comforting and familiar kind of way, confirming her belief that ballet class was basically the same in every country and in every language.

"All right, get your calf raises in, and let's party!" Alice called, rubbing her hands together with evil glee. Heather caught Carly's eye from across the barre and raised her eyebrows.

"Don't say I didn't warn you," she muttered, with a wry smile.

Ninety minutes later, Carly's scalp was drenched with sweat, and her heart was pounding from the speed and difficulty of the petit allegro combinations Alice had set for them. Petit allegro was usually her favorite part of class, because even if you made a mistake, you moved on so quickly to the next jump, the next direction change, that no one would notice, and you could almost forget that the screw up ever happened. Until, of course, you had to do the entire thing on the left side, with all the directions flipped. Most people hated that part, but Carly had always loved the puzzle of it, the way her brain had to communicate with her body, and vice versa. Today she was struggling.

The final group of dancers sautéd in zigzags across the studio, and when they were finished, Alice called out for the pianist to stop. All around Carly, dancers were panting, hunched over with their hands on their knees or leaning on the barre trying to catch their breath.

"Pretty good, guys!" Alice said enthusiastically from the front of the room. "Should we pick the tempo up a bit?"

No one bothered to suppress their groans, but Carly looked around and saw several dancers giving Alice what looked like fond smiles. Apparently this was just the Alice Ho way, and her colleagues had learned to love it. When she retired and was asked to run some company somewhere, she'd have the fittest dancers in the world.

Was that something Carly could do, after she couldn't dance anymore? Run a company? She tried to picture it: teaching company class every day, picking who got promoted and who got let go, meeting with a board stocked with rich donors like her parents, figuring out how to give audiences what they liked without putting the same old shit on stage year after year. It seemed like something she'd be good at. But the question was moot, because only former principals got asked to run companies. No one was handing an artistic director job to Peasant Maiden #4.

"Oi, you're up," someone muttered in her ear, and she started and turned to see a tall blond man looking at her expectantly. Heather had introduced Justin, one of the company's other principals, the first time Carly had taken class here, and she'd noticed his unbelievably good feet immediately. They looked like they'd been photoshopped into the kind of cashew curve that dancers obsessed over. One girl Carly used to dance with had spent hours with her feet under the couch trying to bend them into that shape, but the toe point Justin had been blessed with could only be achieved by some combination of winning the genetic lottery and starting dance training as soon as you exited the womb. Once she was done ogling his feet, she also noticed that Justin was also very cute, with wide green eyes and dimples that flashed whenever he was smiling, which was pretty often.

Right now, though, his dimples were invisible, and his eyebrows were raised in confusion.

"Right, shit, sorry," she muttered back, and stepped forward just in time to start the combination with him and two other dancers. And just in time to immediately bump into Justin.

"Other left, Carly!" Alice called from the front of the room, and Carly swore under her breath again as Justin and the other two dancers carried on without her, bouncing and pivoting across the studio, the women's pointe shoes clacking on the floor in perfect unison each time they landed a jump. She scrambled to catch up, but she could barely remember the combination, let alone flip it and translate everything to the left-hand side. If this ever happened in an NYB class—and she couldn't remember the last time it had—she'd grit her teeth and keep going, unwilling to let the director see her giving up halfway through an exercise. But Alice wasn't a director, and Carly didn't work here.

"Sorry," she waved at Alice, stepping to the side of the room and shaking her head. "Total brain fart. I'll go with the next group." She'd been so distracted by trying, and failing, to envision her hypothetical future that she'd totally spaced out.

"No worries," Alice shrugged, "you killed it on the right. So just . . . kill it backwards and in reverse this time."

Carly gave her a half-hearted smile, then trudged to the back of the room where a handful of dancers were still waiting their turn. Heather, who had already had her turn, caught her eye, looking concerned.

"Are you okay?" she mouthed.

Carly gave her a shrug that she hoped said *I'm fine* and not *I have no idea what I'm doing, with this combination or with the rest of my life*. Heather didn't look convinced. She waved Carly over, and when Carly arrived at her side, Heather gave her a grin.

"Come on, let's do it together. First one to fall on their ass or pass out wins."

Carly laughed despite herself. "You've never once fallen on your ass."

"If anyone can make me do it, it's Alice," Heather shrugged, then reached out and tapped on the shoulder of the tall, reedy dancer in a red Sydney Swans singlet in front of her. "Hey, Matty, do you mind if we join your group?"

In the end, neither of them fell on their ass or passed out. With Heather dancing a foot in front of her, and apparently a little more accustomed to Alice's high-speed, intricate combinations, Carly got through the exercise without messing up again. By the time they were near the front of the studio, Carly caught a glimpse of her own face in the mirror and saw that she was smiling, unable to resist the pleasure of petit allegro, the combination of explosive power and control that had made it her favorite part of class since she and Heather were gangly eleven-year-olds. It felt like magic. Like freedom. Even on the left-hand side.

"Yes, Carly, yes, Carly, yeeeessss!" Alice chanted from the front of the room, clapping her hands with the kind of exuberant delight Carly had never witnessed in a ballet teacher in her entire life. She tried to imagine Mr. K or Catherine behaving like that in a company class and couldn't even conjure it. She liked it, though.

"All right, all right, I'm taking mercy on you all," Alice called, gesturing to the accompanist to stop playing. "You all look great. Don't forget to stretch or you won't be able to walk tomorrow."

"I can barely walk now," Matty grumbled from behind Carly.

"Seriously," she muttered back, but she joined Heather on the floor by their bags, and they took off their pointe shoes to stretch for a few minutes, letting beads of sweat slide into their already-damp leotards and onto the already-slick floor.

"You okay?" Heather asked, before pushing herself up into a downward dog.

Carly hugged one knee to her chest and let out a heavy sigh. How much longer could she keep doing this? Killing herself in class, performing five or six nights a week, waking up stiff and sore and finishing class exhausted? And for what? So she could snatch a few moments of petit allegro joy? So she could wear a giant rat costume in *The Nutcracker* or be one of thirty-two identical wilis in *Giselle*?

"Yeah, I'm okay," she said, needing it to be true. "Just tired. Tired and old."

"Alice makes everyone feel that way, don't worry about it," Heather replied. She pedaled her feet out and groaned. "It's a good thing she's so nice or I'd have to hate her."

"You could never hate me," Alice said, walking over to join them. She was the only person in the room who wasn't panting, sweating, and drooping from exhaustion.

"No, I definitely hated you during that last combination," Carly agreed with Heather. "But it passed."

"Glad to hear it. You look really good!"

"Thanks," Carly sighed, not really believing her. "You're a good teacher. Demonic, but good."

"Ooh, I want that on a business card," Alice grinned. "Okay, I gotta go, but good luck with the big fitting today!"

"They're going to have to pour me into the dress, but thanks," Heather replied. "We'll send pictures."

When Alice was gone, Carly rolled over and reached into her bag for her water bottle, which was almost empty. She drained it, then felt around in her bag and found her phone. Maybe tomorrow would be better, she thought. Maybe tomorrow she'd feel less adrift, and even if she didn't, maybe she'd have the discipline not to get distracted halfway through and—

"Oh, shit," she said, staring at her phone.

"What's wrong?" Heather said instantly.

"Um," Carly scrolled, still staring. "Wow. I . . . we . . . it's very viral."

"What is?" Heather sat up and scooted to her side.

"One of Nick's photos. Holy shit, it's everywhere." It was one of the photos he'd taken in Leura, and she knew he'd been particularly pleased with it—something about the composition that she didn't really understand and couldn't really appreciate. He hadn't let her jump, but he hadn't objected when she'd put both hands on the railing, thrown her head back, and kicked her legs up, the bottom one tucked close to her body and the other arched behind her until her foot almost disappeared into her hair. Her legs looked long and strong, and because it had been toward the end of the session, the sun had dropped a little and the afternoon light had turned warm and golden, and the soles of her feet were dirty, a detail Nick had offered to edit out, but she'd refused to let him. With the falls and the valley behind her and the bright blue sky above her, she looked like she was floating, suspended by her own strength above the iconic Australian landscape.

She pulled up Instagram and her eyes bulged at the reshare number. It was *everywhere*. The official Australia tourism account had shared it, and so had some big-name dancers from the US and the UK she knew by reputation but had never met in real life. One of the recent winners of *So You Think You Can Dance* had shared it, and so had Hugh Jackman. She kept scrolling. She'd been tagged in a dozen or more photos of young dancers recreating the pose on balconies, and in city parks, on bridges, and even one at what looked like an abandoned construction site. There was also at least one parody post, one made by a man who definitely wasn't a dancer but who had tried to mimic the pose and had made it look endearingly awkward and uncomfortable.

Heather grabbed her own bag and seized her phone. "Oh my God, you look *so good* in this one," she gasped. "And look at all those new followers!"

Carly swiped back to her profile. Her follower count had skyrocketed in the two hours since class began and was now at almost eleven thousand. Her phone buzzed in her hand, and the email icon appeared.

From: Ivy Page, The Sydney Morning Sun
To: Carly Montgomery

Hello, Carly—
I'm a senior reporter on the Morning Sun's art desk and
cover Sydney's dance scene, and I was wondering if I could
interview you and Nick Jacobs about the photos you've been
posting from around the city. They're clearly resonating with
people, and I'd love to hear more about them so I can write
up a short story. Do you and Nick have any time to meet
this week?
Thanks,
Ivy Page

Carly let out a shaky breath and held up her phone so Heather could read the email.

"You should do it," Heather said when she'd scanned the message. "Ivy's legit. And once she covers it, other outlets might want to, as well."

"Legit like, she'll help you pull off a grand public gesture so you can get your man back?" Carly said, slyly. Two years ago, when ANB had fired Marcus for breaking the company's no-fraternization policy, Heather had given an interview to the *Morning Sun* in which she criticized the rule—and more or less declared her love for Marcus. And it had worked: the company had revoked the policy and offered Marcus his job back, and Heather and Marcus got their happily ever after.

"Legit like she's a good journalist who was a pretty serious ballet student, so she knows her stuff," Heather shrugged. A smile crept over her face. "But, given the errand we're about to run, you can't argue with her results."

"Okay," Carly nodded. It was working. Their plan was working. She forwarded the email to Nick, then tapped out a quick response to Ivy, saying she'd be happy to speak with her and would get back to her as soon as she knew Nick's availability. She smiled to herself as she hit *send*. Maybe Ivy could help Carly get her own HEA: a Happily Employed After.

The bridal shop was a twenty-minute drive from ANB's studios, an upscale boutique in an even more upscale neighborhood called Double Bay. After Heather pressed a discreet little pearl-white door-bell on the corner of a busy four-lane road, they climbed a set of glossy dark wood steps up to the second floor and stepped onto the plush white carpet of a small, hushed showroom. A chandelier sparkled in the middle of the ceiling, and floor-to-ceiling windows along one wall flooded the place with sunlight while blocking out every trace of the traffic rushing by on the street below. Leanne, Alice, and Izzy had apparently told Heather that the one wedding item she shouldn't skimp on was the dress, and Heather had taken that advice to heart.

A statuesque blonde woman met them as they entered the room, her long hair in perfect soft waves over a sleek and sleeveless pale pink dress.

"Welcome, welcome," she smiled. "So good to see you again, Heather."

"You too," Heather said. "This is my maid of honor, Carly, who's in from New York. Carly, this is Jillian."

Carly shook Jillian's immaculately manicured hand and looked around. There were a dozen or so mannequins set around the room, all dressed in long white gowns. Beads, lace, and white mesh abounded.

"Can I get you ladies a beverage before we start?" Jillian asked. "Sparkling water? Champagne?"

"Champagne for both of us, please," Carly said, before Heather could say anything. "We can recreate the moment Heather said yes to this dress, since I wasn't here to see it."

"Oh, it was love at first sight for this one, wasn't it?" Jillian said to Heather. "I've never seen anyone decide so quickly."

"When you know, you know," Heather shrugged.

"Sure, but I wanted to sit through a whole goofy montage of you trying on dresses, each one bigger and fluffier than the last," Carly said, as Jillian disappeared into a back room to get their drinks.

"Jillian doesn't do big and fluffy," Heather murmured, gesturing around the room. "She's known for sleek and simple. And I don't think she approves of goofy montages. This is a very serious business."

"Well, let's get down to business, then," Carly replied, lifting Heather's dance bag off her shoulder and nodding toward a long silver-grey curtain that had been pinned back to reveal a spacious fitting room with mirrors on all three walls. She sat down on one of several plump velvet loveseats in the middle of the room as Heather disappeared behind the curtain. "I'll be right here with my champagne."

Jillian floated over and set two slender flutes down on the glass coffee table next to Carly's couch, then stood outside the fitting room with a leather sewing kit in one hand.

"Ready?" Heather called through the curtain a few moments later, and Carly sat up a little straighter.

"Only since the day you called to say Marcus proposed," Carly responded, and she heard Heather's chuckle from behind the curtain. Then Jillian pulled the curtain aside and revealed Heather in a low-cut ivory gown with thin straps and a delicate gathering at the side that accentuated her waist. Beneath the ruching, a narrow slit was lined with lace that brushed against her knee and lower thigh as she stepped out into the showroom.

"You have to imagine it with my hair half up and wavy, and not in a damp, post-class ponytail, okay?" Heather said.

Carly didn't say anything. Her throat was suddenly thick and clogged, and her nose was stinging as she watched her friend turn and examine her reflection in all those mirrors. The straps crossed over her shoulder blades, and Carly could just see Heather's heels, still a little pink and inflamed from her pointe shoes, under the fabric. Jillian had clearly hemmed the dress so that Heather could be barefoot on the beach.

"Heather, you look . . ." Carly started, but she stopped to take a deep sniffle. Heather looked perfect. Perfect, happy, ready for this huge step. Carly sniffed again and took a deep breath before she spoke again, feeling pride and love mingle with anxiety and fear. Heather was moving on, moving forward, again. And here Carly was, standing still, unless she could make something magic happen with that interview. She pushed the thought away and focused on what was in front of her: her best friend glowing with anticipation and pleasure and love, beautiful even with her hair in a damp, post-class ponytail.

"You look so happy," she said at last. "You look perfect. This dress is divine. And I hope Jillian won't mind me saying that it makes your ass look spectacular."

Jillian pursed her lips primly and gestured at the slight gathering of fabric at Heather's lower back. "The ruching is subtle but effective," she said.

"Effective at making my ass look spectacular," Heather said, shooting Carly a conspiratorial smile in the mirror. Jillian said nothing and reached out to smooth out one of the straps, no doubt grateful that Carly hadn't been present for Heather's previous appointments.

"I don't think we need to make any more alterations, but take a lap around the room, please, and tell me how it feels," she instructed Heather, who obeyed, walking a careful circle around the circle of couches, looking like one of the leggy mannequins brought to life. The dress swirled gently around her knees and ankles, and Carly was reminded of the way the water at Freshwater frothed and spread in lacy white shallows after the waves broke and slid toward the sand. She pictured Heather walking down the beach, hair caught in the breeze, every step taking her closer to the love of her life. Her heart squeezed at the thought of her best friend finally getting the love she wanted and deserved, after everything she'd been through. What, Carly wondered, would that feel like?

* *

After another few laps around the room, Heather and Jillian agreed that the dress needed no further alterations. Jillian laid it gently into a white dress bag and zipped it up, before carefully lifting the bag and holding it out to Heather.

"I'll take it," Carly said hastily. "Pretty sure that's an official maid of honor job." Jillian looked as if she'd rather not entrust Carly with one of her perfect creations, but Carly reached out and took the dress bag.

Out on the busy, baking street, Heather opened the car, and Carly laid the dress along the back seat with painstaking care.

"Let's get some lunch," Heather suggested, and Carly's stomach rumbled in agreement. A two-hour class followed by champagne on an empty stomach was a recipe for disaster.

They strolled down the bustling commercial street lined with luxury boutiques and chic cafés. Heather led her to an Italian eatery that was serving overstuffed sandwiches and gelato, and they ordered two sandwiches to go.

"There's a park over there, and a nice little beach," Heather said, shading her eyes with one hand and gesturing across the road with the other.

"How long would I have to stay to see every beach in this city?" Carly asked.

"I've been here two years, and I'm nowhere near done. Come on, I'm ravenous."

They ate their sandwiches in silence, seated in the shade at a picnic table that overlooked a long, placid beach. As she chewed, Carly watched a silver-haired man wrestle what looked like his grandchild into a pair of floaties before the small child sprinted down the sand and into the shallow water. A few feet down the beach, two small dogs were chasing each other, throwing plumes of sand into the air as they scrambled in circles. There was a row of colorful kayaks lined up near the shore, and Carly watched a pair of kayakers slide over the calm water and out toward the harbor, where ferries and sailboats were crisscrossing on their way to and from the city. Far on the other side of the harbor, she saw the steep, forbidding face of North Head rising from the water.

Carly swallowed a large mouthful of focaccia. Maybe it was the champagne, or maybe the sight of Heather in her wedding gown, finally, but something made her blurt it out.

"I'm sleeping with Nick."

Heather coughed and spluttered. Maybe Carly should have waited until Heather didn't have a mouthful of sparkling water.

"Sorry, bad timing," she winced, and Heather wiped her mouth, and then her watering eyes. "Swallow your water, then I'll try again."

"It's a bit late for that," Heather laughed. "You just told me you're sleeping with Marcus's best man, and I've already got Pellegrino coming out of my nose."

Carly flushed. "Sorry," she said again.

"Don't apologize, I think it's great," Heather shrugged. "And actually, it's really very late, since you've been doing it for at least a week."

Carly stared across the picnic table. "You knew?"

"Yeah, Carly, I knew."

"How?" Carly frowned.

"You stopped fake smiling at him and started real smiling," Heather shrugged. "You know, that grimace you used to give Mr. K when he'd compliment someone on losing weight? I saw you give Nick that face. But then you stopped. You're a lot of things, honey, but subtle isn't one of them. And then Nick told Marcus he and his girlfriend actually broke up months ago. Between that and how much time you're voluntarily spending with him now, it didn't take Olivia Benson to solve this one."

"Right. Of course," Carly mumbled. So much for her big revelation.

"I kind of wish you'd told me yourself, but I figured it was just another Carly fling, and you didn't need me to know," Heather said, screwing the cap onto her water.

Irritation prodded Carly in the ribs. *Just another Carly fling.* She took a deep breath and reminded herself that Heather hadn't meant to hurt her. Then another deep breath, because the first one didn't work. Neither did the second one.

"Another Carly fling?" she repeated.

"It's not a criticism, I think this is perfect for you," Heather said emphatically. "A short-term thing, which is what you like anyway."

Carly raised her eyebrows, exercising all her self-control to stay silent as Heather kept talking.

"It's just that, you know, you don't keep guys around very long. I figured that even if you weren't leaving next week, this would be what you wanted. Short and sweet, fun and then done."

The prod had become a full-on shove, and Carly could feel her face flushing again, this time with anger. Heather had no idea what she was talking about. Heather thought she *chose* to live this way? Dating a man for a few weeks or months and then calling it quits when she realized that he was just like the one before, and the one before that? Or did Heather just think that she couldn't *hold on to a man*? Who the hell was Heather, with her perfect beach home and perfect principal dancer job and *perfect fucking life*, to judge her?

She opened her mouth to say all this, rage rising in her chest like a hot wave, but then she stopped. Heather wasn't judging her— *Heather* wouldn't judge her. She just really didn't know what she was talking about. She really believed all Carly's relationships were short because Carly had let her think that was what she *wanted*. Heather didn't know the truth. And she didn't know the truth because Carly had kept it from her. Nick had had the courage to come clean to his best friend, and it was about damn time Carly did the same.

Carly took one more deep breath through her nose, and let it out slowly. Then she told her best friend the truth.

"There's a reason I don't keep guys around very long. I have something wrong with my pelvic floor. I've had it since I was a teenager. It makes intercourse really, really painful. I'm seeing a PT about it and that seems to be helping. But it's made dating challenging for a while. Forever, actually."

Heather reached across the table and squeezed her forearm. "Carly, I . . . I'm sorry. I didn't know."

"I know you didn't know. I've never told anyone. Well, that's not true. I told the last guy I was dating, Carter? I told him I couldn't do it for a while, because the PT said so, and he just stopped calling."

"What an asshole," Heather muttered.

Carly shrugged. "He's not the only one. The rest of them never even noticed I was in pain. They just kept plowing away, like they didn't give a shit if I was miserable. Once you realize a man can happily come inside you even if you're about to cry from pain, it's hard to keep him around."

Her eyes burned, and she swallowed hard and blinked away tears.

Heather shook her head, her face crumpled with sympathy. "I'm so sorry, hon. And you never told them?"

"No," Carly said bitterly. "Look what happened the one time I told someone. Ghosted. I wasn't ever going to be enough for him, not unless he could fuck me the way he wanted."

"Did you tell Nick?"

Carly laughed despite herself, and it came out as a gurgle. "Not on purpose, but yeah, Nick knows."

"Not on purpose? What does that mean?"

Carly sighed. "I kind of . . . yelled it at him. In public."

Heather pressed her lips together, as if she was trying not to laugh. "You didn't."

"Oh, I did. I yelled at him. About my vagina. In a hotel lobby."

Heather giggled. "Oh, you *didn't.*"

"Of course I did, have you met me? It was classic Carly. But yeah, Nick knows." She thought about that early morning in her apartment, when he'd come over with coffee and questions that Google couldn't answer. *I want whatever you can give me.* Carly let out a shaky breath. "He surprised me. He's been fine with it. More than fine, really. For a few weeks, at least." Whether he'd start needing more from her and decide that she wasn't enough for him, she had no idea. He probably would, but she'd never find out. Their time was almost up. Fun and done, just like Heather had said.

Heather squeezed her forearm again. "The other men might have surprised you, too. If you'd given them a chance."

Carly sighed. "Who knows? Maybe I should have told them. And I definitely should have told you. I'm sorry I didn't."

Heather stood and came around the picnic table to sit next to Carly, who scooted down to make room for her. As her best friend put an arm over her shoulder and pulled her in for a one-armed hug, Carly breathed out a wobbly sigh. Telling the truth felt like cracking her toe knuckles: it hurt as she was doing it, but the instant relief left her wondering why she hadn't done it sooner.

"I'm sorry you had to suffer alone all this time. And I hope the PT is helping and one day you can have all the intercourse you want. But even if it doesn't," Heather shifted to face her and put her hands on Carly's shoulder, "you are enough. More than enough."

"Right, I'm enough and also kind of a lot," Carly sniffed.

"Yeah, like I said, you're more than enough," Heather smiled and hugged her tight.

"Intercourse is a weird word," Carly said into Heather's shoulder after a moment. Heather giggled again, and Carly squeezed her. She would miss this more than anything once she was back in New York.

Chapter 20

"So, are you going to tell me what the dress looks like?" Nick asked as Carly sat against the headboard, the sheets pulled up to cover her breasts. It was late, and he was planning to be up early to surf with Marcus, but the last thing he wanted to do was sleep.

"I can't tell you, it's a surprise," Carly said in mock outrage. Her cheeks were still flushed and her ponytail was tangled and askew. She looked like someone who had just come, hard, which she was. He licked his lips. He could still taste her.

"It's a surprise for the groom," he corrected. "You have to tell me if she's chosen something that makes her look like a walking pavlova so I can be ready to keep a straight face when I see her coming down the beach at us."

"Heather has impeccable taste in dresses and dessert, and the good sense not to confuse the two. I promise you, the dress is elegant and beautiful, just like she is. And you're polite enough to keep a straight face even if it isn't."

"That's true," he mused, scooting towards her on the bed. "But what about your dress? What am I going to do when I see you coming down the aisle in that strappy teal thing? I'm pretty sure I saw a *very* high slit up one side." With one hand, he pulled her to him, then ran the other hand up her bare thigh, tracing the muscle under the silky skin, feeling soft hairs beneath his fingertips. She sighed, then looked up into his face and gave him a wicked grin.

"Easy, just imagine *I'm* a walking pavlova."

He laughed and kissed her, wishing they could stay up all night bantering and fooling around. But tomorrow was a big day: after he was done at the beach, they had their interview with the *Morning Sun*. His stomach fluttered with nerves as he thought about it. So far, their plan was working. He needed it to keep working until it translated into something more than online followers. He needed those followers to turn into job offers or freelance gigs, and soon. In less than a week, Marcus and Heather would be married, his hotel reservation would end, and he'd have to figure out where to go next and what to do once he got there.

"What's up?" Carly asked, and he realized his shoulders had stiffened under her hands.

"Nothing," he lied, willing his muscles to relax. "Just thinking about tomorrow. We should get some rest."

"But I'm not sleepy," Carly protested, running her hands down his back to squeeze his ass. "I'm horny."

He chuckled. "One of Snow White's lesser-known dwarves."

"Exactly. Strange that Disney didn't include him." One of her hands snaked around and stroked the front of his pants, and his cock responded immediately, like it always did with her.

"*Fuck*," he breathed, and she gave him a wry smile.

"I can't, as you know. But there are other things I can do, and I'm very good at them, as you also know. When you have a broken vagina, you get very good at blow jobs, and you give a whole lot of them. Which in turn only makes you better at them. Practice, perfect, et cetera."

"I'm well aware of how good you are." He smiled dutifully. She joked like this sometimes, making light of her condition and the way she'd coped with it over the years, and though he was glad she could joke about it, he couldn't muster any amusement. The idea of Carly hurting, of her being with men who were content to let her hurt right in front of them, wasn't funny to him at all. He liked penetrative sex, obviously, but he couldn't imagine wanting it enough to hurt someone to get it, or being so oblivious during it that he wouldn't notice that his partner was in pain. Carly was a good actress, but she wasn't that good. He took hold of her wrist and stopped her hand.

"You can practice on me another time, Horny, I promise," he said, kissing her forehead. "But we should really get some rest."

A few short hours later, he and Marcus had rinsed and dried their boards and stopped by the surf club kiosk for a coffee, and he returned to his room to find Carly still dozing in his bed. She stirred as he entered and looked up as he set an iced coffee down on the bedside table next to her.

"Room service for madame," he said.

"Mmmpph," she replied, which he'd learned by now was her usual morning greeting. "Not human yet."

"Well, drink your coffee and get human. I need to shower, and then we've got a journalist to impress."

"Yeah, yeah," she grumbled. "So early."

"I know, Sleepy." He sat on the side of the bed sipping his own coffee, marveling not for the first time at the way her curls took over her entire pillow. Wondering what it would be like to wake up every morning with them straying onto his. Slowly, she sat up and reached for the coffee. The relieved little groan she let out when she swallowed her first mouthful shouldn't have turned him on, but it did. Almost everything about Carly Montgomery turned him on now, even her half-human harrumphs first thing in the morning.

"How's the surf this morning?"

"It's good. Bigger swell than we've had the last few days, but I did all right. Getting my legs back under me after so many years away." Marcus had given him a few pointers last week, and since then he could feel his balance improving and his instinct for how a wave was going to move and shift beneath his board growing. Maybe if he stuck around after the wedding, he'd have a chance to improve further, he thought, studying the lid of his coffee. But that would require a plan for what his life looked like a week from now, and he still didn't know where in the world he'd be or what he'd be doing there.

He looked up to find Carly watching him. "Your hair's all salty," she said, reaching up to rub a few strands of it between her fingers. Nick sat still, letting her work her hand into the damp strands, her fingertips thrillingly cold from her coffee cup. His pulse tripped, and then sped, as he remembered how she'd clung to his hair as she came last night, fingertips scraping against his scalp as she bucked against his mouth and begged him not to stop.

Carly disentangled her fingers from his hair and trailed them down the side of his neck. He was disappointed when she pulled her hand away, but a second later, she slipped a fingertip into her mouth and sucked on it, and his throat went dry. "Tastes salty, too," she said huskily.

"I need a shower," he repeated, watching her mouth. "Would you like to join me in the shower?"

"No, I insist on joining you in the shower," she grinned.

"Thank God," he stood and set both their coffees on the bedside table, and a second later she was laughing as he scooped her out of the bed and carried her into the bathroom.

"Last time we tried this I fell asleep," she said, when he'd set her down on the bathmat and turned on the water.

Nick turned back to face her, his entire body hungry for the taste of her, the way she arched into his hands and whimpered his name. "I promise this time you'll be wide awake. If I have my way, you'll wake the entire hotel."

* *

She was going to hold him to that promise, Carly thought, stepping forward and seizing the hem of his shirt. His skin and board
shorts were damp, but they worked them off together, and by the
time Nick was naked, steam was billowing out of the shower. She
watched the delicious shift of his chest muscles under his skin as
he reached out and pulled her tank top over her head, and the
unmistakable need in his eyes, the determined set in his jaw, as
he tugged her damp panties off her hips and slid them slowly but
deliberately down her thighs. They fell to the ground, leaving her
pussy aching with want. It had only been hours since she'd last
come and it felt like years.

He stepped backward into the shower and tested the water, then
reached and pulled her in gently by her waist. Carly groaned with
relief as the warm water sprayed her shoulders and soaked into
her scalp. He hadn't let go of her, and his large body crowded her
pleasantly, pushing her further under the spray. She wanted to tip
her head back and close her eyes against the water, but that would
mean missing the glisten of his wet skin and the play and slide of
droplets over his chest and down his stomach. She reached out and
brought his hips flush to hers, pulling him closer to the water and
letting his thick, hard cock press against her lower stomach. He
growled and ground against her, the sound desperate and addictive,
then took a small step back and guided her backward until she felt
tiles against her shoulder blades.

She gasped at the sudden press of cold on her back, but he caught
the sound with a fierce kiss, and within a few seconds the sensation
had passed, replaced by a feverish heat that crawled over her skin,
magnifying every stroke of his tongue and slide of his hands. It
only intensified when he pulled his mouth from hers and put his
hands on the tiles on either side of her body, then slowly lowered
himself to his knees.

Distantly, Carly remembered a tipsy conversation she'd had with

Heather, about a year before her engagement to Jack had imploded. They'd been hanging out at Heather's place on a Sunday evening, after a matinee performance, with the promise of Monday off. Jack wasn't there—in hindsight Carly had realized that he was probably out fooling around with one of his many side pieces. She and Heather had sprawled, jelly-legged and wine-loose on Jack's deep velvet couch, and ranked sexual positions from most overrated to least.

"Everyone thinks shower sex is such a good idea," Carly had said, gesturing with a sloshing wine glass for emphasis. "Like, let's go fuck against cold, hard tiles and hope we don't slip and break a wrist before we come."

Heather had giggled and insisted that shower sex had its merits and should be lower on the overrated list. Carly had shook her head, wondering in silence how she was expected to enjoy being repeatedly stabbed in the vagina while her fingertips went pruney from the water. But then, past-Carly had never had shower sex like this.

Nick settled himself on his knees in front of her, the water sliding down his long, taut back, and looked up into her face. Droplets beaded on his dark lashes, threatening to fall into his eyes, but he didn't seem to notice.

"I want to stop if anything hurts, okay?" he said, just like he had last night. Just like he had every time. "Promise you'll tell me."

"Of course," she said, surprised to hear that her voice was steady, a stark contrast to the anticipation and need that were rocketing through her. He nodded but didn't move. "Of *course*," she repeated, realizing as she spoke that she meant it. Of course it would be easy to tell Nick she wanted to stop. He knew the truth about her body. He understood it, and didn't ask her for more than she wanted to give. Not yet, anyway.

He took his time stroking up the insides of her thighs, tracing teasing circles on the slick, sensitive skin, before replacing his fingers with his lips, and then his tongue. One hand slid back up her body, caressing her rib cage, then reaching up to flutter teasingly over one nipple. With the other hand, he anchored himself on her hip, and then, when she thought she might pass out from wanting him to touch her, he dipped his head and ran his tongue lightly, almost imperceptibly, between her slick folds.

The sound that escaped her was something between a sigh and a sob. She knew he heard it, because he repeated the motion with even less pressure, and for a moment she felt a familiar twinge of irritation at him. Of course he was going to tease her. Of course he was going to make her squirm against the tiles, twisting her hips and widening her legs to urge him for more. She wanted to strangle him, but that would interrupt what he was doing, and that was unacceptable.

"Please," she managed, her eyes squeezed shut and the back of her head grinding against the hard tiles. She looked down and met his eyes and saw that he was *grinning*, the absolute bastard.

She was about to tell him that he was an absolute bastard when he flicked his tongue over her clit and she lost the ability to put even that sentence together. With his fingers gently pinching her nipple, his other hand tight on her hip, and his tongue dancing over her most sensitive place, she was incoherent, capable of little more than gasping and whimpering at the ceiling as he moaned against her needy flesh. He was good at this. Of course he was good at this, the absolute bastard.

She felt her climax taking shape, a wave gathering in her muscles, and she chased it, putting a hand in his drenched hair and holding him against her so she could grind against his mouth. He moaned louder, and the vibrations spiraled through her until she was breathless and desperate, until the world beyond this shower, beyond his mouth and his wicked grin and her buzzing, screaming nerve endings, ceased to exist.

"Fuck," she gasped. "Fuck, fuck, fuck, Nick, don't stop."

He didn't stop. Instead, he removed his hand from her hip, moaning against her, and when she looked down, she saw that he'd wrapped it around his cock and was sliding it up and down in firm, rapid strokes to match the rhythm of his tongue on her clit.

The wave broke. She shuddered against his mouth, her fingers scrabbling to find purchase in his hair as that strange sigh-sob escaped her again. A second later, she heard him groan and felt him spasm, and realized that even as he'd come, he'd never stopped lavishing attention on her clit. He kept licking her, his pace gentling as the wave receded and she caught her breath.

After a few minutes, he stood up on shaky legs and kissed her lips, then rinsed himself under the water.

"We should probably turn it off," she said, her voice still breathy. "Isn't there a drought?"

He turned back to her, grin back in place. It did something to her, that grin. Lit up the darkest, hardest to find places in her chest.

"I don't know about a drought," he said, kissing her jaw, then her neck. "Far as I can tell, things around here are *very* wet."

Carly gave him a playful shove, then remembered they were in a shower and put her hand on his waist to steady him in case he slipped. He laughed, turned off the water, then stepped out and passed her a towel. She thanked him with a kiss and watched him walk out of the room, wondering if she could follow on legs that had almost given out in the shower.

"Marcus said they're picking up Heather's mum at the airport this morning," he said, heading to the wardrobe. "What do I need to know about Mrs. Hays before I meet her?"

"Heather didn't write you a one-page briefing memo?"

"No, I think she's counting on you to brief me."

"Well, first of all, it's *Ms.* Hays. Linda. Heather's dad left before she was even born, and Linda never remarried. She's . . . she's nice enough. She worked all the time when Heather was little, because he only paid child support sometimes, so she wasn't around a lot. Heather moved into the dorms when she was fourteen, and she spent a lot of time at my place. Kind of like you and Marcus's family. But Linda loved Jack. *Loved* him. Or the idea of him."

"Why?"

Carly worked her fingers through her hair and sighed.

"He looked stable. He was from a wealthy family, and he was always going to have a job in the ballet world, because of who he was and who his parents were. I think Linda thought he was finally going to give Heather the kind of life she wished she could have given her. He put on a good show of being loving and attentive when the right people were watching, and he fooled her, just like he fooled everyone else."

Nick returned to the bathroom, wearing a pale blue short-sleeve button shirt and a pair of chino shorts. He stepped behind her and met her eyes in the mirror.

"But he didn't fool you." It was a statement, not a question.

"No. I've known Jack since I was five and he was seven. He was an asshole of a kid. Entitled, manipulative. As we got older, he only got worse."

"How does Linda feel about Marcus? They've met, right?"

"We all went out to dinner when Heather was guesting with NYB last year," Carly nodded, reaching for her sunscreen. "I think Linda was skeptical, but Marcus did okay. I was there as a buffer, and I think that helped, too. Linda likes me fine, even if she's always thought I'm a bit of a bad influence on Heather."

"Are you?" he asked, eyebrows raised.

"You're damn right I am," she said quickly, but then she paused. "Heather was such a serious kid, from the very first day she arrived at the NYB school. So obedient and determined and focused. I mean, you've seen the spreadsheets and the to-do lists. A bit of that rubbed off on me, I think, but a bit of my rebellion rubbed off on her, too, which I'm sure Linda didn't appreciate. She really just wants Heather to be settled already, and the last few years have been a bit unsettled. It was the first time Heather ever deviated from her grand plan. It worked out okay, though."

"Better than okay, I'd say. They're great together," he said, and she could feel him watching her as she walked into the bedroom to retrieve her clothes.

So are we, a tiny voice whispered in the back of her mind, and she stopped dead in the middle of pulling on her bra. She glanced over her shoulder, as if Nick could have heard the thought, but he was busy fixing his hair in the bathroom mirror. Ridiculous, she told herself. That voice wasn't real. It was the orgasm talking, that was all. Next week this—this fling, this whatever it was—would be over, before Nick could tire of her. She'd go back to New York, back to work and the real world. She pulled her dress over her head, ignoring the hollow feeling in her stomach at the thought.

Carly and Nick had arranged to meet Ivy Page at a café on the Freshwater main drag. In the twenty-four hours since she'd asked to interview them, their follower counts had both jumped again. The photo Carly had posted this morning from a session they'd done in one of the old shopping arcades in the heart of the city, with shoppers bustling and blurring past her as she posed on pointe on the tiled floor, had amassed thousands of likes already.

Still, Carly was nervous. She didn't have a lot of experience talking to the press. Heather and Nick had done plenty of it, but no one cared much what a corps dancer had to say about anything. She needed to get through this interview without fucking up.

They'd been waiting at a table for about ten minutes, and Carly had already finished her lamington, when a woman entered the café, looked around, and strode over to them. Ivy Page was petite and curvy, with shoulder-length light brown hair tucked behind her ears. She wore glossy black plastic glasses, a snug black dress that reached her shins, and a pair of strappy, block-heeled sandals, without which Carly suspected Ivy would be several inches shorter than her.

"You must be Nick and Carly," she smiled down at them when she reached their table. "I'm Ivy. Thanks for making time for me." They both stood to shake her hand, and Carly's suspicions were confirmed; even with the heels, Nick towered over her.

"I'll just go order a coffee and then we can get started," Ivy said, and Carly nodded silently. As Ivy turned away and walked to the counter at the front of the café, Carly realized how sweaty her hand was and wiped it surreptitiously on her dress. Nick noticed, of course.

"Are you nervous?" he asked as they sat back down.

"A little," she admitted. "I know this isn't a big deal for you, Mr. Big Shot, but I really need this to work."

Nick's gaze dropped to the table, but then he reached down and squeezed her clammy hand. "It *is* working. That's why we're here."

"I know, but . . ."

Nick glanced over his shoulder at Ivy, who was collecting her coffee from the counter. "No buts," he said, turning back to Carly. "You earned this. This whole project was your idea, and you talked me into it even though I didn't want to do it. And if you can win me over after nearly killing me with your luggage trolley, you can do just about anything."

"I didn't nearly kill you," she objected. "It was a light maiming, at most."

"A mild to moderate maiming," he smiled. "And you still managed to bend me to your will."

"Because I'm a ballet brat?" she laughed weakly.

Nick watched her for a few silent seconds. "All right, let's try it this way," he said, straightening up and looking down his nose at her. "You can't do this. I'd like to see you try. You're going to fail. You're going to be Peasant Maiden #4 forever."

Carly's eyes widened as he spoke. What the hell kind of pep talk was that? Honestly, some people deserved to have slates smashed over their heads. She opened her mouth to tell him off, but then he winked.

Oh. *Oh.* Game on, asshole. Challenge accepted. Ballet brat mode activated.

Carly grinned, then quickly schooled her face into a glower. She leaned in close, eyes narrowed. When she spoke, her voice was low and deadly, but he didn't look intimidated.

"It's going to feel *so good* when I prove you wrong, Nick Jacobs."

Nick smiled triumphantly at her as Ivy arrived at the table, and Carly sat back and squared her shoulders. She could do this, she thought. Not because she wanted to prove Nick wrong. Nick believed in her, despite all the evidence she'd given him to the contrary. Despite all the times she'd fucked up and lost her cool in front of him. No, she could do it because she'd spent her life waiting for this opportunity, dancing around in the background with the other nameless peasant maidens, hoping her moment in the spotlight would come. And now it was here. Not because her parents had bought it for her, or because Heather had called in a favor. It was here because Carly had willed it into being. She had convinced Nick to help her, and they'd worked hard together, and now here she was, with a chance to be something other than a body in the background.

Main character energy. That's what she needed right now. As Ivy sat down across from them and pulled out a notebook and a phone, Carly threw her a confident smile.

Chapter 21

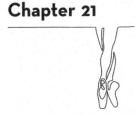

The joint bachelor-bachelorette party was relatively tame until Izzy suggested they play Twister. By that point, they were all several drinks in, buzzed enough to think it was a great idea.

It was not a great idea.

For one thing, all the dancers in the room—which was everyone except Izzy, if you included former dancers—were extremely flexible and strong. For another, they were all very competitive. Finally, the prize for successfully getting your hand or foot on your assigned circle was to take a shot. Which was how Carly ended up in a one-legged downward dog, with Alice folded in half next to her with one hand and both feet all on red, as Heather tried to do a tequila shot while holding a one-armed plank.

Izzy, the evil genius, didn't even play. She just spun the wheel and watched them make absolute drunken fools of themselves.

Eventually, Heather declared that everyone whose body was still their livelihood had to stop playing. "I don't want my wedding to become a mass retirement event," she exclaimed, after she'd fallen over, almost taking Carly with her.

"Former dancers, you're up!" Alice called, shuffling unsteadily over to Marcus and pushing him toward the mat.

"That means you, too, Nick," Izzy called. Nick, who had given up taking photos of the party about an hour ago, was by the drinks station in the kitchen. Between this morning's surf with Marcus and the drinks, his cheeks were flushed an endearing pink, and his hair, which had started the evening in immaculate order, was starting to look worse for wear. Carly's fingers itched to run through it, to mess it up further. To watch his eyes drift closed in desperate pleasure as she tugged gently at the roots, guiding his mouth to where she needed it most.

"Nick, come on!" Heather called from the floor, pulling Carly up short before she drifted too far into fantasy. Neither of them was going to be sober enough to do any of that tonight. For a moment, Nick looked like he was going to refuse Heather—but before she could play the bride card, he poured himself another shot and threw it back, and when they had all finished applauding, he took his place next to Marcus.

Carly threw herself onto the couch and grinned as she watched the two men drunkenly move around the board, talking affectionate trash to each other. When she'd first met Nick, she hadn't believed him capable of joking around like this, but as much as she hated to admit it, she'd been wrong. When Nick was around people he knew and trusted—or, okay, when he'd had several tequila shots—he was loose and laughed easily. He cracked jokes. Sometimes at her expense, but she gave as good as she got.

She thought about the day they'd met three weeks ago, and how she'd shown him the absolute worst of herself from the very first second. The parts of herself she wished away and was working on. All her rage, all her bitterness. God, she'd been a mess in front of him from the moment her cart had run him over. She'd been desperate for help and desperate not to ask for it, and he'd helped her all the same. If she got promoted next month, it would be in no small part because of this man who'd seen all the ugliest parts of her and managed to produce some of the most beautiful images of her.

And when he looked at her . . . She remembered the warm light in his eyes as he watched her answer Ivy's questions this morning. He'd looked at her like he believed she could do anything she wanted, and when he was looking at her like that, his ocean-blue eyes full of confidence and admiration, she believed she could, too. Maybe that was why it had felt so easy to be her best self in front of Ivy—because she'd already been her worst in front of Nick. He'd seen her explode with fury and heard her snark, and he'd sat patiently as she'd explained all the reasons she was broken and not enough for him. And then he'd told her he wasn't afraid of her. Not afraid of the bitterness, or the brokenness. He wanted whatever she could give him, and she wanted—

Fuck, she wanted him. Not just the sex, although being with him felt like falling in love with her own body after years of fighting with it. Like finding a freedom in her muscles and ligaments that she'd once thought possible only when she was dancing. Nick made her body feel like a gift to be treasured despite its brokenness, when all this time she'd tolerated it while wishing it could be different, better. Normal.

But she wanted more than the sex, she realized with horror as he and Marcus maneuvered their bodies awkwardly on the living room floor. She wanted the feeling of kissing him on that lookout beside the waterfall, the sense that they were the only two people in a world full of beauty and danger and possibility. She wanted this, right now. To watch him drunk and goofy enough to forget his starchiness and his perfect posture, messing around with his friends. Their friends.

She tore her eyes away from the Twister mat, where both men were laughing so hard they could barely hold themselves up, and looked around the room. Everyone else was watching the game. Izzy sat on the floor with Alice sprawled half on top of her, Izzy's hand sifting through her hair. On the other end of the couch, Heather was watching Marcus as though she couldn't believe how lucky she was that starting Saturday afternoon, he'd be hers forever. They were all partnered up, all moving on with their lives. Heather's next great adventure was about begin. Marcus was making the most of retirement, and a few years from now he'd be a PT, helping dancers heal and get back on stage. Nick had photography. Alice had years of dancing ahead of her and a girlfriend who adored her. And Carly . . .

Carly was thinking about how much she wanted something she couldn't have. A few days from now, the wedding would be over and she'd be flying back to New York. She *needed* to go back to New York.

She would go, because she deserved that promotion. She'd danced her heart out for over a decade, watching as women who'd danced alongside her in the corps became soloists, taking their bows alone at the front of the stage while she stood behind them in a long line of corps dancers, faceless and forgettable. Thirteen years of conforming. Thirteen years of being told her job was to dance like everyone else so that the audience would see her but wouldn't notice her. Thirteen years of feeling replaceable. If Heather hadn't intervened when Mr. K tried to fire her, she would have vanished from NYB, never to be seen on the Lincoln Center stage again. Some other dancer would have slipped into her peasant maiden costume, and no one out in the theater would even know the difference. Carly had paid her dues, with interest. She had earned this promotion—with some help from Nick—and she wanted what she was owed.

But fuck, she wanted more than that. She wanted something she hadn't let herself want in years. To keep a man around, because she wasn't waiting for him to eventually disappoint her. Or worse, for her to inevitably disappoint him.

When she'd ended things with Carter, when she'd made that *no more fuckboys* vow, she told herself that a man like Nick didn't exist. Oh, she'd thought he should—she'd thought it was bullshit that he didn't—but she'd given up on finding him.

She'd found him now, and she didn't get to keep him. In a few days, this would all be over, and she'd be on her own again. Not the fierce, stubborn independence she'd fought so hard for in the last decade. Not that kind of on her own. The kind that made her chest ache with thoughts of what she could have had.

She hated it already.

When he woke up the morning before the wedding, Nick's first thought was how lucky they all were that they'd run out of tequila halfway through the night. His second thought was that they'd run out of tequila because they'd consumed all the tequila.

"Merrrgh," Carly groaned from beside him. He looked over, moving his head as slowly as he could, but it didn't help. His skull throbbed dangerously as Carly groaned again. It sounded extremely loud.

"Mistakes were made," he agreed. He groped in the direction of the nightstand, hoping he'd had the good drunken sense to put a glass of water by the bed. He hadn't. He also hadn't remembered to close the curtains, and the bright morning light was stabbing him in the eyeballs.

"Merrrgh," he said.

"'S'my line," Carly grumbled, and he couldn't help but smile. He rolled himself carefully off the bed and trudged to the bathroom, trying to remember the last time he'd been this hungover. By the time he'd filled two glasses at the bathroom sink, he'd decided that he'd never been this hungover, and even if he had, last night's exploits had wiped out the brain cells that had stored those memories.

"Water," he said, to Carly's prone form. She opened her eyes and looked up at him blearily, then took the glass he was offering her and took an awkward horizontal gulp. A few droplets ran down her chin, and she didn't object when he lowered himself onto the mattress next to her and wiped them away with his thumb.

"Thanks," she croaked, sitting up a little so she could take another mouthful of water. "The fuck was in that tequila?"

"Tequila. I think Izzy might secretly be trying to kill us all."

Carly nodded, then winced. "Well, it's working. I'm never drinking again."

"Until tomorrow?"

"Oh God," she groaned. "What time is it?"

He glanced at the clock on his bedside table. "Shit, it's almost one. We slept through the entire morning. I'll go get us some coffee."

"No, no, I'll go," she objected. "It's my turn."

He opened his mouth to argue, but she was already peeling herself off the bed. Like him, she'd slept in last night's clothes, and her linen shirt was a rumpled mess, but she didn't seem to notice. He watched as she pulled a hair elastic off her wrist and wrangled her hair into a haphazard high bun.

"I'll be back," she said, crouching to retrieve her bag from the floor. "Or I won't be, because I'll be dead."

"Please don't be dead until you've brought me a coffee," he said, lying back on the bed and closing his eyes. He didn't see it, but he had a very strong feeling she'd stuck her tongue out at him on her way out the door.

He must have dozed off, because the next thing he was aware of was the sound of the door swinging open, followed by rapid footsteps and rustling paper.

"It's out! It's out, it's out!" Carly was saying.

Nick forced his eyes open, squinting against the sunlight. "What's out?"

She stood over him, a half-finished iced coffee in one hand, a hot takeaway cup in the other, and a newspaper tucked under her arm. "Ivy's story! It's in today's paper, front page of the arts section! And they used the best photo from the Blue Mountains. Here, coffee, with an extra shot. You drink, I'll read."

He nodded and took the coffee, taking small sips and hoping he wouldn't throw them up, and Carly leapt back onto the bed.

She shook the newspaper out and cleared her throat dramatically. "The headline is BALLERINA'S SYDNEY HOLIDAY GOES VIRAL IN A SNAP. A solid pun headline."

"Mmm, good job Ivy."

"*Carly Montgomery isn't very good at taking time off.* God, isn't that the truth," she said tartly.

"*The 31-year-old New Yorker, a member of the corps de ballet at the world-famous New York Ballet, scheduled a three-week holiday in Sydney, where her best friend, Australian National Ballet principal dancer Heather Hays, will be married later this week. But rather than soak up the sun and relax on the beach, Montgomery teamed up with Australian dance photographer Nick Jacobs to take a series of scenic photos that have become a viral sensation.*

"*Jacobs, a former professional ballet dancer himself, launched a career in photography after stints dancing in Germany and France. The once-obscure photographer jumped at the chance to combine his photography talent and ballet experience with his picturesque hometown.*"

Carly snorted. "Jumped at the chance? That's not exactly how I remember it, but okay."

Nick opened his eyes to roll them, wished he hadn't, then gestured for her to go on.

"*The result has been viral magic: photos of Montgomery posing in front of the Opera House, at the edge of the pool at Freshwater Beach, and at Bridal Veil Falls in the Blue Mountains have struck a chord, been shared all over the world, and spawned thousands of admirers and hundreds of imitators.*

"*Montgomery says a great deal of work goes into the few shots that make their way onto Instagram. 'For every photo we post, we probably take a hundred that don't make the cut,' she told the* Morning Sun *this week. 'There are plenty of outtakes where I'm falling out of a pose, or my hair's a disaster. But I like the outtakes, even if I don't post them. They're an important reminder that dance photos are just snapshots, and it's easy to make them look neat and perfect. Actual dancing is about movement, and it's always in the moment. So it can get pretty messy.'*

"Jacobs says that outtakes aside, it's easy to capture a good shot of Montgomery, who started training at the famed New York Ballet School when she was just six and has danced in the company's corps de ballet for over a decade.

"'It's hard to take a bad photograph of someone this talented. Even the bad ones are good. She's the best thing that ever happened to my photography.'"

Carly's voice trailed off, and she let out a shaky breath.

"That's it," she said after a moment. He opened his eyes to see her staring down at the paper, clutching her coffee cup with white-tipped fingers.

"Good story," he said, sitting up and reaching for the paper. She didn't object when he pulled it from her hand, and he turned it over to see that the paper had also printed several smaller images: Carly in black and white on Freshwater Beach, Carly kicking her legs up behind her head in Leura, Carly in that perfect tenuous arabesque up on the scrubby cliffside at North Head. She looked striking in all of them, but the real performance had been her interview with Ivy. Carly had been quick and witty, confident without being cocky, and she'd had the reporter chuckling and soaking up her every word within a few minutes. It was like she was born for the spotlight, Nick had thought as he'd watched her charm Ivy a little more with every answer. This was a woman who knew how to captivate an audience. She'd certainly captivated him.

"Thank you," she said quietly, pulling her knees up to her chest. "I know you didn't want to do all this for me, but I'm really grateful that you did. I think it might actually work. It might actually be enough for Catherine to promote me."

Nick took a deep drink of his coffee, then set it and the newspaper down on the nightstand. "I think it might, too. And you never know, it—"

He was interrupted by his phone, which started warbling and vibrating against the bedside table. Wincing at the sound, he grabbed it and answered the call.

"Hello?"

A man's voice with a plummy English accent responded. "Is this Nicholas Jacobs?"

"Euh, yes, this is Nick Jacobs. Who's this?"

"My name is Victor Wilkinson, and I'm the chief photo editor at *Vogue* magazine. Do you have a few moments to speak?"

After several numb moments—or possibly an hour, Nick couldn't say—he ended the call with a trembling thumb and pulled the phone away from his ear.

"*Vogue*," he said to a wide-eyed Carly, who'd been bouncing up and down with impatience and had repeatedly offered him a pen so he could scribble down what the call was about. He'd refused, because he'd been too focused on making sure that Victor Wilkinson was for real.

"*Vogue*?" Carly repeated, looking confused. Even as she said the word, it sounded like something out of a dream. Had that really just happened? Had one phone call just saved his floundering career?

"*Vogue* saw the photos and the article, and they want to hire me. To shoot dancers in couture, all over the world. Wherever I want in the world. He said, and I quote, 'Write your own ticket, name your price—we just want your images in our magazine.'"

"NICK!" Carly shrieked, and he barely noticed the sound plunging a knife into his hungover brain.

"I know," he said weakly, letting the phone drop onto the bed. "They're sending me a contract later today."

She launched herself at him, jumping onto the bed on her knees and throwing her arms around his neck. He caught her by the waist and kissed her, his lips playing against hers and tasting strong coffee. She straddled his hips and deepened the kiss, and he pulled her hard against him as her tongue dueled with his. A second later, she pulled back, panting, and looked into his face. Her mahogany eyes were sparkling with delight and desire.

"I'm so happy for you. This is huge," she said, and he grinned. He took her face in both his hands.

"This never would have happened without you. There wouldn't be any photos without you. Thank you for insisting that we try."

She shrugged and rolled her eyes. "Insisting? You basically made me beg. And to think you almost refused."

He gave his head a little shake, willing her to be serious. "I mean it. Thank you."

She leaned forward to kiss him again, but instead he wrapped his arms around her waist and squeezed tight, breathing out a slow, contented breath when she wound her arms around his neck and pressed her mouth to the skin below his ear. She felt so right there, warm and solid and still. Nick lifted his hand to her head and stroked her curls, feeling them wrap around his fingers, trapping and ensnaring him. Binding him to her.

"I'm so happy for you," she said drowsily a few minutes later, and he felt a contented smile spread over his face. He had the job offer of his dreams, and none of it could have been possible without the woman who was currently drifting into sleep in his lap.

"I'm happy, too. And I know things are going to work out for you, once you get home." He ignored the panic that fluttered in his stomach as he said it. Once she got home, just a few days from now. Once this whatever they'd been doing the last few weeks was over. But what if it didn't have to be over? What if they could . . .

"Hey, Carly," he started, not sure what he'd say next but knowing he had to say it, before he lost his nerve. But before he could continue, she pulled her face from his neck, frowning.

"Wait a sec, I think Ivy made a mistake."

"What do you mean?"

Carly rolled off him and pulled the newspaper off the nightstand. She scanned the article and then began reading aloud again.

"Jacobs is a former professional ballet dancer himself, and launched a career in photography, blah blah blah . . . The *once-obscure* photographer jumped at the chance to combine his photography talent and ballet experience with his picturesque hometown. 'Once-obscure?' You weren't obscure, you were established, and a big deal in Paris. She made a mistake. You should call the paper and ask for a correction."

Nick's pulse quickened as she talked. He licked his suddenly dry lips, trying to decide what to do. He'd spent enough time with Carly to know that she'd insist on asking the *Morning Sun* to correct what she believed was an error in their reporting. But if she did that, she'd have to learn the truth about him from Ivy Page. She'd learn he'd been lying to her, and she wouldn't even hear it from him.

"Nick?" she said, looking up at him with wide eyes, the newspaper still clutched in her hand. "You should make them fix this."

He ran a hand over his hair. "It's not a big deal," he shrugged, hoping he looked unruffled, "and I don't take it as an insult. Plenty of artists do great work in obscurity. And besides, the paper's already printed, so it's too late to change it now."

She shook her head in confusion, then sat up straighter against the bedhead. "It is a big deal! They got it wrong, and they can probably still fix it in the online version." Her face was alight with anger on his behalf, ready to defend him yet again, because he'd let her think he was worth it.

He had to tell her. He ran his hand through his hair again, stalling, putting off the moment when her anger would turn on him and change everything.

"Forget it," she sighed, and for a moment he thought he'd been reprieved. But then she reached for the nightstand again and reached for her phone. "I've got her email address, so I'm going to tell her myself."

Shit. He had to tell her, now.

"Wait a second," he said quickly, and she looked up from her phone. He swallowed hard. "Don't send that to her. She . . . she didn't make a mistake."

Carly frowned, then spoke slowly and clearly, as though explaining something very obvious. "Yes, she did. You were not obscure before the photos went viral."

He forced his mouth to form the words. "I was, though. I . . . things weren't getting off the ground in Paris. I thought I'd done everything right, I worked all my connections in the dance world, but no one wanted to hire me. Aside from a few little shitty gigs, no one wanted yet another dance photographer. I've spent more time pouring drinks lately than I have taking photos."

"Oh my God, the Manhattan recipe. But Marcus said—"

"I know. And I should have corrected him, but I was too embarrassed. And then things kind of . . . got away from me."

Carly's eyes had gone dark, and her face was set in an expressionless mask that made his heart pound with dread. "So you lied to him."

"I—"

"You lied to all of us. You lied to me. To my face." She spoke clearly, every syllable crisp and suffused with anger. She was gripping the newspaper so tightly that the corners were trembling.

"I didn't mean to. I just . . . I didn't want him to know how badly things were going. I didn't want anyone to know."

"So you didn't tell him about your girlfriend, and you didn't tell him about your job," she said, tossing the newspaper off the bed. "You just let him believe a bunch of lies? What kind of friendship is this, Nick?"

A hot wave of shame swept across the back of his neck. "The same kind of friendship where you let your friend believe a bunch lies about your sex life for a decade," he shot back. He heard her sharp intake of breath and regretted his words instantly.

"Fuck you," she hissed. "I would do anything for Heather. I'm here on the other side of the world for her instead of at home trying to get promoted, because she's like my sister, and I would never lie to her. I told her the truth about Jack even when I knew she wouldn't hear it. Even when I knew it would make her hate me." Her voice cracked, and she blinked away a sheen of tears.

She was right. She'd had the courage to tell her friend the truth even though it could have broken the friendship forever, and he couldn't even tell Marcus he was going through a rough patch.

"I'm sorry. Really, I am. I should have told the truth," Nick said. "Because the truth is, I came home feeling really lost, like I didn't know what to do next. But working with you helped me feel like I'm finally on track."

Carly's expression turned thunderous. "I'm so thrilled to hear that, Nick. That's so great for *you*. I'm so glad that *you* feel like you've got *your* shit together. Congratulations."

"I just meant—"

"You just let me believe that you were some big deal photographer, that you were *deigning* to help me. You let me hang my career hopes on a *bartender*," she said, looking at him with betrayal and disgust on her face. "And you didn't just lie to me, you turned me into a liar! All those posts where I talked you up and bragged about what a big deal you were, how talented you are!"

She scrambled off the bed, as though she couldn't stand being near him any more. "God, I'm so stupid," she muttered, pacing the room. "No wonder everyone else has their lives together and I don't. Because the one time I decide that maybe *this* man is different, that *this* man won't fuck me over, he absolutely screws me."

"That's not fair. I did not screw you. I held up my end of the deal!"

"Only after you let me *beg you* for help, when I had no other options," she cried, dashing a few more tears from her eyes. "You let me think you were doing me a favor! Like you didn't need me as much as I needed you, but you did. You needed this as much as I did, maybe more. And now it's worked out perfectly for you, and I'm exactly where I was when we started, which is nowhere!"

"Carly, please, I'm sorry I—"

"Fuck you, and fuck your apologies, Nick Jacobs," she marched over to the desk and snatched her bag from where she'd tossed it the previous night.

"Oh, great, you're going to storm out again?" he said in disbelief. "You're not going to stay and do the hard thing and talk about this? Why am I not surprised, Carly? Storming out is all you know how to do."

She stared at him, her tear-streaked face the picture of wounded rage. Then she took a deep, shuddering breath through her nose. When she spoke, her voice was low and dangerous and white-hot with rage, but it was perfectly steady.

"We will not talk about this. Not to each other, and definitely not to Heather and Marcus. Tomorrow is their *wedding*, and we will be the perfect wedding party for them, because that's what they deserve and that is what we're here to do. But I swear to God, Nick Jacobs, if you come near me for anything other than best man purposes, I will tell everyone you're a fraud. Because that's what *you* deserve."

She didn't even wait for his reply. She gave him one last, disgusted look, then turned and walked out the door.

Carly's hands were still shaking with rage when she arrived at her apartment. She slammed the door behind her and dumped her bag on the floor, wishing she could smash plates or swing a sledgehammer or scream at the top of her lungs. She settled for marching to the couch and screaming into one of the many starfish-covered pillows.

God, she'd been such an idiot to trust Nick. To believe a word out of his mouth when this whole time he'd been lying to her, lying to all of them. She'd bought the lies, and frittered away what precious time she had to secure her promotion.

She was furious at Nick, but just as furious with herself. She'd been so desperate to get promoted that she'd been willing to believe anything. Willing to grovel and plead for his help and feel grateful when he gave it to her. And it had worked out perfectly for him, hadn't it? He was no longer an "obscure" photographer, he'd gotten his little holiday fling, and he'd get to walk away and off into his new job before he could even get sick of her and her broken vagina. Tomorrow Heather and Marcus were going to get married, and Nick was going to ride off into the sunset, *Vogue* contract in hand, and she'd be right where she started, washed up and burned out in her early thirties, with no plan for what came next. As much as she loved Heather, why was it that everyone around her was succeeding and leaving her behind? Nick had just been handed the chance of a lifetime, because of her idea. Her work, her time, her willingness to humble herself and ask for his help after years of working her ass off in the corps and refusing her parent's offers. She'd given ballet everything, and she was still stuck. Standing still while everyone else moved on.

Carly's eyes filled with hot, humiliated tears as she remembered how hopeful she'd felt when she'd read Ivy's article this morning. It had felt like her work was finally paying off, and she'd been so delighted to see those photos in print. Now, her moment in the spotlight felt like a farce. The memory of Nick's words, there on the page, made her stomach roil in disgust. *I love taking photos of her.* For a few brief and idiotic moments, she'd wanted him to tell her that he loved more about her than how well she photographed. God, she was an idiot.

After an hour of sniffling and self-recriminating, she trudged across the living room and pulled her phone out of her bag. She'd missed a call from Heather.

> *Heather, 10:21 AM: Just got a call from the florist, the flowers will be delivered at 10am tomorrow.*
> *Carly, 2:53 PM: Sounds good, I'll be ready for them.*

It was the very last wedding task on her list before the big day really began. Once the flowers, vases, and bouquets were dropped off, she'd put them in the fridge until right before the wedding, so they wouldn't wilt in the sun. Heather had cleared space in the fridge and made sure that Davo bought plenty of ice and a few spare coolers just in case they ran out of room for all the drinks. She'd thought of everything.

> *Heather, 2:54 PM: Great, thanks. I also sent a sample of that tequila to poison control because I've never been this hungover in my life* 😱

Carly let out a watery laugh. She stared down at her phone, wondering if she should tell Heather what had just happened with Nick. She tapped out a few words, wondering where to start. What would she even say? *I thought Nick actually cared about me and I wanted to be right? I thought we were a team but he's been lying to me, to all of us?* She shook her head, then pressed a shaking thumb to the delete button and erased it all.

Carly, 2:56 PM: LOL

Heather didn't need Carly's problems on her plate again, not the day before her wedding. She'd handle this on her own, she thought, tossing the phone onto the couch and taking a deep, steadying inhale. As long as Nick Jacobs stayed the hell away from her, she'd be fine.

Chapter 22

After weeks of sweltering heat, the weather gods smiled on them the morning of the wedding. When Carly woke up, she checked the weather app on her phone and saw that it would be warm but not blistering, breezy but not windy, and there wasn't a drop of rain in the forecast. Heather had made three separate bad weather contingency plans, because of course she had. But it looked like she wouldn't need any of them.

Carly snuck a look at her Instagram account. She'd broken twenty-five thousand followers some time overnight, probably thanks to Ivy's article, and she'd been tagged in dozens more posts where young dancers from all over the world were mimicking her poses. A few other news outlets had followed Ivy's lead, too, and had written up the photos. They all referred to Nick as "formerly unknown," or "under the radar." The words made her want to throw her phone across the room at the seashell wallpaper.

He'd lied to her. He'd lied to all of them, but especially to her. He'd known how reluctant she was to ask him for help, and he'd let her plead for it anyway. And now he was walking away with all the spoils of their project, and she had no way of knowing if this plan—her plan!—was going to work. She glanced back at her follower count and then plopped her phone back on the bed. Sure, she'd racked up a bunch of followers. But it felt like a hollow victory. Where was her *Vogue* phone call?

As much as she wanted to stay in bed plotting ways to destroy Nick Jacobs, today wasn't the day for it. Today was Heather's day. Heather was the reason Carly had flown halfway around the world and blown all her savings on this so-kitschy-it's-almost-cool Airbnb. Heather was the reason she was here instead of back home in New York trying to ensure she had a professional future. Heather was the reason she still kind of sort of believed in true love. So she couldn't destroy Nick Jacobs today. Because today she was going to be what Heather needed her to be: the world's best maid of honor.

Before she got in the shower, she spent a few minutes lying on the couch with a cool washcloth over her eyes, hoping it would bring down the lingering swelling from yesterday's sobfest. Once she'd showered and packed all her makeup and accessories into her bag, she went to the closet and pulled her teal dress out of the closet, then grabbed her phone charger and her phone, trying not to notice as she did that there were no missed calls or texts from Nick. *Good*, she thought. There was nothing he could say to her that she wanted to hear.

She grabbed an iced coffee on the way to Heather and Marcus's and found Marcus walking out of the front gate just as she arrived. She hitched her mouth up into a smile and hoped it looked genuine.

"Good morning, groom!" she called, waving as best she could with her hands full.

"Good morning, maid of honor," he replied, jiggling his garment bag at her in lieu of a wave. "Alice is already here, and Izzy has brought enough hair and makeup stuff for an extremely attractive army. I'm heading over to Nick's place to primp with him and Davo."

Carly swallowed, trying not to think about the three of them gathered in Nick's hotel room, two of them oblivious to what had happened there yesterday. She imagined them toasting to Nick's new job offer and wanted to scream.

"Have a great time, and we'll see you at the end of the aisle," she said, with another attempt at a smile.

Marcus nodded, then stopped. He looked over his shoulder, back at the house, and then down toward the beach where, a few hours from now, he and Heather would be married.

"I'm just so fucking lucky," he said, his voice full of awe. Carly's heart squeezed and suddenly she was blinking away tears, undoing all of that washcloth's good work.

"You're damn right you are. But so is she," she added, and she stepped forward to give him an awkward, hands-full hug. He gave a big sniff over her shoulder, then pulled away.

"Go primp," she said, with a smile that felt like the real thing, and he nodded and headed down the street toward the hotel.

Carly stepped inside the house just in time to hear the sound of a cork popping out of a bottle, followed by whoops and clapping. She made her way down the hallway to the kitchen and dining room, where she found Alice pouring champagne into glass flutes as Izzy laid out the contents of several makeup kits onto the dining table.

"There's the maid of honor!" Alice cried, and Izzy looked up from a handful of brushes and gave her a smile.

"Heather's drying her hair," Izzy said as Alice handed them each a full flute. "We'll do hair first, then makeup. Heather, then Alice, then you. Do you want to see the spreadsheet?"

Carly chuckled. "No, I'm okay. How's she doing?"

Alice wobbled her head, thinking. "She seems a bit nervous, but it's good nerves. Show nerves, you know? The kind that make you sharper and quicker, not the kind that muddle your brain."

Carly took a sip of champagne, wishing she felt that way. Instead, she somehow felt sluggish and enraged at the same time. But that didn't matter today. What mattered was keeping Heather calm, sticking to the schedule and getting her down the aisle without anything going wrong. No fuckups, today of all days. If she couldn't keep that vow for herself, she could keep it for Heather.

A few minutes later, Heather came out of the bathroom wrapped in a plush white robe, bringing the scent of lavender perfume into the room. She beamed when she saw Carly and gave her a quick hug.

"You ready to do this?" Carly asked, squeezing her tight.

"Only for the last two years," Heather said, squeezing her back. "I'm so glad you're here. I wouldn't want to do it without you."

Carly pulled away to see Alice holding out a glass of champagne for Heather.

"A toast," Alice declared. "To my favorite dance partner, Marcus, and his actual partner, Heather."

"To Heather!" Carly and Izzy said, and the four of them clinked their glasses.

Heather took a delicate sip. "Make sure you eat, too, okay? There's cheese and crackers and charcuterie in the kitchen. No one drinks on an empty stomach today—that's how cakes get knocked over."

"As bridezilla requests go, 'Please eat the charcuterie' is pretty manageable," Izzy smirked.

"This is *my wedding*, it's *my day*, and *I demand* you eat some of that goat cheese!" Heather faux glowered at her, and all four of them burst out laughing.

This is fine, Carly thought. She could do this. She'd sit quietly while Izzy did her hair and makeup, and she wouldn't think about the fact that a few hours from now, she'd have to see Nick. Walk down the aisle toward Nick. She took a swig of her champagne and started unpacking her things.

An hour and a half later, Izzy had twisted and pinned half of Heather's long brown hair into an elegant low knot and curled the rest into loose, romantic waves. Alice had opted for a sleek ponytail that would stay out of her face as she was officiating the ceremony. And Carly had asked Izzy to give her a classic French twist with plenty of tendrils left out to frame her face and make the whole thing look slightly more relaxed than an uptight ballet updo.

"You like?" Izzy asked, offering Carly a large handheld mirror. Carly examined her reflection. Her curls looked extra bouncy and defined, which she loved. Her face was still puffy and pale, which she did not love, but Izzy could probably hide that with makeup.

"Looks perfect," Carly said, giving Izzy a quick smile. "And it's almost ten, so I should get ready for the florist."

"All right then. Heather, get your beautiful face over here so I can make it even more beautiful," Izzy said as Carly stood up.

She grabbed her phone, and some cheese and crackers, off the table, hoping that the florist hadn't tried to call her while she was in the chair, but there were no missed calls from them. No missed calls from Nick, either. *Good*, she thought. She didn't want to talk to him. She didn't ever want to see him again, and once this wedding was over, she never would. Her phone vibrated in her hand, and she jumped.

"Must be the florist arriving," she said to the room through a mouthful of cheese, and she headed up the hallway toward the front door.

Halfway down the hallway, she looked down at the screen and saw that it wasn't a text but an email. She swiped to her inbox.

> *Email from: Catherine Lancaster*
> *Subject: Your future at NYB*

Carly's fingers went instantly numb, and she fumbled the phone in her rush to open the email. Had Catherine already decided about promotions? Had she decided to notify people privately, instead of doing it at the end of a company class like she'd done last year?

> *Carly,*
> *I'm aware that you're out of the country at the moment, and I see you've been making the most of your time in Australia; the photos you've been posting are quite wonderful.*

Oh God, she'd seen them. Had she also seen the big boost they'd been to Carly's profile? And would she think it was enough?

> *I wish I had better news to share, but I wanted to let you know privately, before I announce the company's next round of promotions, that I've decided not to promote you at this time. I'm sorry to disappoint you.*

Carly heard a small, alien sound come out of her mouth, something that was half whimper, half sigh.

"Are you okay?" Alice called from the kitchen, and Carly started.

"I'm, I'm fine," Carly said hastily, hoping Alice wouldn't come to check on her. "Just . . . stubbed my toe."

"Guess it's a good thing we're all going barefoot this afternoon," Alice replied. "You want some ice?"

"No, no, I'm— I'm fine," Carly managed, hoping Alice couldn't hear the tears that were thickening her throat.

All that work. All the groveling she'd done to get Nick to work with her, and it was all for nothing. She'd be Peasant Maiden #4 forever, disposable and interchangeable and replaceable, until her body gave out and she retired in obscurity with no prospects and no plan.

> *On another note, I'd like to have a conversation about your future at NYB. Please call my assistant to set up a meeting when you return from Sydney.*
> *Thank you,*
> *Catherine*

Oh God, it was so much worse than she'd imagined. She wasn't getting promoted, she was getting *fired*. Nick fucking Jacobs was getting a job flying around the world taking photos of dancers for *Vogue*, and she . . . she wasn't even going to *be* a dancer anymore. She clapped a hand over her mouth before another one of those noises could come out, then shoved her phone into her pocket and went to the front door to wait for the florist.

Just get through today, she told herself. *Just be present for Heather today. You can deal with this later. You can deal with the giant, gaping hole that is your future and the rest of your life later.*

She stepped out onto the front porch and allowed herself a few quick tears where the others couldn't see or hear her. Then she took a few deep breaths, the kind she'd usually take to get her temper under control when her brain felt like it was on fire. But it wasn't her brain today, it was her heart, which felt like it was cracking under the weight of all of it: Nick's betrayal, Catherine's email, Heather's glowing, beautiful happiness. It was too much.

She was still taking deep breaths when a shiny white van pulled up in front of the house and a woman in an apron climbed out, clipboard in hand.

"Hays-Campbell wedding?" she called from the sidewalk, and Carly nodded. She took one last sniff and squared her shoulders, then marched down the garden path to help unload the flowers.

"You ready?" Nick said, wiggling his toes in the sand.

"I'm ready," Marcus replied firmly.

"Last chance to back out," Davo chimed in.

"Piss off, would you?" Marcus said, with a grin, and Davo obliged, heading down the beach to where forty guests sat on white folding chairs that had been set up in two blocks with an aisle between them. Beyond the chairs, between the guests and the waves, two stakes had been driven into the sand, with white banners fluttering at the top of them.

"Like a white flag of surrender," Davo had said when he'd first seen them, but both Nick and Marcus had ignored him. The weather had cooperated today, and Heather's meticulous planning had ensured that everything and everyone were exactly where they were supposed to be. And now Nick and Marcus were waiting just outside the Freshwater Surf Club, barefoot and tie-less in their suits, waiting for Alice to arrive with Carly and Heather.

Nick looked over at Marcus, who didn't look nearly as nervous as a person ought to look when they were about to bind themselves to someone else for eternity. Forever. What an enormous promise to make, to stay together no matter what. No matter how you changed—or didn't. No matter how you disappointed and failed each other. Together, no matter what. Nick had imagined it with Delphine, once upon a time. And lately he'd allowed himself to imagine it with someone else, someone funny and exasperating who liked his work and made it better. But then he'd messed it all up. And when she left Sydney in a few days, he'd be alone. Again.

Someone cleared their throat behind them, and Marcus whipped around so quickly that Nick realized his best friend might be feeling jumpier than he was letting on. He turned around himself to see Alice, in a black silk camisole tucked into a pair of slim, high-waisted tuxedo pants, with a white leather binder tucked under one arm.

"You boys ready?" Alice asked. She looked completely relaxed, like she'd been officiating weddings for years.

"We're ready," Nick said. Marcus only managed a nod.

"Okay, I'll be waiting at the flags. The ladies are all just inside. Remember, it's Nick and Carly, then Marcus and Leanne, then Heather and Linda."

"Got it," Nick confirmed, his heart clenching at the thought of seeing Carly. He'd barely slept last night, lying in bed replaying yesterday afternoon in his head, wishing he'd had just a few more minutes, just a few more seconds to tell her how he felt about her before everything went to hell. Before he proved her first instincts about him right.

It was just a few dozen metres down the beach. It was only fifteen minutes of standing across the aisle from her. She'd told him to stay the hell away from her, and as much as he wanted to pull her aside and explain himself, to apologize and ask her for another chance, he knew this wasn't the time or the place. He'd have time after the wedding was over.

He and Marcus watched as Alice stopped by Izzy's seat and gave her a quick kiss before taking her place between the two white flags and opening her binder. Then she flashed them the cue they'd decided on, a peace sign, and beamed.

Nick reached out and put his hand on Marcus's shoulder and gave it a gentle squeeze.

"You're going to be a great husband," he said quietly. "Because you're a great friend. And that's all this is: promising to be her best and most loyal friend, no matter what happens. That's what your dad was to your mum, and look what a great husband and father he turned out to be."

Marcus nodded and swallowed hard, and then turned and pulled Nick into a tight hug.

"Thanks for being here," Marcus muttered over his shoulder. Nick nodded and sniffed. There was so much he hadn't been here for, so much he'd missed. Soon he'd be gone again. But today he was here, standing beside the boy who'd been his friend since they were gangly, awkward teenagers. Who wasn't a boy anymore but a man, so deeply in love it shone from his every pore.

Something moved in his peripheral vision, and he pulled away from Marcus to see Carly standing five feet away, watching them with a bouquet of pale pink roses clutched tightly in one hand. His breath caught in his chest at the sight of her. Christ, she was beautiful. Every day, in anything, even in a hideous hotel T-shirt covered in clip art horses, but especially in that dress. The thin teal fabric gathered in delicate folds at her waist and spilled around her feet, which were bare and visible where the cloth was slit halfway up one thigh. It tied at the back of her neck, revealing her strong shoulders and the freckles on her chest. And her hair, so bright and boldly red against the green dress, was perfectly Carly: pinned up in a twist but with curls escaping, bobbing in the breeze. Beautiful, barely controlled chaos.

He had a sudden vision of the first time he'd seen that dress, spilling out of the suitcase he'd thought was his, the suitcase she'd yanked away from him as she yelled at him in the hotel lobby. He'd found her utterly maddening then, a human hand grenade that exploded whenever he got near it. A hand grenade that loathed him. And now . . . well, he still found her maddening. But he knew her now, and *fuck*, he was falling for her. And she loathed him all over again.

He stared at her, willing her to say something to him, but her face was completely impassive. He was about to speak when Leanne and Heather's mum appeared behind her, Linda in a navy blue gown and Leanne in a periwinkle dress that came to her knees. Linda looked slightly uncomfortable wearing a gown without shoes; Leanne looked perfectly at home barefoot on the sand.

"Alice drilled us on the order of operations," Leanne said to Marcus, her eyes twinkling. "So I think you and I should get a wriggle on. And Nicholas, you better be ready, or Sergeant Alice will have your head."

Nick gave her a close-mouthed smile, and then looked over at Carly, who didn't even give him that. But she did walk forward and stand beside him. He offered her his arm, and Nick and Leanne started processing down the sand, and she waited until the last possible moment to take it, touching him so lightly he could barely feel it as they walked down the beach and towards Alice.

"You look beautiful," he murmured, against his better judgment.

Her hand stiffened on his forearm, and he saw her clench her jaw.

"Don't." Her voice was hard and cold as steel.

They arrived at the rows of chairs, and he nodded at Izzy and the handful of dancers he recognized from his time at the ANB school. Carly's eyes were fixed straight ahead, and the second they reached the end of the aisle, she removed her hand from his arm so quickly that Nick saw Alice's eyebrows shoot up her forehead. Carly took her place on Alice's left side, and Nick stepped to the right, and they both turned to face up the aisle as Marcus and Leanne appeared, arm in arm.

By the time Marcus made it halfway down the aisle, both his and Leanne's eyes were shining with unshed tears, and as Marcus helped his mother carefully into her chair in the front row, Nick pulled out a tissue and handed it over. Marcus gave his face a quick wipe, then pocketed the tissue and turned to face the surf club as all the guests stood to watch Heather walk towards them.

Nick tried to keep his eyes on the bride, who looked lovely, but he couldn't keep his gaze from drifting towards Carly. While everyone else was distracted, watching Heather or snapping discreet photos of her with their phones, he drank in Carly's profile. The swell of her lips, the sharp cut of her cheekbone. The long straight line of her neck, such a contrast with the curved, swaying strands of hair that had escaped her bun. Her eyes were sparkling with tears, and as Heather walked the final steps down the aisle, he watched as she blinked them away into the sand. He wanted to hand her a tissue, but he didn't think he could bear the way she'd look at him if he tried.

Heather hugged her mother, who sat down next to Leanne and squeezed the other woman's hand with a quick, sniffling smile. Then Heather stepped forward and turned to face Marcus, her face glowing with love and nerves and excitement.

"Hi," she said breathlessly.

"Hi yourself," he replied, and she giggled.

"Dearly beloved," Alice said, as the guests sat down, "we are gathered here today, on this beautiful beach, to celebrate this beautiful couple and their beautiful love. To honor their commitment to each other and to the life they've built together."

Nick glanced across at Carly, whose jaw was clenched again, and whose eyes were full of tears. He looked down at her hands, which were gripping her bouquet so tightly that her fingertips had gone white. She looked like she was barely holding it together, and all he wanted in that moment was to pull her into his arms and stroke her hair the way he'd done yesterday morning. But he couldn't do that, because *he* was the reason she was barely holding it together.

Alice's remarks were moving but short and to the point, and before long it was time for Heather and Marcus to exchange rings. Nick handed over Heather's ring and watched as Marcus slid it onto her finger, fumbling with nerves on the first try but managing it on the second. Carly's fingers trembled as she handed Marcus's ring to Heather. But Heather's hands were steady, and when the ring was on, she grinned up at Marcus—and before Alice could say anything, she pulled his face down to hers and kissed him.

"Woah, woah, woah, I have to say the thing!" Alice protested as the crowd laughed and clapped and whooped.

Heather broke the kiss and gave Alice a sheepish shrug. "Sorry," she said unconvincingly. "Couldn't wait."

The guests laughed again, and Alice cleared her throat pointedly. "Let's try that again. By the power vested in me by the state of New South Wales, I now declare you married. You may now kiss the—Oi!"

Before she'd even finished, Marcus had thrown his arms around Heather and kissed her deeply, and the guests jumped to their feet and applauded. Nick glanced over and saw that even Carly was smiling now, although he could also see the places where the tears had left streaks in her makeup.

"Please join us all back at Marcus and Heather's place for drinks, dinner, and dancing," Alice called over the commotion, and she closed her binder with a grin.

"So much for Heather's precise plan," she rolled her eyes, and Nick chuckled. "All those spreadsheets and then in the crucial moment she blows her cue? Ah, well, shall we?"

She gestured at the aisle, where Marcus and Heather were already making their way back up the beach.

Nick nodded, then looked over to Carly, hoping for another excuse to touch her and walk with her, but she was already deep in conversation with Linda and studiously avoiding his gaze. He watched her for a moment, hoping she'd turn around, then realized it was hopeless. With a sigh, he started back up the beach alone.

Chapter 23

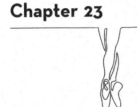

Back at the house, Carly hurried into the kitchen and pulled the remaining flowers out of the fridge. Clutching a few bud vases in each hand, she carried them out into the backyard and arranged them carefully on the half-dozen rented tables that were set and waiting. A few minutes later, Izzy arrived, hands full of vases, and together they ferried back and forth from the kitchen until the fridge was empty and the tables were full.

"Matches?" Izzy asked, looking down at the votive candles on the table in front of her.

"Two boxes on the kitchen windowsill, and a spare box hidden inside the barbecue," Carly said automatically. Heather really had thought of everything.

Izzy strode into the house and returned with two boxes of matches, tossing one to Carly. For a few minutes, they worked in silence, moving slowly along each table to light the candles and drop them carefully back into their little glass holders.

"Hey," Izzy started tentatively from the table behind her, and Carly had an unpleasant suspicion about what was coming next. Apparently she hadn't held it together as well as she'd hoped to today. "Are you okay? You seemed pretty emotional up there. Is something wrong?"

Carly took a deep breath and deposited a lit candle into a cup. The green sign in the middle of the table said GRAND CENTRAL STATION, and the familiar font of the street sign made her suddenly homesick for New York.

"I'm fine," she said to the sign, doing her best to affect a light, happy tone. "Just so happy for Heather, you know?" So happy for Heather, so completely heartbroken for herself. Trying to remember that, today of all days, one was far more important than the other.

It had been hard to remember that fact as she'd stood just behind Heather during the ceremony, barely five feet away from Nick, who looked like a delicious, dashing dream in his suit and his bare feet. Who wouldn't stop looking across the aisle at her. It had taken every ounce of control she possessed to keep it together as she'd listened to Alice talk about friendship and commitment and a love so strong that it broke and then changed ANB's strict no-dating policy. Heather was gaining so much today. A new family, a new future. Carly had stood there, hoping her trickle of tears wouldn't become a flood, and trying to focus on Heather's joy, instead of on how much she herself had lost in the last twenty-four hours.

Carly took a deep sniff, then smiled and turned to face Izzy. "Heather got so close to marrying the wrong person. It makes me happy to see her marry the right one."

Izzy leaned against the table and looked at Carly skeptically. "Sure. But, listen, I don't know you that well, but I know how much she loves you, and I reckon that if something was upsetting you, even on her wedding day, she'd want to know about it. You don't have to tell me, but she'd want you to tell her."

Carly nodded tightly. "I know, but really, I'm fine," she lied.

And even if she weren't, she wouldn't make it Heather's problem today, she thought, turning back to the table to finish lighting the candles. Look what had happened last time she'd asked someone for help. She'd solve her own problems, just like she should have done from the start. She'd fend for herself.

A few minutes later, they heard the sounds of happy chatter filtering from the front of the house, and then guests began arriving through the side gate and wandering into the back yard. They looked around at the transformed space—the twinkle lights hanging over the tables, the wood-fired pizza truck parked in one corner, the speakers and slabs of wood Davo had laid down to create a dance floor between the tables. Before long, people were wandering up to the back deck, where the friends of Alice's brother who had agreed to do the catering had set up a bar and were offering up beer, wine, and the cocktails she and Nick had invented together.

Carly went up to the deck and tucked the matches inside the barbecue, then grabbed a Freshwater 75 from the table, wishing she could just swipe the gin bottle from behind the bar. By the time she'd downed half her drink, the backyard was full of guests chatting and laughing. She spotted Davo and Justin, plus a few other dancers she recognized from ANB company class, but she felt no desire to join in their joyful conversations.

As she watched guests mingle and locate their assigned seats, Alice and Nick came through the side gate. Alice looked delighted, glowing with triumph from officiating the wedding. Nick looked like he was trying to look happy, and as she watched him, Carly felt hot liquid rage rush through her veins. What the hell did he have to be unhappy about? He'd gotten everything he wanted. He had his dream job, the kind of real professional success he'd been faking this whole time. Plus a little holiday fucking around on the side, without ever having to dump her once he got sick of her and her broken vagina. He had *everything*, and he had the nerve to look unhappy about it.

At that moment, Nick glanced around the garden, and before she could look away, his eyes found her. He froze and stared at her as Alice chattered beside him, and even from twenty feet away, she could see the deep, fathomless blue of his eyes, and the wrinkle of a frown across his forehead. She saw him take a step toward the deck, but a second later, Alice glanced over her shoulder, then turned back to face the guests, grinning.

"All right everyone, grab yourselves a drink and take a seat, and please welcome, for the first time as a married couple, Marcus and Heather!"

Heather and Marcus appeared in the corner of the garden hand in hand, both of them beaming, the picture of love and slightly dazed delight. Everyone, including the bartender next to her, burst into applause, and Justin put two fingers in his mouth and whistled loudly. Carly's eyes found Nick again, but he was no longer watching her.

She drained her drink. "Another one, please. Heavy on the gin if you can," she told the bartender, who gave her a knowing nod and grabbed the bottle from beneath the bar.

Every wedding reception should have a wood-fired pizza truck, Nick had decided. Who wanted to chew rubbery chicken or lukewarm pasta in an airless hotel function room when you could eat fresh hot pizza by the slice under the pink and orange sky and crisscrossing lines of fairy lights?

The pizza had almost been enough to distract from the loud silence between him and Carly as they'd sat across the table from each other. She'd avoided his eyes throughout the entire meal, maintaining a determined conversation first with Linda, who was seated on one side of her, and then with Izzy, who was on the other. Every now and then, Nick noticed Izzy flicking a questioning glance at him, and then at Carly, but he ignored it. He would have time to get Carly alone and apologize to her, to explain everything, he reminded himself.

At the head of the table, Marcus and Heather were all smiles, leaning briefly away from each other to chat with the people next to them, or with guests who stopped by the table on the way to the bar, but swaying back towards each other immediately, as if each was the other's magnetic pole. He looked across the table at Carly, who was deep in conversation with Linda again, and who seemed to be leaning away from him as if they were each the north end of a different magnet. His heart gave a painful throb.

"Leanne, Linda, Carly," Alice called down the table. "About ten minutes, and then we'll do speeches, okay?"

Nick saw Carly nod and mutter something to Linda. Then she picked her purse up from the table and headed up onto the back deck and disappeared into the house. He hesitated for a moment, indecisive and fully aware that Izzy was watching him again. Then he stood and strode into the house.

Inside the kitchen, every available surface was covered in dirty rented plates and glasses, and every available container was full of ice. The one exception was the countertop next to the stove, where a three-tiered wedding cake sat waiting on a white paper doily. Artistically uneven white icing covered the layers, and perched on the top tier was a small and carefully painted New York–style street sign that matched the table numbers out back. It read "Heather and Marcus Ave."

Carly wasn't in the kitchen, and he was about to go in search of her when he heard the toilet flush and the sink run. A moment later she emerged with her purse in her hand, wearing freshly applied lipstick that made it even harder than usual to keep his eyes from her mouth. She stopped short when she saw him, and then made to walk past him.

"Wait," he said, stepping forward to block her path. "Please, just let me explain."

"There's nothing to explain," she said firmly, her eyes on the end of the hallway.

"I called *Vogue* and asked if you can be part of the first shoot I do for them. I told them I didn't want to work for them if I couldn't work with you, and they were fine with that. I know it's not the promotion you wanted, but it'll boost your profile more than Instagram posts ever could, and that might help with promotion. I owe it to you, Carly. I wouldn't have gotten this job without you."

She still wouldn't look at him. "Will you please just listen to me, just hear me out?" he pleaded.

She took a deep breath and he thought he saw her counting in her head again. Then she turned to look at him, her face a picture of cold fury.

"I did listen to you, Nick, and that's the problem. I listened to you when you told me you were a big deal photographer who was doing me a huge favor by helping me. I listened to you when you told me you loved taking photos of me. I listened to you—I *trusted you*—when you told me you were single and successful and so happy to take whatever I had to offer you, and it was all bullshit. So forgive me if I don't want to hear more of your bullshit now."

"It wasn't bullshit!" he cried. "Yes, I let you all believe that my career was going better than it really was, but I wasn't trying to screw over you or anyone else. I was just scared that I wasn't far along enough in my life, that I didn't have it all together like Marcus and Heather and everyone else we know. Don't tell me you don't know what that feels like."

Her eyes filled with tears, then narrowed in anger. "Of course I know what that feels like. *You* made me feel that way. And then you made me feel like I *was* enough, but that was a lie, too."

His stomach dropped, but before he could say anything else, she pushed past him and stalked down the hall towards the kitchen. He followed her, unwilling to let her out of his sight before he could apologize, explain.

"Carly, please, just stop. I need you to listen to me, because I'm trying to tell you that I'm sorry and I'm fucking falling in love with you!" He caught up to her at the kitchen doorway and grabbed her forearm to keep her from walking out the back door. He tugged on her arm and she whirled around to face him. Her eyes were sparkling with tears again, and she looked more furious than he'd ever imagined her.

"I swear to God, Nick, I don't want to hear your bullshit apologies. I don't want your pity job. And I sure as shit don't want to hear that you're falling for me. You lied to me. Over and over. And Alice is standing out there and she's about to hand me a microphone, so unless you want me to light your ass up in front of all those people, I suggest you let me *go!*" She yanked her arm out of his grasp, probably expecting him to hold on to her, but he let her slip through his fingers, and as she pulled her arm back from him, her purse flew out of her hand.

They both watched in horror as it sailed across the room towards the countertop and whacked into the second tier of the cake.

"Fuck," they gasped in unison, and they both lurched towards the cake as the middle tier collapsed. But neither of them got there in time to stop the top tier from toppling over and splattering onto the floor.

"Oh my God," Carly squeaked, jumping back to avoid getting icing and cake all over her feet. She stared at the demolished cake, which was now nothing but a pile of white rubble lying on top of the bottom tier. "Oh my God, oh no, no, *shit.*"

She looked at him, eyes wide and mouth open in mortification, and before he could move, she stooped and picked up her purse, and then turned around and ran down the hallway. A second later he heard the front door slam.

Carly ran down the garden path and out onto the street, barely registering the hot, hard pavement under her bare feet. She ran to the end of the block, adrenaline racing through her body and making her legs move faster than she'd known they could.

She'd fucked everything up. Everything. She'd fucked up by fooling around with Nick. She'd wasted her chance to get promoted. She'd lost her job. She'd destroyed Heather's wedding day. *Classic fucking Carly.*

She ran until she reached the front door of her rental, not caring how strange she must have looked running barefoot down the street in a gown and in tears at four in the afternoon. She fumbled with the keys and let herself inside and sprinted up the stairs, hearing nothing but her own wet, gulping breaths.

Once inside, she stood panting and shaking and stared unseeing at the beach house decor around her.

She had to leave. She had to get out of here. Out of this apartment, out of this city, out of this country. She had to go home. Now.

But she still had another three days left in Sydney before her flight, and a last-minute flight change would cost money she just didn't have. She stared around again, thinking hard. When her breath had settled enough to speak, she dug into her purse for her phone and dialed. She only had to wait two rings before the call went through.

"Hi, Dad, it's me. I, um, I need your help."

Chapter 24

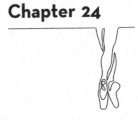

When Nick woke up the morning after the wedding, he allowed himself a brief, delusional moment of hope that when he rolled over, he'd find Carly asleep beside him. It was stupid, he knew, but he couldn't help himself. After a few seconds, he turned over under the sheet and saw exactly what he'd known he would find: an empty, Carly-less bed.

He laid on his back and let out a deep sigh, letting his memories of the night before wash over him. After Carly had vanished from the house, he'd gone outside and grabbed Alice and Davo as discreetly as he could. Alice had been horrified by the damage Carly's purse had done to her brother's magnificent cake creation. Davo said nothing, which was standard for him.

"Davo, how much have you had to drink? Can you drive?" Alice had asked in a decisive tone, once she'd recovered herself.

"Uh, yeah, but—"

"Good. Get your keys, and go up the street to the bakery. Buy the biggest pavlova they have. Bring it back here, *carefully*, and we'll put it on top of the bottom layer. We can clean the cake topper off and put it back on top."

"I don't know if that'll work," he replied, looking at the messy remnants of the cake.

"It's either that or get them both so drunk they don't notice their wedding cake looks like a car crash," she said. "Go. Nick and I will stall the speeches and the cake cutting until you get back."

Davo gave her a skeptical shrug, but he dug his keys out of his pocket and headed for the front door.

Once he was gone, Alice turned to Nick. "What the hell happened?"

"Carly and I were arguing, and she threw her purse."

"At you?"

"No, although she probably wanted to," he muttered.

"Do I want to know what got her mad enough to throw her purse at her best friend's wedding cake?" Alice raised her eyebrows expectantly.

"It wasn't like that," he said defensively. "It was an accident. She didn't really throw it, it just . . . flew out of her hand."

"Where is she?"

Nick's stomach churned miserably. "She left. A few minutes ago. She was pretty upset."

"When is she coming back? According to Heather's run sheet she's supposed to be giving a toast in—" Alice checked the time on the microwave "—three minutes ago."

Nick stared at his feet, and at the chunks of cake and white icing all over the kitchen floor. "I don't know."

He could feel Alice staring at him in disbelief. No doubt she blamed him for Carly's disappearance, and she wasn't wrong.

"Okay, here's what we're going to do," she said in a firm, quiet voice. "You're going to clean this up. I'm going to go tell Heather and Marcus that there's a problem with the cake and we're working on it. And I'll say that Carly's not feeling well but that she told us all we should carry on without her and she'll be back soon."

Nick nodded, and once she left out the back door, he pulled a handful of paper towels off the roll and started picking chunks of cake off the floor and wiping icing off the cabinets. But as he watched from the window as Alice slipped into her seat and leant over to talk to Marcus and Heather, he knew that Carly—who would do just about anything for Heather, even if it meant teaming up with someone she hated and missing her chance at a promotion—wouldn't be back to give her toast at her best friend's wedding. And he knew it was all his fault.

Morning light streamed into his hotel room, warm and bright and hopeful. He felt none of those things. Alice and Davo's cobbled-together pavlova-cake had turned out fine, and Heather and Marcus had seemed so happy to be toasting and eating cake with their loved ones that they'd laughed off the last minute cake swap.

"I guess it was BYO cake after all," Heather had grinned.

As Marcus and Heather fed each other mouthfuls of store-bought pavlova, Nick had caught Alice's eye across the table, and they'd both let out a sigh of relief. Alice had saved the day, but Carly never returned to the reception. He'd noticed that as the night went on, Heather looked more and more worried. Shit, he was worried, too, and part of him wanted to go find Carly and make sure she was all right. But he also knew that she wanted nothing to do with him. Still, with every big moment—Leanne's moving toast about her son, Marcus and Heather's first dance—he thought, *she should be here.*

"Text her in the morning," Nick heard Alice say to Heather, as Heather glanced over her shoulder at the back door yet again. "I'm sure she'll be fine by then."

Nick sat up slowly in bed and felt his hamstrings object to the movement. He hadn't danced much last night, but at one point Izzy had dragged him onto the dance floor and made him whirl her around, and this morning he could feel it in his legs and his lower back. He was definitely out of ballet shape if one dance to "Wham!" could leave him feeling like this the next day.

He checked his phone. No texts or calls from Carly. But there was an email from Victor Wilkinson waiting in his inbox. Contracts for him to sign, and a note asking him to propose the first three locations where he wanted to shoot, and the dancers he wanted to use as his models.

Anywhere, was his first thought. *I'll go anywhere, and the only dancer I want is Carly.*

He was in the middle of typing out a response to Victor when his phone vibrated with a text from Alice, sent to him, Davo, and Carly.

Alice, 9:48 AM: Clean up crew, assemble! Shouldn't take more than a few hours if we all pitch in. Iz and I will bring coffee and some of Will's cheesymite scrolls.
Nick, 9:49 AM: Be there in 30.

* *

Transpacific Airlines, 10:07 AM: Thanks for flying with Transpacific! Your plane is at the gate and boarding will begin soon. We look forward to welcoming you on board.

There was a special place in hell reserved for the people who designed the lighting in airport bathrooms, Carly thought once again, as she stared at her own reflection in the mirror over the sink. But even if the lighting had been photo-shoot quality, she knew she looked like hell. Her eyes were pink and puffy, and her hair was still crunchy with the products Izzy had sprayed on it yesterday morning. She bent over and splashed her face with water, then patted it dry with a scratchy paper towel. It didn't help.

As she walked to her gate, her phone vibrated in her pocket yet again, and she didn't have to check to know who it was. She'd already tried to call three times this morning.

Heather, 10:09 AM: Please call when you wake up, I'm worried about you.

Carly tucked herself behind a pillar and looked out at the tar-
mac. Bright, blinding sunshine was bouncing off the nose of her
plane, and the blue sky was dotted with puffy, plump, pearly-
white clouds. A perfect summer day. Yet another thing she could
ruin for Heather.

She took a deep breath and put her headphones in. She didn't
need all of Sydney Airport to hear this conversation.

After half a ring, Heather's face popped onto the screen. She
was wearing a pair of ice-blue silk pajamas, and her hair was in
big just-woke-up waves.

"Are you okay?" she asked immediately.

"I'm fine," Carly nodded, even though nothing could have been
further from the truth.

"What happened last night? Did you get food poisoning or
some— Wait, where are you right now?"

Carly swallowed. "I'm at the airport. I'm going home."

"What's wrong? Did something happen to Edward and Marlene?"

"No, they're fine. Listen, I'm sorry I wasn't there last night. I
screwed everything up."

"What are you talking about? Are you okay?" Heather asked
again, frowning and leaning closer to the screen to look at Carly's
face.

Carly's eyes started to water. "No, I'm not. I messed everything
up. I ruined your cake, and I wasn't there for the toast, and Catherine's going to fire me, and I'm so, so sorry, Heather."

"What are you talking ab—"

"And now I'm making it your problem again instead of figuring
it out for myself, and I'm just . . . I'm so sorry. I screwed up again,"
she sobbed loudly. In her peripheral vision, she saw someone stop
walking and stare at her. So much for Sydney Airport not witnessing
the Carly Montgomery Traveling Shitshow.

"Honey, stop. Take a deep breath," Heather said. Carly obeyed,
breathing through her mouth because her nose was too clogged.
"Okay. One thing at a time. What happened with Catherine?"

"The plan didn't work. The photos I took with—" She couldn't even say his name. "The photos we took in Sydney, they didn't work. Catherine told me she's not promoting me, and she's going to fire me instead."

"What makes you think that?"

"It doesn't matter, I'm just . . . I'm so sorry I wasn't there, Heather."

Heather sighed and leaned back on the pillow behind her. "I am too, hon. I missed you all night, and it sucked." Guilt swirled so violently in Carly's stomach she wondered if she was going to throw up.

"But," Heather went on, "I know how badly you wanted to be there, which means something really awful must have happened to make you leave. Did you get sick? Did something happen with Nick?"

"I don't want to talk about . . . about him. He's not important. I'm so sorry, Heather. I hate that I didn't show up for you. I hate that I'm always asking you to help me and save me and pull me out of trouble."

Heather frowned. "What are you talking about? You're the one who helps *me*."

"No, I'm not, I'm—"

"You're the one who flew over here and ran errands for three weeks straight," Heather interrupted stubbornly. "You're the one who helped me see the truth about Jack. You helped me get to Sydney, and you helped me get Marcus back when I thought I'd lost him forever. You're the reason I woke up married this morning!"

Carly sniffed and wiped her nose on the back of her hand. Her tiny image in the corner of the screen looked completely pathetic. But she wanted to believe what Heather was saying.

"I just feel like such a fuckup. I ruined your wedding, I ruined my chance at a promotion, I'm just . . . I'm nowhere."

"Carly, listen to me. You're not a fuckup. You've spent over ten years dancing in one of the most prestigious companies in the world, for God's sake. Okay, so you won't retire as a principal dancer, but you're still exceptional. This isn't all or nothing. Ballet makes you feel like life is all or nothing, like you're perfect or you're worthless, but let me tell you, when I was in New York I had it all, and it all came to nothing. You're talented, and tenacious, and you're going to figure out what comes next. I know you feel like you're nowhere right now, but you're going to be okay, I promise."

Carly felt hot tears running down her cheeks and didn't bother to wipe them away. She was so tired of feeling like she wasn't enough. For Catherine, for the men she dated, for herself. But Heather was telling her that she was enough for her, even after she'd screwed up so completely.

"I should have been there," she said quietly.

"Yes, you should have," Heather replied. "Next time I get married, I expect you to stay for the whole night."

Carly managed a small smile, but relief was a cold drink on a hot day. She hadn't ruined everything. She hadn't ruined the most important thing.

"If I thought that was ever going to happen, I'd promise to be there," she said. "But I know you and Marcus are forever."

Heather sniffed. "So are we. You and me. And at least you ran out before you could tell any embarrassing stories about me."

Carly's smile became a grin. "I did, didn't I? But that doesn't mean I can't tell them now."

"No, don't," Heather objected, but Carly was already pulling up the notes app on her phone.

"Come on, if I'm the world's best maid of honor, I need to give the world's best maid of honor toast," she said, and Heather responded with a watery laugh. "Aren't you a little curious to know which embarrassing story I picked?"

"Kind of," Heather admitted.

"Well, then," Carly cleared her throat and glanced around her to make sure none of the passengers at the gate were listening in. Then she began.

"Ladies and gentlemen, my name is Carly Montgomery, and Heather has been my best friend since we were eleven years old. Which means that since the very first day she arrived at the NYB school, she's been looking out for me. Taking care of me, talking me down, helping me clean up my messes. We're both only children, but she's a big sister like that. On the day I got kicked out of ballet class for doing cartwheels, Heather went to the teacher and begged her to give me a second chance, and when she refused, Heather told her calmly that she was planning to teach the entire class to do cartwheels if I wasn't allowed back into class. She'd planned a whole cartwheel clinic, just like she planned this whole beautiful wedding."

Carly stopped to wipe away the tears that were running steadily down her cheeks. It didn't matter that Linda had nearly had a stroke when she'd found out what Heather had done, and it didn't matter that it was fear of losing her parents' donations that had actually convinced the school to let Carly come back to class. What mattered was that Heather had fought for her. She glanced back down at her notes.

"That's who Heather Hays was: the kindest, most stubborn, most terrifyingly organized child you'd ever met. And that's who she still is. I used to think there was no one in the world who deserved a lifetime of Heather. And I still think that. But Marcus comes damn close, and I know he's going to make her happy every day."

Heather made a strangled sobbing sound and wiped her eyes with the back of her hand.

"And then I'd tell everyone to raise their glasses to Heather and the luckiest man alive, Marcus."

"Cheers!" Heather said, with another loud sniff. Carly wiped her own face quickly and closed the notes app.

"Thank you," Heather said. "I wish you'd been here to give it last night. Are you sure you have to leave?"

Carly shook her head. "I need to go home. If Catherine's going to fire me, I need to make a new plan."

Heather's shoulders drooped in disappointment, but she gave Carly a kind smile. "I'll help, if you want. Apparently I'm pretty good with plans."

Carly hesitated for a long moment. Then she nodded again. "I'd like that."

Chapter 25

Nick arrived at Marcus and Heather's place to find Heather having a friendly argument with Alice.

"Absolutely not," Alice was saying as she washed a wine glass and handed it to Izzy, who wiped it dry and put it in the plastic rental case. "Sit down and eat your cheesymite scroll and don't even think of helping."

"I can't just sit here while you clean up my wedding," Heather objected.

"Yes, you can," Izzy chimed in. "You planned the whole thing, at least let us clean it up for you. And she's right about the scrolls. Will says these are a failed batch, but he's crazy, because they're perfect."

"Just let me—" Heather stood and reached for a dirty glass.

"Sit!" both women said, and she sat, smiling and shaking her head at her friends.

"We've got this handled. The guys are going to take down the tables and the lights, and when Carly arrives we'll put her to work as well," Alice said, and Heather bit her lip.

"Uh, Carly's not coming," she said, her eyes darting towards Nick.

"Is she okay?" Nick asked, before he could stop himself. Alice and Izzy asked the same thing at precisely the same time.

"Not really. She's not hurt or sick, but she was pretty upset when I spoke to her this morning." Heather was looking at Alice and Izzy, but Nick had the distinct impression that her words were meant for him. "This obviously isn't public yet, but it sounds like NYB isn't going to renew her contract, and she's devastated."

"Oh, shit," Alice said, her hands stilling around a soapy wine glass.

Oh shit was right, Nick thought. Why hadn't Carly told him about this? *Because she doesn't trust you, you idiot.* And why would she, after he lied to her? After their project, *her* project idea, won him the chance of a professional lifetime?

He glanced over his shoulder, towards the front door. "Where is she?" he asked Heather.

Heather paused, chewing on her bottom lip. This time, when she spoke, she wasn't looking at Alice and Izzy. She looked right at Nick, her expression a mix of helplessness and sympathy.

"She's gone. Her flight back to New York just took off."

"But . . . I thought she wasn't leaving for a few more days?" Nick objected, not bothering to conceal the pleading note in his own voice. Alice and Izzy looked at him, surprised, but he ignored their synchronized raised eyebrows. He'd thought he had more time. More time to explain, to apologize, to make her understand why he'd done what he'd done. To make clear how he felt about her.

"I'm sorry," Heather sighed, giving him a knowing look. "I wanted her to stick around, too. She should land in about twenty hours if you, uh, want to call her."

He didn't want to call her, he wanted to kiss her. Wanted to hold her as she fell asleep and watch her argue with her pillow and win.

"It's fine," he muttered. "Hope she has a safe flight. I'm going to go help Davo." Without waiting for Heather's reply, he strode across the kitchen and yanked the back door open.

The backyard was strewn with the remnants of last night: A napkin had blown into the bushes, and there were a few wine glasses lying on the grass. The white linen tablecloths had been left out overnight and bore scattered wet patches where the dew hadn't dried yet. In the corner of the garden, Davo was on a large stepladder, pulling the fairy lights down from where they'd been fastened to a pole lashed to the fence.

"G'day," Davo grunted, giving Nick a curt nod before returning to the string of lights.

"You want a hand?" Nick asked. Moving would help. Doing something, completing a task, would make it feel less like his chest was cracking in two. He remembered this feeling, from when Delphine had dumped him, but he didn't remember it being this disorienting, like he could barely remember his own name.

"Nah, I'm right. Can you pull up the dance floor, though?"

Nick nodded and got to work.

Half an hour later, he'd pulled the three heavy sheets of painted plywood off the grass and carried them over to the back gate, ready for loading onto Davo's ute. He'd folded the tablecloths and collapsed the tables and had just started collecting the abandoned napkins and glasses when the back door slid open and Marcus appeared with a glass of water in each hand.

"Finally, the married man emerges," Davo called, his arms full of tangled fairy lights. "How does it feel? You miss your freedom yet?"

Marcus looked at Nick and rolled his eyes, then did a double take and frowned. He elbowed the back door shut, walked over to Davo and handed him a glass, then crossed the garden to talk to Nick.

"What's wrong with you?" he asked, quiet enough that Davo couldn't hear.

"I'm fine," Nick said, taking the water from his friend's hand.

"You're full of it," Marcus said, looking at him closely. "Heather said something about Carly leaving in a hurry? Do you know anything about that?"

Nick took a big gulp of water and took his time swallowing it. Marcus watched him patiently, with an expression that clearly said he wasn't having it. "I don't want to talk about it," Nick lied.

Marcus watched him for another moment, then seemed to decide something.

"Oi, Davo, we're going on a coffee run. You want your usual?"

Davo grunted in response, and Marcus gave Nick a decisive nod. "Let's go."

They were around the block before Marcus tried again.

"What happened with Carly? She disappeared last night, and now she's on the first flight back to New York?"

Nick sighed. He needed to tell his friend the truth, at last.

"Things haven't been going that well for me lately. With Delphine, and with retirement, it's been a hard year. And, well, the photography thing wasn't going that well, either," he said to the concrete three feet in front of them. "I know it looked like I was doing okay, and I didn't say anything when you all thought I was making it work, but the truth is I wasn't. I was floundering. And when I came home from Paris, I had no idea what I was going to do next. If I'd have to figure out something else entirely, because dance photography wasn't working out."

"I'm sorry, mate. Why didn't you just tell us that? Or tell me, at least?"

"Because you were handling retirement so well. You have a new career lined up, you're married now, you're . . . You're moving forward, and I was just flailing."

Marcus didn't stop walking, but he did turn to stare at Nick. "I got fired. After a year of recovering from surgery, and right after my dad died. You think I don't know what flailing feels like?"

"Right," Nick agreed, "but then you figured it out."

"Yeah, mate, I figured it out with help. From Shaz and the physio team at the company, from Alice, from Heather, even from Davo in a weird way. I couldn't handle it all on my own."

"I know, I just . . . I didn't want to add more stuff to your plate."

"Bullshit," Marcus said flatly. "That's crap and you know it."

They stopped at a crossing, and Nick forced himself to look at Marcus. It was crap. He'd been insecure, and jealous of his friend's new life.

He swallowed hard and told himself that Marcus would understand. "I'm sorry. I should have told you the truth, but I hated the truth. I don't want to be jealous of you. You deserve everything you have, everything you worked for."

Marcus was quiet for a long moment. "They make you take a liberal arts class if you want to be a physio, don't ask me why. I ended up in a poetry seminar, and I thought I would hate it, but one day we read this poem that made the last couple of years make sense to me. *Let everything happen to you: beauty and terror. Just keep going. No feeling is final.* I really needed to hear that." He put his hand on Nick's shoulder, just like Nick had done before they'd walked down the aisle the day before. "No feeling is final. The shit ones, the depressed ones, even the great ones, they're all temporary. You have to remember that, or they'll swallow you whole. There are only a few things in life that are truly forever and truly unfixable. Everything else, you can get through. And you can get through the unfixable stuff, too. Trust me."

Marcus's eyes glittered with tears, and Nick felt his throat thicken with emotion. Marcus gave his shoulder another squeeze, then he dropped his hand and they crossed the road together. Nick turned the words over in his mind as they walked. *Let everything happen to you: beauty and terror.* He thought about the famous Australian poem he'd loved as a kid. *I love her far horizons, I love her jewel sea. Her beauty and her terror, the wide brown land for me.* He thought about Carly, how she'd stormed into his life, stunned him, and stormed out again. How she'd *happened* to him, all beauty and terror and delight and confusion. Chaos. Control. Contentment, for a few precious moments there, before they'd allowed their insecurities to destroy it all.

No feeling was final. He wouldn't feel rootless forever. He wouldn't feel insecure forever. He wouldn't miss Carly forever.

"You didn't really answer my question, though," Marcus said, after another block. "What happened with Carly?"

Nick sighed. Might as well come all the way clean. "The photos we were taking? I got a job offer out of them. A big one, from *Vogue*. They want me to go all over the world photographing dancers for them. I found out the day before the wedding."

"Mate, that's huge, congratulations."

"Thanks," Nick replied quickly, "but that wasn't what was supposed to happen. The whole point was to help Carly get promoted, and it didn't work. They're not renewing her contract, and she found out I'd been lying about my own work, and, well."

"She did a Carly," Marcus finished.

"Big time," Nick said. "Which I deserved, because I should have told her the truth, too, but the thing is—"

"You're crazy about her." It was a statement, not a question.

"I— How did you know?"

Marcus laughed, and Nick stared at him in surprise.

"Please don't take this the wrong way," Marcus grinned, sounding frankly delighted that he got to be the one to break the news to Nick, "but it was super fucking obvious last night. The way you were looking at her? Like she was holding your heart in her hands? Anyone watching you would have known in two seconds that you were head over heels for her."

Nick opened his mouth to argue, but he couldn't think of anything to say. Marcus was right. He was head over heels for Carly Montgomery. The problem was, the woman who was holding his heart in her hands was on a plane, headed for the other side of the world.

"I don't know what to do," he sighed. "The *Vogue* thing is such a huge deal, and I should be happy about it. And being back here just makes it more complicated, because it's home, but it's not, and

I'm from here, but I don't live here, and I . . . I just feel unmoored, you know? And now, she's gone, too."

"My mum still doesn't want to sell the house," Marcus said, as they approached the coffee shop, and Nick frowned at the sudden non sequitur. "We tried for a while, Davo and me, to get her to give it up, but she's still so attached to it, because of Dad, because of us. And one day I asked her why she couldn't make a home somewhere else, an apartment or something without stairs and stuff. You can make any place feel like home. Home is where the heart is, right? And she said, 'No, home is wherever it hurts the most to leave.'

"And I don't know if I agree with that, but maybe home doesn't have to be a place. Maybe it can be a sound, a taste, a feeling. A person. Maybe it's where you feel the most like yourself. Or maybe it's more than one thing at once. You can still call Australia home," Marcus said, gesturing over Nick's shoulder at the beach, "but I think the luckiest people get to call multiple places home."

Nick nodded, his throat too thick with tears to say anything, and let Marcus order his coffee for him. They walked back in silence, down the frangipani-scented street and towards the salt spray wafting off the beach.

He had left home a long time ago, and now, it didn't hurt to leave any place. But it sure as hell hurt to be left.

Chapter 26

Carly trudged away from the baggage carousel at JFK airport, having checked three times that the suitcase she'd pulled off it was actually hers. She didn't bother with a luggage cart this time. She might never risk a luggage cart ever again.

To her surprise, she saw a familiar man waving at her and holding up a tablet with her full name on it. Of course her parents had sent Timur, the family's longtime driver, to collect her.

Exhausted from two long and sleepless flights, Carly returned his wave with far less enthusiasm and followed him out to the curb, where a sleek black town car was waiting. It was already dark at 5:00 PM, and freezing rain pelted them as he loaded her suitcase into the trunk.

"In, in!" he urged her, and she fell into the backseat, plopping her backpack at her feet with a sigh.

"Hello, Caroline."

Carly started. Her mother was sitting on the other side of the pebbled leather seat, looking at her appraisingly.

"Hi, Mom," she managed, weakly.

Marlene Parker-Montgomery looked flawless as ever, every strand of her shoulder-length auburn hair in perfect place, as though it had just been blown out at the salon. Which, Carly reminded herself, it probably had been. She was wearing a classic Marlene outfit: black wool slacks and an immaculately crisp white silk blouse under a Burberry trench coat. Her camel-colored kitten-heeled boots were made of a leather that looked so soft Carly would have used it for washcloth, and a Hermes scarf was tied carefully around her neck, not quite concealing her usual two-strand pearl necklace, which she always wore with matching pearl earrings. The entire interior of the car smelled like her custom-blended perfume, the familiar peppery-floral scent that announced that Marlene was in the building.

"You look well," her mother said, in a tone that made it very clear that she was only being polite.

Carly resisted the urge to roll her eyes. "It's a long flight back, and I'm tired."

"You could have flown in first, you know. Your father and I would have been very happy to—"

"I know, Mom," Carly interrupted tersely, but she tried to soften her tone. It had made her feel like even more of a failure to call her parents and ask them for the money to change her ticket, but they'd helped her without hesitation, and she was grateful. "Coach isn't so bad, really. And it's a long flight no matter where you're sitting."

"Mmm," Marlene replied doubtfully. Marlene Parker-Montgomery had never flown coach in her life, and she never would.

Timur drove them out of the clogged underpasses around the airport, and soon they were speeding along the highway toward Manhattan. Sunday night traffic was light, and Carly let her head fall back against the soft leather headrest, thinking that at least she'd be in her own bed in less than an hour. But when they arrived in the city, Timur turned uptown.

"Hang on," Carly objected, as the car rolled in the wrong direction.

"I'm taking you home," her mother said quickly.

"You mean to your home. *My* home is downtown," Carly said. She just wanted to be alone in her little apartment. Dingy and inadequate as her parents clearly thought it was, it was hers. Well, it was her landlord's, but the money on every single rent check was hers.

"Yes, to our home," Marlene confirmed. "You can spend the night with us and go to your home tomorrow."

"Mom, please, I really want to—"

"Caroline," her mother interrupted crisply. "You called us from the other side of the world. You asked us for help for the first time in over a decade. You look as though you've spent the last two days crying. Something is obviously wrong. We are your parents. I am your *mother*. I understand that you have some kind of allergy to accepting our money, but please, accept our hospitality. Your old room is all ready, and if you want to sneak out at dawn and disappear downtown, that's your business. But I insist you come home with me tonight."

Carly stared at her mother's usually composed face, which was flushed with frustration, and found that she was too tired to argue. And that she didn't want to argue, anyway. Her mother might not understand her, but she did love her. And when you loved someone, you wanted to help them. And it hurt when you couldn't. She knew that all too well from spending years trying to help Heather see the truth about Jack.

Nick offered to help you the other night, a voice in her head reminded her, unhelpfully. *He offered to help you even before you asked him.*

She sighed and nodded. "Okay, Mom. Let's go home."

Nick could go fuck himself with a purple sparkly dilator.

When Carly woke up the next morning, she could feel every single one of the hours she'd spent in transit in her body. Her back ached, and her hip flexors felt as if they were wound too tightly for her to walk. She rolled over with a groan and pressed herself into the mattress, stretching out her lower back.

She could smell him. She could smell Nick's spicy, citrusy scent in her childhood bedroom. She looked around the room, at the soaring ceiling, which was still painted to look like a calm blue sky full of fluffy clouds, a project her parents had commissioned for her eighth birthday. At the thick jacquard curtains around the bed, which they'd installed when she'd swooned over the curtained bed on stage the first time she'd seen NYB's production of *Romeo and Juliet*. And then down at the T-shirt she was wearing, the first garment she'd pulled out of her suitcase when she'd arrived here last night: the Leura House T-shirt.

For one long, weak moment, she looked down at the hideous stock art horses on her chest and let herself inhale the lingering notes of Nick that remained on the fabric. Let herself remember that exhausting, exhilarating night up in the Blue Mountains, when they'd mixed drinks all night, and he'd crept into bed and called her "*ma puce.*" *My flea*, literally. But really, *my darling*.

Except she wasn't his darling. She was the jobless woman with a broken vagina that he'd lied to even as they'd been working together. Sleeping together.

She sat up and pulled the shirt over her head and threw it in the direction of her suitcase, but it slid under the ornate antique desk her parents had bought at Sotheby's when she started junior high and started bringing homework home. She climbed out of bed and walked to the en suite to shower, not bothering to retrieve it.

When she padded down the hall and into the dining room half an hour later, she was greeted by the same sight that had started her mornings every day when she was growing up: her mother sitting at the long mahogany table, drinking coffee and reading the *Wall Street Journal*. Marlene wasn't yet dressed for the day, but she still looked impeccable in a cashmere lounge set and custom-made velvet house slippers. As long as Carly could remember, her mother had sat at this table and read the paper from start to finish before retreating to her dressing room and re-emerging looking chic and ready to start a day of board meetings, charity lunches, or appointments with art dealers or personal shoppers or who knew who else.

Carly paused in the doorway, watching her mother scan the pages and sip elegantly from her light-as-air porcelain cup. Marlene had red hair, too, though hers was darker and more subdued than Carly's. For the last decade or so, grays had begun to creep in, and to Carly's surprise, Marlene hadn't tried to hide them. She hadn't resorted to Botox or plastic surgery like so many of the wealthy women walking these streets, and as a result, she looked her age. When she frowned, her whole face moved and wrinkled, which was a rarity around here. As Carly watched, a frown appeared, and Marlene looked up from the paper.

"Good morning," her mother said cautiously. "Are you hungry? Camille can make you something if you are."

"I'm okay," Carly shrugged. "But could I have some coffee?"

Marlene nodded and opened her mouth to call out to the chef, who was almost certainly working on dinner already.

"It's fine, Mom, I'll get it myself," Carly said quickly.

"Of course you will," she heard Marlene say under her breath as she headed for the kitchen.

When she returned a few minutes later with a comically small cup of coffee—what she wouldn't give for a giant iced coffee right now, even an Australian one—her mother had finished with the real estate section and had moved on to the arts pages. Carly sat down as unobtrusively as she could and took a few careful sips, feeling, like she often had, as though she was too loud for this huge, quiet place, with its high ceilings and lush fabrics.

She took a few more sips and sighed, feeling the caffeine work its way into her system. At the sound, her mother looked up, and Carly was about to apologize for the disruption when Marlene spoke.

"You came back early."

"Not that early, just . . . just a few days." Just early enough to miss half of her best friend's wedding and break her years-long streak of not asking her parents for help.

"What happened?" Maybe Marlene didn't mean to sound disappointed, or accusing, but she definitely did.

"Nothing happened," Carly said defensively. "I just needed to come home. Why do you assume something happened?"

Marlene pursed her lips slightly, and Carly thought she might be about to drop the subject. She should have known better. Her mother was nothing if not persistent.

Marlene set the paper down. "I'm not *assuming* anything, I'm observing a set of facts. Your father said you sounded distressed when you called. You asked for our help. And then you agreed to spend the night here, and you were here when I woke up. You even accepted a cup of coffee just now. So I am *observing* that something has changed, and since it's clearly not your attitude, I have to imagine that it's your circumstances. In other words, something happened."

Irritation nipped at the back of Carly's neck. She hated when her mother talked to her this way, in that cool but clearly frustrated tone. Carly didn't enjoy the guilty, smoldering aftermath of yelling at someone, but at least it felt better in the moment than this clipped performance of civility.

"Nothing happened," she told Marlene firmly, and she saw her mother's squared shoulders droop slightly. In disappointment? Frustration? Confusion? Probably all three, which shouldn't surprise Marlene: Carly had spent most of her life as a confusing, frustrating disappointment.

Except, that wasn't true, was it? Okay, so her parents didn't understand her. But they'd also leapt into action to help her the second she'd asked, and now, her mother only wanted to know *why* she'd asked. She looked across the table at Marlene and tried to remember what Heather had told her at the airport. It didn't have to be all or nothing. She didn't have to reveal absolutely nothing to her mother, just like she didn't have to refuse absolutely all help from her parents.

"Okay, something happened," she conceded, and her mother's eyebrows rose. "Or is about to happen. I have a meeting with

Catherine Lancaster the day after tomorrow, and she's going to tell me that she's not renewing my contract. So this season will be my last, and then I'll have to figure out what comes next."

Marlene's forehead creased in a concerned frown. "Why aren't they renewing your contract?"

"I'm old," Carly shrugged, feigning a calm acceptance she didn't feel. "I'm not principal material, I'm Peasant Maiden #4 material. I've had a good run, but I guess they're moving on. Which means I need to move on, too."

Marlene nodded slowly, processing this information, and Carly took her silence as an opportunity to drink more coffee. *I need to move on, too.* From ballet, from her hope of being promoted. From Nick, from her hope that there was at least one man out there she could trust with her body. With her heart. She would figure it out, she told herself.

"What will you do next?" Marlene asked.

Carly shrugged again. "I don't know. I'm . . . Well, I'm scared. I don't know how to do anything but dance, because it's all I've ever wanted to do. And I got to do it, and I'm really grateful. But I don't know what comes next. But I'll figure it out."

"Your father and I would be very happy to—"

"Mom," Carly said firmly, and Marlene stopped talking, her mouth still open. "I'll figure it out."

Marlene closed her mouth, looking defeated but unsurprised.

"But if I need your help, I'll ask for it. I promise. Okay?"

Marlene squared her shoulders again and gave her a close-mouthed smile. "Understood, Carly," she said.

"Okay." Carly drained the rest of her coffee and stood, groaning slightly at the stiffness in her quads and hips. "I should go home. Thank you for the coffee, and for letting me stay. And for getting me home."

"You're very welcome. Should I bother offering to ask Timur to drive you downtown?" Marlene asked, picking up her paper.

"No," Carly smiled. "But I'll take some coffee for the road. Please."

Marlene nodded and returned her smile. "Help yourself," she said.

Nick's phone rang as he was packing the last of his cameras into his suitcase. His carry-on this time. Better safe than sorry. He flipped the suitcase closed with one hand and grabbed his phone with the other, and froze when he saw the name on the caller ID.

"Dad?" he answered carefully.

"Nick." His father's voice was low and terse, and he'd said Nick's name like a full sentence.

"Is, euh, is everything okay?" His dad hadn't called him in years. Had something happened to Nina or his mum?

"How was the wedding?"

Nick frowned. *How was the wedding?* From the man who seemed constitutionally incapable of small talk? The man whose house Nick had stormed out of barely a week ago?

"It was fine," Nick said slowly. Then, because he was still worried, he repeated: "Is everything okay?"

"Yes. I just wanted to congratulate you on the article in the paper," his dad said stiffly. Nick could picture him sitting on the couch in the living room overlooking the valley, or at the kitchen table with a steaming mug of tea, which he drank year-round, sweltering Australian summers be damned. It had never occurred to Nick that his dad, devoted newspaper reader that he was, would see Ivy's story. Nina had already texted him about it, of course, and had threatened to get it framed for his next birthday present.

"Thanks," Nick said carefully. "Is that all?"

There was a long pause, and Nick was about to pull the phone away from his ear to make sure the call hadn't dropped when his father spoke again.

"I also wanted to tell you that I'm proud of you. I know I haven't acted like it, but I am. Your, uh, American friend was a little forceful in making her point, but she was right. What you've achieved is very impressive."

Nick's chest constricted at the mention of Carly. At the memory of her flying to her feet and telling his dad how great Nick was, how proud they all should be of him. He took a deep breath, trying to loosen the snug bands of pain around his ribs.

"Thanks, Dad," he said softly. He swallowed hard against the tide of emotions welling in his throat. How long had he been waiting to hear those words come out of his father's mouth? Long enough that he'd stopped hoping, without even realizing he'd given up on it ever happening.

His dad cleared his throat, and Nick realized there was more. "I also wanted to say I understand if you've made a home somewhere else. But you'll always be welcome here, however long you want to stay."

Nick pressed his lips together, trying to chase away the sting at the bridge of his nose. "Okay," he managed, not trusting himself to say any more without his voice cracking. After a long moment, he collected himself enough to speak.

"I'm sorry for the way I left, Dad. I shouldn't have gone behind your back. I know I hurt you and Mum, and I'm sorry."

"You were right to do it." Rod's voice was scratchy now, too. "I didn't understand it at the time, but I see now that it was the only way for you to have the career you wanted."

Nick nodded, then remembered his dad couldn't see him. "Right. But still, I'm sorry. Because those first few years were really hard. I was so young, and I didn't know anyone, and the company worked us into the ground in the corps—and I couldn't call you and tell you any of that. I was too proud to admit I might have made a mistake."

"But you got through it, didn't you? And look at you now."

Right. Look at him now. Finally a successful photographer, just like he'd pretended to be. And still nowhere to call home. Not really. And still a giant ache between his ribs every time he thought about Carly. *No feeling is final*, he reminded himself. *And home doesn't have to be a place.*

"She's quite the firecracker, your American," his dad said, and the ache only intensified. *Not my American.*

"Yeah, she's a lot," Nick said, managing a small smile. *She's so much. So much passion and rage and fierce loyalty. She's all of it. Everything.*

"She clearly thinks the world of you," his dad replied. *She used to,* Nick wanted to say, but he wasn't ready to reveal all that to his dad today. This mending felt too new and tenuous, and he didn't totally trust it yet. "And she looks beautiful in those photos you took."

Nick pressed his lips together again, with no idea of how to respond to that. Luckily, his dad saved him.

"Your sister told us she won't be the messenger anymore. That if I wanted to know about your life, I'd have to ask you myself."

God bless Nina. She'd finally figured out that she couldn't fix this mess for him. Nick's throat went tight.

"I see," he managed. He waited to see if his father was going to act on Nina's new rule, or if it was too soon.

"So, where are you off to next?"

"Euh, Santorini. Greece. I've always wanted to go."

"I hear it's beautiful. And after that?"

"I don't know."

"All right. Will you be coming home any time soon? Not to stay, I mean. To visit?"

Nick couldn't miss the hope in his dad's voice, and it made him wish he didn't have to get on a plane in a few hours.

"I don't know, but soon. I promise."

"All right." His dad let out a sigh. "You can always come home. We'll—I'll—always be glad to see you. That's all we were trying to say. You can always come home."

Chapter 27

Catherine Lancaster's office was on the sixteenth floor of the building that housed the NYB school and the company's administrative staff, and as Carly rode the elevator from the lobby, which was around the corner from Lincoln Center, she felt the same roiling nerves she'd always felt when she'd been called to an appointment with the artistic director. Perched on the firm leather couch in the waiting room, she remembered the last time she'd been called to this office, when Mr. K had informed her that he was firing her effective immediately, because Jack Andersen had asked him to choose between his golden boy and some random, replaceable woman in the corps.

Despite her nerves, she smiled grimly to herself. So few people got to say they'd been hired by NYB. Even fewer got to say they'd been fired by NYB twice. She'd woken up this morning in her own bed downtown and had spent a few minutes staring at the ceiling thinking about the coming season, which would be her last with the company. What would it be like to wake up and not go to company class? Or to wake up and not feel the previous night's performance in her calves and ankles and hips? She'd find out soon enough.

A phone rang on Catherine's assistant's desk.

"Carly," Barbara said a moment later, "she's ready for you."

Carly gave her a mute, nervous nod and stood. *Here we go*, she thought. *Time to get fired.*

Catherine stood as she entered, revealing the usual chic all-black outfit she wore on days when she wasn't teaching company class. She gestured Carly toward one of several seats on the other side of the desk, then sat down. In Mr. K's day, the desk had faced away from the floor-to-ceiling windows, which looked out over Lincoln Center Plaza and the grand white theater where the company performed, so that you couldn't look at the man without remembering that he was in charge of everything that happened in that huge, impressive building. Catherine had turned the desk ninety degrees, so that you still got the view, but only if you looked for it. Carly didn't want to look at it. She didn't want to think about the fact that her time on that stage was now so limited.

"Thanks for coming to see me," Catherine smiled, once Carly had sat down.

Carly tried to match her smile but couldn't quite manage it. Catherine had been a principal dancer at NYB until a few years ago, so Carly had known her for years, but it was still something of a surprise to see her in a sweater, slacks, and heels instead of a leotard, tights, and pointe shoes. She'd cut her hair to shoulder length since retiring, and she wore a little more makeup than she had when she'd been sweating at work all day long.

"Thanks for . . . asking me," Carly returned weakly. Had she just *thanked* Catherine for firing her in person?

"How was the wedding?"

"Oh, it was fine," Carly said, caught off guard. Were they going to engage in social small talk before Catherine lowered the ax? "Lovely, really. Heather is really happy down there, and it was a beautiful trip." *Except for the bit where the best man betrayed me and I found out I'm out of a job.*

"Looks like a beautiful city," Catherine nodded, "and you certainly made it look its best. The photos were fantastic, truly. A nice bit of positive press attention for NYB."

"Uh, thanks?" Carly said. If the photos were so great and press attention was so positive, why wasn't she getting promoted? Why was she getting fired?

"Like I said in my email, I want to talk to you about your future at the company," Catherine started, and Carly steeled herself. It would be fine. She would be fine. She would make a new plan. One that didn't involve Nick Jacobs's "help." And she'd be fine.

"As I'm sure you know, I didn't have any experience running a ballet company before they gave me this job. I didn't have any experience running any kind of company. I virtually went straight from being a principal dancer to being artistic director, in charge of this entire operation, with very little preparation and certainly no training beforehand."

Carly nodded. What did this have to do with Carly's contract?

"Obviously, I know the dancer's experience inside and out, but there are so many other people who make the company run: ballet mistresses, choreographers, costume designers, doctors, lighting designers, sales, marketing, philanthropists, the board." Her eyes widened, and she gave her head a little shake. "And that doesn't include everything on the school side: dealing with teachers, and parents, and funders, and the list goes on. It's so many things I had no idea how to do, and the learning curve has been extremely steep. I'm more than a year in and I still don't truly feel I know how to do it all well."

Carly nodded again, understanding even less why Catherine was telling her this. But she had no doubt it was all true: most companies picked their next artistic director out of the ranks of retiring principal dancers, and plenty of former NYB dancers were running companies around the country. If the board hadn't picked Catherine for this role, Mr. K probably would have tapped some other dancer—like Jack, God forbid—who would have transitioned straight from dancing into directing with basically no way of knowing if he'd be any good at a completely different kind of job. Carly suppressed a shudder at the idea of Heather's abusive, drunken ex being put in charge of her career and everyone else's.

"All of this is to say, I'm very grateful to have this job, but I think the model is broken," Catherine said. "Just because someone is a good dancer doesn't mean they know how to run a company."

"Okay . . ." Carly said, cautiously. She agreed, but she still didn't understand what this had to do with her own job.

"As I've told you, I've decided not to promote you this season," Catherine said gently. *Ah, here it comes.* "Instead, I'd like you to start shadowing me in this role. I'd like you to get a sense of what it requires and if it's something you'd like to start work toward. When you're ready to stop dancing, that is."

Carly stared at her.

"So I'm not getting fired?" she blurted out.

Catherine frowned. "No, you're not getting *fired*. But none of us can dance forever, and I think you have a future at this company. There's no way to know that until you've had some exposure to the job, of course. As I've said, it's very different from being a dancer, and not the kind of thing anyone should do without preparation and some kind of training. So I'd like you to spend some of your time this season here with me. You'll be paid for that time, of course. And if you enjoy the administrative and leadership side of the company, and think you'd like to do more of it, that's a conversation we'll have when you decide to stop performing."

Relief knocked all the air out of Carly's lungs. She still had a job. She was being offered the chance to explore another one. It was a future, a plan. A way to fend for herself after ballet.

"Is that something that interests you?" Catherine asked, after a moment.

"Yes," Carly said quickly, giving her a shaky smile. "Yes, absolutely. But I have to ask you something."

"Of course."

"I hope you understand that if I were to take this opportunity, or any role that came of it, it would be just me. Not my parents and their checkbook. I know that fundraising is a large part of running a company, but they haven't given to NYB or the school in years, and I wouldn't ask them to start giving again. Does that change things?"

Catherine shook her head slowly. "No, that's not a problem."

"You're sure?" Carly pressed.

"Yes, I'm sure," Catherine said, with a small, amused smile. "With all due respect to your parents, there are a lot of checkbooks in this city."

Carly laughed. "I guess that's true." She fell silent for a moment.

"Is something wrong?" Catherine asked. "If you want to take some time to think about this, you should."

"No, it's not that. I'm just in shock."

"You shouldn't be," Catherine shrugged. "You're observant and opinionated, and an excellent advocate for other dancers. That photo project makes me think you have a good sense of what modern balletgoers want and what gets them excited about ballet. Which is important, because we can't rely on, forgive me, rich old New Yorkers forever. The world is changing, and I think you understand that ballet will have to change with it. Assuming you don't mind the other, less enjoyable parts of the job, I suspect you'll find this work very gratifying. And you'd be doing me a favor, too," she added conspiratorially.

"Why?"

"Well, I want to stay in this job for as long as I can, but I'd be silly not to think about my successor. This current model for finding one is clearly broken, but unless I can find some other way of doing things, I won't be able to get the board to understand that. If we can show that this new way can work, we can set an example for other companies, and they can make sure that they're picking the best people for the job, not just the people they've always picked. It's not just about NYB, it's about ballet as a whole."

Carly gave her another smile, a full one this time. "You want to lead," she said.

"I do," Catherine agreed. "I'm sick of the Great Man model of ballet. I want great women, great people, a great collective. I want people who care about the future of ballet more than its past, and I don't want to figure this all out on my own."

For the first time in days, Carly's limbs didn't feel heavy with dread. She stood and shook Catherine's hand and walked out of the office, pride and relief warring in her chest. She had a job, and more than that, she had Catherine's trust and admiration. She'd *earned* that. All by herself.

Well, not all by herself. Nick had helped. But Nick was gone now, far away in Sydney or Scotland or Chiang Mai or whatever photogenic location he'd chosen for his first *Vogue* photo shoot. She was on her own now, and she was fine with that. Perfectly fine. As the elevator opened and she slumped against its mirrored walls, she could almost believe it.

Out on the plaza, she zipped her coat up to her throat and flipped up her hood. It was hard to believe that just a few days ago, she'd been sweltering in the Sydney sunshine. The trees around Lincoln Center were spindly and bare, and chunks of dirty gray snow were scattered around the stretch of grass next to the opera house. The pond had been drained, and the fountain was still. She dug her hands into her pockets and felt her phone vibrate. For a split second, she hoped it was Nick, but she squashed that hope as quickly as it had flared. She needed to tell Heather what had just happened. Quickly, with fingers numb from shock and cold, she checked the time in Sydney. Too late to call—if Heather was even awake, she was almost certainly busy with honeymoon-type activities.

Carly, 11:37 AM: Not fired! Not only not fired, but Catherine wants me to shadow her to see if I'd be any good at running a company. Call me when you can . . . I want to make a plan.

She paused, then sent another text.

Carly, 11:38 AM: Don't call me until AFTER opening night.
The plan can wait.

She stared down at her screen, hovering her thumb over Nick's name. She didn't know where in the world he was now, and she didn't want to care. She didn't want to start every morning remembering how it had felt to wake up next to him, his warm body curled elegantly around hers. She didn't want to think about his Freshwater-blue eyes every time she made eye contact with another man. She missed him enough to make her ribs ache, and she wanted to tell him that their plan had worked in a roundabout way, and she was furious with him, and she didn't want to feel any of that.

Forty minutes later, she climbed out of the subway station at Canal Street and dragged her jetlagged limbs up the stairs to her apartment, letting herself in the door with a deep, bone-tired sigh. She'd just flopped down on the couch and let her body sink into the saggy old cushions when there was a sharp knock at her door.

Carly sat up with a start and for a second all she could do was stare, suddenly alert, at the door. When another knock came, she pulled herself off the couch and opened the front door to find a messenger in a bright yellow jacket and matching beanie waiting for her, a package in one hand and a table in the other.

"Carly Montgomery?" he asked.

Carly nodded, and he held out the tablet. "Sign here, please."

She signed without thinking, and he handed over the package, which was about the size of a book but weighed almost nothing. "Thanks," she said numbly, and he nodded and hurried toward the stairwell.

Carly closed the door behind her and leaned against it, gazing down at the package in her hands. It was wrapped in thick, dark green paper she thought she recognized. Trying to ignore the way her heart had raced at the knock on the door, then sank when she saw the courier, she slipped a finger under the seam of the paper and prised it open. Of course Nick hadn't followed her back to New York, she chastised herself. Of course he hadn't dropped his fancy *Vogue* contract to beg for her forgiveness—and that was good, because she didn't want him to. He'd lied to her, over and over again. She didn't want him, at all. Nodding decisively, and ignoring the lingering ache of disappointment that throbbed in her chest, she lifted the paper away.

And revealed her hideous, Nick-scented T-shirt, ironed and carefully folded into a neat rectangle, with a piece of sturdy, green-trimmed paper pinned to the chest. The initials at the top of the card were MPM. Marlene Parker-Montgomery.

You left this behind, her mother had written in her distinctive, looping hand, *and I thought you might want it back.*

Chapter 27

Santorini was everything Nick had been promised. The light was so sharp, the colors so bold and bright. White, turquoise, ochre. The air was crisp and salty, the water was clear, the food put Sydney and Paris and Berlin to shame. The days reminded him of winter in Sydney: a chill in the air, but a warm, low sun that stuck around well into the evening. And because it was low season, he and the small *Vogue* crew had all the most picturesque and tourist-friendly locations to themselves. On this shoot, his models were a South Korean dancer named Hana and a former principal from the Birmingham Royal Ballet named Stella. They were both gorgeous and easy to work with—experienced at modeling and easy to coach. The night before their first shoot, they'd all gone out to a little beachside restaurant and stayed for hours, drinking Greek wine and sharing stories about their dance careers until the waiters started stacking chairs on tables.

After five days of shooting all over the island—on a black sand beach, on a yacht moored next to a volcanic island, in a hillside monastery—they were almost done. Hana and Stella had each been photographed in a closet's worth of couture, and Hana had asked the shoot director at least three times if she could keep the marigold-yellow gown she'd worn on the yacht. Beth, the production director, had answered every time with a firm no—"Not unless you have a spare $3,000"—which was about what each of the women had been paid for the week. Stella had shaken her head ruefully and told Hana to take the money.

From Santorini, he'd head to London, then to Portugal, then to Croatia, and then to India. He'd never be in one place for more than ten days, but he found the prospect of constant motion thrilling. Last time he'd stayed put for a few weeks, he'd made the biggest mistake of his life. Better to keep moving, even if it meant going where the wind took him.

Beside him, Beth checked her laptop, where she could see the images he was taking in close to real time.

"Do you think you have everything you need?" he asked, as he took a few more shots of Stella, who was posing against the ancient stone wall of the monastery, pulling up her swirling shell-pink gown just enough for the camera to see her relevéd feet. It was the last outfit of the day and the last day of the shoot.

"I think so," Beth muttered, not looking away from the screen. "You?"

"Yeah, I think so," he agreed. It had been a long week, and the back of his neck was prickling with the beginnings of a sunburn.

"Let's call it, then," Beth said, and he nodded.

"All right, everyone," Beth called to Stella and the assembled production and styling assistants, "that's a wrap on Santorini. Thanks for your work this week. Go relax and rest up, but not so much that you miss the shuttle tomorrow. We will leave for the airport with or without you."

That night, he did what he'd done most evenings: showered, changed into warmer clothes, and had a quick meal before the sun dropped too far in the sky, then grabbed his Nikon and headed out to stroll the narrow lanes that curved and wound around the stark white houses hanging on the hillsides. The constant glimpses of water reminded him of the Sydney headlands, and the cobblestones made him think of the Marais. After an hour or so of wandering, he sat down at a small café and ordered a glass of wine. He didn't know what, if anything, he'd do with these photos, but after so many months of producing work he didn't like, it felt like a precious relief to take photos without doubting. Without wondering if he'd ever be a real photographer.

He was a real photographer now. A real big deal photographer, just like he'd pretended to be in Sydney. Just last week, another magazine had asked him to call them when his contract with *Vogue* was up, and a representative for a young recent Oscar winner had reached out to him, emailed him an NDA, and then inquired if he was available to shoot the actress's pregnancy reveal photos.

A waiter arrived with a glass of red wine. "*Efcharistó*," Nick thanked him in his best Greek, which wasn't very good.

"You're welcome," the young man replied, and Nick chuckled.

The sun had slipped below the water, and the light was fading. He took a few sips of wine, then turned his camera back on and began scrolling through the night's work. The colors here were otherworldly, almost too rich and concentrated to seem real. Santorini, the original #nofilter. As he had a hundred times this week, he thought of the old proprietor of that little camera shop in Sydney and wondered where in Greece he'd emigrated from. Had he lived here before he crossed the world and started calling Australia home?

Under the darkening sky, he scrolled back through a week's worth of evening strolls, past shopfronts full of mouthwatering desserts and white buildings washed in golden-hour light. He scrolled all the way back to the very first photo he'd taken here. And then, even though he knew he shouldn't, he kept going, and there she was.

Carly jumping on the steps of the Opera House. Carly ankle-deep in the water at Bronte Baths. Carly hovering over the Megalong Valley, feet grubby and pointed and high above the earth. Every morning, he woke with an ache in his chest, like his heart had cracked open and some essential part of him was leaking slowly, painfully, out of his body. He hadn't heard from her, and he hadn't had the courage to ask Marcus how she was doing. All he knew was that she'd run out of the wedding after they'd fought, after he'd told her he had feelings for her, and then she'd run out of the country. Was she okay? Was she going to find another job? He had no idea, and he knew her well enough to know that if she wasn't okay, she certainly wasn't going to ask him for help again.

He kept scrolling all the way back to the beginning, to their first shoot together on North Head. He clicked and clicked, his self control unraveling, until he found what he wanted—one of the very first photos of his that she'd liked, one they hadn't agreed to post. One that was just for them. It was as absurd and unusable as he'd remembered: her body sharp and powerful, her head a blurry fireball as the wind blew her curls across her face. Chaos and control. That was Carly, but he knew now there was more to her than that. She was proud and loyal and determined to the point of stubborn. She was fiercely protective of the people she cared about. She was funny and sharp and principled, and *exhausting* at times, and he had watched through his lens as she'd taken a risk and tried to make a new life for herself.

Nick thought about that disastrous dinner at his parents' place, when Carly had nearly flipped the table defending the person she'd thought he was, then stormed away like only she could. He wished he'd taken a picture of her at that dinner, or at his front door, where that long poem about Australia had hung on the wall his whole childhood. *An opal-hearted country, a willful, lavish land. All you who have not loved her, you will not understand.*

That was Carly. Opal hearted. Willful, lavish. For a few short weeks, he'd seen her, held her. Let her be fierce with him and protective of him.

He stared at the photo for another long moment, then closed his eyes and tried to conjure the sound of her laugh when she'd seen it. Her throaty, musical giggle had filled the car and stolen his breath. He could almost remember it. And almost remembering would have to be enough, because he'd never hear Carly Montgomery laugh again.

Chapter 29

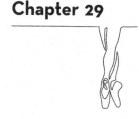

Four months later

Carly had always imagined that her final performance with NYB would be a grim, dour night, that she'd spend the day feeling weepy and nostalgic as she prepared to walk the plank, out of the only job she'd ever wanted, and plunge into the depths of the great unknown.

But it didn't feel like that at all. Okay, she was still weepy and nostalgic, but she didn't feel grim or afraid at all. She put the final touches on her hair and let another dancer spray it to within an inch of its life, feeling nothing but gratitude for the sisterhood that thrived inside a crowded, nervous dressing room. She lined her false lashes with glue and felt relief that, after tonight, she'd never have to wear lashes again unless she absolutely wanted to, which she couldn't imagine ever doing. And she danced through her final company preshow warm-up class feeling nostalgic for the days when she could dance with far less pain and fatigue. Her body was telling her that it was time to stop now, and she was going to listen to it.

Because she wasn't a principal dancer, her retirement performance wasn't a big public affair. When principals retired, their final shows were hyped up and ticket prices skyrocketed, and when they took their final bows, current and former dancers joined them on stage to applaud their years of service as confetti fell from the ceiling and the audience tossed bouquets onto the stage.

It wasn't like that for Carly. Catherine gave a short speech after warm-up, and all Carly's soon-to-be-former colleagues applauded her as she sniffled and tried not to mess up her eye makeup. Then it was upstairs and into the wings, onto the stage for one final performance with her dozens of fellow corps de ballet dancers. Carly took her final bow, not alone at the front of the stage, but in a long line of fellow dancers, shoulder to shoulder with the women she'd worked alongside for the last decade.

When the curtain came down for the last time, the rest of them heaved sighs of relief: the spring season was finally over. Carly watched them filter off the stage and into the wings, all sweaty and tired and eager to begin their two-week break from daily classes and rehearsals. She stayed behind, taking in the stage and the heavy gold curtain one last time. She would be back, but next time she stepped onto this stage, she wouldn't be a dancer anymore. She glanced up into the rafters, where rows of lights hung below the walkway, thinking about the dozens of ballets she'd danced on this stage, and her chest filled with a sense of fulfillment. She had grown up here, had developed into a person she was becoming proud to be here. And when she returned from her own two-week break, she would keep going.

She'd spent three afternoons a week in Catherine's office this season, listening and taking notes as Catherine explained her decision-making process for hiring a new choreographer, or walked her through her preparations for the next board meeting. Heather had offered to make Carly a spreadsheet where she could keep track of what she'd learned and what she had questions about, and she had gladly accepted her friend's help. She wasn't stuck or flailing. She was moving forward, and she wasn't afraid.

Back in the dressing room, in between sweaty hugs from the other women, she hung her tutu on the hanger with her name on it and peeled off her lashes for the last time. Makeup free and back in her street clothes, she said goodbye to the last straggling dancers, then started loading the contents of her dressing table and her cubby into a box that she'd addressed to herself earlier in the day. The company would ship it to her later. She pulled a photo of her and Heather, taken during their first season in the company, off the mirror and smiled down at it. A lifetime ago.

She'd just put the photo in the box when someone knocked on the door.

"Yeah, come in," she said vaguely. Then she glanced up at the mirror in front of her and stared.

Nick Jacobs was standing in the doorway behind her, watching her, a bouquet of pink roses in one hand.

"I thought you were in India," she said, before she could stop herself. She'd unfollowed him on Instagram, but against her better judgment, she still checked his account a few times a week. He'd been posting images from all over the world, most recently from a magnificent garden in Jaipur, where he'd found prowling peacocks and pink flowers so vivid she could almost smell them through the screen. Hashtag on assignment. Hashtag *Vogue*.

"I'm not in India," he stated the very obvious, not taking his eyes off the mirror, off her shocked face. His eyes were bluer than she remembered, his lashes even longer and darker. But the way he looked at her was just as intense, just as all-seeing as she remembered, and it made the hairs stand up on her forearms.

She turned to face him, suddenly furious at him. All these months of silence, and he showed up now? At her retirement performance?

"I'm sorry I didn't call or text first. I got a last-minute flight here, and then I bought a ticket off a scalper outside. Highway robbery," he said, with a tentative smile. She kept her face as stony as she could. He had *Vogue* money now, so he could afford a criminally marked-up ticket to the ballet.

"Okay," she said stiffly. What the fuck was he doing here? What did he want from her? And why was she so horrifyingly relieved to see him after all this time?

"You're a beautiful dancer, Carly. I already knew that, but watching you tonight, with the lights, and the music, it's . . . you're a gorgeous dancer."

"Was. I was a gorgeous dancer. This was my last show. I'm taking a job in the administration next month. I'm moving on." She glared at him, hoping her meaning was perfectly clear. *I don't think about you. I don't miss you.*

"That's fantastic, congratulations," Nick smiled, and she felt her glare waver. How dare his smile still make her pulse flutter like that? How dare he look so happy at her success? "But I'm not."

"Not what?"

"Not moving on. I mean, work is fine; it's better than fine. I'm having a good time and taking good pictures, and the response has been really positive for the first two issues. I think *Vogue* will keep me on for another year, if it keeps up like this."

"Did you pay a scalper all that money just to rub your success in my face?" Carly interjected. "Because you could have waited at the stage door and done it for free."

He smiled to himself, as though he'd known exactly how she'd respond to his showing up out of nowhere. The sight of his smile made her stomach swoop with pleasure, which was quickly chased by irritation at how well he knew her. Then an ache. He *knew* her. He watched her silently and ran a hand over his hair. His hair was a little shorter than it had been in Sydney, and to her irritation, it suited him even better now.

"No, I didn't. I wanted to see you dance. And I wanted to tell you something, which is that I fucked up and I'm sorry. I shouldn't have lied to you, or to everyone. I was insecure and jealous, and I decided that was more important than being honest with people. But I'm not doing that anymore. I'm telling the truth even when it's frightening, even when I'd rather hide from people. Which is why I'm here."

Carly crossed her arms and said nothing, so he kept talking.

"I spent all that time in Sydney with you, walking around this place that used to be my home and feeling like I didn't belong there anymore. And then you left and I realized that home doesn't have to be one place. It can be two different places, or five. It can be wherever you feel safest or wherever you became the version of yourself you always wanted to be. Or it can be the place it hurts the most to leave. And nothing ever hurt like when you left Sydney. And for a while I couldn't figure out why, but then I realized it was because I was at home with you."

Carly had a sudden vision of the lost, confused look on his face the day he'd gone looking for the old photography shop and found a café in its place, and felt her heart squeeze in her chest. She crossed her arms tighter, wishing his words hadn't moved her at all. She didn't want to be moved by Nick Jacobs.

"It was just a fling, Nick," she said firmly.

Except, that wasn't true, was it? It wasn't everything, but it wasn't nothing, either. What she had felt for Nick, what she still felt now, despite all her efforts to move on, it wasn't nothing.

"And even if we'd had more time," she barreled on, determined to make her point, "it was never going to last. We had fun, until we didn't, and if it had lasted any longer . . ."

She didn't finish the sentence aloud. If it had lasted any longer, he would have tired of her, would have realized that she wasn't enough for him. That was the Carly Montgomery story: kind of a lot, but never enough.

"If it had lasted any longer, I only would have fallen deeper in love with you," he said, taking a few steps into the room, but stopping well short of close to her. He swallowed hard, and she remembered what he'd said about telling the truth even when it was frightening.

Except that he'd had so many chances to tell her the truth, and he'd wasted them all. And now he was back here, just as she was moving on with her life, telling her he still wanted her?

"It was just sex, Nick, okay? And it wasn't even real sex." It didn't even count.

"You know that's not true. You know what we did was real. It was sex, and it was more than just that. It . . . it meant something to me. It made me want more of you. All of you."

"You can't have all of me. No one can."

"Not like that. I don't want you like that. I want you like this. Mad, and stubborn, and making me be better, and making me work to be all the things I want to be. I want you. I want to love you. That's the truth."

Carly's eyes had filled with tears, but she blinked them away, her heart suddenly raw and throbbing like it had been the day she left Sydney. She wanted to believe him—she hated that she wanted to believe him—but she'd believed him before, ignored all her instincts in order to trust him and let him under her skin, into places no one else had seen before. She wouldn't make that mistake again.

"It's too late, Nick. You had your chance. We had our chance, and it didn't work."

"Carly, please," his voice cracked a little.

She tightened her arms across her chest and stared at the floor between his feet, too exhausted to yell or stalk away. Too tired to go through all this pain again.

"Just go, Nick. I need to finish packing." She turned away and went back to pulling photos and good luck cards off the mirror, arranging them carefully in the box so that she only heard, and didn't see, when he backed out of the room and turned down the hall.

She kept piling things into the box, trying to ignore the tremble in her hands and the ache in her chest. They would fade. They'd faded last time. She'd come back to New York and begun building herself a new life, something she once thought she didn't know how to do. But she'd done it, just like Heather had. Just like Nick had. He had a new life full of real glamor and real success. All the things he'd pretended to have. He had *Vogue* money.

But he'd come here to tell her that none of it was enough if he didn't have her. That he didn't want to build his new life without her. Carly looked up and stared at her face in the mirror. Even the warm light from the yellow-gold bulbs couldn't conceal the pink rimming her eyes. She looked like a mess. She remembered what Nick had told Ivy Page about all the photos he'd taken of her. *Even the bad ones are good.* Even when she was a mess, when she was angry and hurt and storming out of rooms, he still saw her. Saw who she was trying to be, even when she fell short.

It was just sex, she repeated to herself. But that wasn't true, was it? In only having the sex with him that she really wanted to have, she'd ended up being far more intimate with him than she'd been with any other partner. He hadn't had all of her, but he had seen all her. He knew all of her. And he still wanted her.

I want you like this. Mad and stubborn.

She was mad. She was mad at Nick Jacobs for throwing himself in front of her luggage cart and making her question everything she thought she knew. She was mad at him for lying to her. And she was so damn stubborn that she'd just made him leave even though she wanted him to stay. Forever.

"Shit," she breathed. *Shit, shit, shit.* She loved Nick Jacobs, and she'd sent him away. *Classic fucking Carly.*

She dropped the card she was holding and turned, running out of the dressing room and down the corridor as fast as she could. The hallways were almost empty, and as she pelted along the concrete floor, a member of the stage crew flattened herself against the wall in surprise.

"Sorry!" Carly yelled, but the woman was already five feet behind her. She kept going until she reached the stairs to the stage door, and took them two at a time, shoving the door with all her body weight and stumbling out onto the side of Lincoln Center Plaza, her pulse pounding in her ears.

There was no one there. The fans hoping to catch a glimpse of a principal dancer, the little girls clutching programs and waiting for autographs, had all gone home. Carly ran out into the plaza and looked up and down Columbus Avenue, desperate to find him before it was too late.

"Nick!" she yelled at a distant figure. "Nick, wait!"

A second later, the figure slowed, then stopped and turned. Carly ran, faster than she'd ever run toward anything.

She stopped a few feet from him, panting in the middle of the sidewalk. He watched her, a guarded hope on his face and the flowers still in his hand.

"I'm sorry," she said, when she'd caught her breath. "I'm sorry. I should have heard you out at the wedding. I should have heard you out back there. I have a temper, I don't know if you've noticed." She paused, chest still heaving, waiting for him to say something, but he didn't.

"I have a temper, and I'm working on it. I'm working on only getting angry at the people who deserve it. And not getting angry when I'm really just scared. I want to try that again, and hear you out this time."

Nick stared at her for a long moment, his face unreadable, and as she watched him she felt all the adrenaline of the run drain out of her, leaving her empty. Finally, he spoke.

"You can't," he said decisively.

"Can't what?"

"You can't hear me out. You once told me that the easiest way to get you to do something was to tell you that someone, somewhere, had made a rule saying you can't. So, Carly, you can't." The side of his mouth lifted in a tiny, cautious smile.

Carly let out half a sob, and she took a step toward him. "Watch me," she said, with her best attempt at a glower. It was hard to glower when relief and hope were threading through her body, filling her chest like cool water.

Nick stepped closer, and she could smell his cologne, spicy and warm and unmistakably him.

"I've taken so many photos in the last few months, and people seem to love them," he said, his voice quiet but steady. "But I can't stop looking at the photos I took of you. The photos we took together. I have so many photos of you I've memorized your face. Every freckle, every frown. Did you know you have six different kinds of frowns?"

"I do?"

"You do. Six of them." He held up his hand and started counting on his fingers. "The *I need coffee* frown. The *I don't understand* frown. The *I understand but I don't like it* frown. The *this guy is being a jerk* frown. The *I wish I hadn't yelled quite so loudly at the jerk* frown."

Carly smiled. Why did he have to be like this? So perceptive, so intimately acquainted with all of her, even the worst of her? A few months ago, she would have hated it, but now, she didn't know how she'd ever lived without it.

"That's only five frowns," she pointed out. He chuckled, and the sound demolished any remaining anger. She had missed that sound more than her pride had let her admit.

"Well, the sixth is my favorite, so I saved it for last. It's the *I hate Nick Jacobs but I really want to kiss him* frown. I've seen that one a lot. You're wearing it right now," he said quietly.

She took a step toward him and saw hope flicker across his face as she moved. He had seen the worst of her, and he still wanted more. He still wanted everything. Brow furrowed, she searched his face, drinking in the sharp cheekbones and soft lips and endless blue eyes, and she knew. She wanted everything, too.

"You're wrong," she said stubbornly, taking another step and putting a hand on his chest. "You missed a frown. This isn't the *I hate Nick Jacobs but I really want to kiss him* frown. It's my *I like Nick Jacobs and I demand to kiss him* frown."

Nick reached out and put a hand on each side of her waist, pulling her to him. "That's awfully pedantic of you," he murmured, looking down into her face with a cautious smile.

"Not pedantic, per se, just precise," she corrected, and before she could say another word, he kissed her. She smiled against his mouth and opened her lips so her tongue could meet his, and he sighed as her fingers found their way into his hair. His lips were just as soft as she remembered, his mouth greeting hers like the last few months had never happened. But they had happened, and they'd taught her that even though she could fend for herself, she wanted Nick in her life. In her arms, in her bed. By her side.

After a few minutes, or possibly an hour, they broke apart and smiled at each other. Nick twisted one of her curls around his finger and pressed his forehead to hers.

"I want you, Nick Jacobs," she whispered, and the relief at finally saying the words she'd been fighting for months made her want to dance.

"And I want all of you," he whispered back. "The insecure parts, the scared parts. The parts you think aren't good enough yet, I want it all. I want to love it all. I want you, Carly Montgomery. You're the best kind of challenge. And I love a challenge."

He ducked down and briefly pressed his mouth to hers again, as though he was afraid she would vanish if he didn't keep kissing her.

"Where are you staying?" she finally asked.

"Not staying, actually. Living," he said, with a tentative smile. "I can keep traveling if I want to, but I told the magazine I want to come home for a bit. And as long as you're here, here is home."

"You got a place here?"

"A short-term corporate rental, near Penn Station. It's kind of sterile, but it's convenient."

"And what about that offer to shoot with me again? Does that still stand?" Carly felt an intoxicating sense of possibility gathering and swelling in her chest. He was here. He was *staying* here. For her.

"I don't see why not. Where do you want to go?"

"Anywhere. Everywhere."

"Then let's go anywhere and everywhere," he said, bending down to kiss her again. "But first can we go back to your place?"

She smiled up into his stupid, handsome face, the face she'd memorized and wanted to wake up to tomorrow morning. Every morning.

"Yes, let's go back to my place. My parents had a bottle of unbelievably expensive champagne delivered, and I can't drink it alone." She took the flowers from him and slipped her hand into his. He was watching her avidly, drinking her in. "Well, I *can* do it alone, but I don't want to."

"I'll pop the champagne—make yourself at home," Carly said as she led him into the apartment and flicked on the bright entryway light. When he didn't move, she set her bags down and smiled at him expectantly, waiting for him to step further into the apartment. Instead, he stood a few feet away, cataloging every inch of her. Her flushed cheeks, her strong legs, her lean, freckled arms. Her incredible hair, fiery and unruly, but not nearly as fiery and unruly as she was. His breath was short in his chest, and not only because of the five flights of stairs up to her apartment. He'd felt short of breath the whole ride home, holding her hand in the back seat of the taxi, resisting the urge to release it and run his fingers up her thigh, even when she placed their clasped hands on top of her leg and arched an eyebrow at him invitingly. He'd waited months to see her again, to touch her again, he'd told himself. He could wait a few more minutes.

But he couldn't wait now. Not when he'd spent all those weeks wishing for her. For the silk of her inner thighs, the sharp catch of her gasp. The way she kissed and came like she did everything else—with her whole body and without restraint.

Nick stepped towards her until their bodies met, and kept moving until he felt her lower back hit the wall gently and Carly's surprised intake of breath melted into a moan.

"What are you doing?" she asked coyly, as if she wasn't already arching against him, tipping her head up until her lips were mere inches from his.

"Making myself at home," he murmured, and before he could say another word, she captured his mouth, kissing him slow and deep. As if they had all night, and even longer than that. And Nick let her take him, let her kiss him and pull him harder against her. Let her welcome him home.

He'd thought he'd missed her before. He had felt the ache in his gut every morning and had dragged it around with him every day. That was why he'd told the creative director he needed to stay put for a while, and he'd bought a ticket to New York, and then a ticket to tonight's NYB performance. Even though he didn't know if Carly would ever talk to him again, he just needed to be near her. He'd thought he'd missed her, but as she kissed him now, as she pressed her lips against his neck and he heard her breathe him in, he realized that it had been far more than mere missing. He had not truly felt like himself in his skin when she was so far away, and when he hadn't known if she felt the same way about him. He had needed her. He was going to need her for a long, long time.

Eventually, Carly broke the kiss and leant her head against the wall, looking up at him with sparkling, mischievous eyes. "Feeling at home yet?"

"I should probably see the bedroom."

She raised her eyebrows, then reached up to nip at his lower lip, and she might as well have run her hand over his crotch.

"It's through there," she tipped her head slightly, and a second later he'd scooped her up and was striding down the narrow hallway as Carly giggled and clung to his neck. He shouldered the door open and dropped her unceremoniously on the bed, relief and joy and need thundering through him.

Carly kicked her shoes off and scooted back, and Nick removed his shoes as fast as he could without falling over. A second later, he had joined her on the bed and covered her body with his, relishing the gasp she let out as he rolled his weight on top of her. She felt perfect beneath him, her muscles tightly coiled and her skin soft, and he felt himself get almost painfully hard as she wrapped one powerful leg around his lower back and pinned his hips against hers.

He propped himself up on one hand, freeing the other to snake lightly up her bare leg, loving the tiny whimpers that escaped her when his fingers brushed the satiny skin of her inner thigh. Forget champagne. He wanted to get drunk on that sound. He wanted to devour it, drown in it. He let his hand continue, pushing the hem of her shirt away and tracing the lines of muscle around her hip bones, feeling her squirm and arch beneath his teasing fingers. As his hand climbed higher, playing with the band of her bra, he lowered his face to the place where her neck met her shoulder, caressing the long slope of straining muscle with gentle presses of his lips, swirling swipes of his tongue, and tender nips with his teeth. The whimpers were louder now, more insistent, and with every one he felt his cock harden and press against the front of his briefs.

"Please," she gasped, and he smiled against her skin. So impatient, his tiny American cyclone.

He lifted his head so he could look into her face. "Please what?" he asked, with a teasing smile.

She met his eyes, her lips parted and her breath quick.

"Please touch me before I die."

He smiled, tracing his fingers up over the swell of her breast, tracing them lightly, slowly, over her hardened nipple, feeling it bead even tighter through the thin fabric. She gasped and then groaned, and pressed her head into the pillow until her ribs flared and her flesh pressed into his hand.

"You're not going to die," he murmured, repeating the movement with more pressure this time.

"Fuck," she groaned, arching into his hand again, one hand clutching at the bed sheet and the other grabbing a fistful of his shirt. "Then please touch me before I kill you," she growled, and he grinned. So impatient. So passionate. So imperfect, and so perfectly Carly. How could he refuse?

He ran his hand over her ribcage, feeling her muscles shift under his palm as he slid it downward until he reached the waistband of her shorts. His hand trembled slightly as he worked the button out of its hole and got hold of the zipper, and he'd just pulled it all the way down when Carly put both hands on his chest, pushed him onto his side, and kissed him hungrily. For a moment, her hand was buried in his hair, her nails scraping lightly, maddeningly, against the suddenly tight and sensitive skin of his scalp. Then it ran down his body and mimicked the motion he'd made a moment ago, unbuttoning his fly and sliding his zipper down. He moaned into her mouth as his cock throbbed and strained, desperate for her inches-away touch.

For a moment, they stayed like that, lips playing and tongues searching, his fingertips brushing against the top of her panties and hers trapped gently under the waistband of his briefs. Her skin was smooth and warm, but her breath was ragged and hot, and she broke the kiss and pulled her head back on the pillow, meeting his eyes as she slid her hand past his waistband and wrapped it around his cock. He hissed with relief and need, and he saw triumph flicker in her warm brown eyes as she began to stroke him slowly. Two can play that game, he wanted to say, but all that came out was a moan, and besides, actions were better than words. He slid his hand into her dampened panties and ran a careful finger up between her drenched folds, and she answered with another intoxicating whimper and a wobbling, distracted stroke of his cock.

He repeated the motion, pulling even more wetness into his fingers and towards her clit, so that when he drew a slow, light circle around the tender bud, it was slick and slippery, the most arousing thing he'd ever touched. She gasped and pressed her forehead against his, tightening her grip on his cock and stroking him firmly from base to tip, sending electric pleasure rocketing up his spine. He answered by pressing the heel of his hand on her clit, freeing his fingers to gently stroke her folds as he gave her circles of pressure and she ground a slow, insistent rhythm against him.

Nick closed his eyes against the sensation, overwhelmed by the feeling of her hand on his cock, her breath on his cheek, her drenched pussy in his hand, her forehead on his. He heard nothing but her moans and sighs mingling with his own as she stroked him, smelled nothing but her arousal and the smoky rose scent of her skin. Nothing but Carly, the impatient, exhausting, unpredictable human hurricane who made him want to scream and laugh and come all in the same breath.

"Shit, Nick, don't stop," she gasped, rolling her hips against his hand and stroking him faster. He wasn't going to stop. He didn't ever want to stop, he thought, as his breath quickened and he felt his release gathering at the base of his spine. He never wanted to stop taking photos of her, never wanted to stop waking up with her, or kissing her, or making her gasp and moan like this. He leant forward and kissed her, sweeping his tongue into her mouth, knowing that it was too soon to say all that, not when they were starting fresh here in New York. But one day, he'd tell her. He'd show her every day until she believed it in her bones. Carly whimpered against his lips, and at last he felt her whole body tense and then tremble as her orgasm broke over her. Her hips bucked against his hand, but he followed their motion, making sure his hand never left her as she rode her climax, gasping and shaking against him. A second later, he came so hard that he saw white spots, emptying himself into her hand as he kissed her clumsily, desperately.

Her hand stilled against him, and they lay facing each other, their panting the only sound in the dimly lit room. Legs loose and exhausted, they slowly came back to their own bodies. Nick looked across the pillow at Carly, whose eyes were closed and whose chest was still rising and falling deeply as her breath steadied. He studied her face, tracing the constellations of freckles on her cheeks and nose, and the firm, expressive lines of her brows, and the full, flushed pink pillows of her lips. He leaned forward and pressed a careful kiss against them, and she sighed contentedly. Nick extricated his feet from hers so he could stand up, and returned a few seconds later with a handful of tissues. She watched as he wiped her hand down and tossed the damp wad into a bin in the corner of the room. When he climbed back into bed, she whispered her thanks and scooted towards him until her face was nuzzled into his neck.

Nick held her for a long time, feeling her breath on his collarbone, her ribs expanding against the side of his body. He listened to the sounds of the city beyond her window, the honking cars, the distant rumble of the subway, the occasional shrieks of Saturday night revellers. It sounded nothing like Springwood or Sydney, nothing like Munich or Paris. It sounded nothing like any home he'd known. But then Carly breathed another happy, sated sigh against his skin, and hummed quietly as he pulled her closer, held her tighter. And he knew he was home.

Epilogue

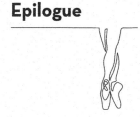

One year later

The fragile white paper crinkled under Carly's legs as she sat down on the table, watching Angela pull on her rubber gloves. Next would come the Q-tip test, then the lube. She lay back and shifted under the sheet until her lower back was happy with her position, then waited for Angela to sit on the rolling stool at the foot of the table and get to work.

"I'm going to touch you now, okay?" Angela said.

"Okay," Carly nodded, and she didn't even flinch as Angela ran the Q-tip over her vulva.

"Any pain?" Angela asked.

"Nope," Carly grinned, just like she had at every appointment for the last few months, and Angela responded with a satisfied *hmm*.

Next came Angela's first finger, then a second, and Carly lay there, breathing deeply and keeping her pelvic floor relaxed, as Angela pressed on various points around her opening and on her vaginal walls. She felt no pain and no resistance. She'd practiced this so many times in the last year with her dilators, and her body had become accustomed to this kind of penetration. Last month, she'd leveled up to the biggest dilator the clinic offered, a thick white cylinder that had felt like a stretch, but that, to her relief, hadn't caused her any pain.

After a few minutes of internal massage, Angela slowly withdrew her hand and peeled off her gloves.

"Things look pretty good to me," she said, tossing the gloves in the bin. She sat down on the stool and wheeled it along the table so Carly didn't have to crane her neck to see her. "How is it feeling when you do your exercises?"

"It feels fine," Carly said. "Good even. I didn't realize how much of a difference it would make to stop dancing all day. The rest of me feels weaker, but I think my pelvic floor is the strongest it's ever been."

Angela nodded as Carly spoke, then gave her a tiny *I told you so* shrug. "Well, you've been extremely diligent about your exercises, which obviously helps a lot."

Carly felt a swell of pride. Some people would call her stubborn, but Nick preferred "persistent." She'd persisted at this, and look at the results.

"I *think*," Angela said slowly, "that if you wanted to attempt intercourse now, it would probably be okay."

Carly stared at her. It had been well over a year since Angela had told her to stop having penetrative sex, since that disastrous final date with Carter. She and Nick had had a lot of sex since then—like, a lot—because it turned out that there was plenty of sex to be had without putting a penis in a vagina. It was something she probably should have realized a long time ago, something Nick had helped her to understand: Sex wasn't a hierarchy with penetration at the top. Sex was just sex, and as long as everyone was enjoying it, it didn't really matter which body parts were going where.

All the same, Angela had just said something she'd been waiting a long time to hear.

"Are you saying I no longer have a broken vagina?" Carly blurted.

Angela laughed and shook her head indulgently, but when she replied, her voice was firm. "I wouldn't say you ever had a broken vagina, so I can't say you no longer have one. I think you've worked hard to retrain your muscles and to strengthen them, and that penetration with my finger or your dilator no longer hurts. So it stands to reason that with proper preparation, and enough lube, other kinds of penetration won't hurt either."

Carly pulled at the sheet so that it covered her legs, and turned Angela's words over in her mind. She'd hoped this day would come eventually, but now that it had arrived, she didn't know what to do with it. She liked her sex life with Nick, and if the look on his face as they'd dried each other off after their shower this morning was anything to go by, he liked it, too. What would he say when she told him the news, though? As Angela jotted down some notes on her clipboard, Carly sat up and felt a flicker of foreboding. She assumed he'd be happy, but what if he was jubilant? What if he'd been waiting and hoping this whole time, putting up with her limitations but secretly hoping they'd be able to fuck soon?

She bit her lip, then remembered what he'd told her when he'd come to her apartment in Sydney, iced coffee in hand. *I want whatever you can give me.* He'd taken it, too. He'd taken all all her chaos, all her mess, all her *persistence*, and any kind of sex she was willing to share with him. He'd treated them all as gifts. She gave her head a tiny shake and reminded herself of what she knew to be true, now. She was enough for him, as she was. She was enough, period.

Out in the reception area, Carly booked her next two appointments with Angela, then grabbed a bite-size Reese's cup from the bowl on the counter and headed out into the warm spring day. On her way to the bus stop, she texted Heather.

Carly, 9:13 AM: Huge news: I'm cleared for --intercourse--! 🧦🧦🧦

By the time her bus had arrived, Heather had texted back.

Heather, 9:21 AM: OMG, so exciting! But be careful, or you'll end up like me 🤰

Carly grinned and rolled her eyes. As if Heather hadn't planned her pregnancy as carefully as she planned everything else in her life. That baby was coming out of the womb with a spreadsheet in her hand. Still, Carly thought, she should figure out her birth control situation, and soon.

As the bus trundled across town, she pulled up her calendar and looked at the day ahead. She and Catherine had a meeting with the director and deputy director of the NYB school, then lunch with a potential donor, and then Catherine wanted to stop by a rehearsal to observe a choreographer who was making her first ever work on the company.

Carly was fully adjusted to office life now, and for the last nine months, she'd been acting as Catherine's assistant and right-hand woman, watching how Catherine made decisions about promotions and casting, about which choreographers to hire and which donors to cultivate. The learning curve had been steep, but once a month Catherine sat down with her and answered her questions and explained anything Carly felt she hadn't understood in the moment. Carly doubted she'd ever be put in charge of NYB, but she was developing the skills and knowledge to run *something*, and she liked how competent she felt, even when she came home from work exhausted by all the information swirling around her brain. It was a different kind of exhaustion than the kind she'd felt at the end of a day of rehearsing or a night of performing, but she was getting accustomed to it. Tonight, though, she'd try not to come home exhausted, because Nick had planned a belated celebration dinner, since he'd been on a weeklong shoot in the Caribbean on the one-year anniversary of them getting together for real.

The bus pulled up beside Lincoln Center, and Carly hopped off, waving at a few of her former colleagues as they headed to the theater for company class. There were days when she missed dancing, she conceded as she walked toward the administrative building on the other side of the plaza, but most days she only felt gratitude. For her new life, for her new future. And for the fact that she was choosing them for herself.

The workday passed at its usual breakneck pace, and at 5:15, Catherine popped her head into Carly's cubicle and told her to go home.

"You're sure?" Carly asked, even though she was itching to throw her bag over her shoulder and race to the subway.

"Mmhmm, I've got a few more hours of work, but nothing you need to worry about. Plus I know you've got a special occasion to get to," Catherine said with a smile, which widened as Carly leapt to her feet.

"Okay, thanks, see you tomorrow, bye!" she said quickly, grabbing her bag and nearly knocking a pile of binders off her desk as she rushed to the elevator. She might be an office worker now, but she was still occasionally, as Nick had once lovingly described her, a human hurricane.

Nick checked his reflection in the mirror for what must have been the forty-seventh time that evening and straightened his collar yet again. Everything was in place. The chicken was in the oven. The candles were lit, a bottle of champagne, the same exorbitant French brand they'd drunk the night of Carly's retirement, was chilling in the fridge, and his anniversary present was wrapped and waiting on the coffee table. It had taken longer than expected for it to arrive from Australia, and Nick was secretly grateful that they'd had to delay their anniversary celebration. He hoped she liked the gift, even though it was goofy. If she didn't like it, he reminded himself, she'd certainly like the other present he had for her.

He checked the mirror one last time, then resumed pacing. After a few laps of the living room, his phone buzzed.

Carly, 6:17 PM: Almost home, 1 train was delayed again 😑

Nick let out a shaky breath and kept pacing. He didn't know why he was nervous. After all, he knew what her answer would be. He'd sent some potential ring designs to Heather, who had encouraged him to "add more sparkle," and he knew their friendship well enough to suspect that this piece of feedback was not, in fact, from Heather. Still. He'd never proposed to anyone before, and the gravity of what he was about to do made him feel like his lungs were too big for his body and his skin too tight.

The past year had made a lot of things clear to Nick. The first was that he could make a home anywhere, if he wanted to. Living in New York had been utterly draining at first; the city had everything you could possibly want or need, but in exchange it took all your energy. Getting to know Carly's hometown made him understand Carly better, in that respect. That first summer, as she'd been settling in to her new job, Nick had spent the weeks he wasn't on location walking around the city trying to get his bearings, trying to learn the subway system, trying to adjust to the pace of New York, which was faster and more demanding than either Paris or Munich. But after a few months, he'd started to feel at home. Now, every time he returned from a shoot, he felt a sense of calm settle over him when he sank into the back seat of an airport cab and gave the driver the address of Carly's apartment.

The second thing that had become clear in the last year was that he really was a talented photographer. When his *Vogue* contract had come up for renewal at the end of a year—after his photos had been featured in five issues, and once on the cover—he'd found himself more in demand than he'd ever imagined possible. He'd shot three luxury brand ad campaigns and had several more lined up. Carly's parents had been impressed by those campaigns, but Carly herself had been more excited when he'd been approached by a nonprofit photography collective that was trying to diversify stock image footage of ballet dancers. His first shoot, with a group of Black, brown, fat, and disabled dancers, was scheduled for next week.

The final thing, and the only thing that truly mattered, and the reason he was pacing anxiously around the living room they now shared, was that he wanted to spend the rest of his life making Carly Montgomery happy. Furious, occasionally, if the last year was anything to go by, but happy. She was still a human hand grenade at times, but he knew now that when she exploded, it was usually because she was feeling insecure or misunderstood. It helped that she had switched from a free meditation app to actual therapy. Ballet companies still had hang-ups about dancers who needed mental health care, but no one thought twice about an office worker who needed a therapist. And now when she exploded, she didn't storm out. She stayed, and they talked things out until they understood each other.

And the better he understood her, the more he loved her. He wanted years and years of her rolling her eyes at his bad puns and fierce, loving disagreement. Decades of waking up in the morning with her hair invading his pillow. He knew there had been years of his life, a whole career on a whole different continent, when he didn't love Carly. Didn't even know she existed. But it was hard to remember that time now. It was impossible to imagine his life, or his heart, without her, and he had no interest in trying.

He heard a key in the lock and froze, midstride, and turned towards the front door. A second later, the door swung open, and Carly appeared, her low ponytail draped over the shoulder of her sleek floral-print dress. Her cheeks were a little flushed, as though she'd rushed from the subway and all the way up the tight, dimly lit stairwell. The moment she entered the apartment and smiled at him, his nerves vanished. His lungs returned to their normal size, and his skin felt perfectly fine. He slipped his hand into his pocket and squeezed the small velvet box as she dropped her bag on the table in the entryway and walked towards him.

"Happy anniversary," she said, rising up on her toes to kiss him. He wrapped his arms around her waist and held her close.

"Belated anniversary," he said apologetically.

"Pedant," she said, "and I don't mind. Sounds like you had a great time over there. Next time take me with you."

"Deal," he agreed, and he kissed her back gently, mentally adding Anguilla to a list of potential honeymoon destinations.

"Mmm," she murmured against his mouth, then pulled away and glanced towards the tiny kitchen. "Something smells good."

"Roast chicken," he said. "It needs another twenty minutes or so. And I've got a present for you in the meantime."

She pulled back and frowned. "We said no presents! Remember, a nice meal, no gifts necessary?"

"I remember," he said, "but then I thought of the perfect gift for you and I couldn't resist."

"Oh yeah?" she asked slyly. "Is it a sexy gift?"

"Absolutely not," he said firmly, and her smile faltered a little. "In fact, I hope you don't find it sexy."

She raised her eyebrows, looking mystified, and watched him cross the room to the coffee table and return with the strangely shaped package. He handed it to her, and she weighed it in her hands curiously, then gave it a testing squeeze. Then she flipped it over and slipped her finger under the tape, and a second later the paper fell away to reveal—

"Oh my God, *no*!" she laughed. She threw her head back and cackled, hugging the horse-head pillow to her chest in delight. "How did you get this?"

"I emailed the B&B and asked them where they bought their hideous, cursed pillows, and they gave me the name of their deranged interior decorator. Don't worry, I didn't phrase it like that," he added.

Carly grinned down at the absurd pillow and shook her head in stunned disbelief. "It's awful, and I love it. It'll go perfectly with my T-shirt. Thank you. I'm going to go see how it looks on the bed."

She all but skipped off to the bedroom, and he followed her, thrilled by her response. He stood in the doorway and watched as she rearranged the other throw pillows—simple, tasteful, normal throw pillows—to make room for the new addition. She stood back to admire her work and cackled again, and as he watched her, he put his hand back in his pocket.

"It's perfect," she sighed. "We're going to wake up in *The Godfather* every single morning." She turned around and saw him standing in the doorway, with a box open in his hand and an opal ring winking in the light, and froze.

Nick loved the sound of her voice, but he still enjoyed the sight of Carly Montgomery speechless.

He slowly lowered himself to one knee, feeling his quads shake a little from the sudden rush of adrenaline.

"I love you more than I ever imagined possible," he said, trying to keep his voice steady against the emotion that was clogging his throat. "You once told me that we only get so much luck in this life, and I didn't know it at the time, but the luckiest thing that ever happened to me was getting run over by your luggage cart. Wherever I am in the world, however far I go, you're home for me. You're it for me. You are *indispensable* to me. And I want to spend the rest of my life loving you. Will you—"

"Yes!" she blurted, and he couldn't resist a laugh.

"God, you're not impatient at all, are you?"

"Sorry, sorry, you were saying. You love me and you want to spend the rest of your life with me."

He shook his head and smiled up at her, then got to his feet and pulled her to him. He pressed his forehead to hers and took a deep breath, taking in the scent of her and thinking of all the thousands of breaths he'd have with her.

"I love you, too, Nick Fucking Jacobs," she whispered. "And I *insist* on spending the rest of my life with you."

She nipped at his bottom lip, and Nick held her as tight as he dared. She kissed him deeply, fiercely, and with her whole body, and he chuckled against her mouth, finally feeling rooted and secure— and, as always, a little dazed by her. By Carly Montgomery, human hurricane, and his, forever.

A Note to the Reader by Cari Everhart

I am a physical therapist at the University of Iowa Hospitals & Clinics and have been treating pelvic floor conditions for eighteen years, in addition to dealing with these issues firsthand. First, I am here to validate the pelvic pain experience. It is a particularly distressing, embarrassing, and excruciatingly painful condition. Pelvic pain affects daily activities, disrupts relationships, decreases workplace productivity, and can interfere with the ability to urinate and evacuate the bowel. Pain with penetrative sex turns something that by all societal accounts should be a pleasurable experience into a stressful and in some cases intolerable one.

I also know how isolating it can be to suffer from this kind of pain. Because of the secrecy American culture encourages around our sexual organs and intimacy, it can feel like no one else in the world has these issues. But you are not as alone as it seems: research tells us that pelvic pain and painful sex may affect up to one in five people with a vagina.

Most importantly, I am here to tell you that these problems can be treated! Find an ob-gyn who will listen to you and validate your concerns. Don't accept anything less than this; there are a lot of compassionate and well-informed doctors out there who will help to identify any issues that need to be treated with medical interventions, including anatomical issues or skin conditions. Find a good pelvic floor physical therapist. It isn't as strange as it seems! Physical therapists treat muscles, and the pelvic floor muscles can be stiff or sore just like any other muscle—they're just a little harder to get to. While pelvic floor physical therapy often involves internal exams and home exercises, you will be able to start with whatever makes you feel the most comfortable. Just like Angela is for Carly, your PT can be an ally who supports and gently guides you along the road to recovery.

Finally, I want you to fully believe that you deserve a romantic partner who supports you regardless of whether penetrative intercourse is working out for you or not. We have created a very narrow view of what "counts" as sex, especially for heterosexual couples, when in fact there are a plethora of ways to create intimacy and experience sexual pleasure that don't involve penetration. Although Nick is a fictional character, he's not a fantasy. There are plenty of real-life partners out there that will believe you, support you, and fully enjoy sexual intimacy with you in a way that feels good to *your* body.

Best wishes in your journey,

Cari Everhart, PT

To find a provider:
www.aptapelvichealth.org/ptlocator
www.hermanwallace.com/practitioner-directory
www.isswsh.org
www.pelvicpain.org/public
www.pelvicguru.com
www.pelvicpain.org.au

Other helpful websites:
www.tightlipped.org
www.hopeandher.com
www.pelvicpainrehab.com

Acknowledgements

This book would not exist without the readers who preordered, bought, borrowed, recommended, or reviewed my first novel, *Pas de Don't*. Thank you for making it possible for me to do this dance all over again; I'm so lucky. So many of you told me you were hungry for Carly's story, and thanks to you, here it is. I hope you love it.

Thank you also to the booksellers who championed *Pas de Don't* and told me how excited they were for the next book, especially the indies of Iowa, including Sidekick Coffee & Books, Prairie Lights, Dog-Eared Books, and Beaverdale Books. Thanks to HEA Book Boutique for making sure this book can still get out in the world while I'm snuggled up at home taking care of my family.

My agent JL Stermer has had my back through every step of this process, and has never let me forget it. Alicia Sparrow edited Carly and Nick's story with her trademark care and enthusiasm, and helped them become the enemies and lovers I wanted them to be. Michelle Williams and Devon Freeny carried Carly and Nick over the finish line, and the whole team at Chicago Review Press—Serena

Knudson, Lauren Chartuk, Melanie Roth, Candysse Miller, and Valerie Pedroche—helped them find their audience. Thank you all so much.

Hot damn, Sarah Gavagan, this cover. You killed it. *Again.*

Cari Everhart, thank you for being willing to try something new and for extending your compassion and expertise to my readers. To all the pelvic floor PTs out there, thank you for your essential, life-changing work.

Thank you to all the authors who helped spread the word about this book, and to everyone who read drafts in various stages of development and offered me encouragement and ideas to make it better: Julie Anna Block, Sarah Chabolla, Olivia Dade, Cécile Dehesdin, Amanda Litman, Jessica Luther, Brittney Mmutle, Jess Morales Rocketto, Emma Weinert, Ellen O'Connell Whittet, Emily Wilcox, and Vanessa Zoltan. Thank you to Denise Williams and Rachel Mans McKenny for welcoming me into the Iowa romance writers' community, and to the writers of the Romance Craft Club and Romance Schmooze Discords for their company and support. Special thanks to Zeb Wahls, who helped me figure out the third act as I confidently drove us twenty miles in the wrong direction in the pouring rain (that's not a metaphor, it's a thing I really did).

Finally, thank you to Zach Wahls, who never once let me feel anything less than whole, wanted, and worthy. I love you so.

ABOUT THE AUTHOR

CHLOE ANGYAL is the author of the novel *Pas de Don't* as well as *Turning Pointe: How a New Generation of Dancers Is Saving Ballet from Itself*, which the Boston Globe called "incisive and unsparing" and "an important read for ballet lovers and an essential part of any conversation moving forward." Chloe holds a BA from Princeton and a PhD in arts and media from the University of New South Wales, where she wrote a dissertation about romantic comedies. She grew up in Sydney, Australia, and lives in Iowa.